THE GRAPHIC NOVEL
William Shakespeare

ORIGINAL TEXT VERSION

Script Adaptation: John McDonald
American English Adaptation: Joe Sutliff Sanders
Character Designs & Original Artwork: Jon Haward
Inking: Gary Erskine
Coloring & Lettering: Nigel Dobbyn
Design & Layout: Jo Wheeler & Carl Andrews

Editor in Chief: Clive Bryant

The Tempest: The Graphic Novel
Original Text Version

William Shakespeare

First US Edition

Published by: Classical Comics Ltd
Copyright ©2009 Classical Comics Ltd.

Acknowledgments: Every effort has been made to trace copyright holders of
material reproduced in this book. Any rights not acknowledged here will be
acknowledged in subsequent editions if notice is given to Classical Comics Ltd.

Images on page 135 reproduced with the kind permission of The Shakespeare Birthplace Trust.

All enquiries should be addressed to:
Classical Comics Ltd.
PO Box 7280
Litchborough
Towcester
NN12 9AR
United Kingdom
Tel: +44 (0)845 812 3000

info@classicalcomics.com
www.classicalcomics.com

ISBN: 978-1-906332-69-3

Printed in the USA

This book is printed by CG Book Printers using environmentally safe inks, on environmentally
friendly paper which is FSC (Forest Stewardship Council) certified (SW-COC-003110). This material
can be disposed of by recycling, incineration for energy recovery, composting and biodegradation.

The publisher wishes to acknowledge and thank Greg Powell
for his help in the completion of this book.

The rights of John McDonald, Joe Sutliff Sanders, Jon Haward, Gary Erskine and Nigel Dobbyn
to be identified as the artists of this work have been asserted in accordance with
the Copyright, Designs and Patents Act 1988 sections 77 and 78.

Contents

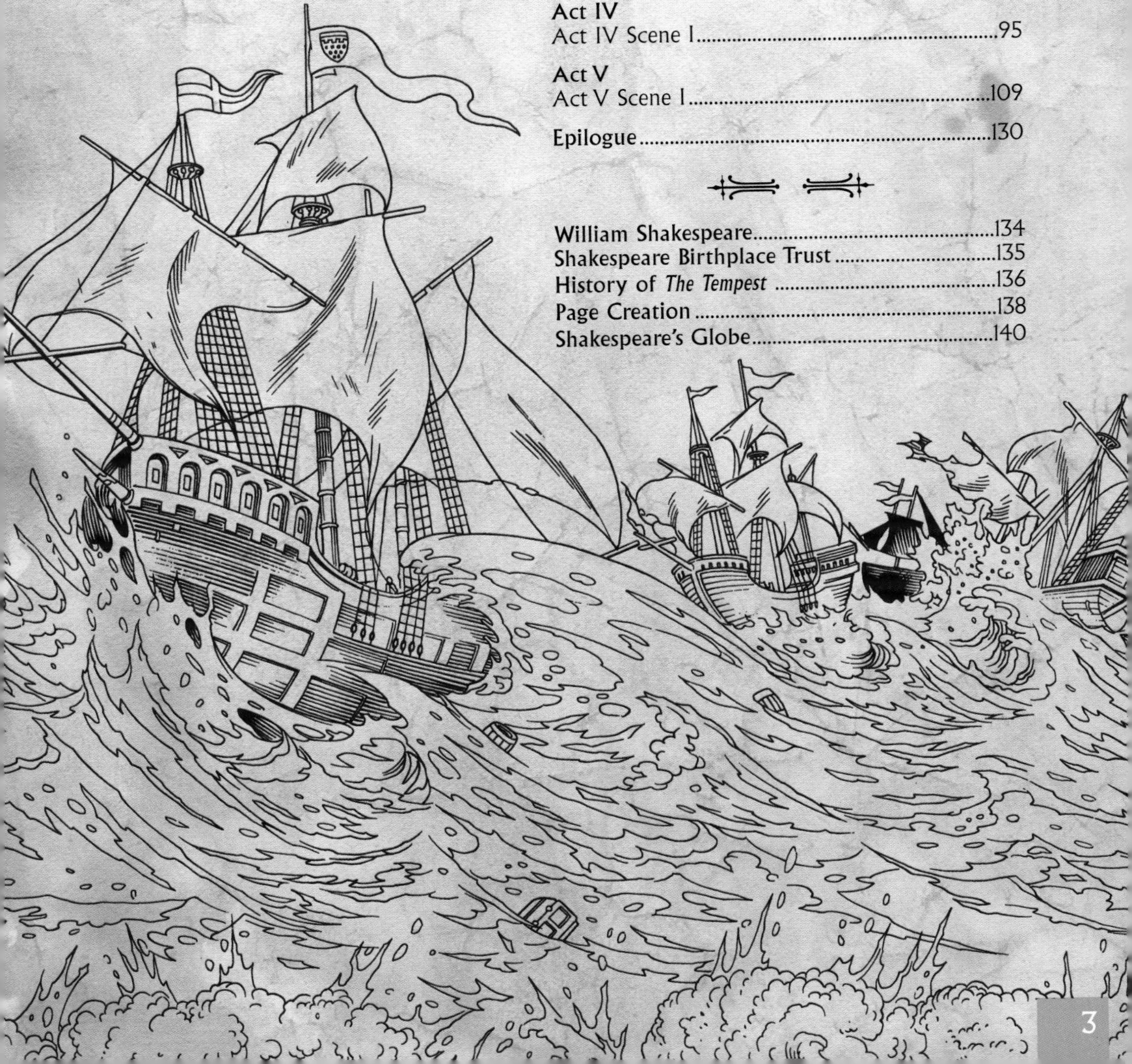

Dramatis Personæ

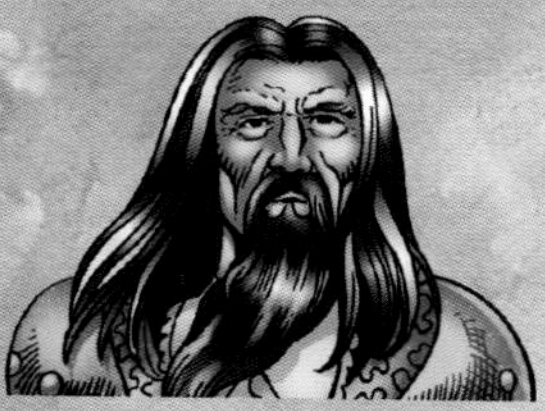

Prospero
The right Duke of Milan

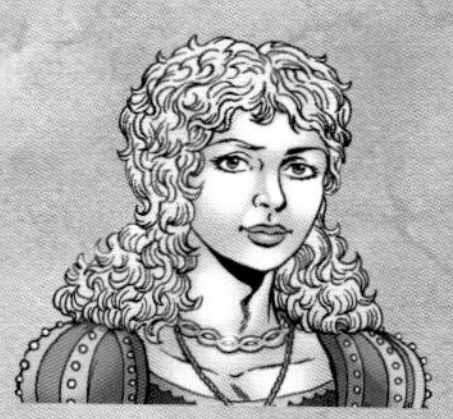

Miranda
Prospero's daughter

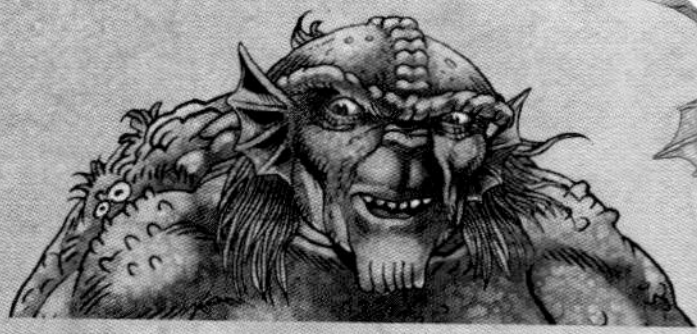

Caliban
A savage and deformed slave

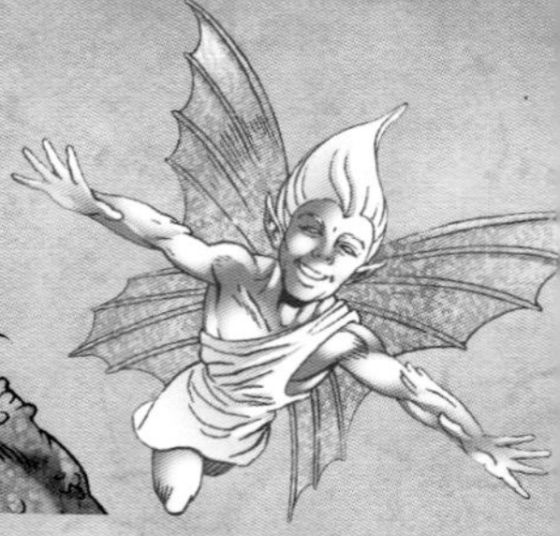

Ariel
An airy Spirit

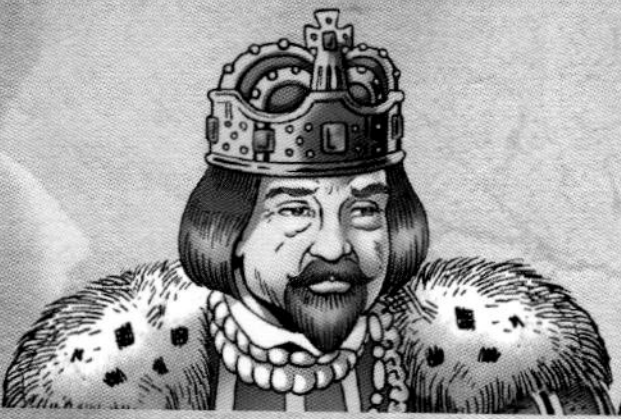

Alonso
King of Naples

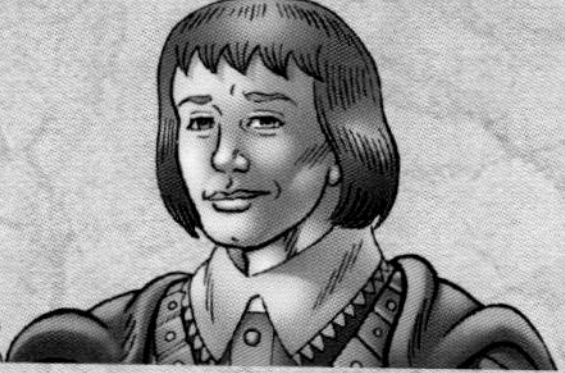

Ferdinand
The King's son

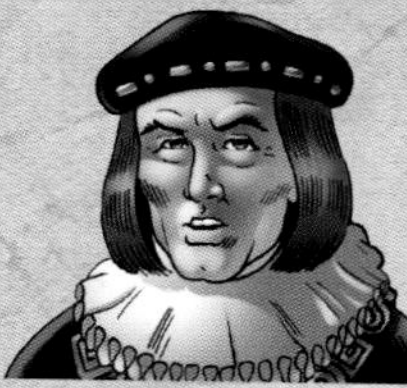

Sebastian
The King's brother

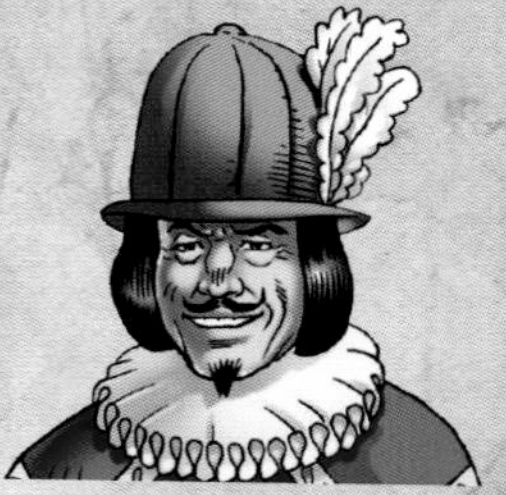

Antonio
Prospero's brother, the usurping Duke of Milan

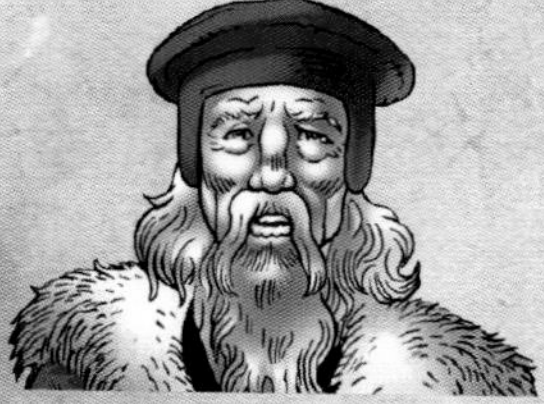

Gonzalo
An honest old counselor

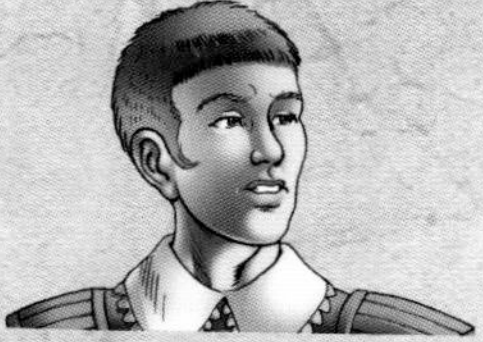

Adrian
A lord

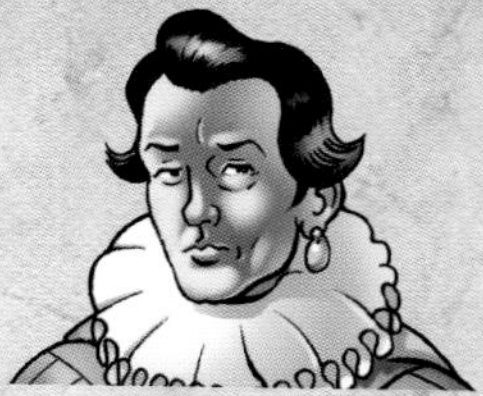

Francisco
A lord

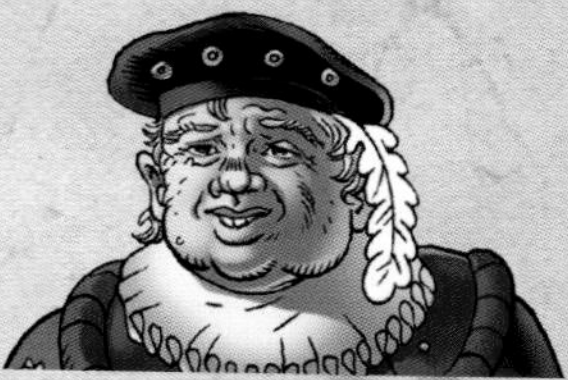

Stephano
A drunken butler

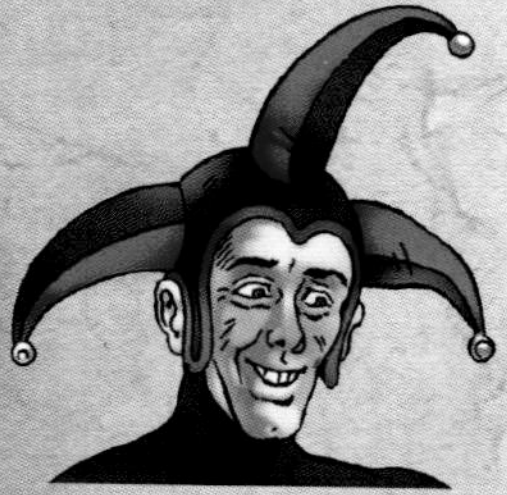

Trinculo
A jester

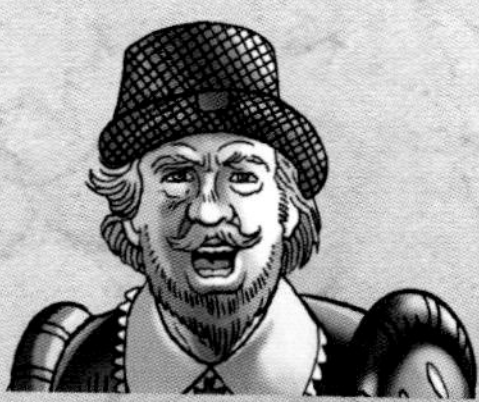

Master of the ship

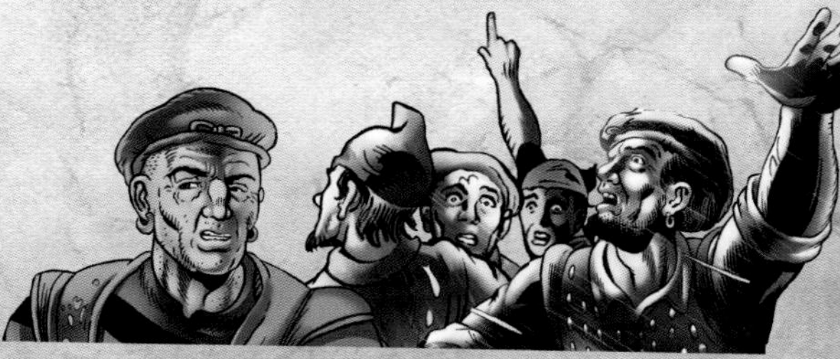

Boatswain of the ship
(pronounced "Bosun")

Mariners of the ship

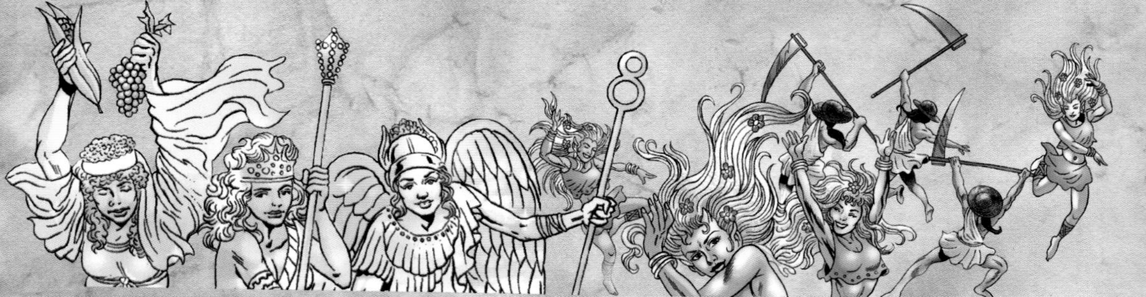

Ceres, Juno and Iris
Spirits, commanded by Prospero

Spirits and Reapers
Commanded by Prospero

Prologue

A royal ship, carrying the King of Naples and his entourage, is part of a small fleet sailing home from Tunis in North Africa. They are returning from the wedding of the King's daughter, Claribel, to the King of Tunis. The King of Naples is accompanied by his son Ferdinand, his brother Sebastian, and his trusty advisor Gonzalo. Also with the party is the King's friend Antonio, Duke of Milan. Antonio took the title of Duke from his older brother Prospero, who disappeared suddenly one night, never to be seen again…

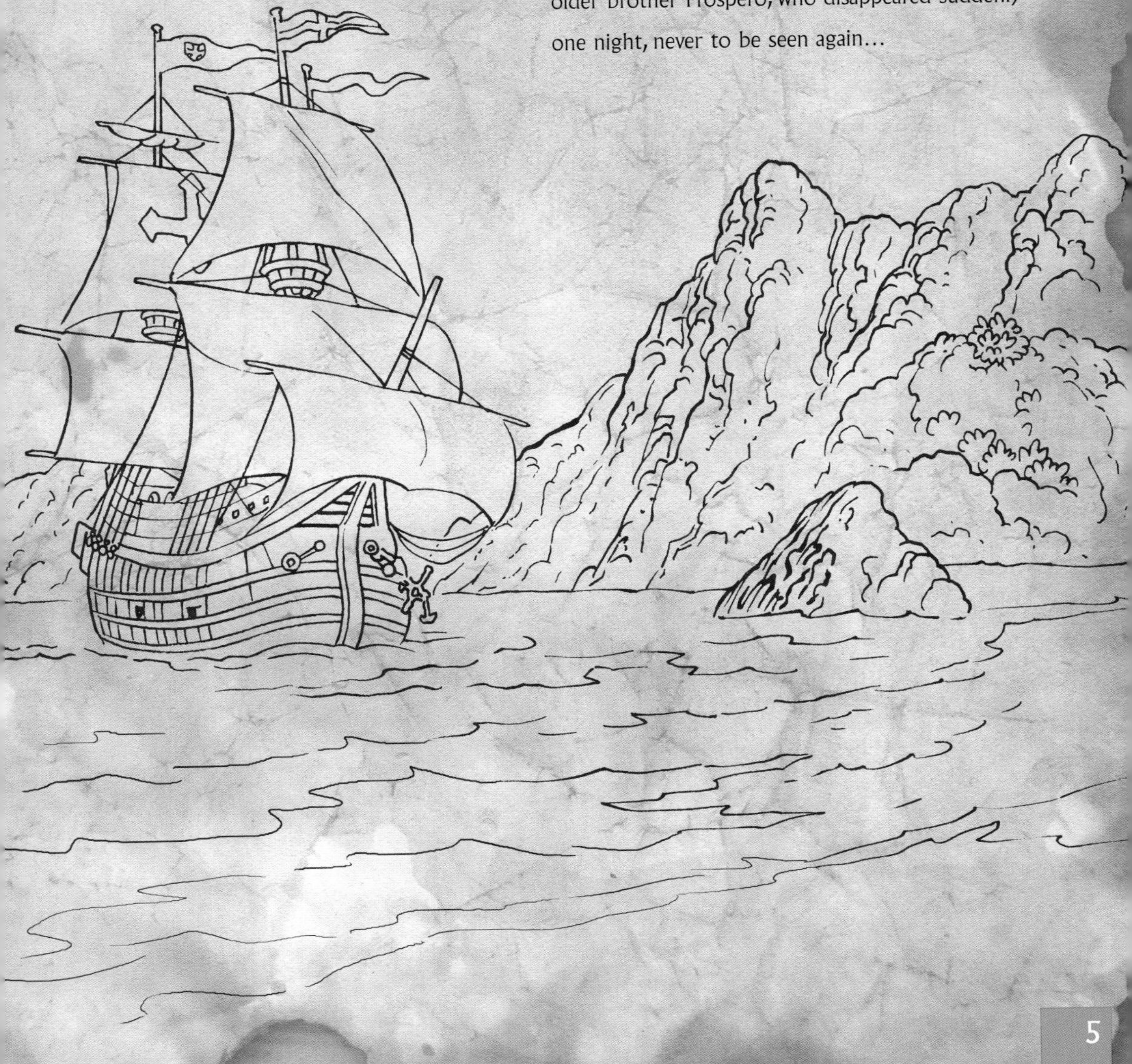

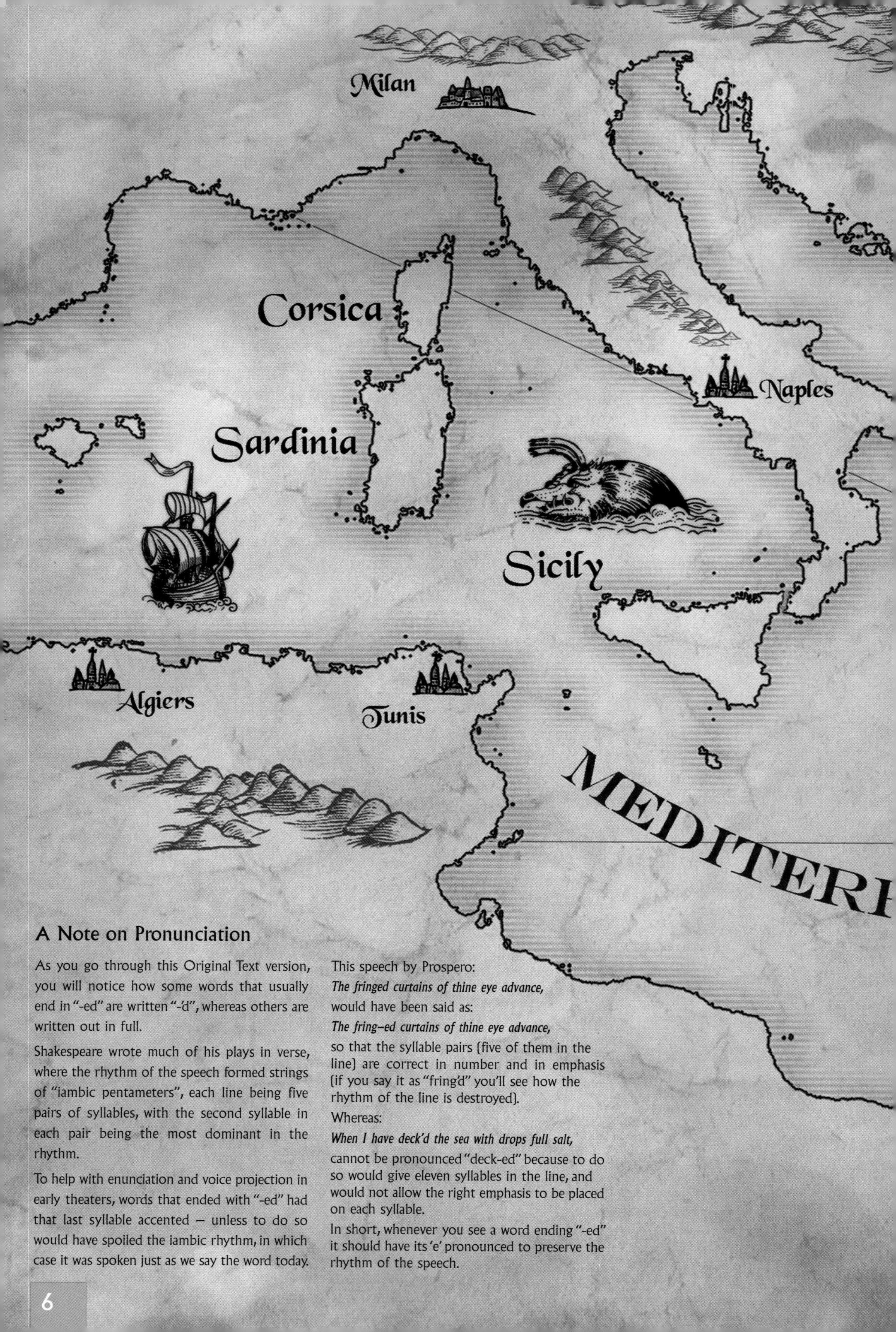

Milan
Corsica
Naples
Sardinia
Sicily
Algiers
Tunis
MEDITERI

A Note on Pronunciation

As you go through this Original Text version, you will notice how some words that usually end in "-ed" are written "-'d", whereas others are written out in full.

Shakespeare wrote much of his plays in verse, where the rhythm of the speech formed strings of "iambic pentameters", each line being five pairs of syllables, with the second syllable in each pair being the most dominant in the rhythm.

To help with enunciation and voice projection in early theaters, words that ended with "-ed" had that last syllable accented – unless to do so would have spoiled the iambic rhythm, in which case it was spoken just as we say the word today.

This speech by Prospero:

The fringed curtains of thine eye advance,

would have been said as:

The fring–ed curtains of thine eye advance,

so that the syllable pairs (five of them in the line) are correct in number and in emphasis (if you say it as "fring'd" you'll see how the rhythm of the line is destroyed).

Whereas:

When I have deck'd the sea with drops full salt,

cannot be pronounced "deck-ed" because to do so would give eleven syllables in the line, and would not allow the right emphasis to be placed on each syllable.

In short, whenever you see a word ending "-ed" it should have its 'e' pronounced to preserve the rhythm of the speech.

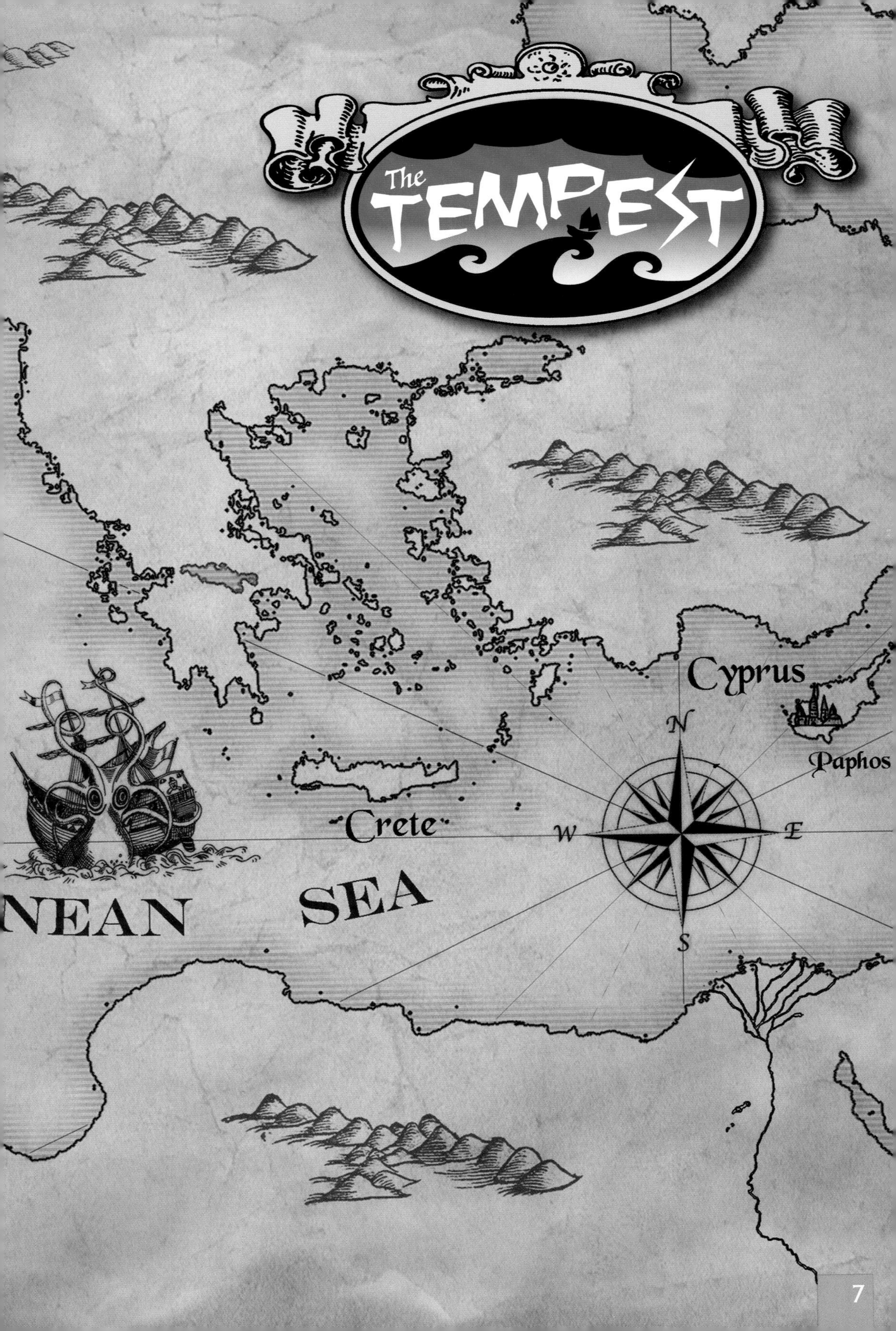
The TEMPEST
Cyprus
Paphos
N
W
E
S
Crete
NEAN
SEA

Act 1
Scene 1

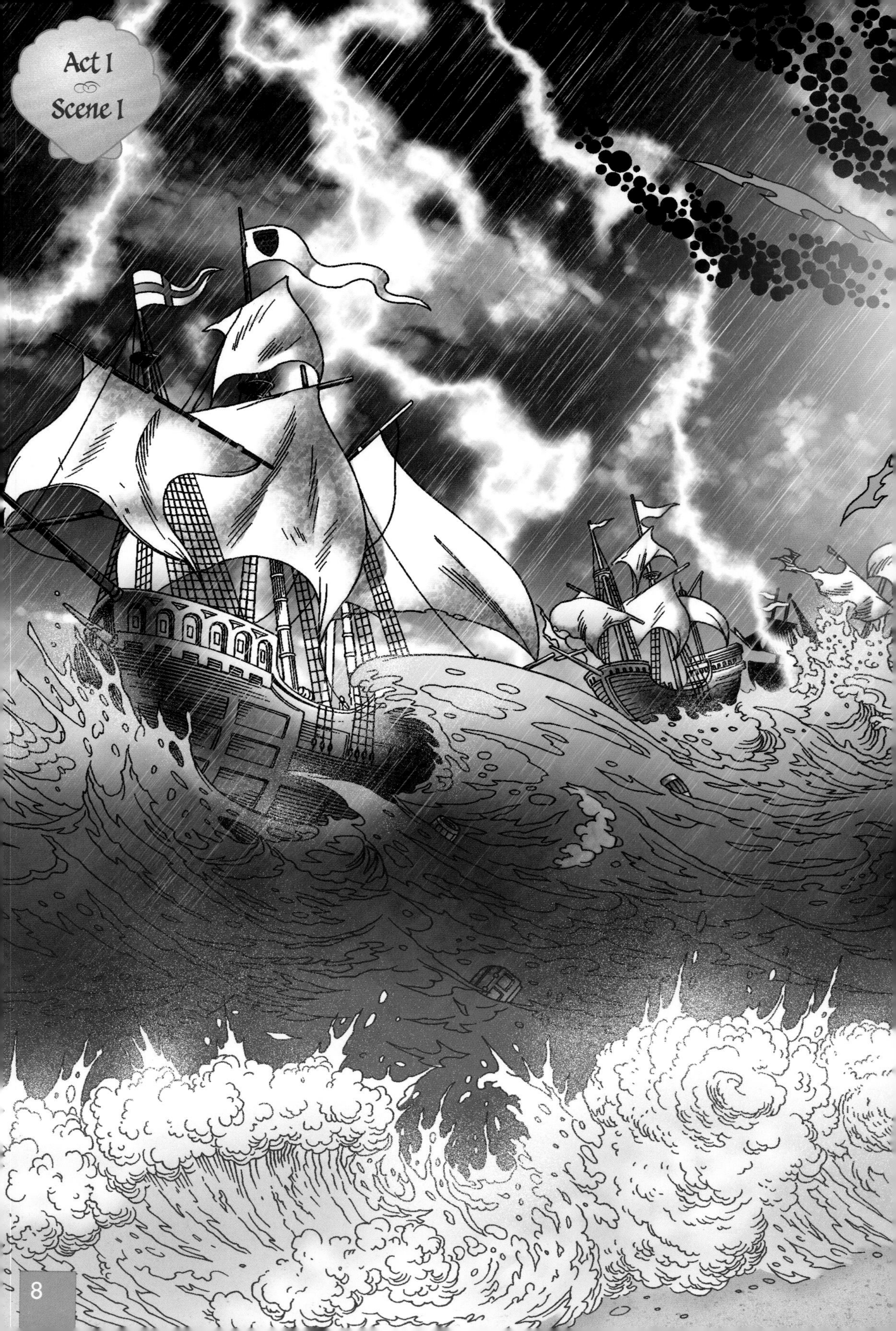

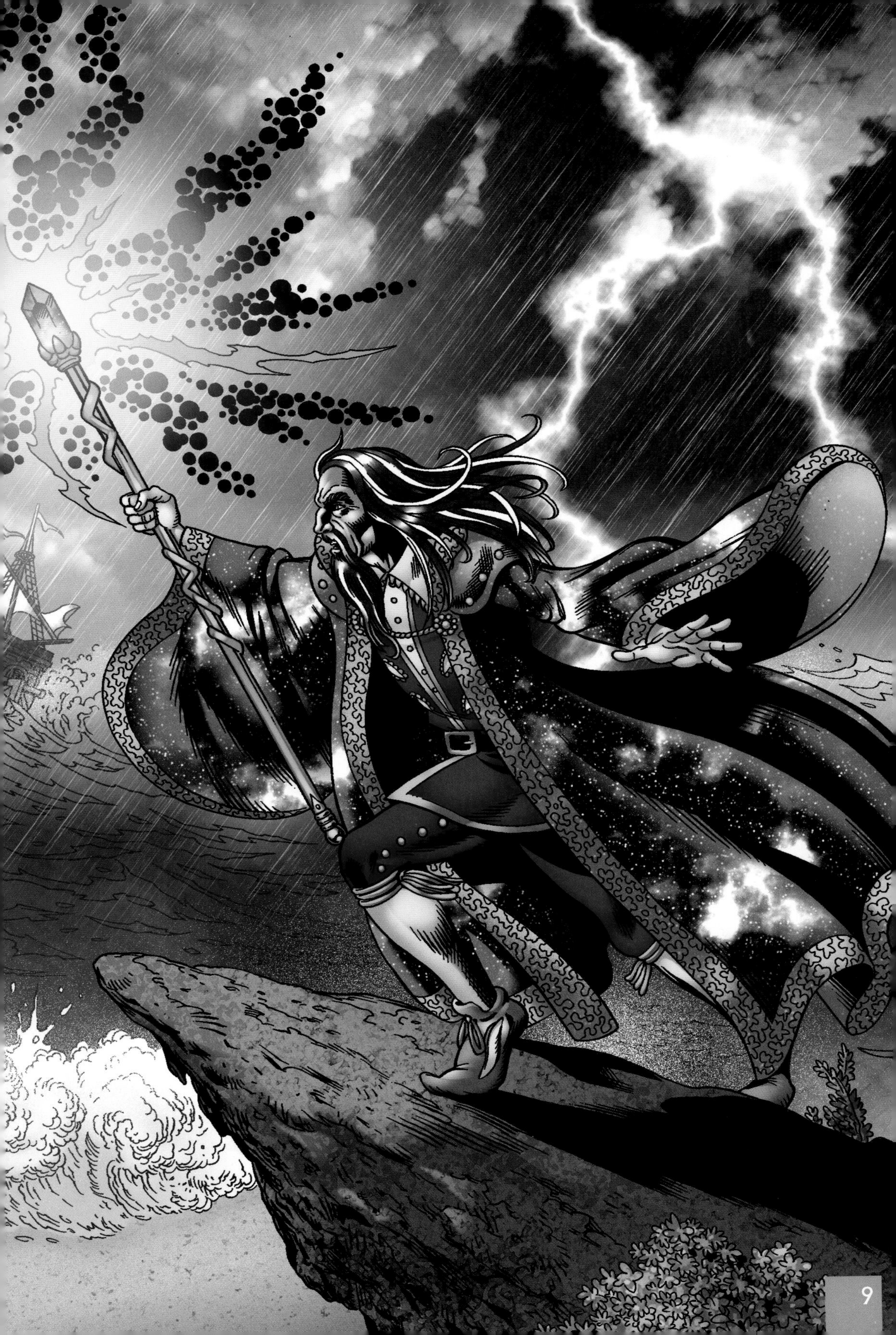

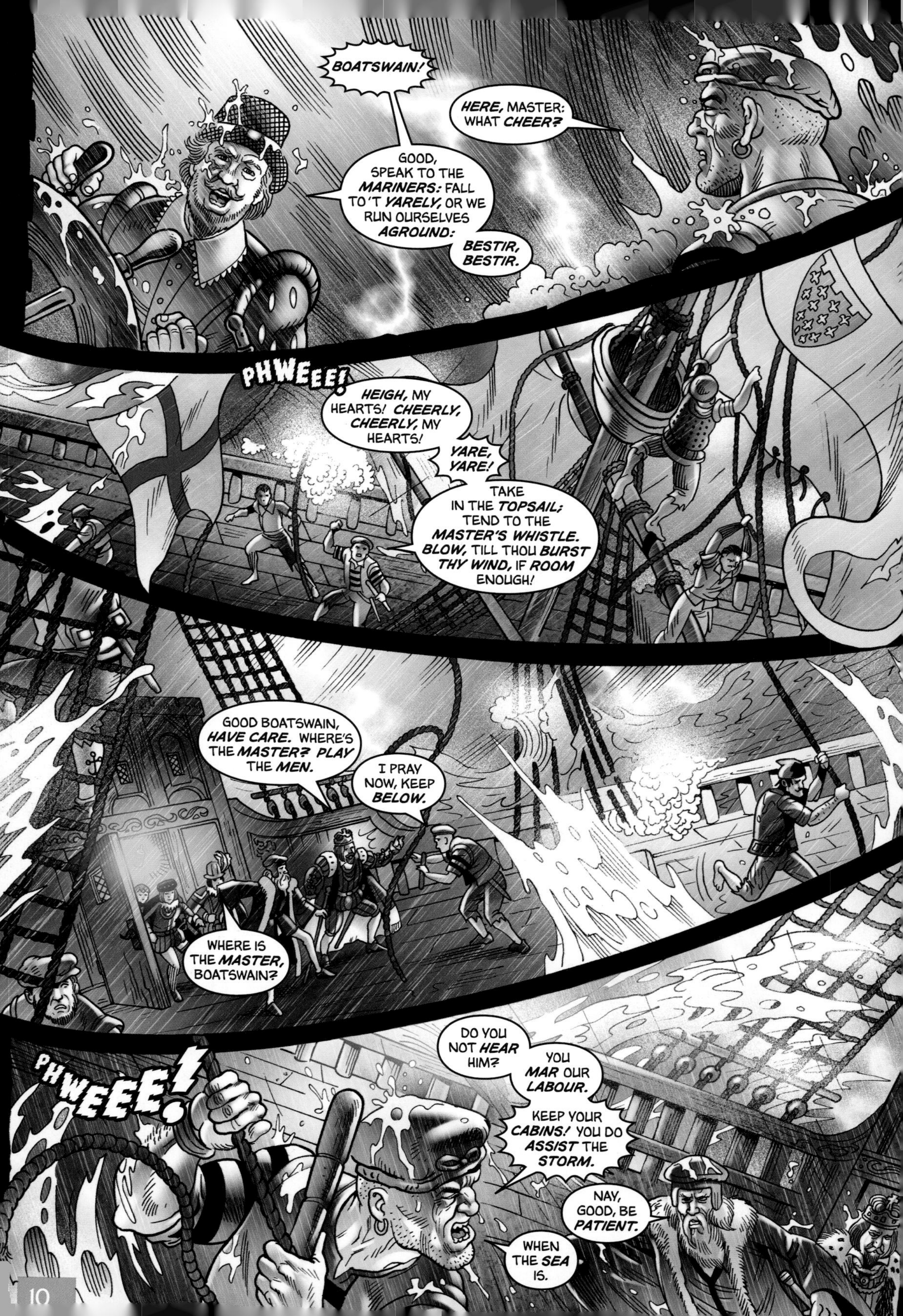
BOATSWAIN!
HERE, MASTER: WHAT CHEER?
GOOD, SPEAK TO THE MARINERS: FALL TO'T YARELY, OR WE RUN OURSELVES AGROUND:
BESTIR, BESTIR.
PHWEEE!
HEIGH, MY HEARTS! CHEERLY, CHEERLY, MY HEARTS!
YARE, YARE!
TAKE IN THE TOPSAIL; TEND TO THE MASTER'S WHISTLE. BLOW, TILL THOU BURST THY WIND, IF ROOM ENOUGH!
GOOD BOATSWAIN, HAVE CARE. WHERE'S THE MASTER? PLAY THE MEN.
I PRAY NOW, KEEP BELOW.
WHERE IS THE MASTER, BOATSWAIN?
PHWEEE!
DO YOU NOT HEAR HIM?
YOU MAR OUR LABOUR.
KEEP YOUR CABINS! YOU DO ASSIST THE STORM.
NAY, GOOD, BE PATIENT.
WHEN THE SEA IS.

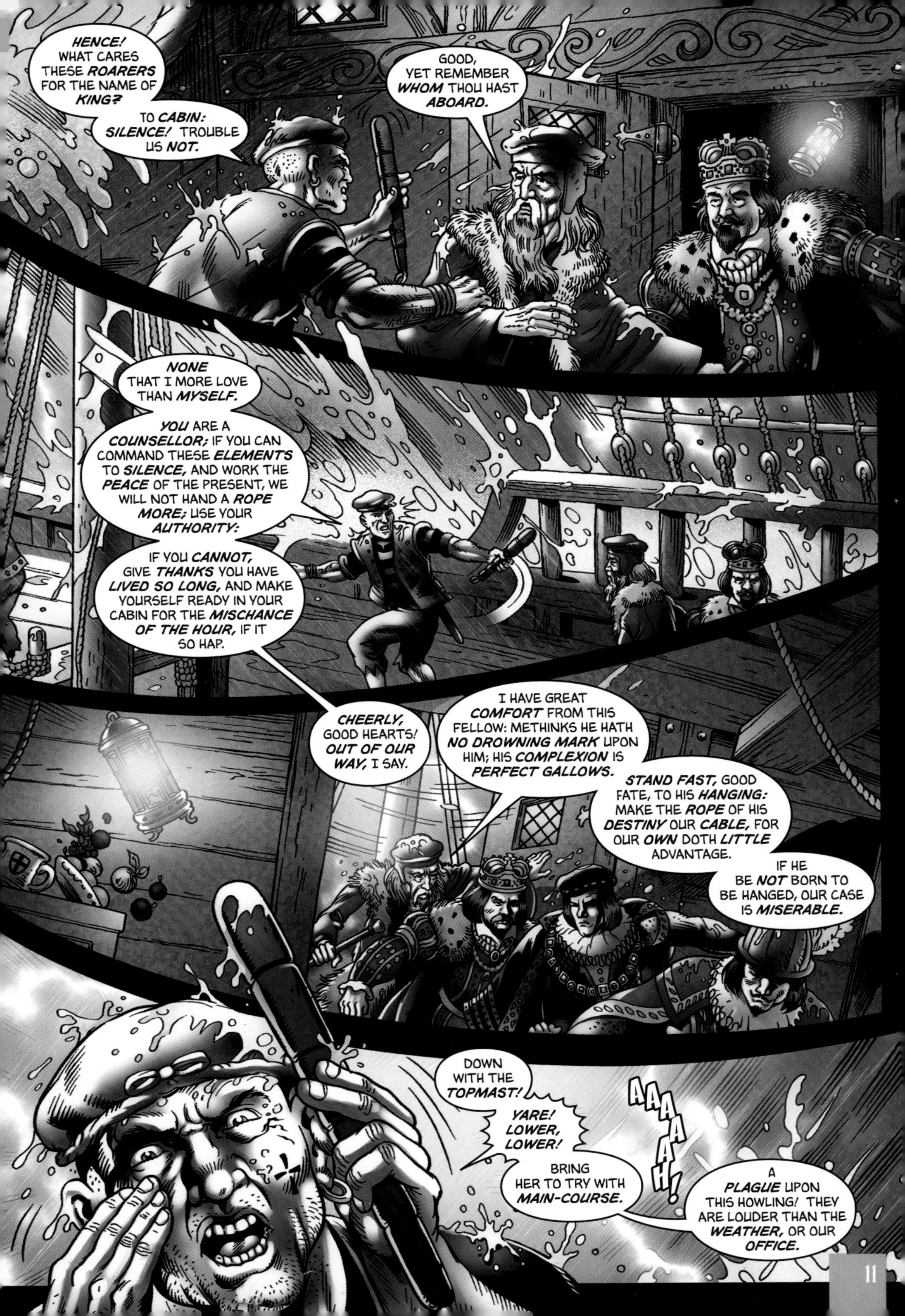

HENCE! WHAT CARES THESE ROARERS FOR THE NAME OF KING?
TO CABIN: SILENCE! TROUBLE US NOT.
GOOD, YET REMEMBER WHOM THOU HAST ABOARD.
NONE THAT I MORE LOVE THAN MYSELF.
YOU ARE A COUNSELLOR; IF YOU CAN COMMAND THESE ELEMENTS TO SILENCE, AND WORK THE PEACE OF THE PRESENT, WE WILL NOT HAND A ROPE MORE; USE YOUR AUTHORITY:
IF YOU CANNOT, GIVE THANKS YOU HAVE LIVED SO LONG, AND MAKE YOURSELF READY IN YOUR CABIN FOR THE MISCHANCE OF THE HOUR, IF IT SO HAP.
CHEERLY, GOOD HEARTS! OUT OF OUR WAY, I SAY.
I HAVE GREAT COMFORT FROM THIS FELLOW: METHINKS HE HATH NO DROWNING MARK UPON HIM; HIS COMPLEXION IS PERFECT GALLOWS.
STAND FAST, GOOD FATE, TO HIS HANGING: MAKE THE ROPE OF HIS DESTINY OUR CABLE, FOR OUR OWN DOTH LITTLE ADVANTAGE.
IF HE BE NOT BORN TO BE HANGED, OUR CASE IS MISERABLE.
DOWN WITH THE TOPMAST!
YARE! LOWER, LOWER!
BRING HER TO TRY WITH MAIN-COURSE.
AAAAAAH!
A PLAGUE UPON THIS HOWLING! THEY ARE LOUDER THAN THE WEATHER, OR OUR OFFICE.

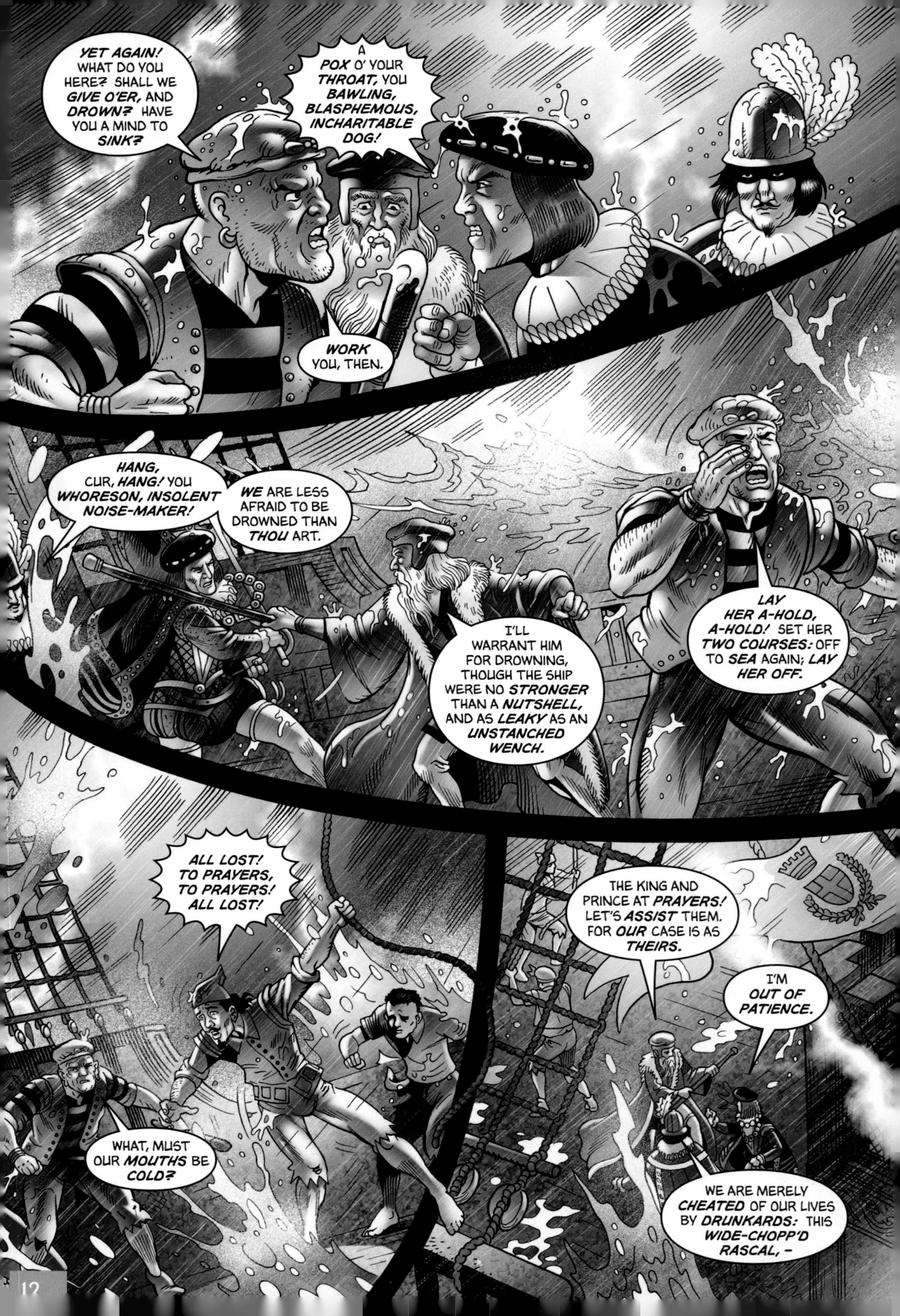

YET AGAIN! WHAT DO YOU HERE? SHALL WE GIVE O'ER, AND DROWN? HAVE YOU A MIND TO SINK?
A POX O' YOUR THROAT, YOU BAWLING, BLASPHEMOUS, INCHARITABLE DOG!
WORK YOU, THEN.
HANG, CUR, HANG! YOU WHORESON, INSOLENT NOISE-MAKER!
WE ARE LESS AFRAID TO BE DROWNED THAN THOU ART.
I'LL WARRANT HIM FOR DROWNING, THOUGH THE SHIP WERE NO STRONGER THAN A NUTSHELL, AND AS LEAKY AS AN UNSTANCHED WENCH.
LAY HER A-HOLD, A-HOLD! SET HER TWO COURSES: OFF TO SEA AGAIN; LAY HER OFF.
ALL LOST! TO PRAYERS, TO PRAYERS! ALL LOST!
WHAT, MUST OUR MOUTHS BE COLD?
THE KING AND PRINCE AT PRAYERS! LET'S ASSIST THEM. FOR OUR CASE IS AS THEIRS.
I'M OUT OF PATIENCE.
WE ARE MERELY CHEATED OF OUR LIVES BY DRUNKARDS: THIS WIDE-CHOPP'D RASCAL, –

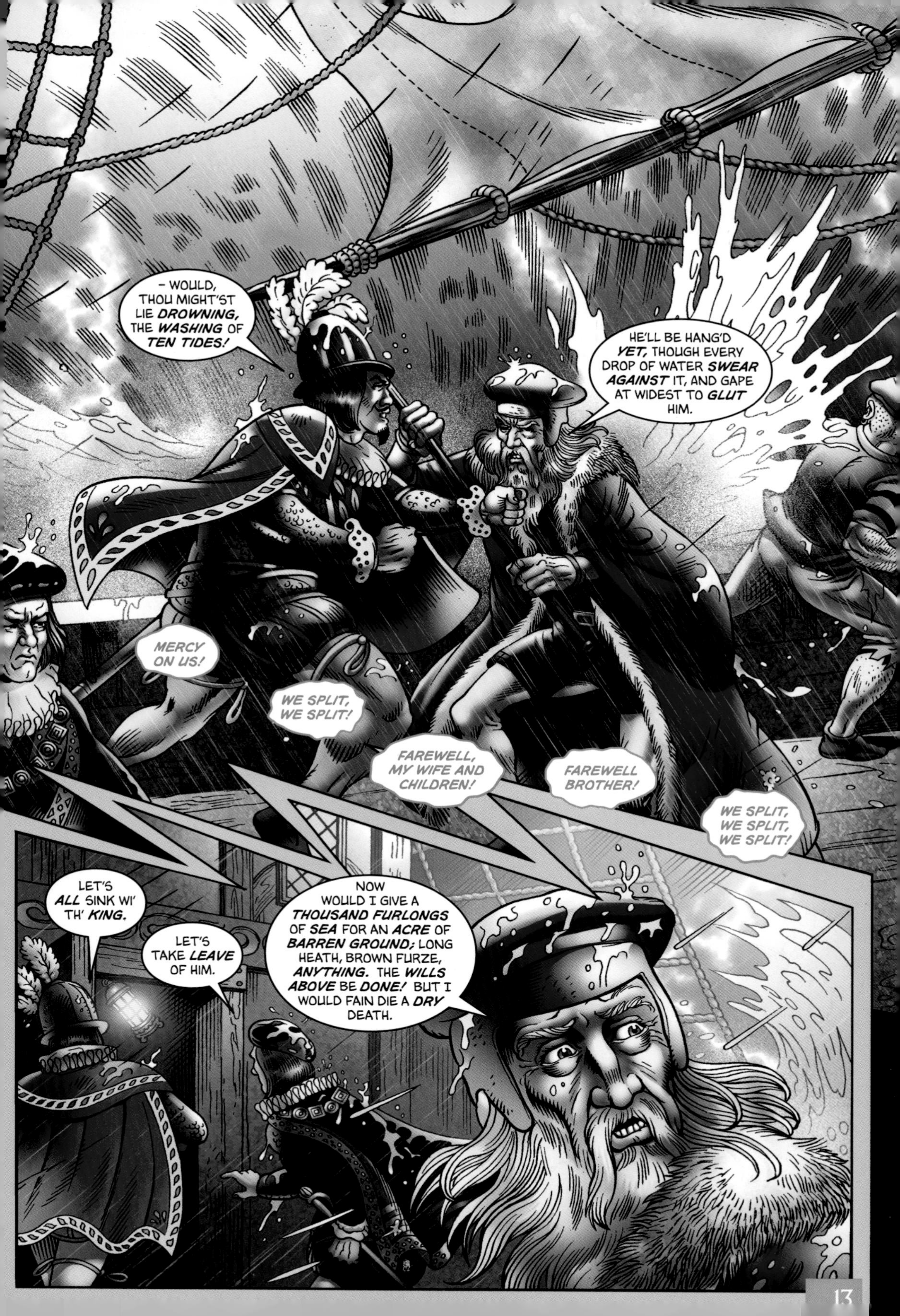
– WOULD, THOU MIGHT'ST LIE DROWNING, THE WASHING OF TEN TIDES!
HE'LL BE HANG'D YET, THOUGH EVERY DROP OF WATER SWEAR AGAINST IT, AND GAPE AT WIDEST TO GLUT HIM.
MERCY ON US!
WE SPLIT, WE SPLIT!
FAREWELL, MY WIFE AND CHILDREN!
FAREWELL BROTHER!
WE SPLIT, WE SPLIT, WE SPLIT!
LET'S ALL SINK WI' TH' KING.
LET'S TAKE LEAVE OF HIM.
NOW WOULD I GIVE A THOUSAND FURLONGS OF SEA FOR AN ACRE OF BARREN GROUND; LONG HEATH, BROWN FURZE, ANYTHING. THE WILLS ABOVE BE DONE! BUT I WOULD FAIN DIE A DRY DEATH.

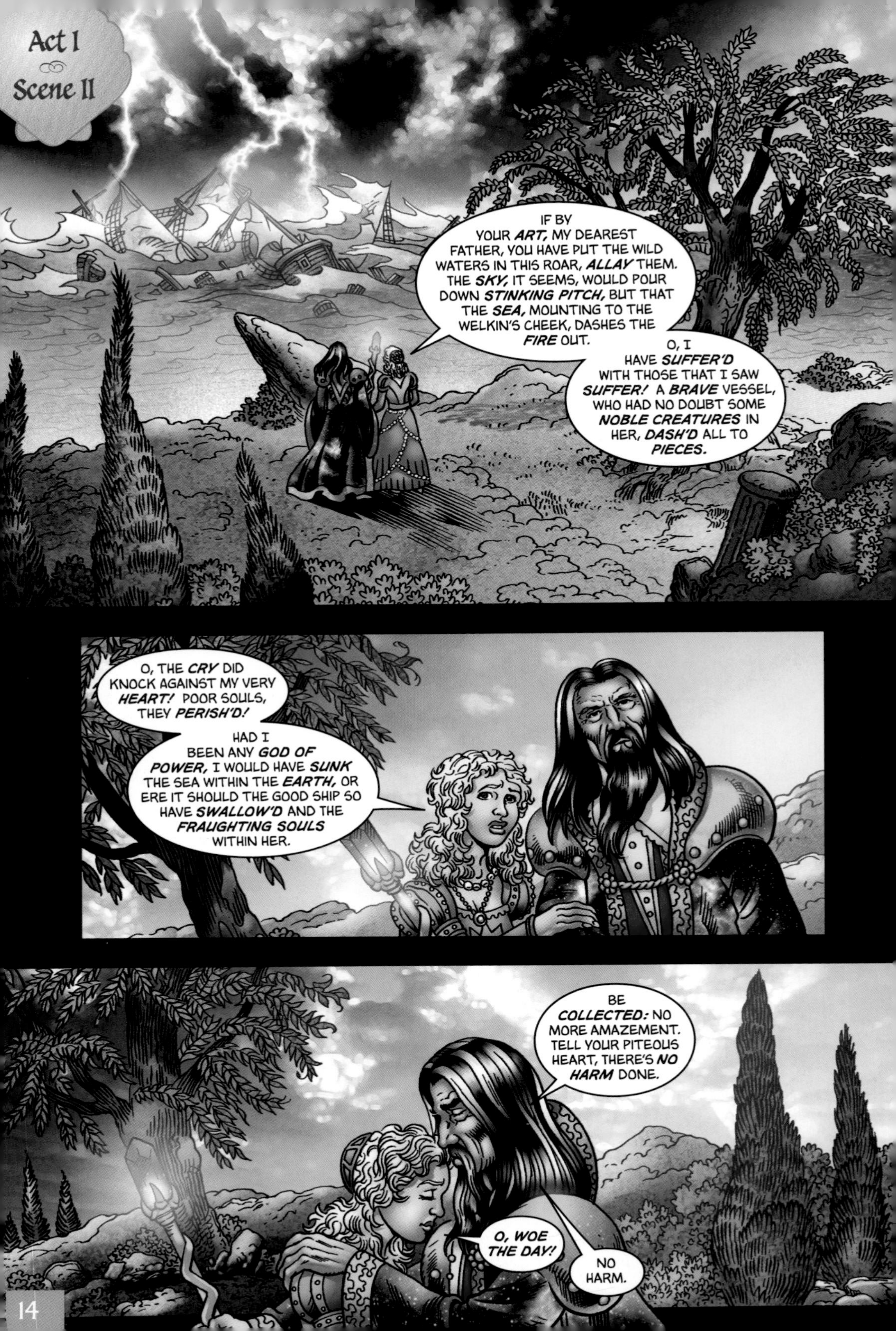
Act I Scene II
IF BY YOUR ART, MY DEAREST FATHER, YOU HAVE PUT THE WILD WATERS IN THIS ROAR, ALLAY THEM. THE SKY, IT SEEMS, WOULD POUR DOWN STINKING PITCH, BUT THAT THE SEA, MOUNTING TO THE WELKIN'S CHEEK, DASHES THE FIRE OUT.
O, I HAVE SUFFER'D WITH THOSE THAT I SAW SUFFER! A BRAVE VESSEL, WHO HAD NO DOUBT SOME NOBLE CREATURES IN HER, DASH'D ALL TO PIECES.
O, THE CRY DID KNOCK AGAINST MY VERY HEART! POOR SOULS, THEY PERISH'D!
HAD I BEEN ANY GOD OF POWER, I WOULD HAVE SUNK THE SEA WITHIN THE EARTH, OR ERE IT SHOULD THE GOOD SHIP SO HAVE SWALLOW'D AND THE FRAUGHTING SOULS WITHIN HER.
BE COLLECTED: NO MORE AMAZEMENT. TELL YOUR PITEOUS HEART, THERE'S NO HARM DONE.
O, WOE THE DAY!
NO HARM.

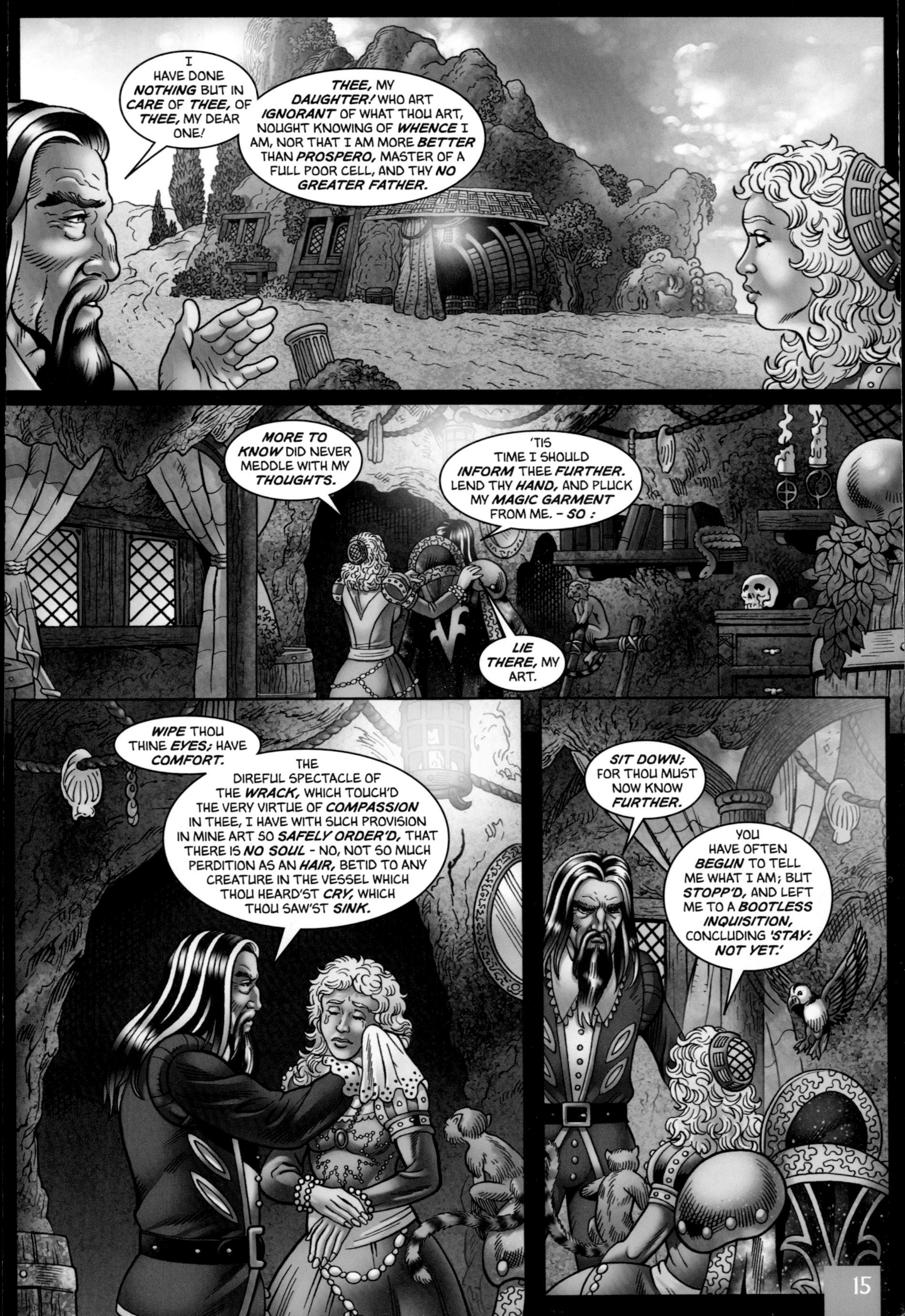
I HAVE DONE NOTHING BUT IN CARE OF THEE, OF THEE, MY DEAR ONE!
THEE, MY DAUGHTER! WHO ART IGNORANT OF WHAT THOU ART, NOUGHT KNOWING OF WHENCE I AM, NOR THAT I AM MORE BETTER THAN PROSPERO, MASTER OF A FULL POOR CELL, AND THY NO GREATER FATHER.
MORE TO KNOW DID NEVER MEDDLE WITH MY THOUGHTS.
'TIS TIME I SHOULD INFORM THEE FURTHER. LEND THY HAND, AND PLUCK MY MAGIC GARMENT FROM ME. - SO :
LIE THERE, MY ART.
WIPE THOU THINE EYES; HAVE COMFORT.
THE DIREFUL SPECTACLE OF THE WRACK, WHICH TOUCH'D THE VERY VIRTUE OF COMPASSION IN THEE, I HAVE WITH SUCH PROVISION IN MINE ART SO SAFELY ORDER'D, THAT THERE IS NO SOUL - NO, NOT SO MUCH PERDITION AS AN HAIR, BETID TO ANY CREATURE IN THE VESSEL WHICH THOU HEARD'ST CRY, WHICH THOU SAW'ST SINK.
SIT DOWN; FOR THOU MUST NOW KNOW FURTHER.
YOU HAVE OFTEN BEGUN TO TELL ME WHAT I AM; BUT STOPP'D, AND LEFT ME TO A BOOTLESS INQUISITION, CONCLUDING 'STAY: NOT YET.'

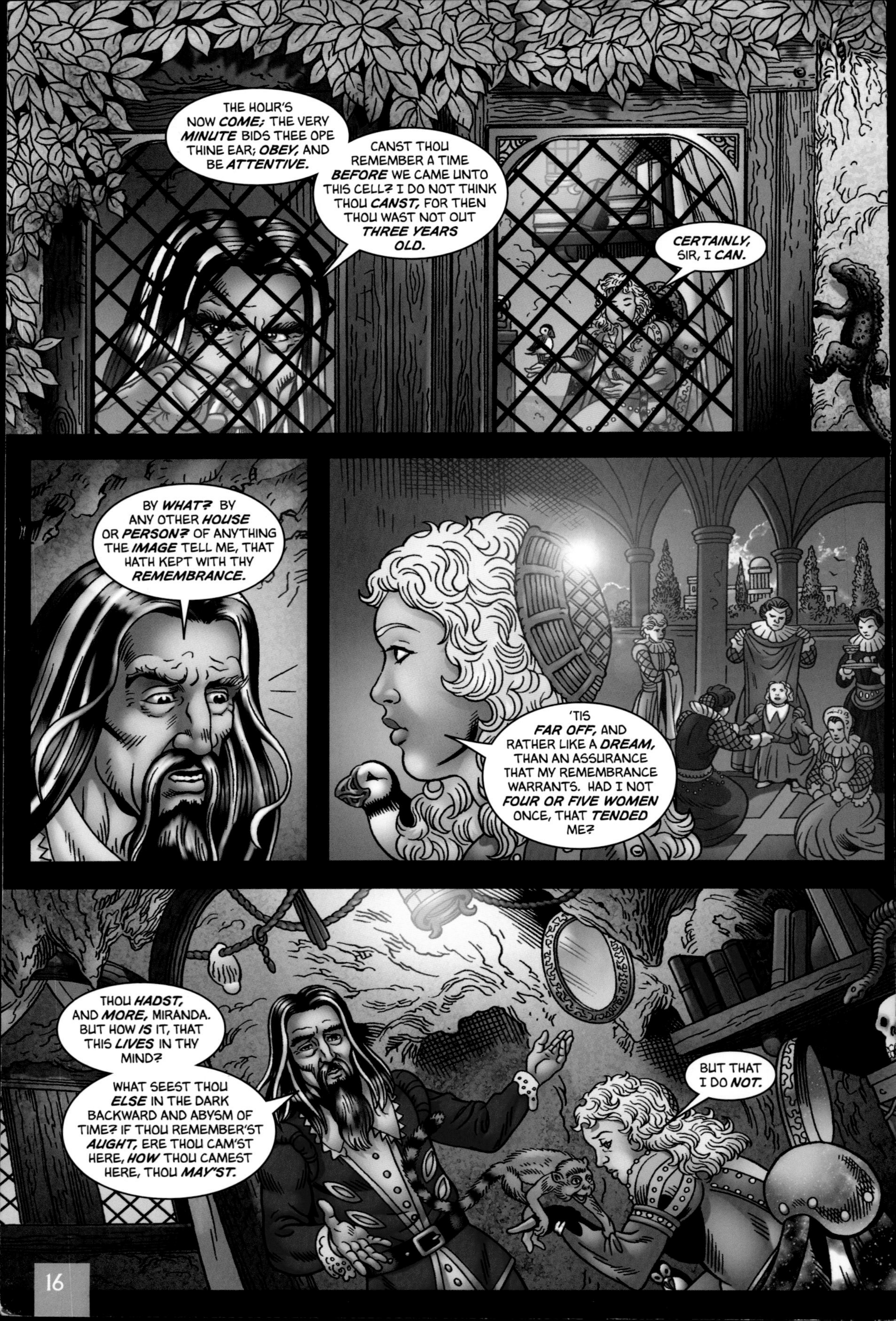
THE HOUR'S NOW COME; THE VERY MINUTE BIDS THEE OPE THINE EAR; OBEY, AND BE ATTENTIVE.
CANST THOU REMEMBER A TIME BEFORE WE CAME UNTO THIS CELL? I DO NOT THINK THOU CANST, FOR THEN THOU WAST NOT OUT THREE YEARS OLD.
CERTAINLY, SIR, I CAN.
BY WHAT? BY ANY OTHER HOUSE OR PERSON? OF ANYTHING THE IMAGE TELL ME, THAT HATH KEPT WITH THY REMEMBRANCE.
'TIS FAR OFF, AND RATHER LIKE A DREAM, THAN AN ASSURANCE THAT MY REMEMBRANCE WARRANTS. HAD I NOT FOUR OR FIVE WOMEN ONCE, THAT TENDED ME?
THOU HADST, AND MORE, MIRANDA. BUT HOW IS IT, THAT THIS LIVES IN THY MIND?
WHAT SEEST THOU ELSE IN THE DARK BACKWARD AND ABYSM OF TIME? IF THOU REMEMBER'ST AUGHT, ERE THOU CAM'ST HERE, HOW THOU CAMEST HERE, THOU MAY'ST.
BUT THAT I DO NOT.

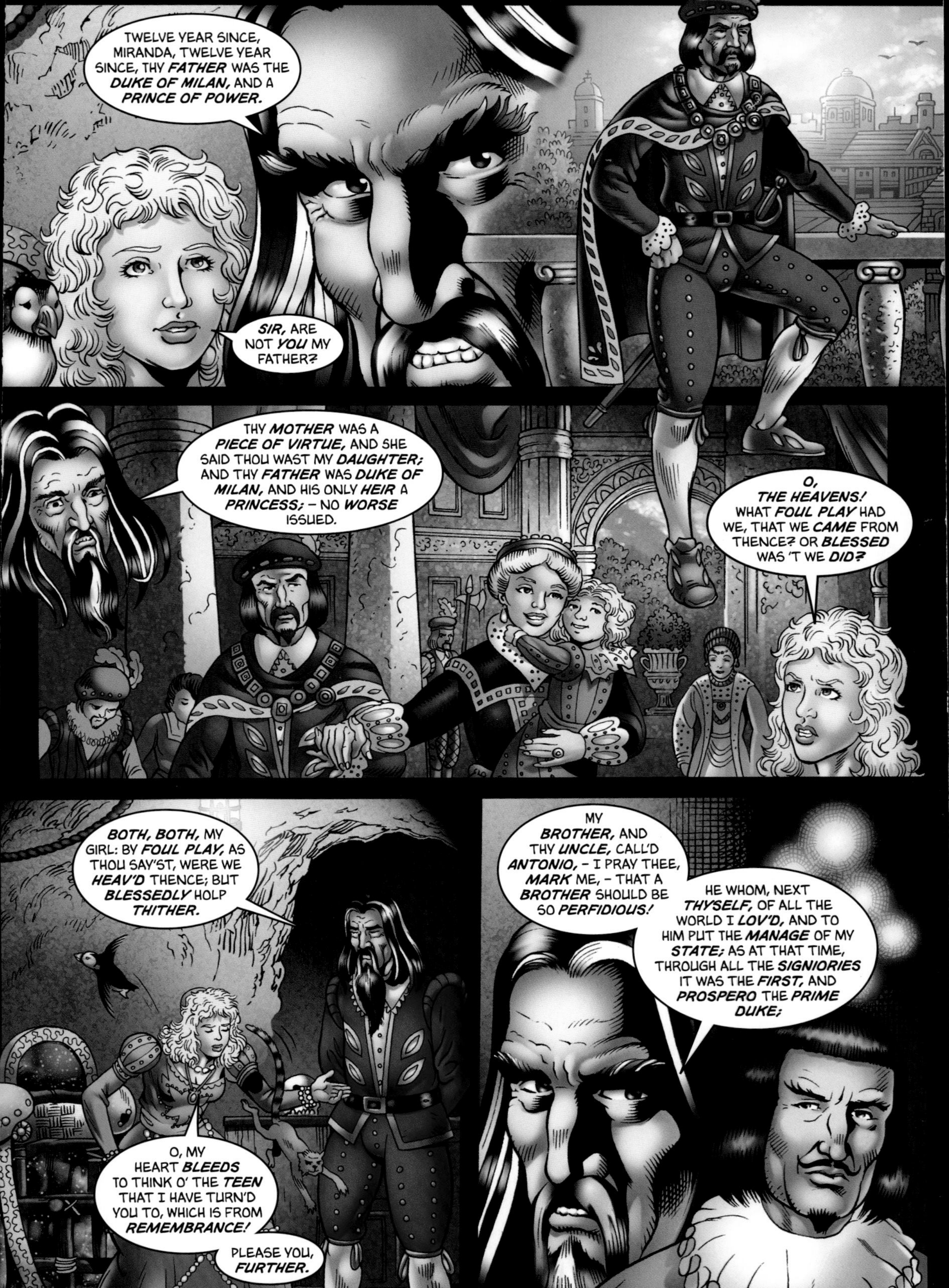

TWELVE YEAR SINCE, MIRANDA, TWELVE YEAR SINCE, THY *FATHER* WAS THE *DUKE OF MILAN,* AND A *PRINCE OF POWER.*
SIR, ARE NOT *YOU* MY FATHER?
THY *MOTHER* WAS A *PIECE OF VIRTUE,* AND SHE SAID THOU WAST MY *DAUGHTER;* AND THY *FATHER* WAS *DUKE OF MILAN,* AND HIS ONLY *HEIR* A *PRINCESS;* – NO *WORSE* ISSUED.
O, THE HEAVENS! WHAT *FOUL PLAY* HAD WE, THAT WE *CAME* FROM THENCE? OR *BLESSED* WAS 'T WE *DID?*
BOTH, BOTH, MY GIRL: BY *FOUL PLAY,* AS THOU SAY'ST, WERE WE *HEAV'D* THENCE; BUT *BLESSEDLY* HOLP *THITHER.*
O, MY HEART *BLEEDS* TO THINK O' THE *TEEN* THAT I HAVE TURN'D YOU TO, WHICH IS FROM *REMEMBRANCE!*
PLEASE YOU, *FURTHER.*
MY *BROTHER,* AND THY *UNCLE,* CALL'D *ANTONIO,* – I PRAY THEE, *MARK* ME, – THAT A *BROTHER* SHOULD BE SO *PERFIDIOUS!*
HE WHOM, NEXT *THYSELF,* OF ALL THE WORLD I *LOV'D,* AND TO HIM PUT THE *MANAGE* OF MY *STATE;* AS AT THAT TIME, THROUGH ALL THE *SIGNIORIES* IT WAS THE *FIRST,* AND *PROSPERO* THE *PRIME DUKE;*

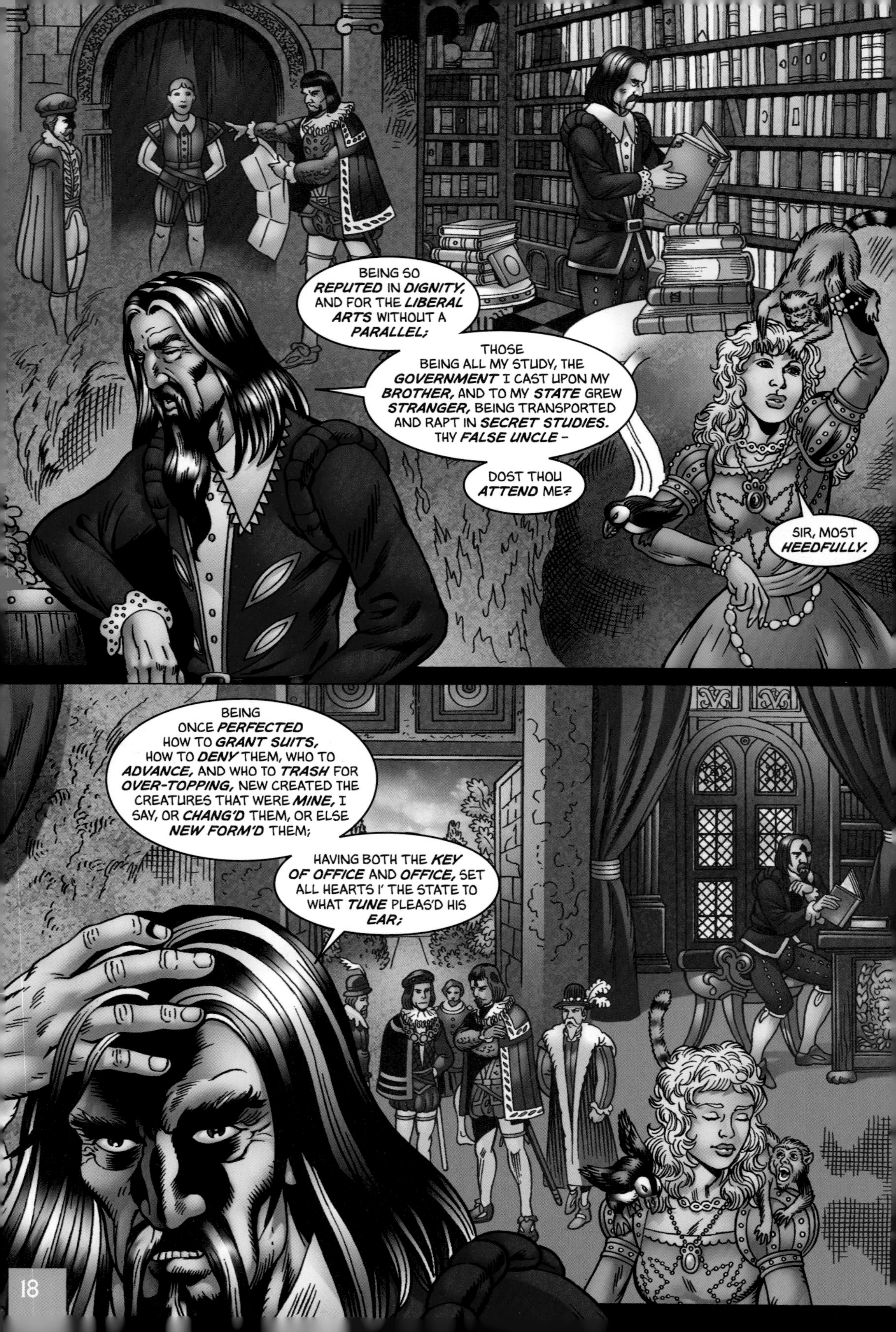

BEING SO REPUTED IN DIGNITY, AND FOR THE LIBERAL ARTS WITHOUT A PARALLEL;
THOSE BEING ALL MY STUDY, THE GOVERNMENT I CAST UPON MY BROTHER, AND TO MY STATE GREW STRANGER, BEING TRANSPORTED AND RAPT IN SECRET STUDIES. THY FALSE UNCLE –
DOST THOU ATTEND ME?
SIR, MOST HEEDFULLY.
BEING ONCE PERFECTED HOW TO GRANT SUITS, HOW TO DENY THEM, WHO TO ADVANCE, AND WHO TO TRASH FOR OVER-TOPPING, NEW CREATED THE CREATURES THAT WERE MINE, I SAY, OR CHANG'D THEM, OR ELSE NEW FORM'D THEM;
HAVING BOTH THE KEY OF OFFICE AND OFFICE, SET ALL HEARTS I' THE STATE TO WHAT TUNE PLEAS'D HIS EAR;

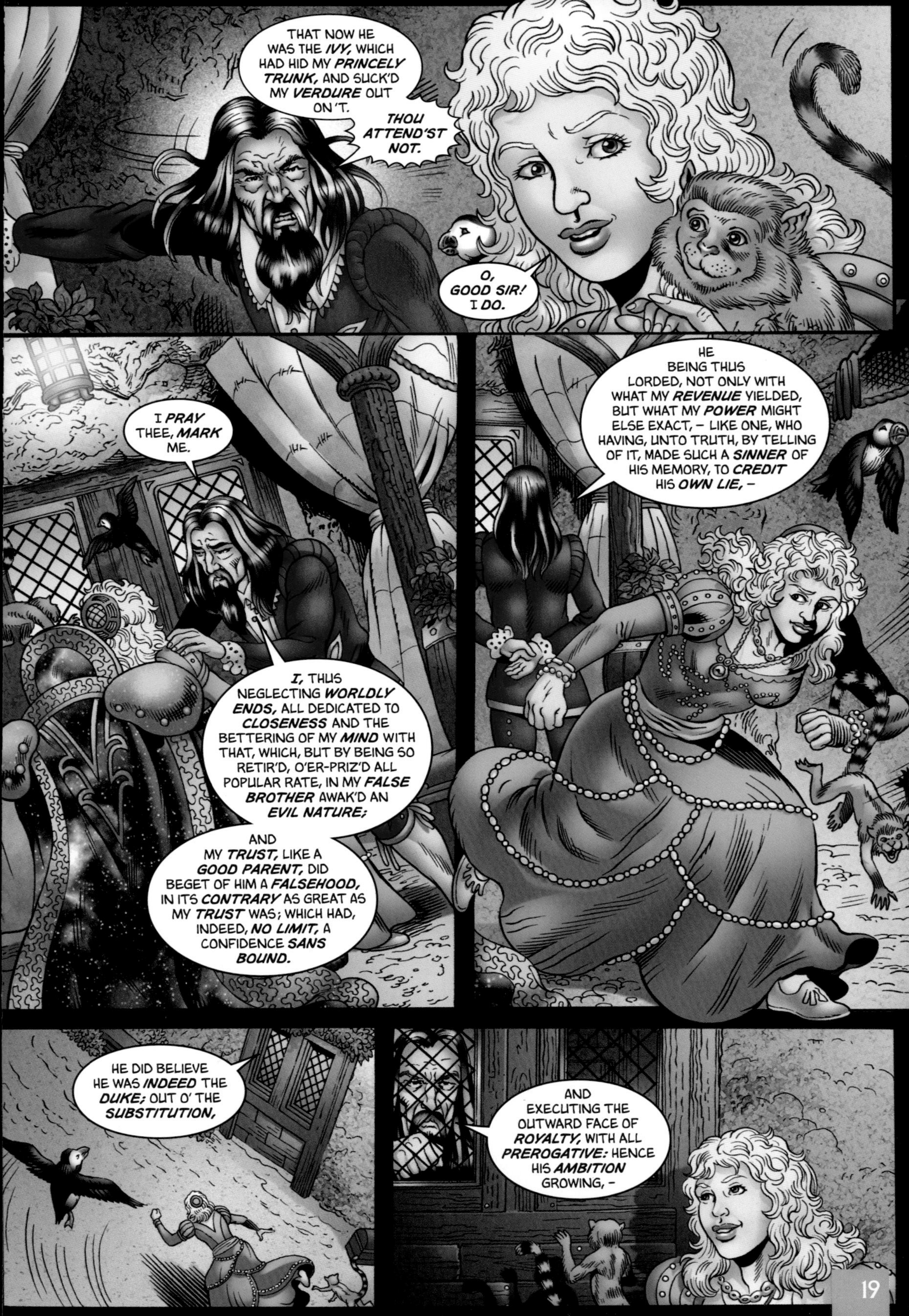

THAT NOW HE WAS THE IVY, WHICH HAD HID MY PRINCELY TRUNK, AND SUCK'D MY VERDURE OUT ON'T.
THOU ATTEND'ST NOT.
O, GOOD SIR! I DO.
I PRAY THEE, MARK ME.
I, THUS NEGLECTING WORLDLY ENDS, ALL DEDICATED TO CLOSENESS AND THE BETTERING OF MY MIND WITH THAT, WHICH, BUT BY BEING SO RETIR'D, O'ER-PRIZ'D ALL POPULAR RATE, IN MY FALSE BROTHER AWAK'D AN EVIL NATURE;
AND MY TRUST, LIKE A GOOD PARENT, DID BEGET OF HIM A FALSEHOOD, IN ITS CONTRARY AS GREAT AS MY TRUST WAS; WHICH HAD, INDEED, NO LIMIT, A CONFIDENCE SANS BOUND.
HE BEING THUS LORDED, NOT ONLY WITH WHAT MY REVENUE YIELDED, BUT WHAT MY POWER MIGHT ELSE EXACT, – LIKE ONE, WHO HAVING, UNTO TRUTH, BY TELLING OF IT, MADE SUCH A SINNER OF HIS MEMORY, TO CREDIT HIS OWN LIE, –
HE DID BELIEVE HE WAS INDEED THE DUKE; OUT O' THE SUBSTITUTION,
AND EXECUTING THE OUTWARD FACE OF ROYALTY, WITH ALL PREROGATIVE: HENCE HIS AMBITION GROWING, –

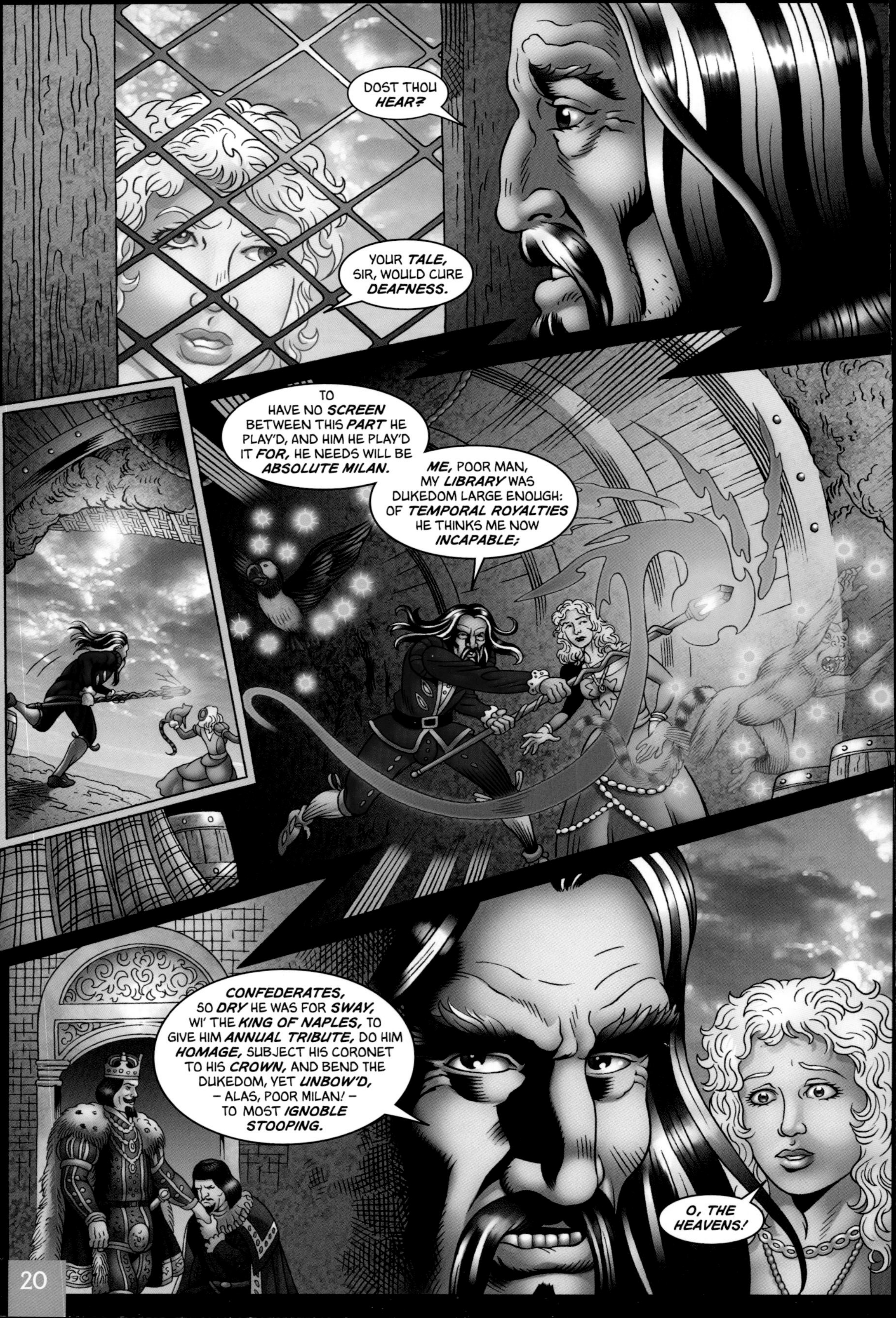
DOST THOU HEAR?
YOUR TALE, SIR, WOULD CURE DEAFNESS.
TO HAVE NO SCREEN BETWEEN THIS PART HE PLAY'D, AND HIM HE PLAY'D IT FOR, HE NEEDS WILL BE ABSOLUTE MILAN.
ME, POOR MAN, MY LIBRARY WAS DUKEDOM LARGE ENOUGH: OF TEMPORAL ROYALTIES HE THINKS ME NOW INCAPABLE;
CONFEDERATES, SO DRY HE WAS FOR SWAY, WI' THE KING OF NAPLES, TO GIVE HIM ANNUAL TRIBUTE, DO HIM HOMAGE, SUBJECT HIS CORONET TO HIS CROWN, AND BEND THE DUKEDOM, YET UNBOW'D, – ALAS, POOR MILAN! – TO MOST IGNOBLE STOOPING.
O, THE HEAVENS!

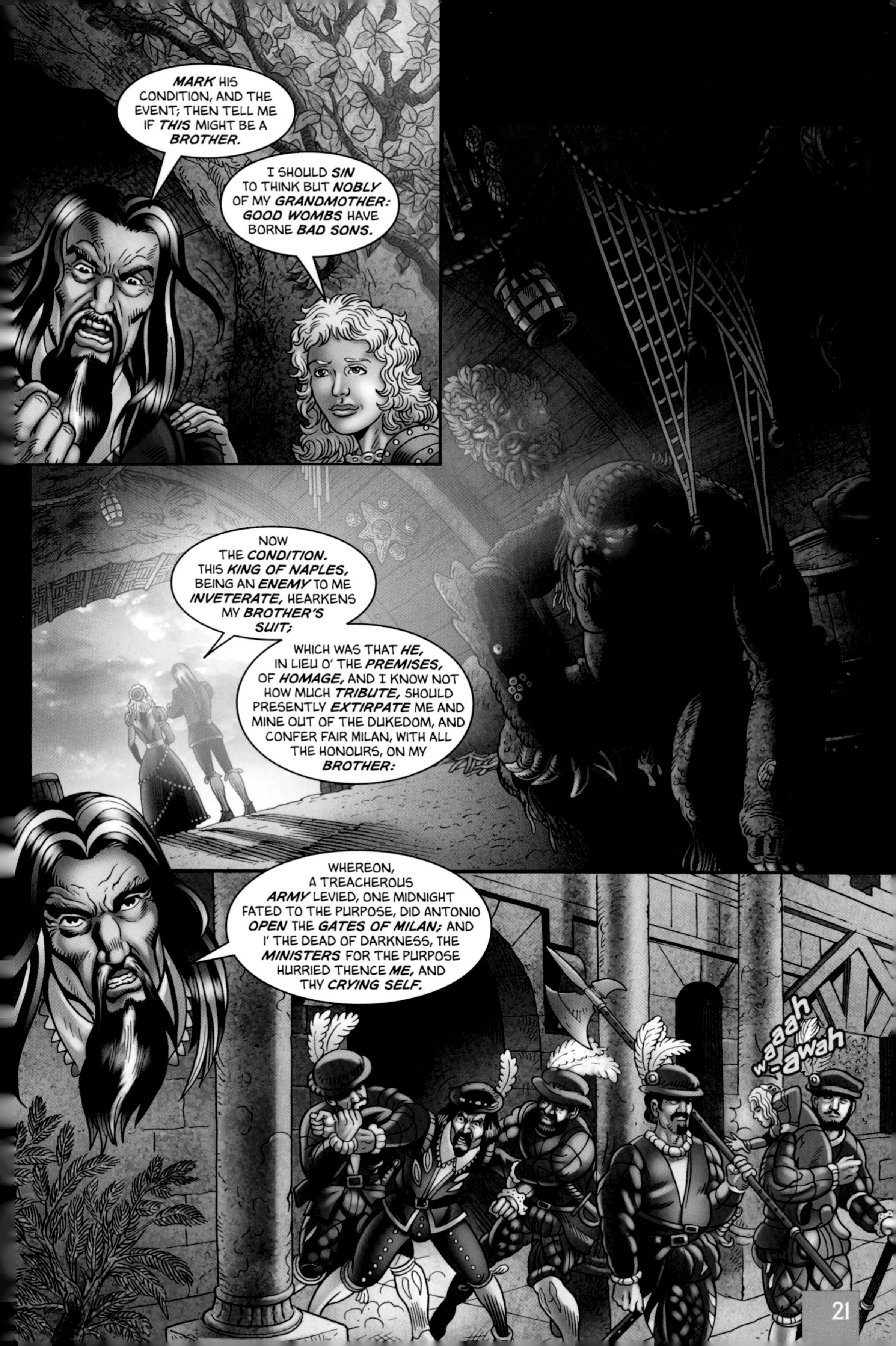

MARK HIS CONDITION, AND THE EVENT; THEN TELL ME IF THIS MIGHT BE A BROTHER.
I SHOULD SIN TO THINK BUT NOBLY OF MY GRANDMOTHER: GOOD WOMBS HAVE BORNE BAD SONS.
NOW THE CONDITION. THIS KING OF NAPLES, BEING AN ENEMY TO ME INVETERATE, HEARKENS MY BROTHER'S SUIT;
WHICH WAS THAT HE, IN LIEU O' THE PREMISES, OF HOMAGE, AND I KNOW NOT HOW MUCH TRIBUTE, SHOULD PRESENTLY EXTIRPATE ME AND MINE OUT OF THE DUKEDOM, AND CONFER FAIR MILAN, WITH ALL THE HONOURS, ON MY BROTHER:
WHEREON, A TREACHEROUS ARMY LEVIED, ONE MIDNIGHT FATED TO THE PURPOSE, DID ANTONIO OPEN THE GATES OF MILAN; AND I' THE DEAD OF DARKNESS, THE MINISTERS FOR THE PURPOSE HURRIED THENCE ME, AND THY CRYING SELF.
waaah wa-awah

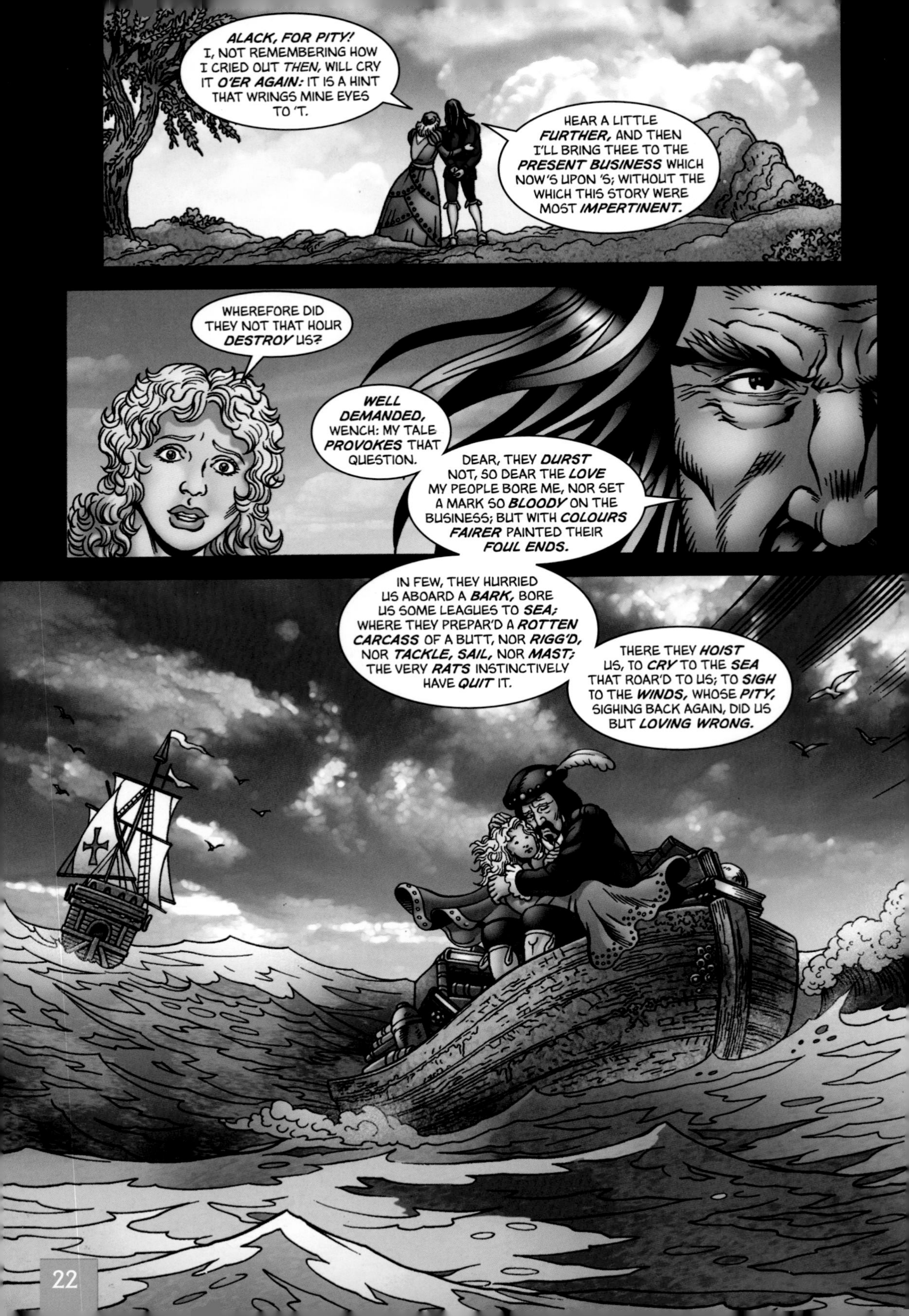
ALACK, FOR PITY! I, NOT REMEMBERING HOW I CRIED OUT THEN, WILL CRY IT O'ER AGAIN: IT IS A HINT THAT WRINGS MINE EYES TO 'T.
HEAR A LITTLE FURTHER, AND THEN I'LL BRING THEE TO THE PRESENT BUSINESS WHICH NOW'S UPON 'S; WITHOUT THE WHICH THIS STORY WERE MOST IMPERTINENT.
WHEREFORE DID THEY NOT THAT HOUR DESTROY US?
WELL DEMANDED, WENCH: MY TALE PROVOKES THAT QUESTION.
DEAR, THEY DURST NOT, SO DEAR THE LOVE MY PEOPLE BORE ME, NOR SET A MARK SO BLOODY ON THE BUSINESS; BUT WITH COLOURS FAIRER PAINTED THEIR FOUL ENDS.
IN FEW, THEY HURRIED US ABOARD A BARK, BORE US SOME LEAGUES TO SEA; WHERE THEY PREPAR'D A ROTTEN CARCASS OF A BUTT, NOR RIGG'D, NOR TACKLE, SAIL, NOR MAST; THE VERY RATS INSTINCTIVELY HAVE QUIT IT.
THERE THEY HOIST US, TO CRY TO THE SEA THAT ROAR'D TO US; TO SIGH TO THE WINDS, WHOSE PITY, SIGHING BACK AGAIN, DID US BUT LOVING WRONG.

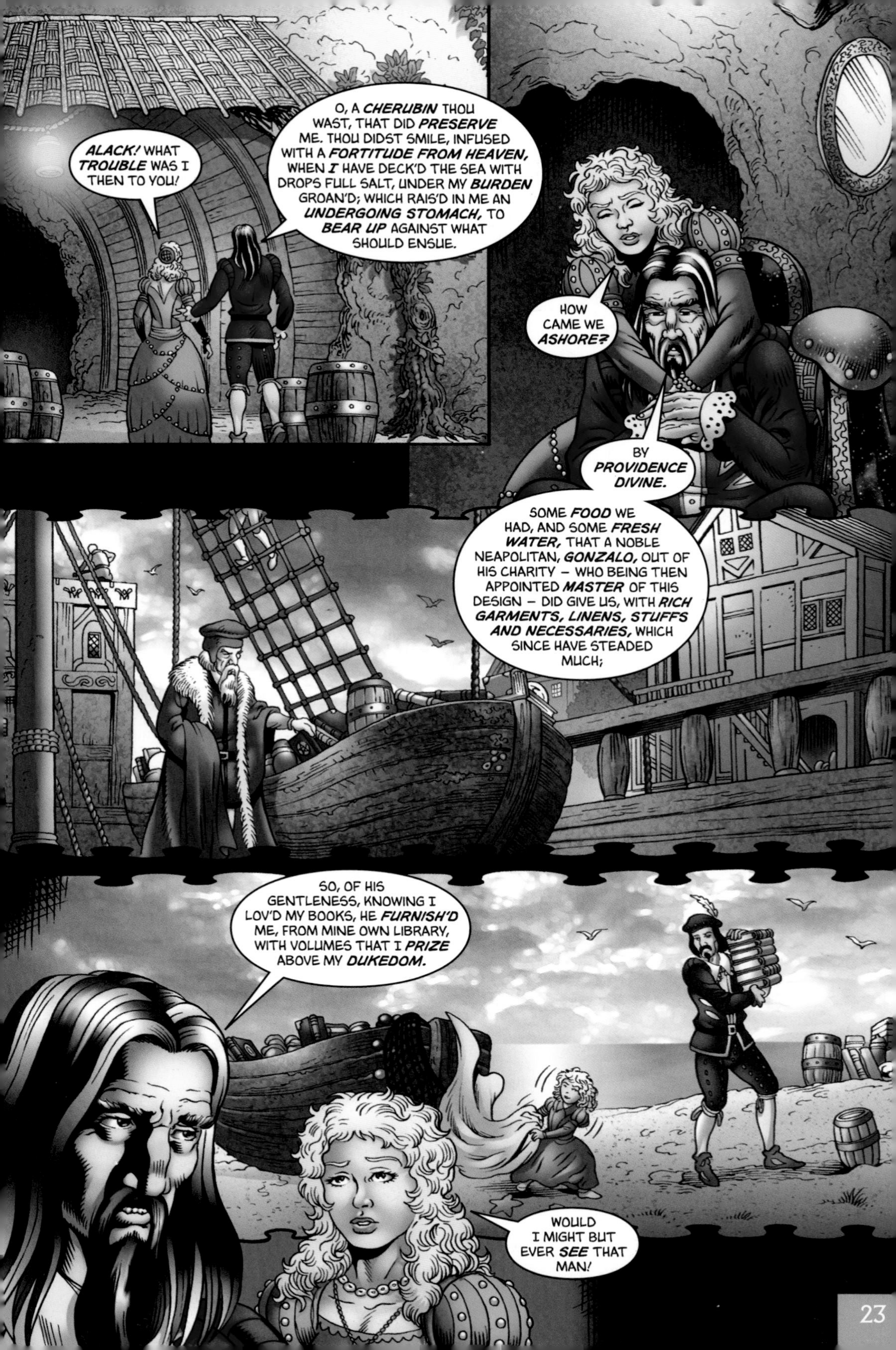
ALACK! WHAT TROUBLE WAS I THEN TO YOU!
O, A CHERUBIN THOU WAST, THAT DID PRESERVE ME. THOU DIDST SMILE, INFUSED WITH A FORTITUDE FROM HEAVEN, WHEN I HAVE DECK'D THE SEA WITH DROPS FULL SALT, UNDER MY BURDEN GROAN'D; WHICH RAIS'D IN ME AN UNDERGOING STOMACH, TO BEAR UP AGAINST WHAT SHOULD ENSUE.
HOW CAME WE ASHORE?
BY PROVIDENCE DIVINE.
SOME FOOD WE HAD, AND SOME FRESH WATER, THAT A NOBLE NEAPOLITAN, GONZALO, OUT OF HIS CHARITY – WHO BEING THEN APPOINTED MASTER OF THIS DESIGN – DID GIVE US, WITH RICH GARMENTS, LINENS, STUFFS AND NECESSARIES, WHICH SINCE HAVE STEADED MUCH;
SO, OF HIS GENTLENESS, KNOWING I LOV'D MY BOOKS, HE FURNISH'D ME, FROM MINE OWN LIBRARY, WITH VOLUMES THAT I PRIZE ABOVE MY DUKEDOM.
WOULD I MIGHT BUT EVER SEE THAT MAN!

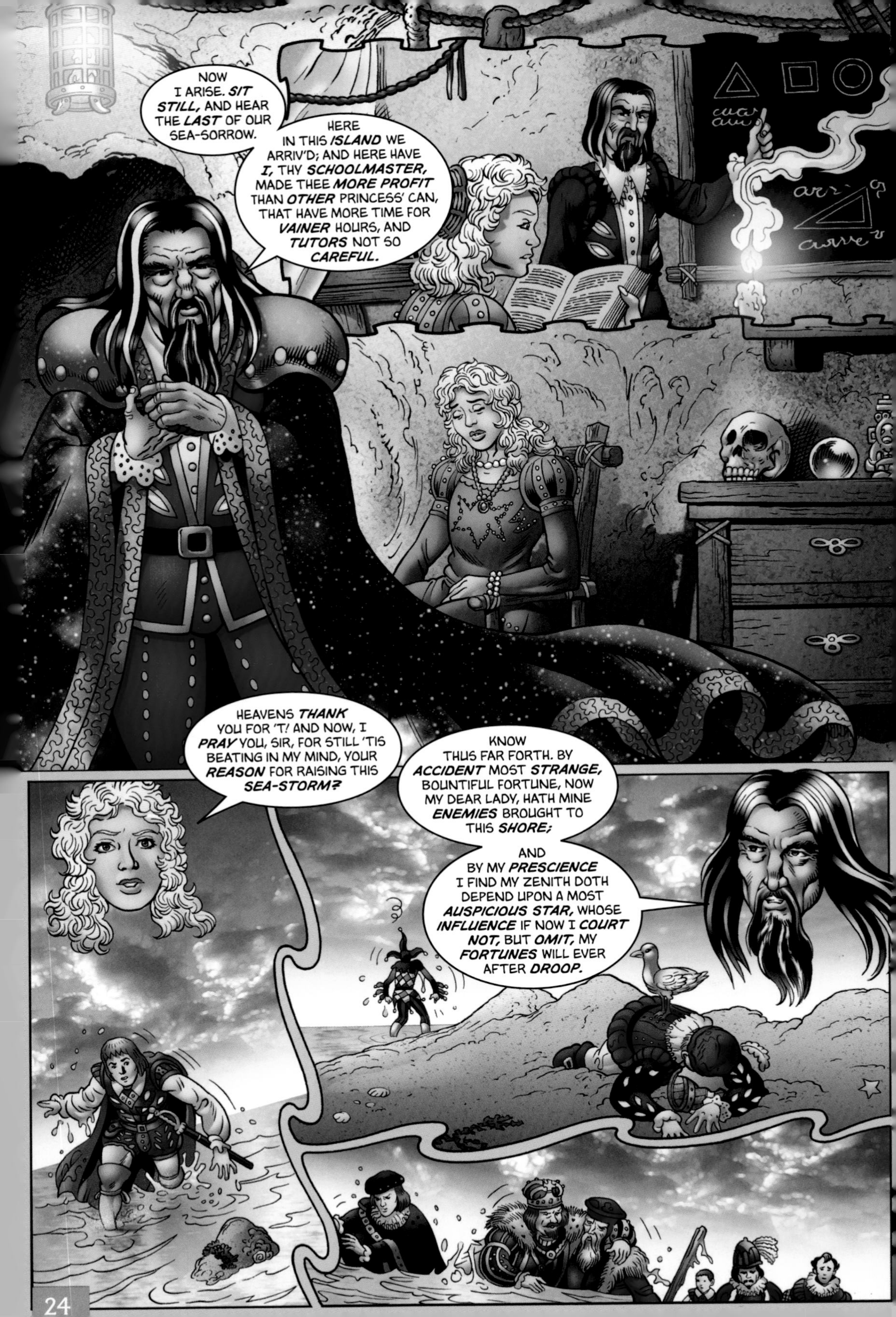
NOW I ARISE. SIT STILL, AND HEAR THE LAST OF OUR SEA-SORROW.
HERE IN THIS ISLAND WE ARRIV'D; AND HERE HAVE I, THY SCHOOLMASTER, MADE THEE MORE PROFIT THAN OTHER PRINCESS' CAN, THAT HAVE MORE TIME FOR VAINER HOURS, AND TUTORS NOT SO CAREFUL.
HEAVENS THANK YOU FOR 'T! AND NOW, I PRAY YOU, SIR, FOR STILL 'TIS BEATING IN MY MIND, YOUR REASON FOR RAISING THIS SEA-STORM?
KNOW THUS FAR FORTH. BY ACCIDENT MOST STRANGE, BOUNTIFUL FORTUNE, NOW MY DEAR LADY, HATH MINE ENEMIES BROUGHT TO THIS SHORE;
AND BY MY PRESCIENCE I FIND MY ZENITH DOTH DEPEND UPON A MOST AUSPICIOUS STAR, WHOSE INFLUENCE IF NOW I COURT NOT, BUT OMIT, MY FORTUNES WILL EVER AFTER DROOP.

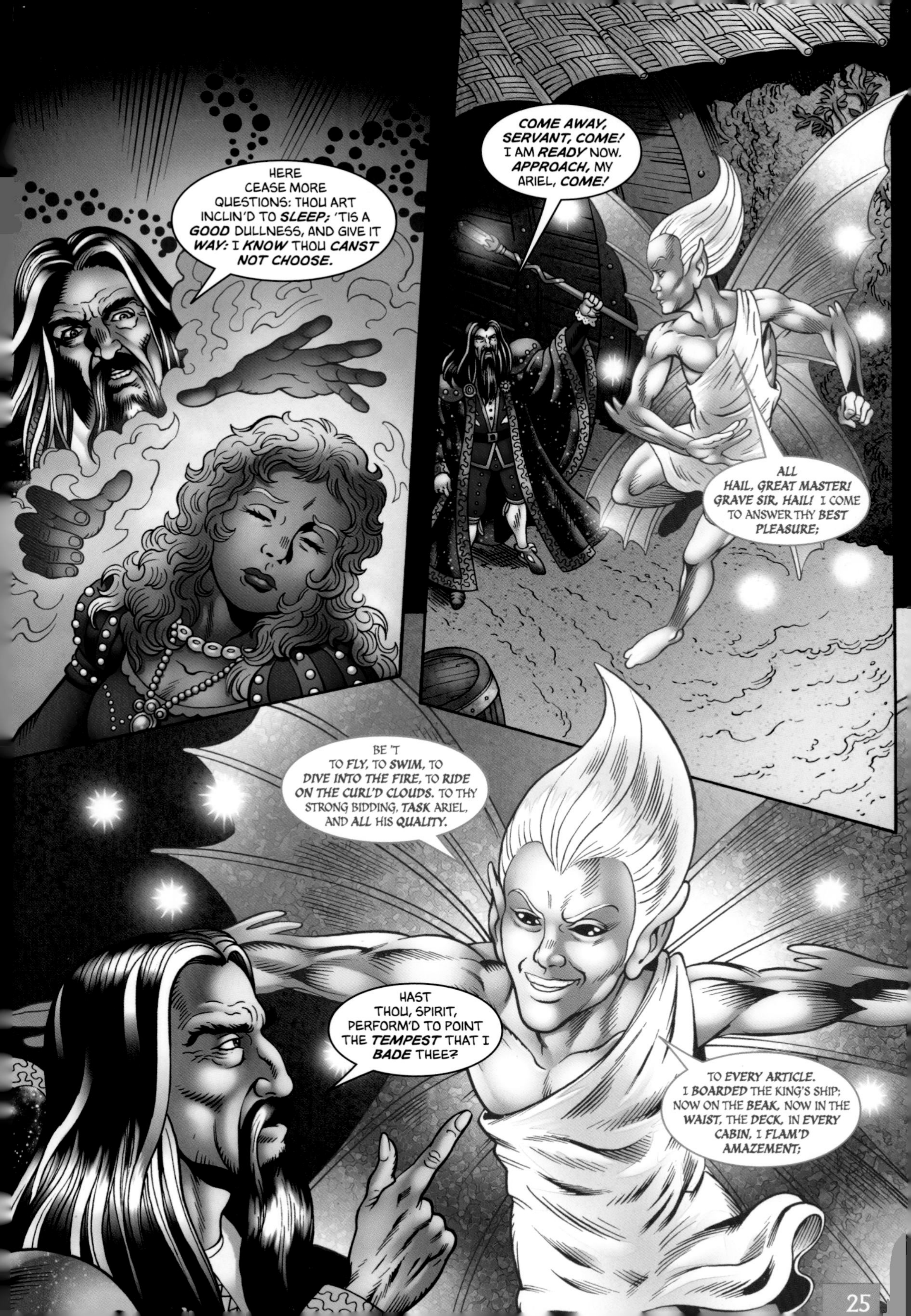
HERE CEASE MORE QUESTIONS: THOU ART INCLIN'D TO SLEEP; 'TIS A GOOD DULLNESS, AND GIVE IT WAY: I KNOW THOU CANST NOT CHOOSE.
COME AWAY, SERVANT, COME! I AM READY NOW. APPROACH, MY ARIEL, COME!
ALL HAIL, GREAT MASTER! GRAVE SIR, HAIL! I COME TO ANSWER THY BEST PLEASURE;
BE 'T TO FLY, TO SWIM, TO DIVE INTO THE FIRE, TO RIDE ON THE CURL'D CLOUDS. TO THY STRONG BIDDING, TASK ARIEL, AND ALL HIS QUALITY.
HAST THOU, SPIRIT, PERFORM'D TO POINT THE TEMPEST THAT I BADE THEE?
TO EVERY ARTICLE. I BOARDED THE KING'S SHIP; NOW ON THE BEAK, NOW IN THE WAIST, THE DECK, IN EVERY CABIN, I FLAM'D AMAZEMENT;

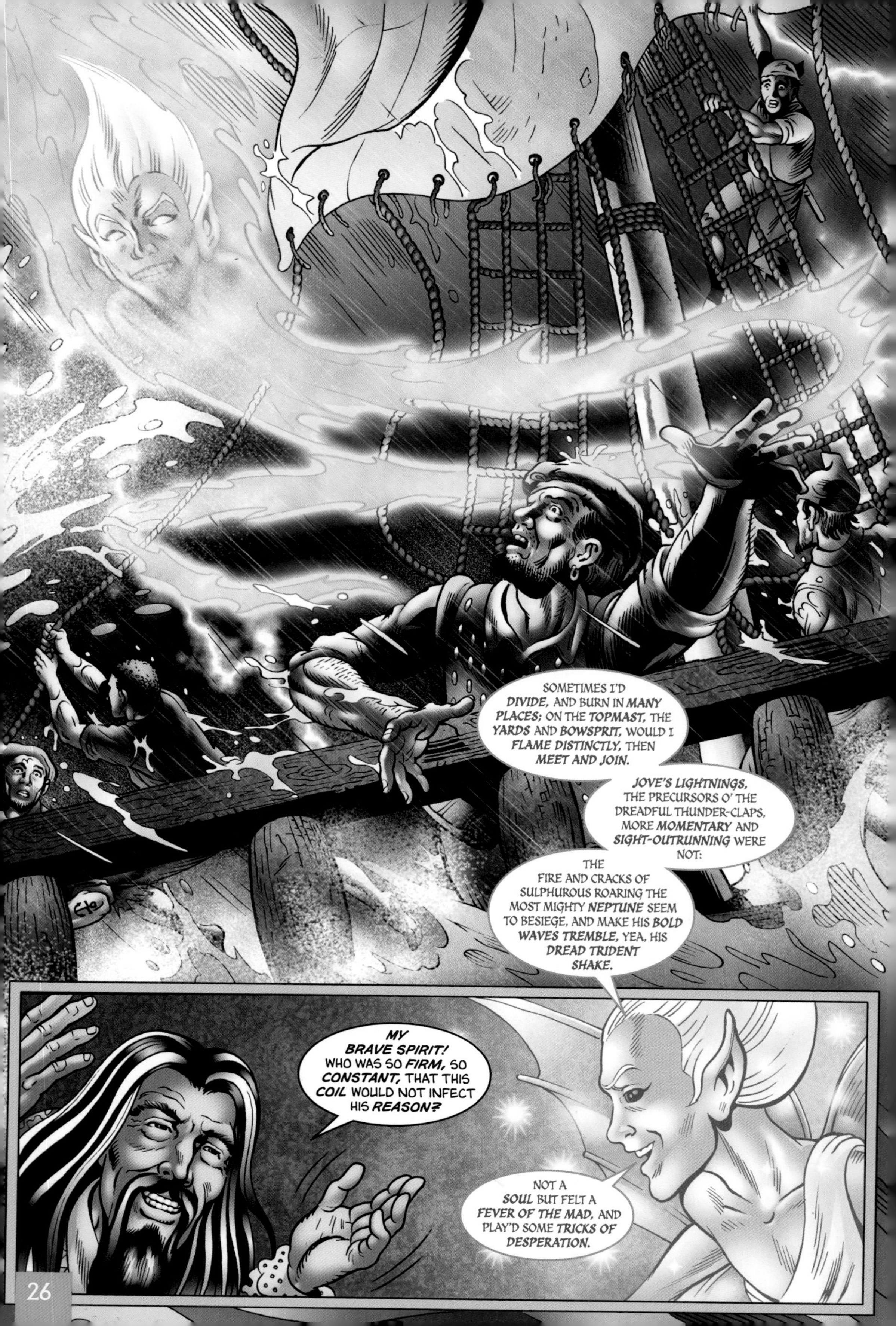
SOMETIMES I'D DIVIDE, AND BURN IN MANY PLACES; ON THE TOPMAST, THE YARDS AND BOWSPRIT, WOULD I FLAME DISTINCTLY, THEN MEET AND JOIN.
JOVE'S LIGHTNINGS, THE PRECURSORS O' THE DREADFUL THUNDER-CLAPS, MORE MOMENTARY AND SIGHT-OUTRUNNING WERE NOT:
THE FIRE AND CRACKS OF SULPHUROUS ROARING THE MOST MIGHTY NEPTUNE SEEM TO BESIEGE, AND MAKE HIS BOLD WAVES TREMBLE, YEA, HIS DREAD TRIDENT SHAKE.
MY BRAVE SPIRIT! WHO WAS SO FIRM, SO CONSTANT, THAT THIS COIL WOULD NOT INFECT HIS REASON?
NOT A SOUL BUT FELT A FEVER OF THE MAD, AND PLAY'D SOME TRICKS OF DESPERATION.

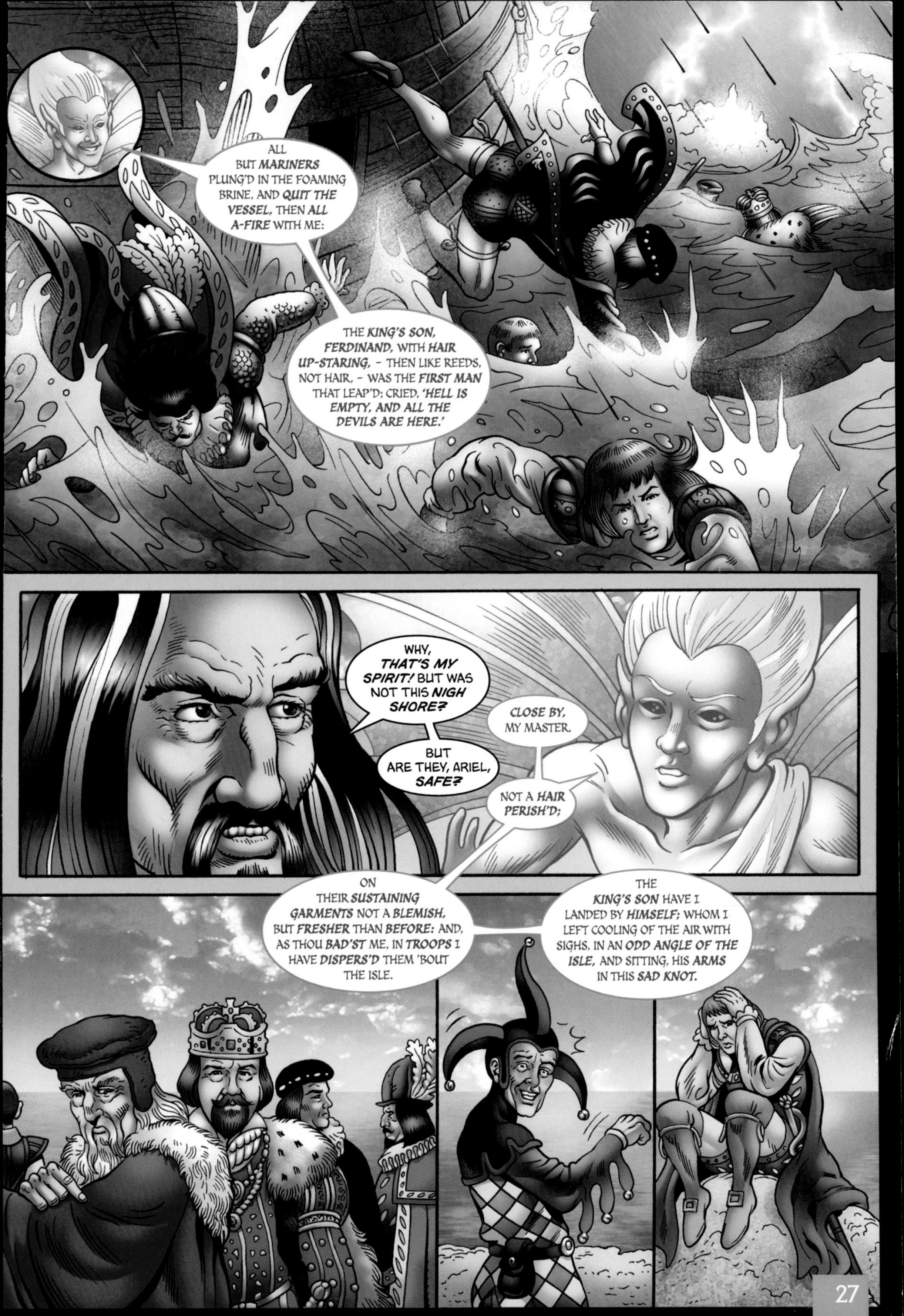
ALL BUT MARINERS PLUNG'D IN THE FOAMING BRINE, AND QUIT THE VESSEL, THEN ALL A-FIRE WITH ME:
THE KING'S SON, FERDINAND, WITH HAIR UP-STARING, - THEN LIKE REEDS, NOT HAIR, - WAS THE FIRST MAN THAT LEAP'D; CRIED, 'HELL IS EMPTY, AND ALL THE DEVILS ARE HERE.'
WHY, THAT'S MY SPIRIT! BUT WAS NOT THIS NIGH SHORE?
CLOSE BY, MY MASTER.
BUT ARE THEY, ARIEL, SAFE?
NOT A HAIR PERISH'D;
ON THEIR SUSTAINING GARMENTS NOT A BLEMISH, BUT FRESHER THAN BEFORE: AND, AS THOU BAD'ST ME, IN TROOPS I HAVE DISPERS'D THEM 'BOUT THE ISLE.
THE KING'S SON HAVE I LANDED BY HIMSELF; WHOM I LEFT COOLING OF THE AIR WITH SIGHS, IN AN ODD ANGLE OF THE ISLE, AND SITTING, HIS ARMS IN THIS SAD KNOT.

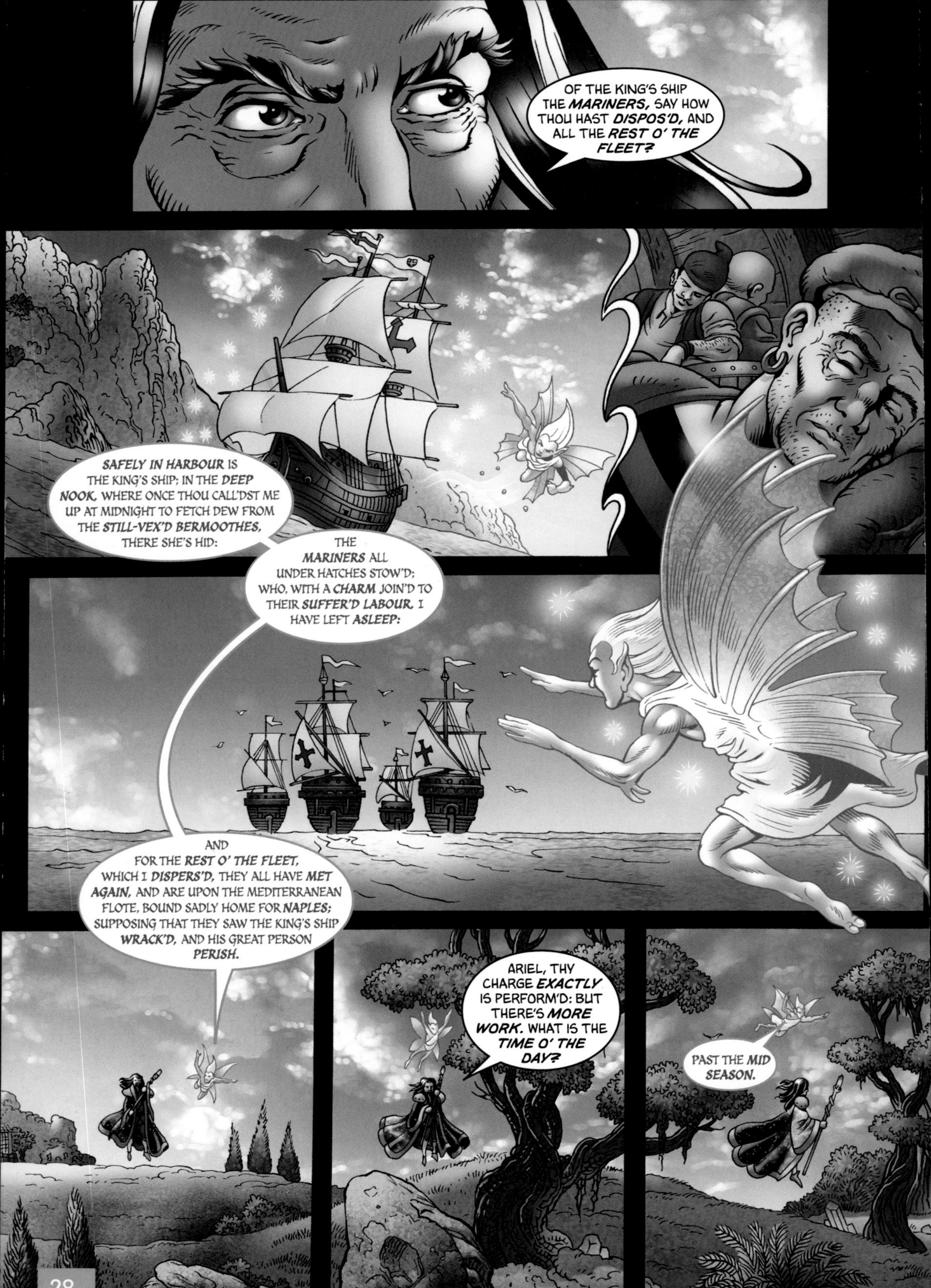

OF THE KING'S SHIP THE MARINERS, SAY HOW THOU HAST DISPOS'D, AND ALL THE REST O' THE FLEET?
SAFELY IN HARBOUR IS THE KING'S SHIP; IN THE DEEP NOOK, WHERE ONCE THOU CALL'DST ME UP AT MIDNIGHT TO FETCH DEW FROM THE STILL-VEX'D BERMOOTHES, THERE SHE'S HID:
THE MARINERS ALL UNDER HATCHES STOW'D; WHO, WITH A CHARM JOIN'D TO THEIR SUFFER'D LABOUR, I HAVE LEFT ASLEEP:
AND FOR THE REST O' THE FLEET, WHICH I DISPERS'D, THEY ALL HAVE MET AGAIN, AND ARE UPON THE MEDITERRANEAN FLOTE, BOUND SADLY HOME FOR NAPLES; SUPPOSING THAT THEY SAW THE KING'S SHIP WRACK'D, AND HIS GREAT PERSON PERISH.
ARIEL, THY CHARGE EXACTLY IS PERFORM'D: BUT THERE'S MORE WORK. WHAT IS THE TIME O' THE DAY?
PAST THE MID SEASON.

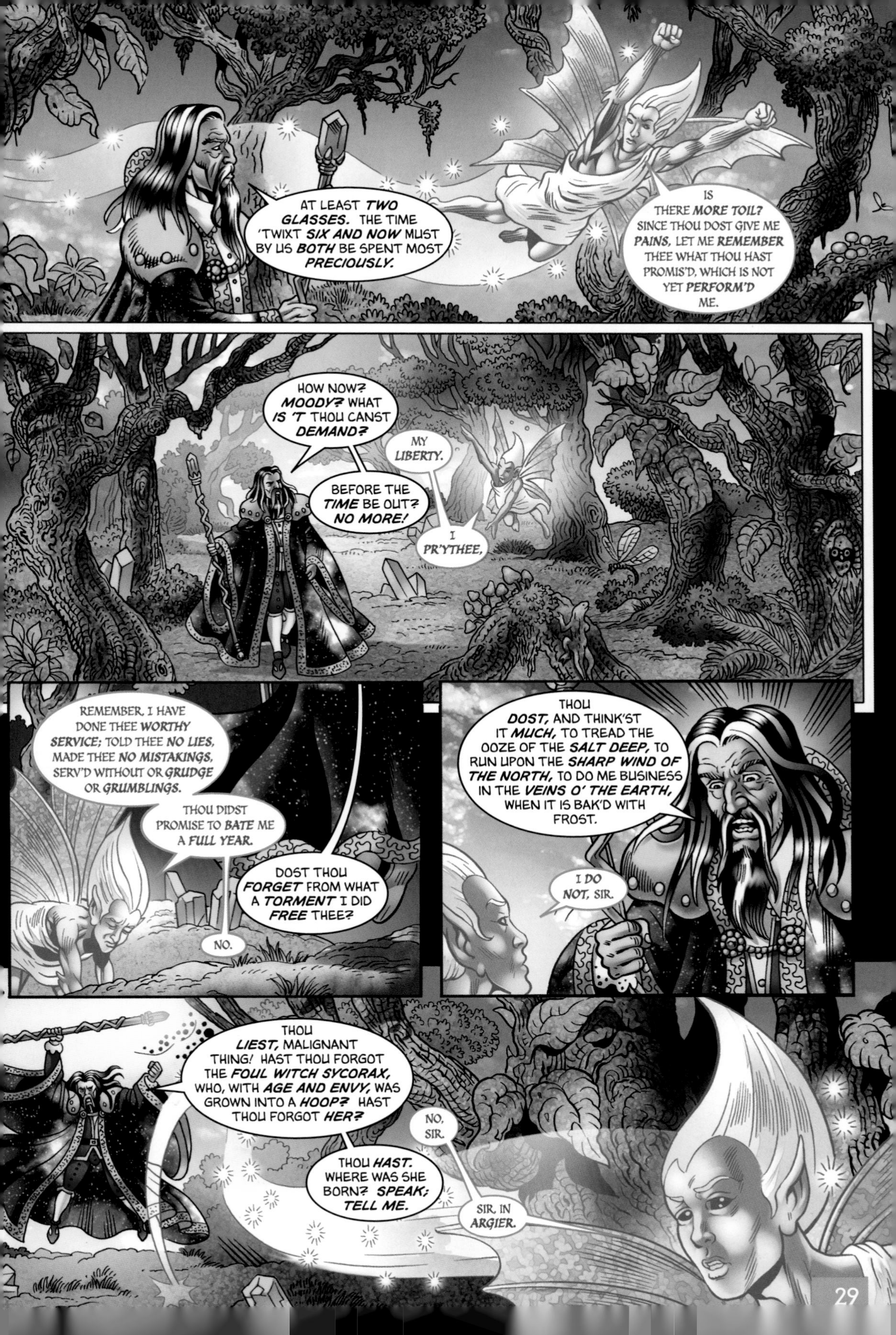
AT LEAST TWO GLASSES. THE TIME 'TWIXT SIX AND NOW MUST BY US BOTH BE SPENT MOST PRECIOUSLY.
IS THERE MORE TOIL? SINCE THOU DOST GIVE ME PAINS, LET ME REMEMBER THEE WHAT THOU HAST PROMIS'D, WHICH IS NOT YET PERFORM'D ME.
HOW NOW? MOODY? WHAT IS 'T THOU CANST DEMAND?
MY LIBERTY.
BEFORE THE TIME BE OUT? NO MORE!
I PR'YTHEE,
REMEMBER, I HAVE DONE THEE WORTHY SERVICE; TOLD THEE NO LIES, MADE THEE NO MISTAKINGS, SERV'D WITHOUT OR GRUDGE OR GRUMBLINGS.
THOU DIDST PROMISE TO BATE ME A FULL YEAR.
DOST THOU FORGET FROM WHAT A TORMENT I DID FREE THEE?
NO.
THOU DOST, AND THINK'ST IT MUCH, TO TREAD THE OOZE OF THE SALT DEEP, TO RUN UPON THE SHARP WIND OF THE NORTH, TO DO ME BUSINESS IN THE VEINS O' THE EARTH, WHEN IT IS BAK'D WITH FROST.
I DO NOT, SIR.
THOU LIEST, MALIGNANT THING! HAST THOU FORGOT THE FOUL WITCH SYCORAX, WHO, WITH AGE AND ENVY, WAS GROWN INTO A HOOP? HAST THOU FORGOT HER?
NO, SIR.
THOU HAST. WHERE WAS SHE BORN? SPEAK; TELL ME.
SIR, IN ARGIER.

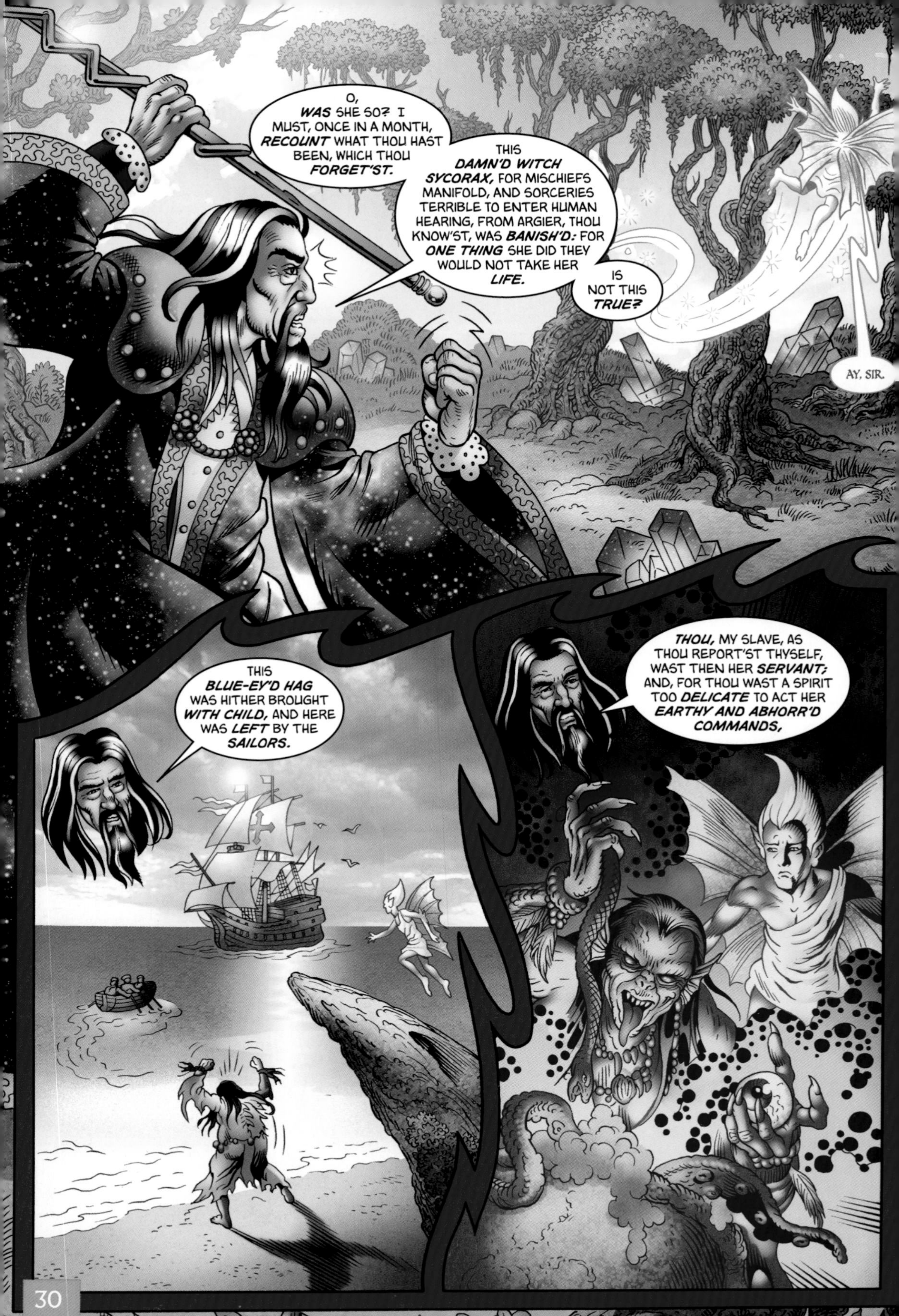

O, WAS SHE SO? I MUST, ONCE IN A MONTH, RECOUNT WHAT THOU HAST BEEN, WHICH THOU FORGET'ST.
THIS DAMN'D WITCH SYCORAX, FOR MISCHIEFS MANIFOLD, AND SORCERIES TERRIBLE TO ENTER HUMAN HEARING, FROM ARGIER, THOU KNOW'ST, WAS BANISH'D: FOR ONE THING SHE DID THEY WOULD NOT TAKE HER LIFE.
IS NOT THIS TRUE?
AY, SIR.
THIS BLUE-EY'D HAG WAS HITHER BROUGHT WITH CHILD, AND HERE WAS LEFT BY THE SAILORS.
THOU, MY SLAVE, AS THOU REPORT'ST THYSELF, WAST THEN HER SERVANT; AND, FOR THOU WAST A SPIRIT TOO DELICATE TO ACT HER EARTHY AND ABHORR'D COMMANDS,

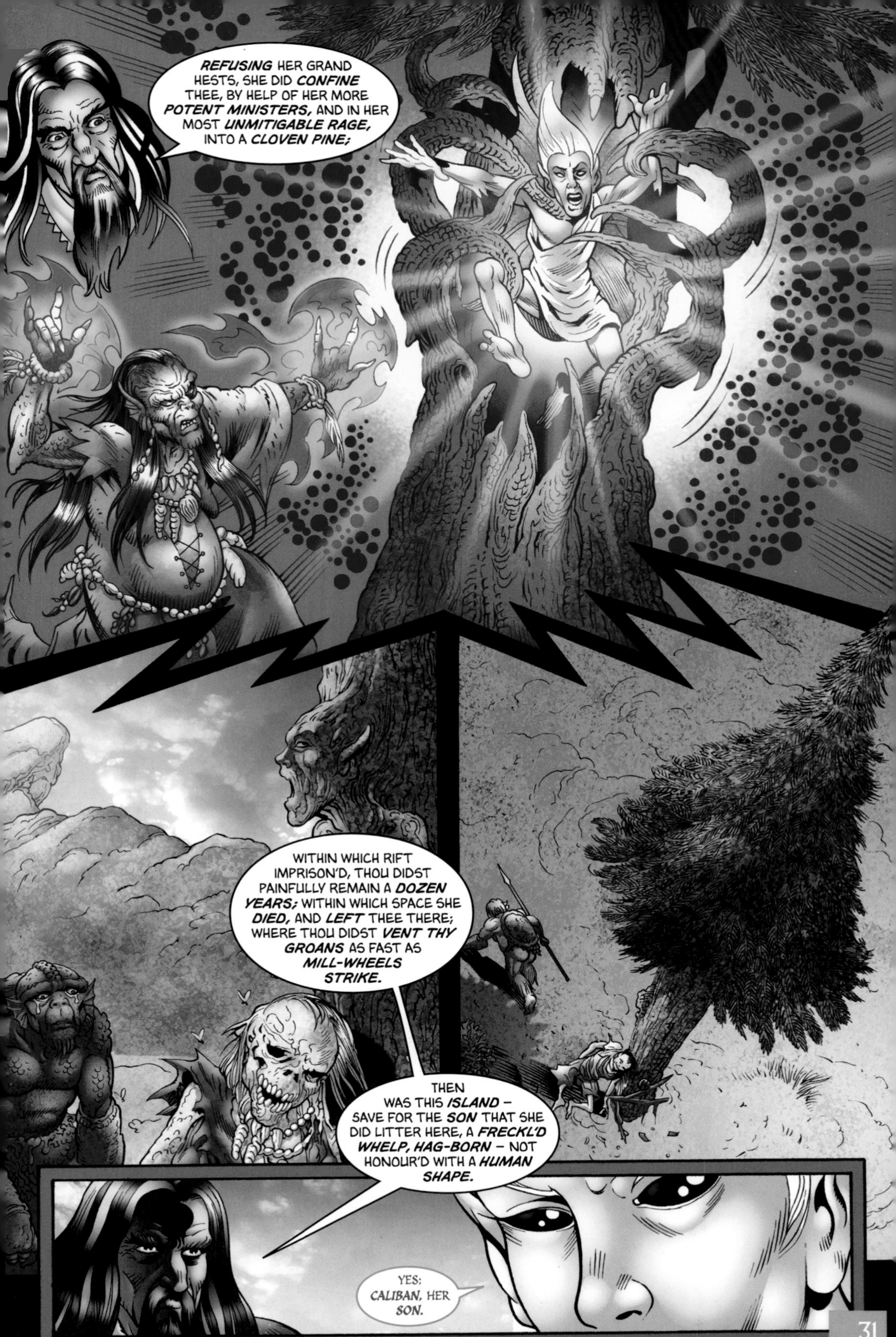
REFUSING HER GRAND HESTS, SHE DID CONFINE THEE, BY HELP OF HER MORE POTENT MINISTERS, AND IN HER MOST UNMITIGABLE RAGE, INTO A CLOVEN PINE;
WITHIN WHICH RIFT IMPRISON'D, THOU DIDST PAINFULLY REMAIN A DOZEN YEARS; WITHIN WHICH SPACE SHE DIED, AND LEFT THEE THERE; WHERE THOU DIDST VENT THY GROANS AS FAST AS MILL-WHEELS STRIKE.
THEN WAS THIS ISLAND – SAVE FOR THE SON THAT SHE DID LITTER HERE, A FRECKL'D WHELP, HAG-BORN – NOT HONOUR'D WITH A HUMAN SHAPE.
YES: CALIBAN, HER SON.

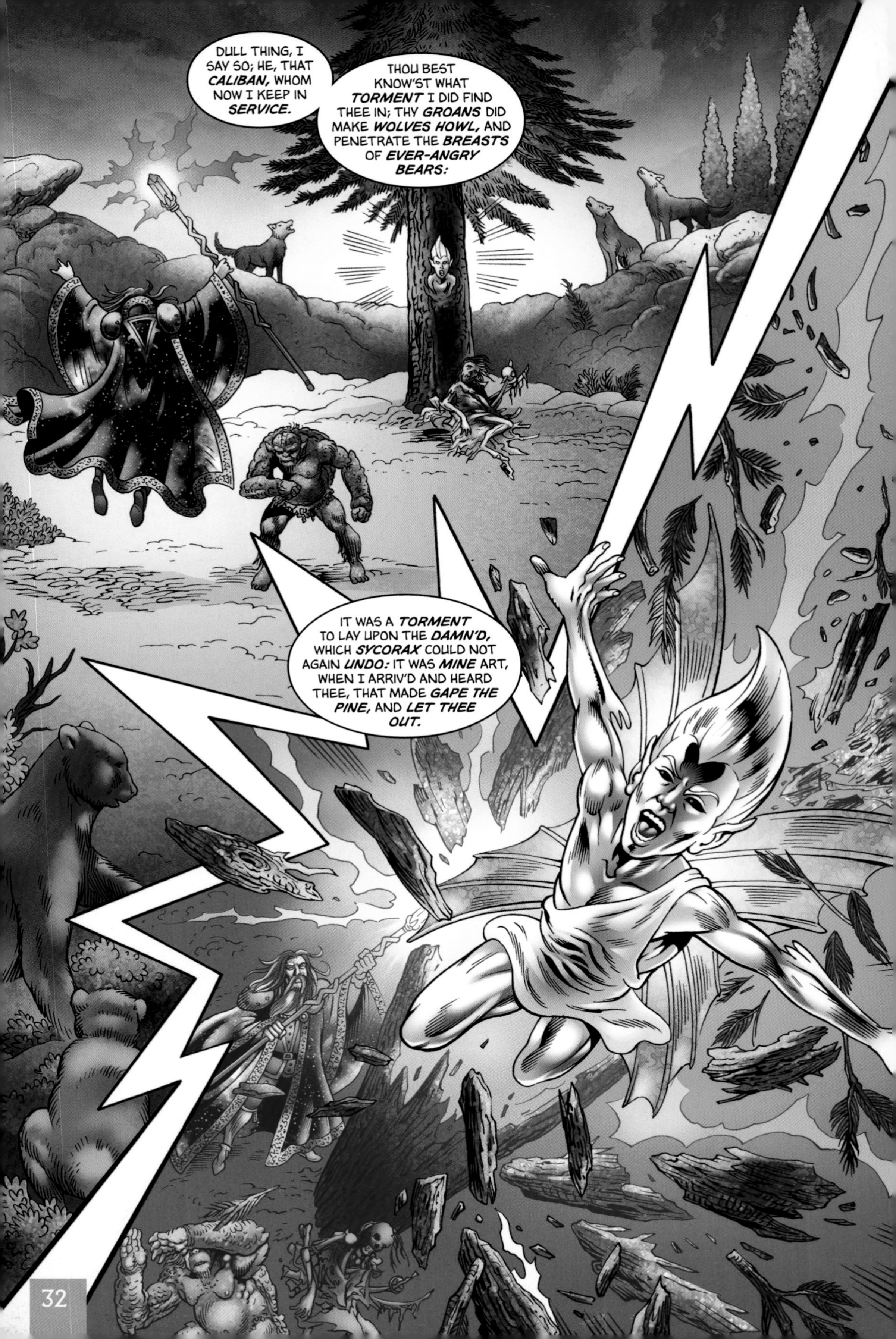
DULL THING, I SAY SO; HE, THAT CALIBAN, WHOM NOW I KEEP IN SERVICE.
THOU BEST KNOW'ST WHAT TORMENT I DID FIND THEE IN; THY GROANS DID MAKE WOLVES HOWL, AND PENETRATE THE BREASTS OF EVER-ANGRY BEARS:
IT WAS A TORMENT TO LAY UPON THE DAMN'D, WHICH SYCORAX COULD NOT AGAIN UNDO: IT WAS MINE ART, WHEN I ARRIV'D AND HEARD THEE, THAT MADE GAPE THE PINE, AND LET THEE OUT.

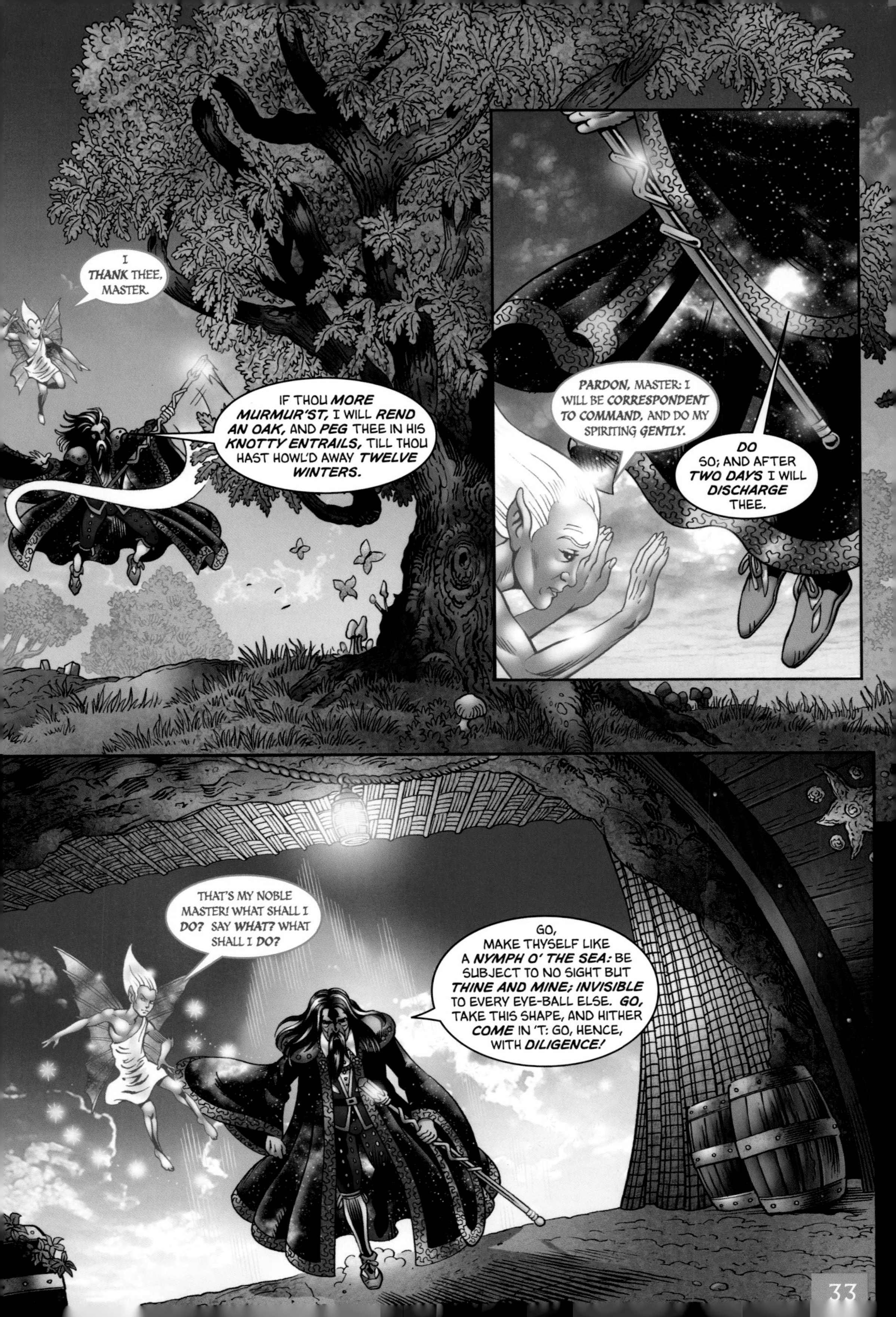
I THANK THEE, MASTER.
IF THOU MORE MURMUR'ST, I WILL REND AN OAK, AND PEG THEE IN HIS KNOTTY ENTRAILS, TILL THOU HAST HOWL'D AWAY TWELVE WINTERS.
PARDON, MASTER: I WILL BE CORRESPONDENT TO COMMAND, AND DO MY SPIRITING GENTLY.
DO SO; AND AFTER TWO DAYS I WILL DISCHARGE THEE.
THAT'S MY NOBLE MASTER! WHAT SHALL I DO? SAY WHAT? WHAT SHALL I DO?
GO, MAKE THYSELF LIKE A NYMPH O' THE SEA: BE SUBJECT TO NO SIGHT BUT THINE AND MINE; INVISIBLE TO EVERY EYE-BALL ELSE. GO, TAKE THIS SHAPE, AND HITHER COME IN 'T: GO, HENCE, WITH DILIGENCE!

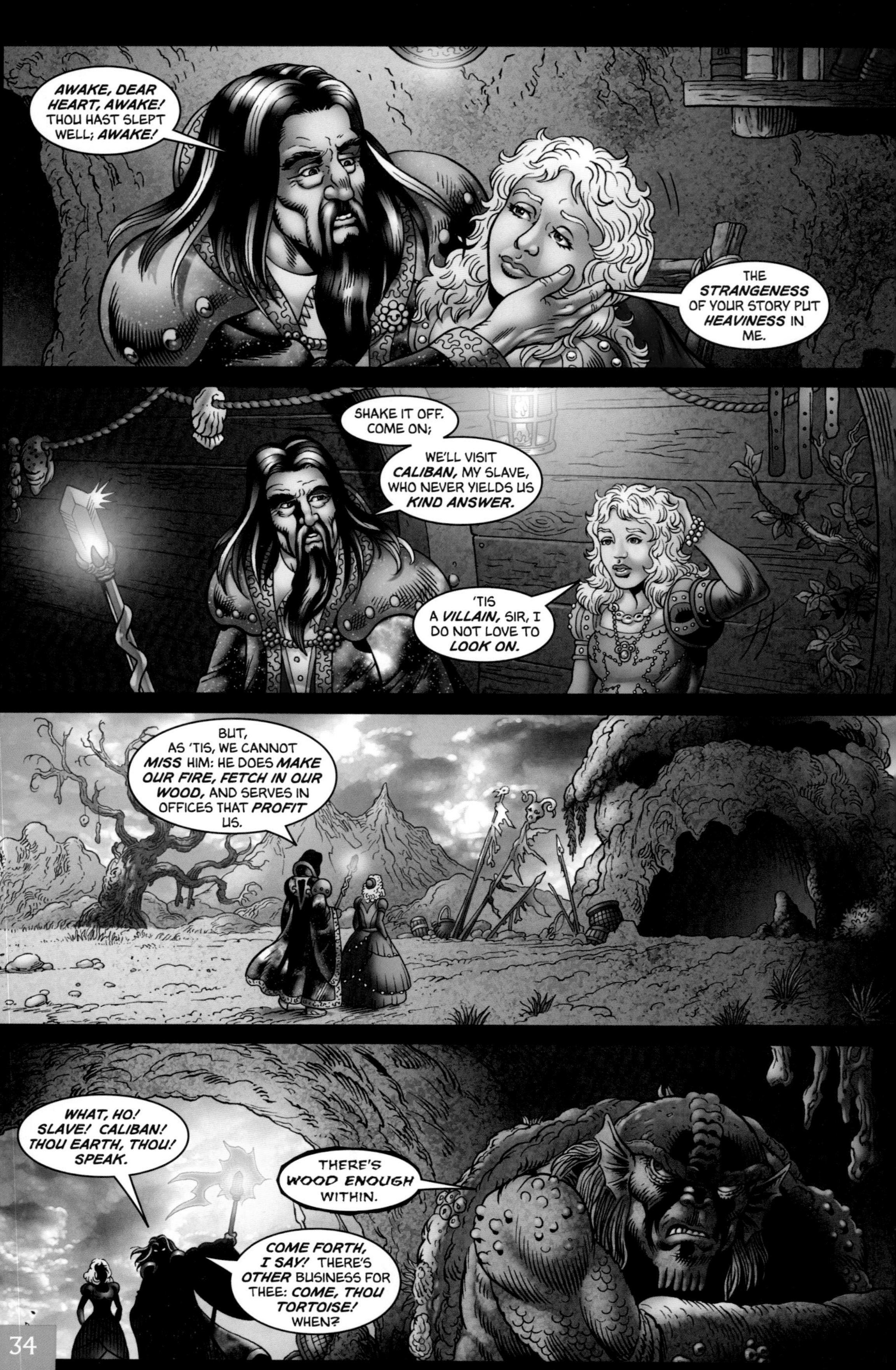
AWAKE, DEAR HEART, AWAKE! THOU HAST SLEPT WELL; AWAKE!
THE STRANGENESS OF YOUR STORY PUT HEAVINESS IN ME.
SHAKE IT OFF. COME ON;
WE'LL VISIT CALIBAN, MY SLAVE, WHO NEVER YIELDS US KIND ANSWER.
'TIS A VILLAIN, SIR, I DO NOT LOVE TO LOOK ON.
BUT, AS 'TIS, WE CANNOT MISS HIM: HE DOES MAKE OUR FIRE, FETCH IN OUR WOOD, AND SERVES IN OFFICES THAT PROFIT US.
WHAT, HO! SLAVE! CALIBAN! THOU EARTH, THOU! SPEAK.
THERE'S WOOD ENOUGH WITHIN.
COME FORTH, I SAY! THERE'S OTHER BUSINESS FOR THEE: COME, THOU TORTOISE! WHEN?

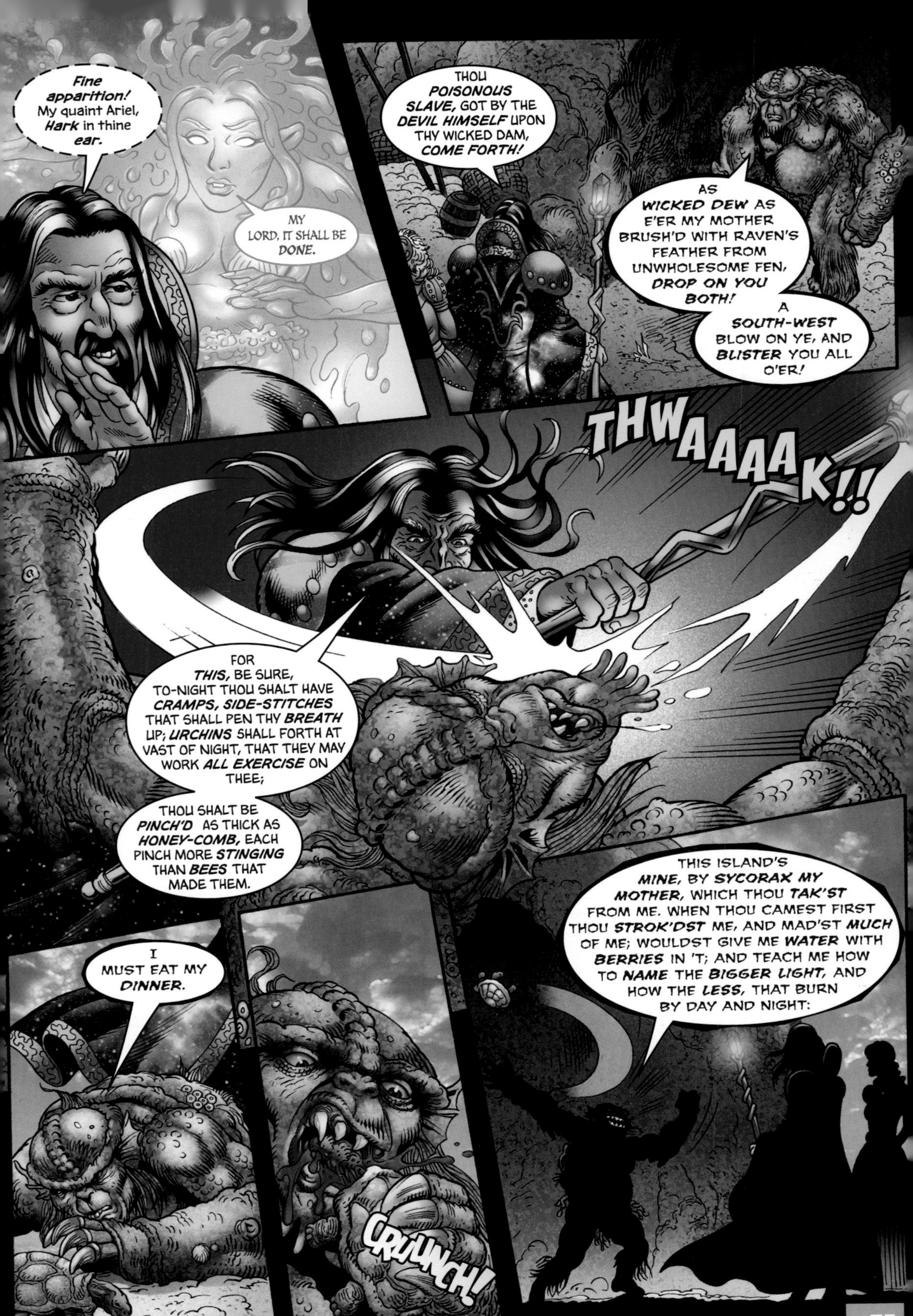

Fine apparition! My quaint Ariel, Hark in thine ear.
MY LORD, IT SHALL BE DONE.
THOU POISONOUS SLAVE, GOT BY THE DEVIL HIMSELF UPON THY WICKED DAM, COME FORTH!
AS WICKED DEW AS E'ER MY MOTHER BRUSH'D WITH RAVEN'S FEATHER FROM UNWHOLESOME FEN, DROP ON YOU BOTH!
A SOUTH-WEST BLOW ON YE, AND BLISTER YOU ALL O'ER!
THWAAAAK!!
FOR THIS, BE SURE, TO-NIGHT THOU SHALT HAVE CRAMPS, SIDE-STITCHES THAT SHALL PEN THY BREATH UP; URCHINS SHALL FORTH AT VAST OF NIGHT, THAT THEY MAY WORK ALL EXERCISE ON THEE;
THOU SHALT BE PINCH'D AS THICK AS HONEY-COMB, EACH PINCH MORE STINGING THAN BEES THAT MADE THEM.
I MUST EAT MY DINNER.
CRUUNCH!
THIS ISLAND'S MINE, BY SYCORAX MY MOTHER, WHICH THOU TAK'ST FROM ME. WHEN THOU CAMEST FIRST THOU STROK'DST ME, AND MAD'ST MUCH OF ME; WOULDST GIVE ME WATER WITH BERRIES IN 'T; AND TEACH ME HOW TO NAME THE BIGGER LIGHT, AND HOW THE LESS, THAT BURN BY DAY AND NIGHT:

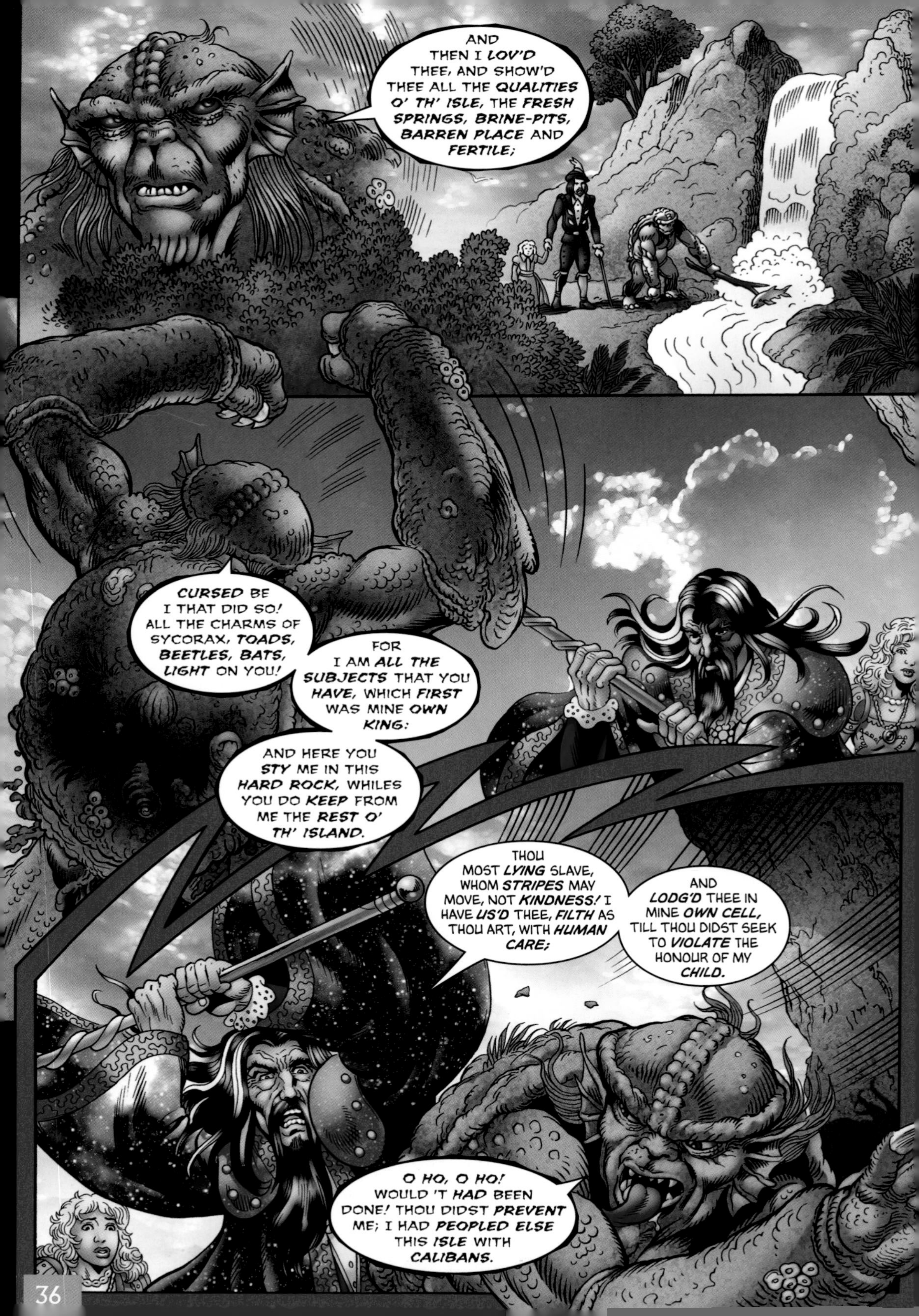
AND THEN I LOV'D THEE, AND SHOW'D THEE ALL THE QUALITIES O' TH' ISLE, THE FRESH SPRINGS, BRINE-PITS, BARREN PLACE AND FERTILE;
CURSED BE I THAT DID SO! ALL THE CHARMS OF SYCORAX, TOADS, BEETLES, BATS, LIGHT ON YOU!
FOR I AM ALL THE SUBJECTS THAT YOU HAVE, WHICH FIRST WAS MINE OWN KING:
AND HERE YOU STY ME IN THIS HARD ROCK, WHILES YOU DO KEEP FROM ME THE REST O' TH' ISLAND.
THOU MOST LYING SLAVE, WHOM STRIPES MAY MOVE, NOT KINDNESS! I HAVE US'D THEE, FILTH AS THOU ART, WITH HUMAN CARE;
AND LODG'D THEE IN MINE OWN CELL, TILL THOU DIDST SEEK TO VIOLATE THE HONOUR OF MY CHILD.
O HO, O HO! WOULD 'T HAD BEEN DONE! THOU DIDST PREVENT ME; I HAD PEOPLED ELSE THIS ISLE WITH CALIBANS.

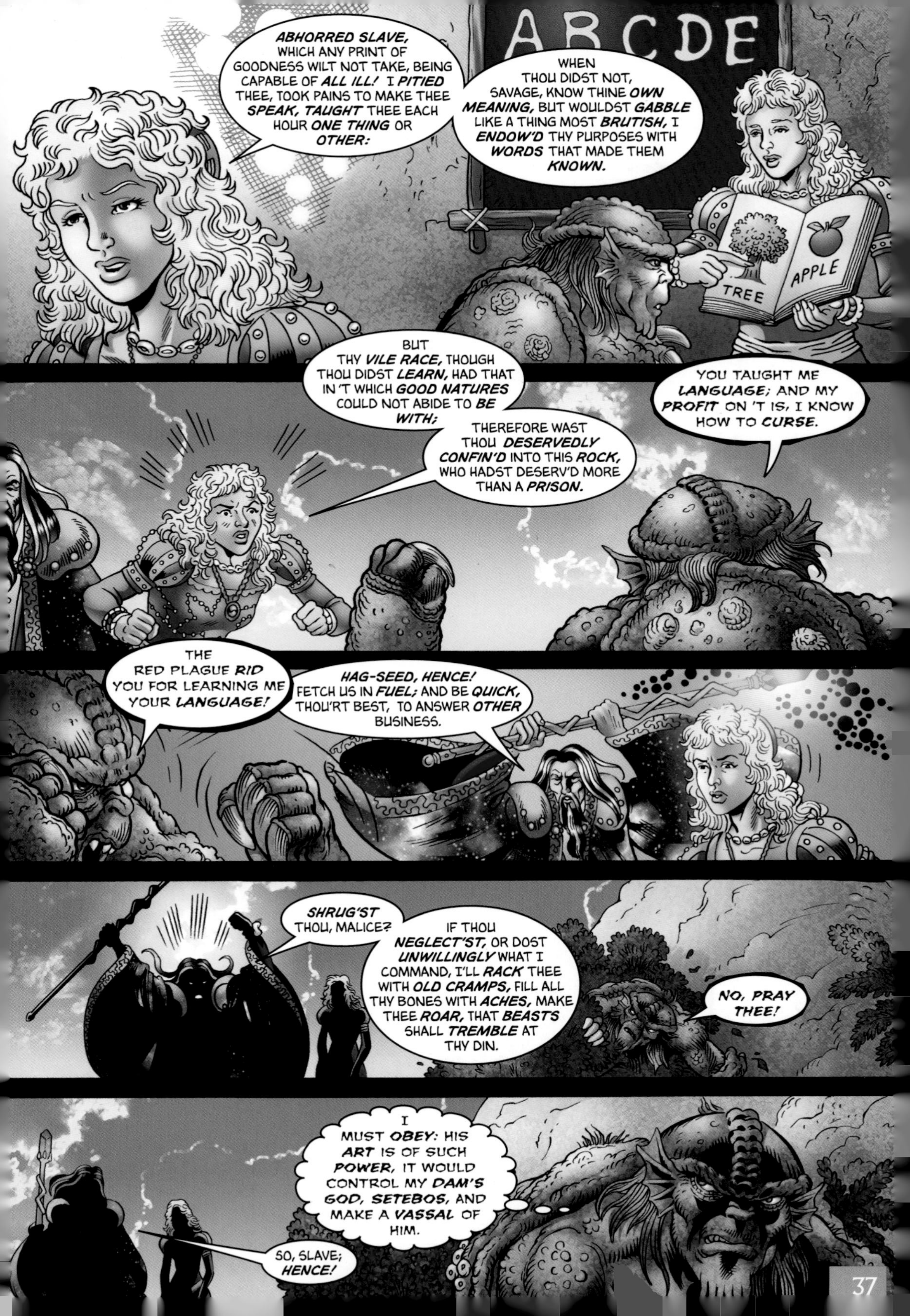
ABHORRED SLAVE, WHICH ANY PRINT OF GOODNESS WILT NOT TAKE, BEING CAPABLE OF ALL ILL! I PITIED THEE, TOOK PAINS TO MAKE THEE SPEAK, TAUGHT THEE EACH HOUR ONE THING OR OTHER:
A B C D E
WHEN THOU DIDST NOT, SAVAGE, KNOW THINE OWN MEANING, BUT WOULDST GABBLE LIKE A THING MOST BRUTISH, I ENDOW'D THY PURPOSES WITH WORDS THAT MADE THEM KNOWN.
TREE
APPLE
BUT THY VILE RACE, THOUGH THOU DIDST LEARN, HAD THAT IN 'T WHICH GOOD NATURES COULD NOT ABIDE TO BE WITH;
THEREFORE WAST THOU DESERVEDLY CONFIN'D INTO THIS ROCK, WHO HADST DESERV'D MORE THAN A PRISON.
YOU TAUGHT ME LANGUAGE; AND MY PROFIT ON 'T IS, I KNOW HOW TO CURSE.
THE RED PLAGUE RID YOU FOR LEARNING ME YOUR LANGUAGE!
HAG-SEED, HENCE! FETCH US IN FUEL; AND BE QUICK, THOU'RT BEST, TO ANSWER OTHER BUSINESS.
SHRUG'ST THOU, MALICE?
IF THOU NEGLECT'ST, OR DOST UNWILLINGLY WHAT I COMMAND, I'LL RACK THEE WITH OLD CRAMPS, FILL ALL THY BONES WITH ACHES, MAKE THEE ROAR, THAT BEASTS SHALL TREMBLE AT THY DIN.
NO, PRAY THEE!
I MUST OBEY: HIS ART IS OF SUCH POWER, IT WOULD CONTROL MY DAM'S GOD, SETEBOS, AND MAKE A VASSAL OF HIM.
SO, SLAVE; HENCE!

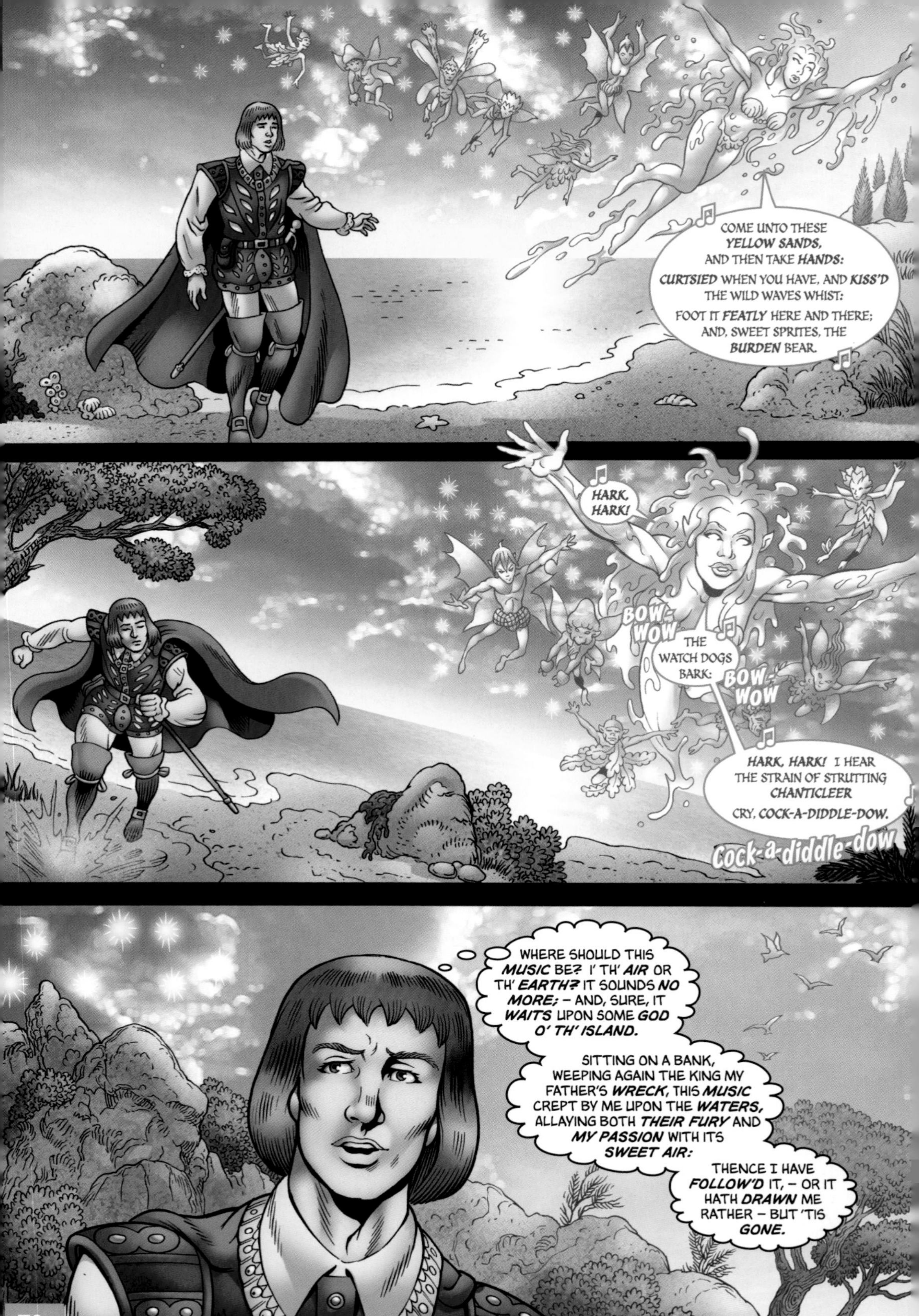
COME UNTO THESE YELLOW SANDS, AND THEN TAKE HANDS: CURTSIED WHEN YOU HAVE, AND KISS'D THE WILD WAVES WHIST: FOOT IT FEATLY HERE AND THERE; AND, SWEET SPRITES, THE BURDEN BEAR.
HARK, HARK!
BOW-WOW
THE WATCH DOGS BARK:
BOW WOW
HARK, HARK! I HEAR THE STRAIN OF STRUTTING CHANTICLEER CRY, COCK-A-DIDDLE-DOW.
Cock-a-diddle-dow
WHERE SHOULD THIS MUSIC BE? I' TH' AIR OR TH' EARTH? IT SOUNDS NO MORE; – AND, SURE, IT WAITS UPON SOME GOD O' TH' ISLAND.
SITTING ON A BANK, WEEPING AGAIN THE KING MY FATHER'S WRECK, THIS MUSIC CREPT BY ME UPON THE WATERS, ALLAYING BOTH THEIR FURY AND MY PASSION WITH ITS SWEET AIR:
THENCE I HAVE FOLLOW'D IT, – OR IT HATH DRAWN ME RATHER – BUT 'TIS GONE.

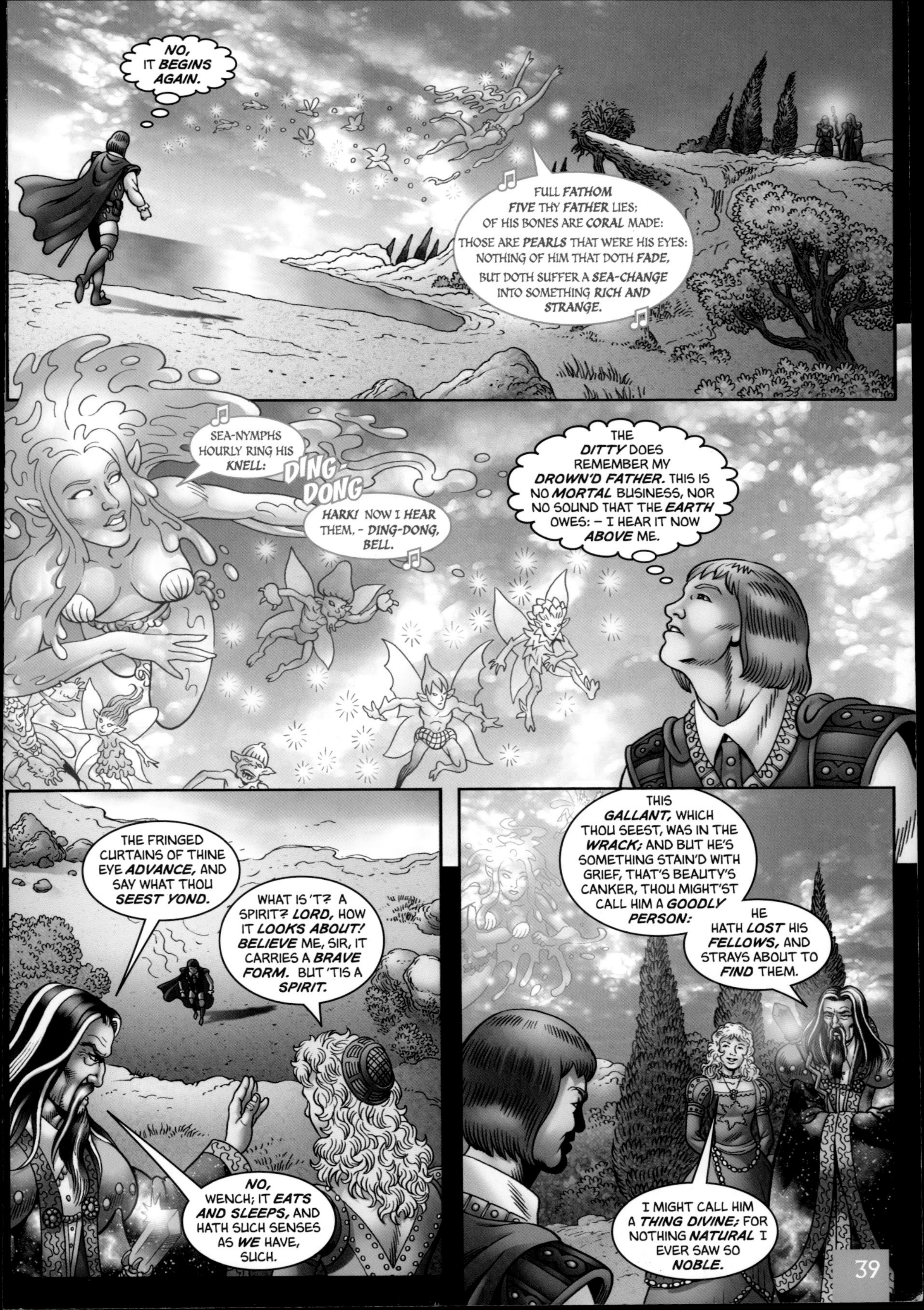
NO, IT BEGINS AGAIN.
FULL FATHOM FIVE THY FATHER LIES; OF HIS BONES ARE CORAL MADE: THOSE ARE PEARLS THAT WERE HIS EYES: NOTHING OF HIM THAT DOTH FADE, BUT DOTH SUFFER A SEA-CHANGE INTO SOMETHING RICH AND STRANGE.
SEA-NYMPHS HOURLY RING HIS KNELL:
DING-DONG
HARK! NOW I HEAR THEM, - DING-DONG, BELL.
THE DITTY DOES REMEMBER MY DROWN'D FATHER. THIS IS NO MORTAL BUSINESS, NOR NO SOUND THAT THE EARTH OWES: - I HEAR IT NOW ABOVE ME.
THE FRINGED CURTAINS OF THINE EYE ADVANCE, AND SAY WHAT THOU SEEST YOND.
WHAT IS 'T? A SPIRIT? LORD, HOW IT LOOKS ABOUT! BELIEVE ME, SIR, IT CARRIES A BRAVE FORM. BUT 'TIS A SPIRIT.
NO, WENCH; IT EATS AND SLEEPS, AND HATH SUCH SENSES AS WE HAVE, SUCH.
THIS GALLANT, WHICH THOU SEEST, WAS IN THE WRACK; AND BUT HE'S SOMETHING STAIN'D WITH GRIEF, THAT'S BEAUTY'S CANKER, THOU MIGHT'ST CALL HIM A GOODLY PERSON:
HE HATH LOST HIS FELLOWS, AND STRAYS ABOUT TO FIND THEM.
I MIGHT CALL HIM A THING DIVINE; FOR NOTHING NATURAL I EVER SAW SO NOBLE.

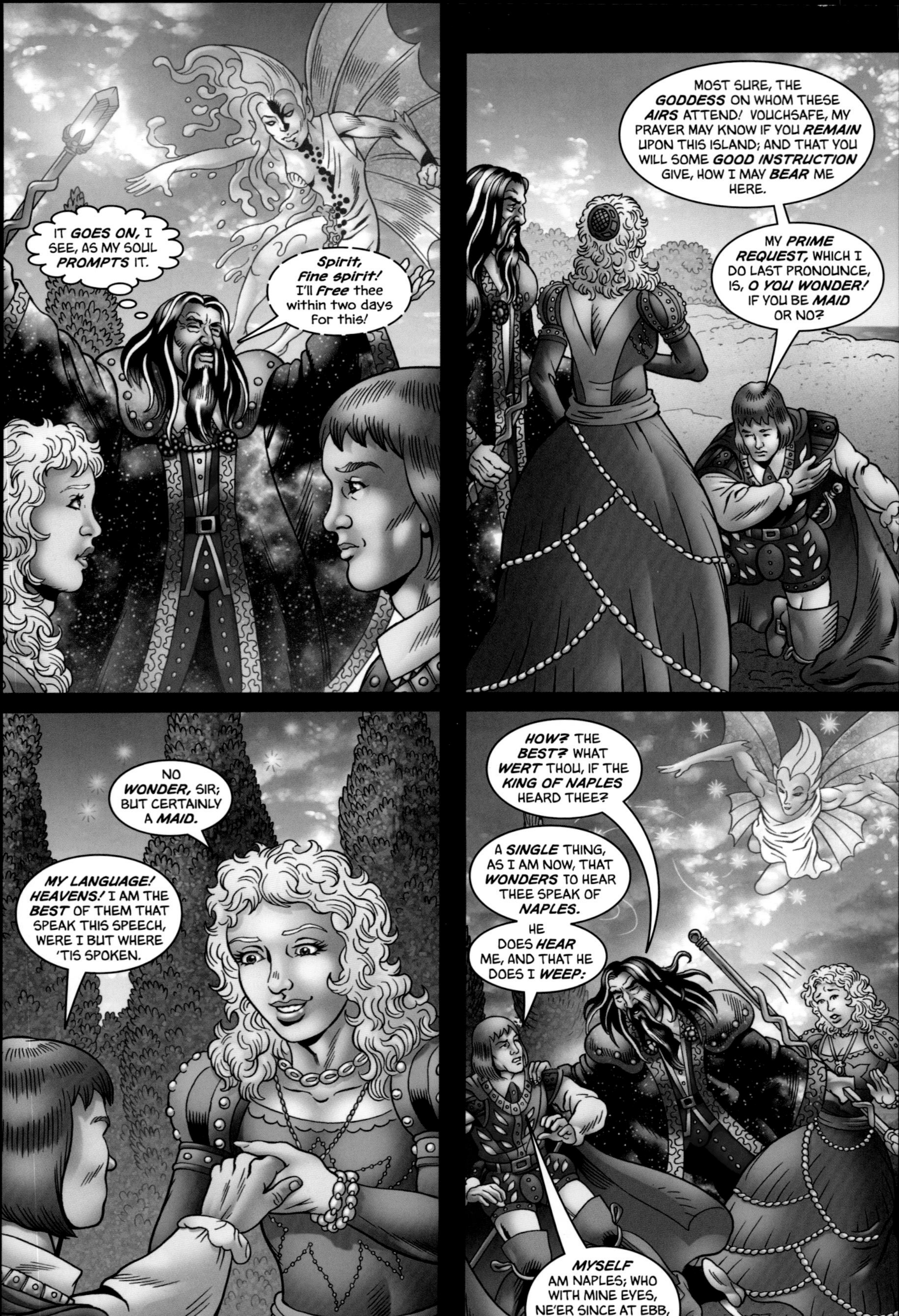
IT GOES ON, I SEE, AS MY SOUL PROMPTS IT.
Spirit, Fine spirit! I'll Free thee within two days for this!
MOST SURE, THE GODDESS ON WHOM THESE AIRS ATTEND! VOUCHSAFE, MY PRAYER MAY KNOW IF YOU REMAIN UPON THIS ISLAND; AND THAT YOU WILL SOME GOOD INSTRUCTION GIVE, HOW I MAY BEAR ME HERE.
MY PRIME REQUEST, WHICH I DO LAST PRONOUNCE, IS, O YOU WONDER! IF YOU BE MAID OR NO?
NO WONDER, SIR; BUT CERTAINLY A MAID.
MY LANGUAGE! HEAVENS! I AM THE BEST OF THEM THAT SPEAK THIS SPEECH, WERE I BUT WHERE 'TIS SPOKEN.
HOW? THE BEST? WHAT WERT THOU, IF THE KING OF NAPLES HEARD THEE?
A SINGLE THING, AS I AM NOW, THAT WONDERS TO HEAR THEE SPEAK OF NAPLES.
HE DOES HEAR ME, AND THAT HE DOES I WEEP:
MYSELF AM NAPLES; WHO WITH MINE EYES, NE'ER SINCE AT EBB, BEHELD THE KING MY FATHER WRACK'D.

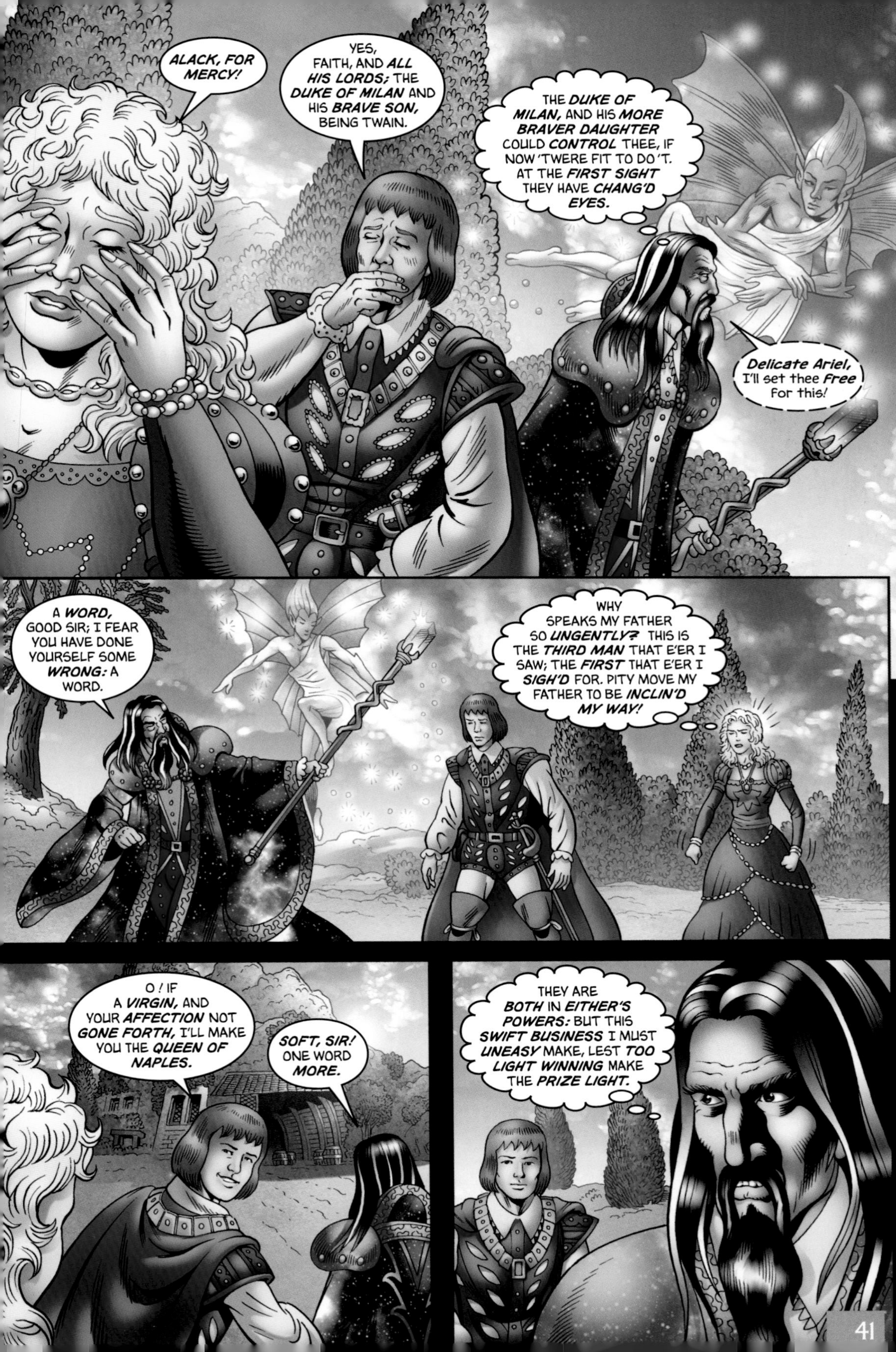
ALACK, FOR MERCY!
YES, FAITH, AND ALL HIS LORDS; THE DUKE OF MILAN AND HIS BRAVE SON, BEING TWAIN.
THE DUKE OF MILAN, AND HIS MORE BRAVER DAUGHTER COULD CONTROL THEE, IF NOW 'TWERE FIT TO DO 'T. AT THE FIRST SIGHT THEY HAVE CHANG'D EYES.
Delicate Ariel, I'll set thee Free for this!
A WORD, GOOD SIR; I FEAR YOU HAVE DONE YOURSELF SOME WRONG: A WORD.
WHY SPEAKS MY FATHER SO UNGENTLY? THIS IS THE THIRD MAN THAT E'ER I SAW; THE FIRST THAT E'ER I SIGH'D FOR. PITY MOVE MY FATHER TO BE INCLIN'D MY WAY!
O! IF A VIRGIN, AND YOUR AFFECTION NOT GONE FORTH, I'LL MAKE YOU THE QUEEN OF NAPLES.
SOFT, SIR! ONE WORD MORE.
THEY ARE BOTH IN EITHER'S POWERS: BUT THIS SWIFT BUSINESS I MUST UNEASY MAKE, LEST TOO LIGHT WINNING MAKE THE PRIZE LIGHT.

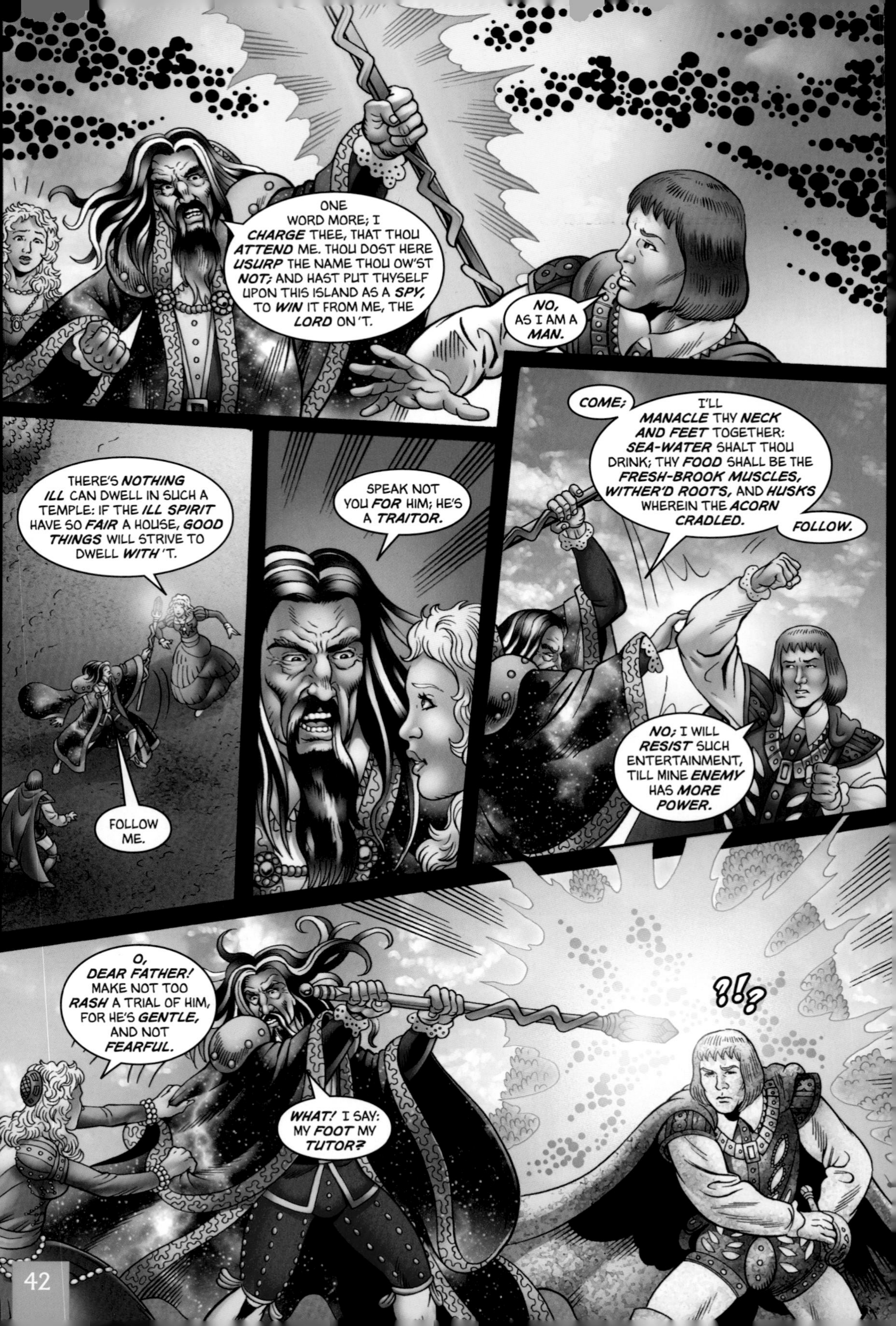
ONE WORD MORE; I CHARGE THEE, THAT THOU ATTEND ME. THOU DOST HERE USURP THE NAME THOU OW'ST NOT; AND HAST PUT THYSELF UPON THIS ISLAND AS A SPY, TO WIN IT FROM ME, THE LORD ON 'T.
NO, AS I AM A MAN.
THERE'S NOTHING ILL CAN DWELL IN SUCH A TEMPLE: IF THE ILL SPIRIT HAVE SO FAIR A HOUSE, GOOD THINGS WILL STRIVE TO DWELL WITH 'T.
FOLLOW ME.
SPEAK NOT YOU FOR HIM; HE'S A TRAITOR.
COME;
I'LL MANACLE THY NECK AND FEET TOGETHER: SEA-WATER SHALT THOU DRINK; THY FOOD SHALL BE THE FRESH-BROOK MUSCLES, WITHER'D ROOTS, AND HUSKS WHEREIN THE ACORN CRADLED.
FOLLOW.
NO; I WILL RESIST SUCH ENTERTAINMENT, TILL MINE ENEMY HAS MORE POWER.
O, DEAR FATHER! MAKE NOT TOO RASH A TRIAL OF HIM, FOR HE'S GENTLE, AND NOT FEARFUL.
?!?
WHAT! I SAY: MY FOOT MY TUTOR?

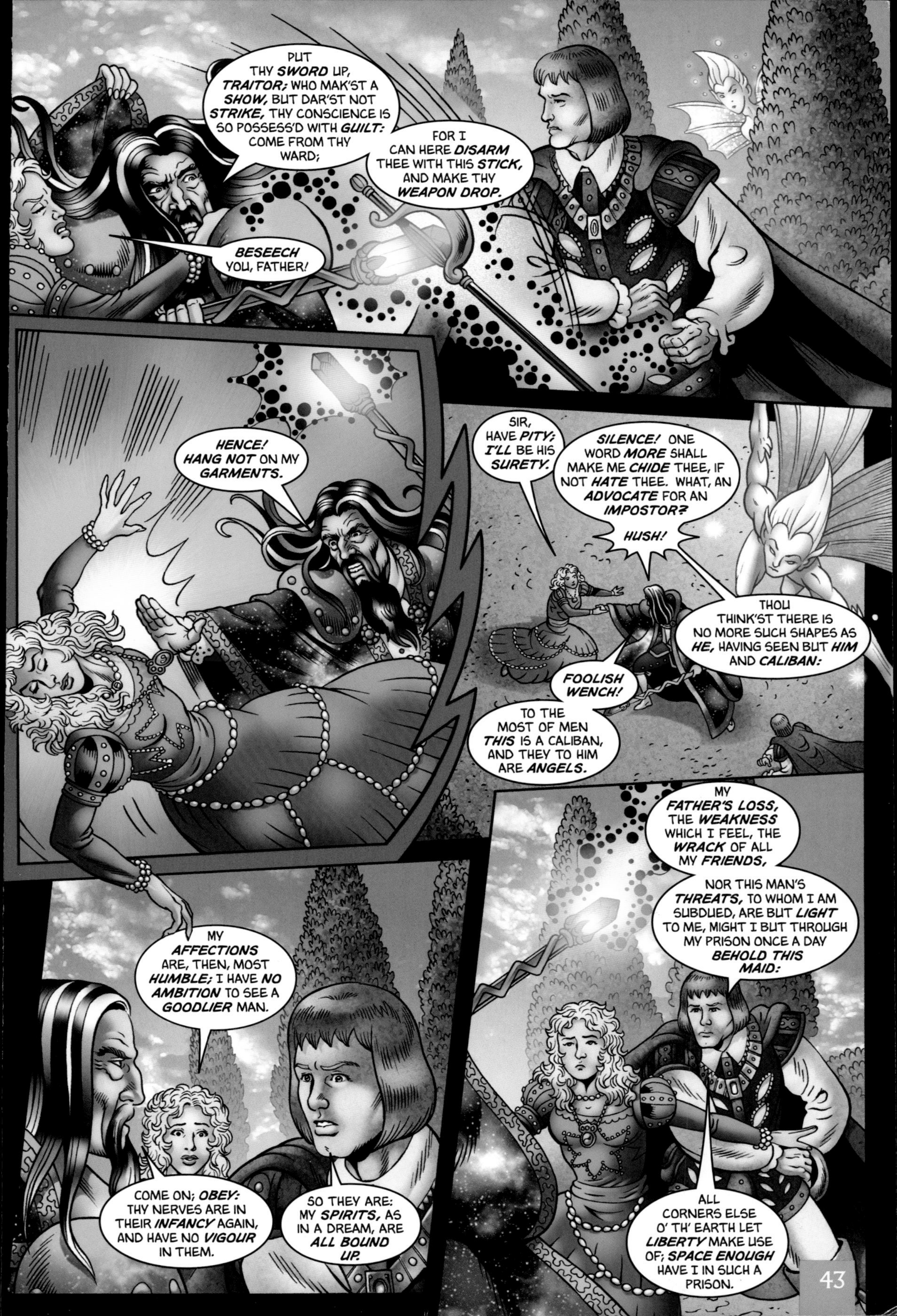
PUT THY SWORD UP, TRAITOR; WHO MAK'ST A SHOW, BUT DAR'ST NOT STRIKE, THY CONSCIENCE IS SO POSSESS'D WITH GUILT: COME FROM THY WARD;
FOR I CAN HERE DISARM THEE WITH THIS STICK, AND MAKE THY WEAPON DROP.
BESEECH YOU, FATHER!
HENCE! HANG NOT ON MY GARMENTS.
SIR, HAVE PITY; I'LL BE HIS SURETY.
SILENCE! ONE WORD MORE SHALL MAKE ME CHIDE THEE, IF NOT HATE THEE. WHAT, AN ADVOCATE FOR AN IMPOSTOR?
HUSH!
THOU THINK'ST THERE IS NO MORE SUCH SHAPES AS HE, HAVING SEEN BUT HIM AND CALIBAN:
FOOLISH WENCH!
TO THE MOST OF MEN THIS IS A CALIBAN, AND THEY TO HIM ARE ANGELS.
MY AFFECTIONS ARE, THEN, MOST HUMBLE; I HAVE NO AMBITION TO SEE A GOODLIER MAN.
COME ON; OBEY: THY NERVES ARE IN THEIR INFANCY AGAIN, AND HAVE NO VIGOUR IN THEM.
SO THEY ARE: MY SPIRITS, AS IN A DREAM, ARE ALL BOUND UP.
MY FATHER'S LOSS, THE WEAKNESS WHICH I FEEL, THE WRACK OF ALL MY FRIENDS,
NOR THIS MAN'S THREATS, TO WHOM I AM SUBDUED, ARE BUT LIGHT TO ME, MIGHT I BUT THROUGH MY PRISON ONCE A DAY BEHOLD THIS MAID:
ALL CORNERS ELSE O' TH' EARTH LET LIBERTY MAKE USE OF; SPACE ENOUGH HAVE I IN SUCH A PRISON.

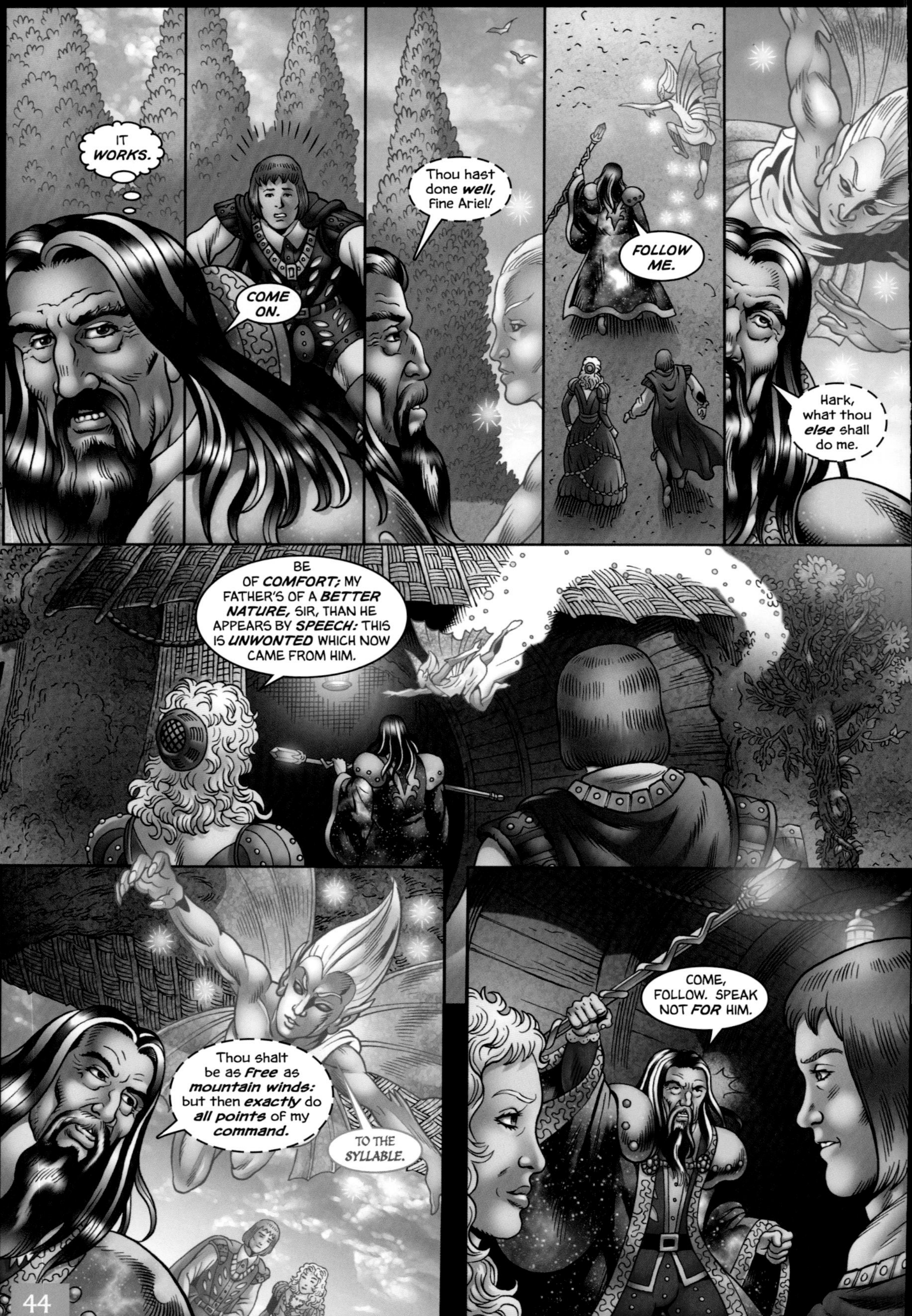
IT WORKS.
COME ON.
Thou hast done well, fine Ariel!
FOLLOW ME.
Hark, what thou else shall do me.
BE OF COMFORT; MY FATHER'S OF A BETTER NATURE, SIR, THAN HE APPEARS BY SPEECH: THIS IS UNWONTED WHICH NOW CAME FROM HIM.
Thou shalt be as free as mountain winds: but then exactly do all points of my command.
TO THE SYLLABLE.
COME, FOLLOW. SPEAK NOT FOR HIM.

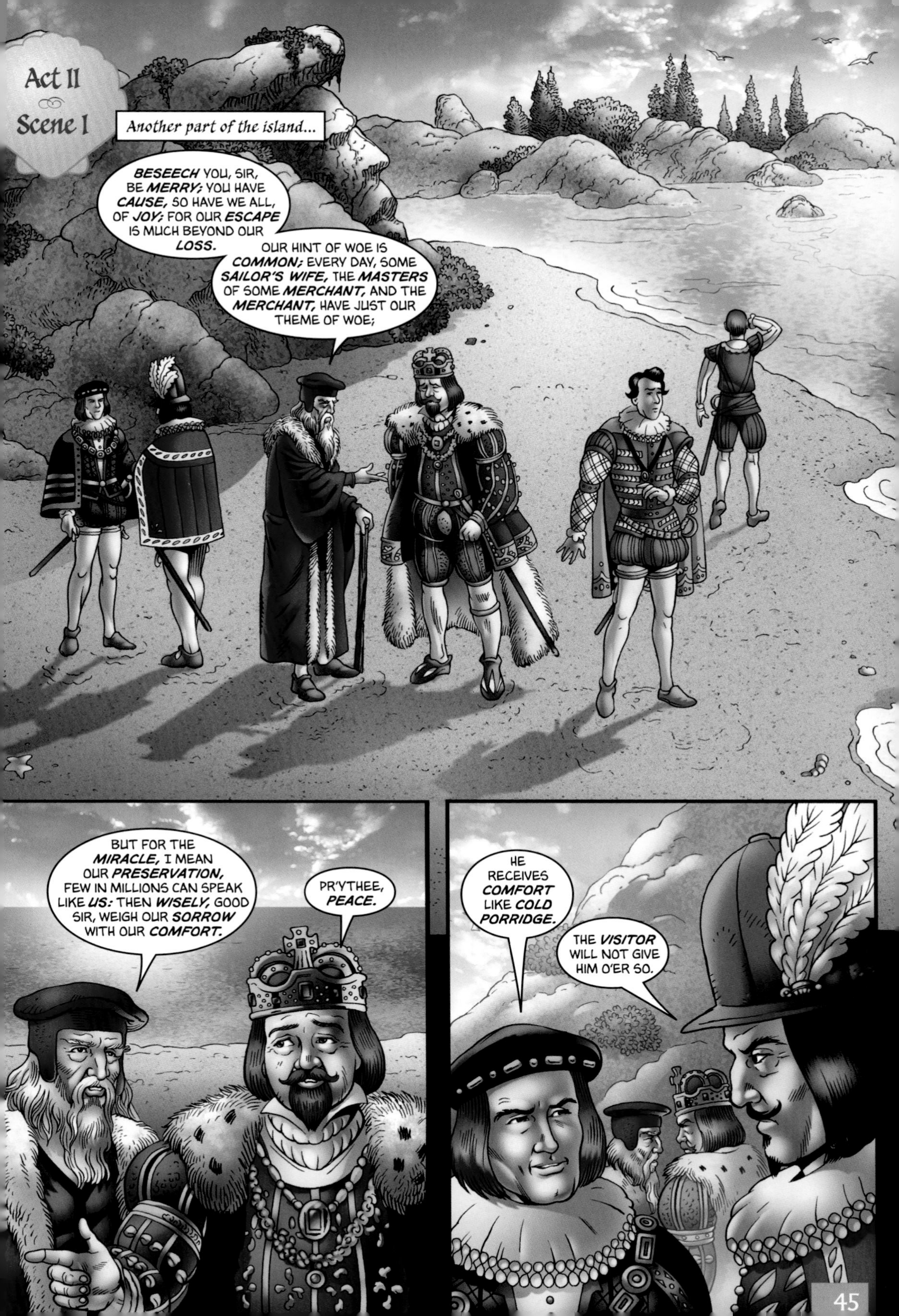
Act II Scene I
Another part of the island...
BESEECH YOU, SIR, BE MERRY; YOU HAVE CAUSE, SO HAVE WE ALL, OF JOY; FOR OUR ESCAPE IS MUCH BEYOND OUR LOSS.
OUR HINT OF WOE IS COMMON; EVERY DAY, SOME SAILOR'S WIFE, THE MASTERS OF SOME MERCHANT, AND THE MERCHANT, HAVE JUST OUR THEME OF WOE;
BUT FOR THE MIRACLE, I MEAN OUR PRESERVATION, FEW IN MILLIONS CAN SPEAK LIKE US: THEN WISELY, GOOD SIR, WEIGH OUR SORROW WITH OUR COMFORT.
PR'YTHEE, PEACE.
HE RECEIVES COMFORT LIKE COLD PORRIDGE.
THE VISITOR WILL NOT GIVE HIM O'ER SO.

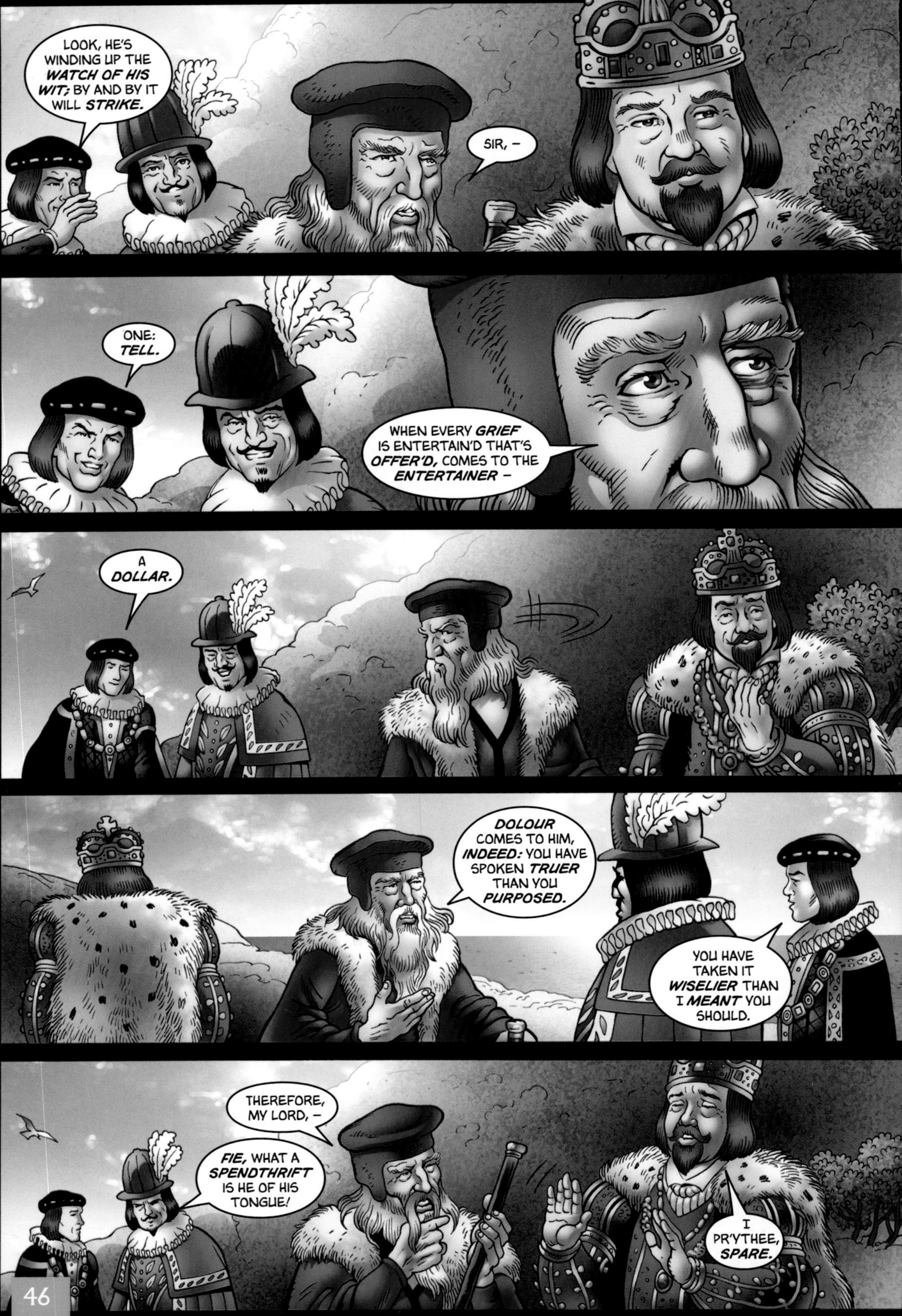
LOOK, HE'S WINDING UP THE WATCH OF HIS WIT; BY AND BY IT WILL STRIKE.
SIR, –
ONE: TELL.
WHEN EVERY GRIEF IS ENTERTAIN'D THAT'S OFFER'D, COMES TO THE ENTERTAINER –
A DOLLAR.
DOLOUR COMES TO HIM, INDEED: YOU HAVE SPOKEN TRUER THAN YOU PURPOSED.
YOU HAVE TAKEN IT WISELIER THAN I MEANT YOU SHOULD.
THEREFORE, MY LORD, –
FIE, WHAT A SPENDTHRIFT IS HE OF HIS TONGUE!
I PR'YTHEE, SPARE.

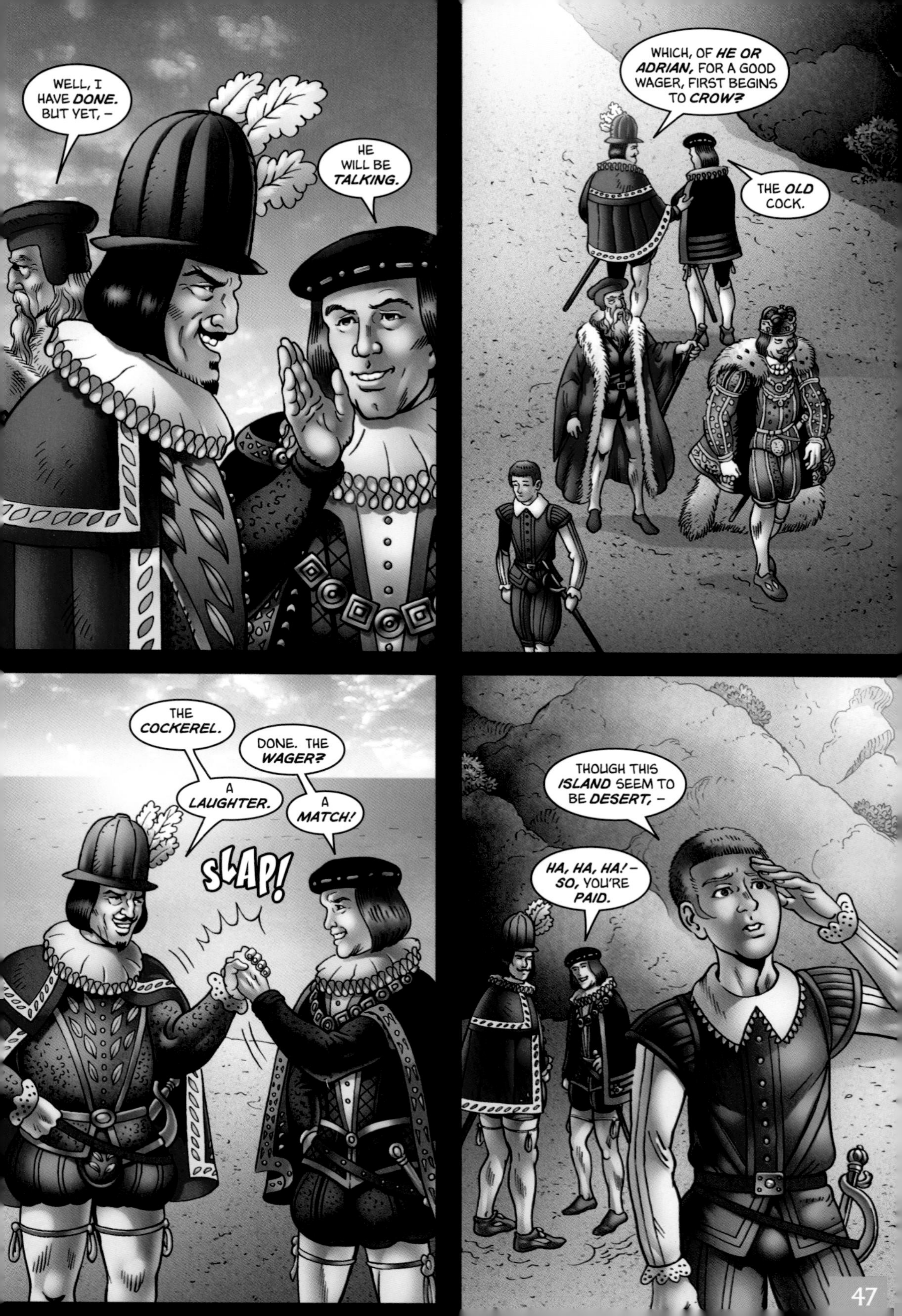
WELL, I HAVE DONE. BUT YET, –
HE WILL BE TALKING.
WHICH, OF HE OR ADRIAN, FOR A GOOD WAGER, FIRST BEGINS TO CROW?
THE OLD COCK.
THE COCKEREL.
DONE. THE WAGER?
A LAUGHTER.
A MATCH!
SLAP!
THOUGH THIS ISLAND SEEM TO BE DESERT, –
HA, HA, HA! – SO, YOU'RE PAID.

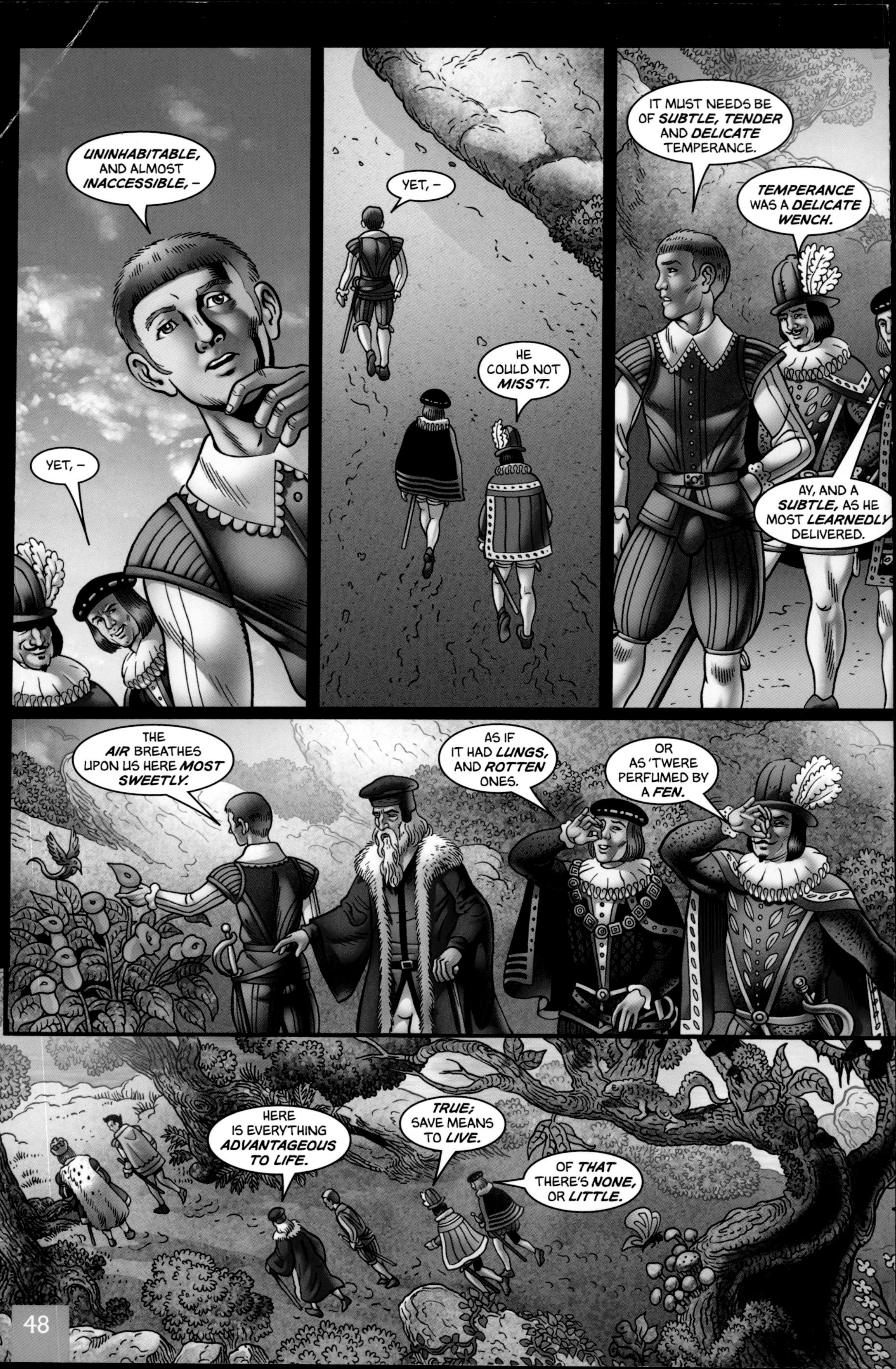
UNINHABITABLE, AND ALMOST INACCESSIBLE, –
YET, –
YET, –
HE COULD NOT MISS'T.
IT MUST NEEDS BE OF SUBTLE, TENDER AND DELICATE TEMPERANCE.
TEMPERANCE WAS A DELICATE WENCH.
AY, AND A SUBTLE, AS HE MOST LEARNEDLY DELIVERED.
THE AIR BREATHES UPON US HERE MOST SWEETLY.
AS IF IT HAD LUNGS, AND ROTTEN ONES.
OR AS 'TWERE PERFUMED BY A FEN.
HERE IS EVERYTHING ADVANTAGEOUS TO LIFE.
TRUE; SAVE MEANS TO LIVE.
OF THAT THERE'S NONE, OR LITTLE.

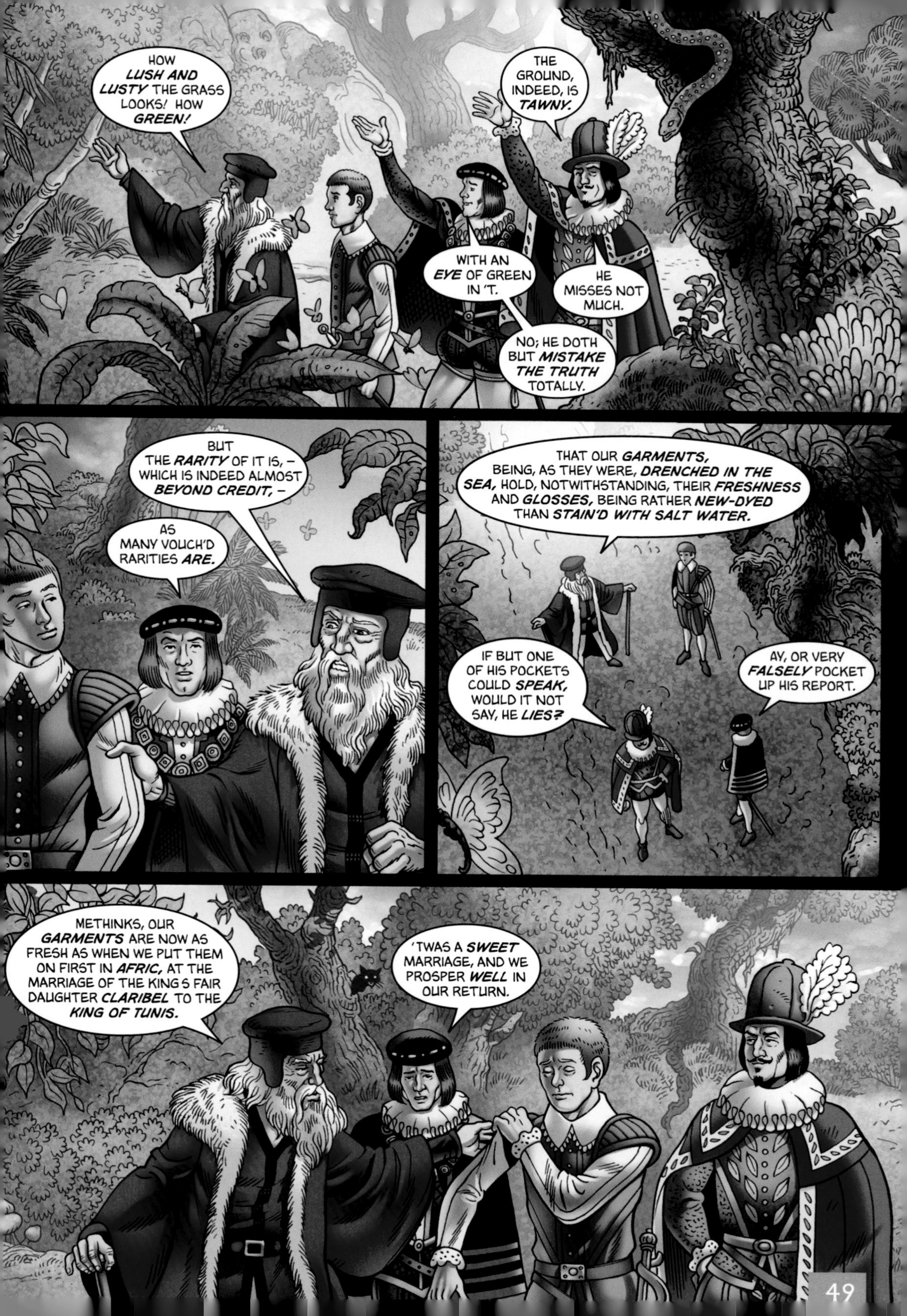
HOW LUSH AND LUSTY THE GRASS LOOKS! HOW GREEN!
THE GROUND, INDEED, IS TAWNY.
WITH AN EYE OF GREEN IN 'T.
HE MISSES NOT MUCH.
NO; HE DOTH BUT MISTAKE THE TRUTH TOTALLY.
BUT THE RARITY OF IT IS, – WHICH IS INDEED ALMOST BEYOND CREDIT, –
AS MANY VOUCH'D RARITIES ARE.
THAT OUR GARMENTS, BEING, AS THEY WERE, DRENCHED IN THE SEA, HOLD, NOTWITHSTANDING, THEIR FRESHNESS AND GLOSSES, BEING RATHER NEW-DYED THAN STAIN'D WITH SALT WATER.
IF BUT ONE OF HIS POCKETS COULD SPEAK, WOULD IT NOT SAY, HE LIES?
AY, OR VERY FALSELY POCKET UP HIS REPORT.
METHINKS, OUR GARMENTS ARE NOW AS FRESH AS WHEN WE PUT THEM ON FIRST IN AFRIC, AT THE MARRIAGE OF THE KING'S FAIR DAUGHTER CLARIBEL TO THE KING OF TUNIS.
'TWAS A SWEET MARRIAGE, AND WE PROSPER WELL IN OUR RETURN.

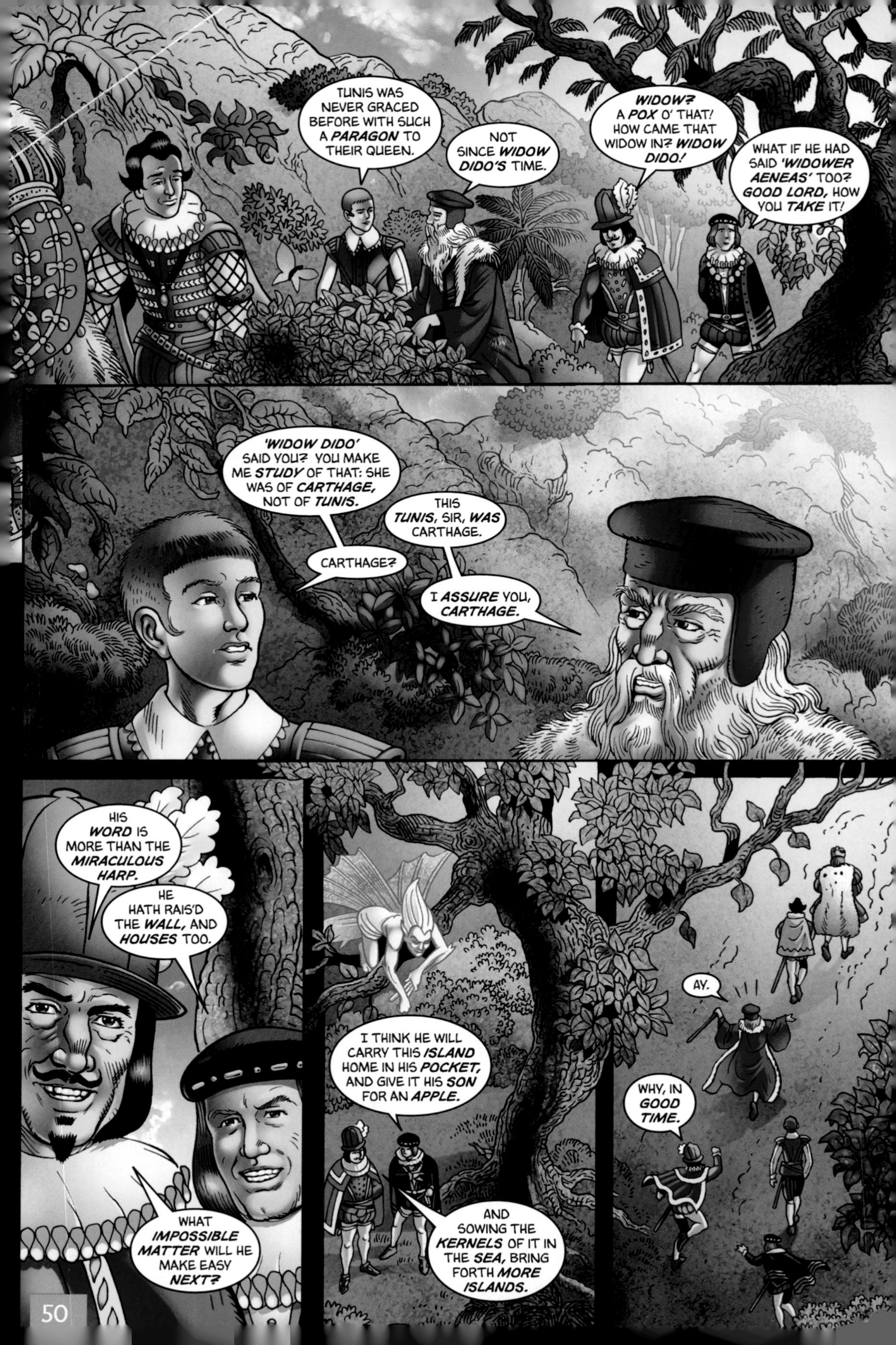
TUNIS WAS NEVER GRACED BEFORE WITH SUCH A PARAGON TO THEIR QUEEN.
NOT SINCE WIDOW DIDO'S TIME.
WIDOW? A POX O' THAT! HOW CAME THAT WIDOW IN? WIDOW DIDO!
WHAT IF HE HAD SAID 'WIDOWER AENEAS' TOO? GOOD LORD, HOW YOU TAKE IT!
'WIDOW DIDO' SAID YOU? YOU MAKE ME STUDY OF THAT: SHE WAS OF CARTHAGE, NOT OF TUNIS.
THIS TUNIS, SIR, WAS CARTHAGE.
CARTHAGE?
I ASSURE YOU, CARTHAGE.
HIS WORD IS MORE THAN THE MIRACULOUS HARP.
HE HATH RAIS'D THE WALL, AND HOUSES TOO.
WHAT IMPOSSIBLE MATTER WILL HE MAKE EASY NEXT?
I THINK HE WILL CARRY THIS ISLAND HOME IN HIS POCKET, AND GIVE IT HIS SON FOR AN APPLE.
AND SOWING THE KERNELS OF IT IN THE SEA, BRING FORTH MORE ISLANDS.
AY.
WHY, IN GOOD TIME.

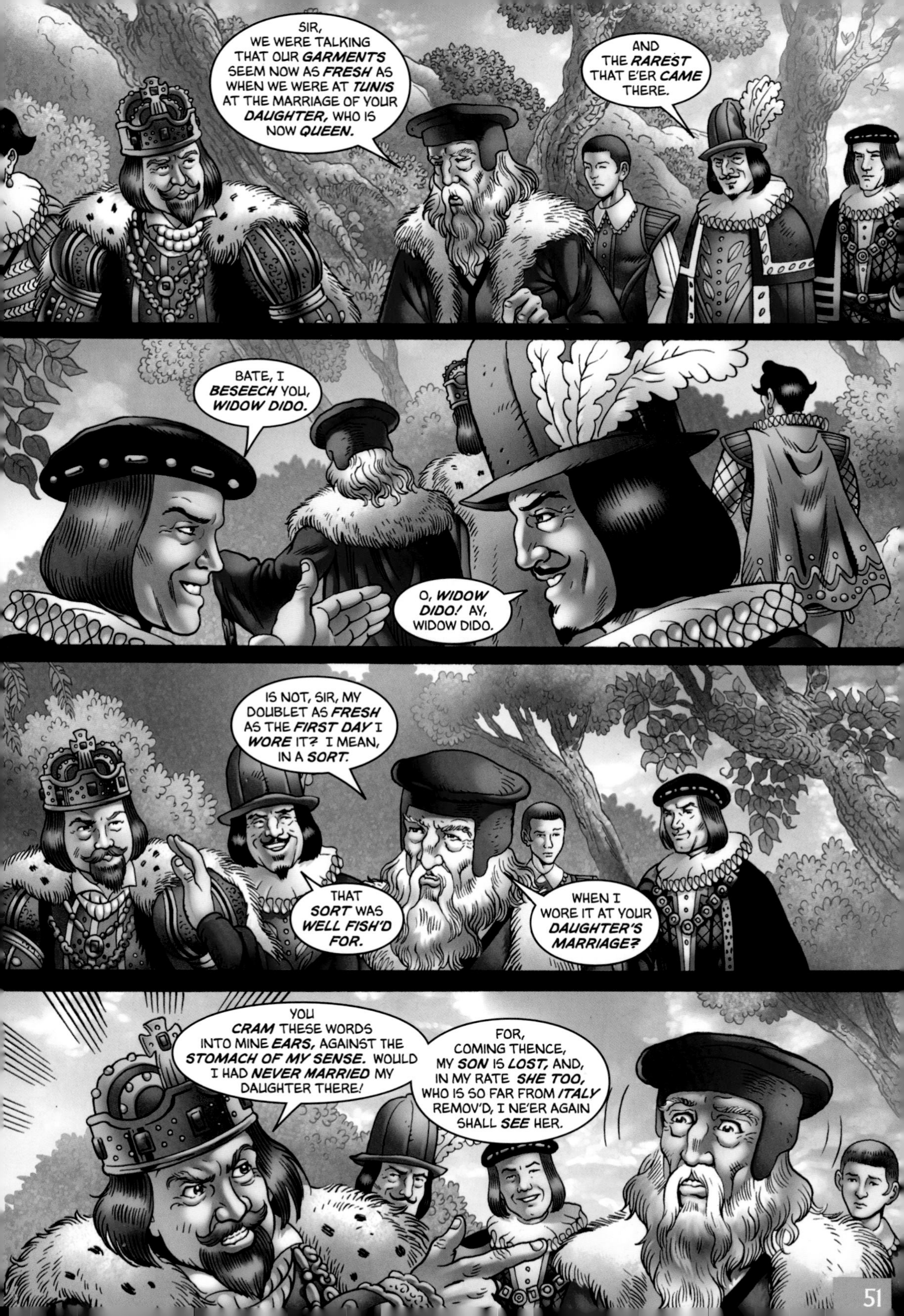
SIR, WE WERE TALKING THAT OUR GARMENTS SEEM NOW AS FRESH AS WHEN WE WERE AT TUNIS AT THE MARRIAGE OF YOUR DAUGHTER, WHO IS NOW QUEEN.
AND THE RAREST THAT E'ER CAME THERE.
BATE, I BESEECH YOU, WIDOW DIDO.
O, WIDOW DIDO! AY, WIDOW DIDO.
IS NOT, SIR, MY DOUBLET AS FRESH AS THE FIRST DAY I WORE IT? I MEAN, IN A SORT.
THAT SORT WAS WELL FISH'D FOR.
WHEN I WORE IT AT YOUR DAUGHTER'S MARRIAGE?
YOU CRAM THESE WORDS INTO MINE EARS, AGAINST THE STOMACH OF MY SENSE. WOULD I HAD NEVER MARRIED MY DAUGHTER THERE!
FOR, COMING THENCE, MY SON IS LOST, AND, IN MY RATE SHE TOO, WHO IS SO FAR FROM ITALY REMOV'D, I NE'ER AGAIN SHALL SEE HER.

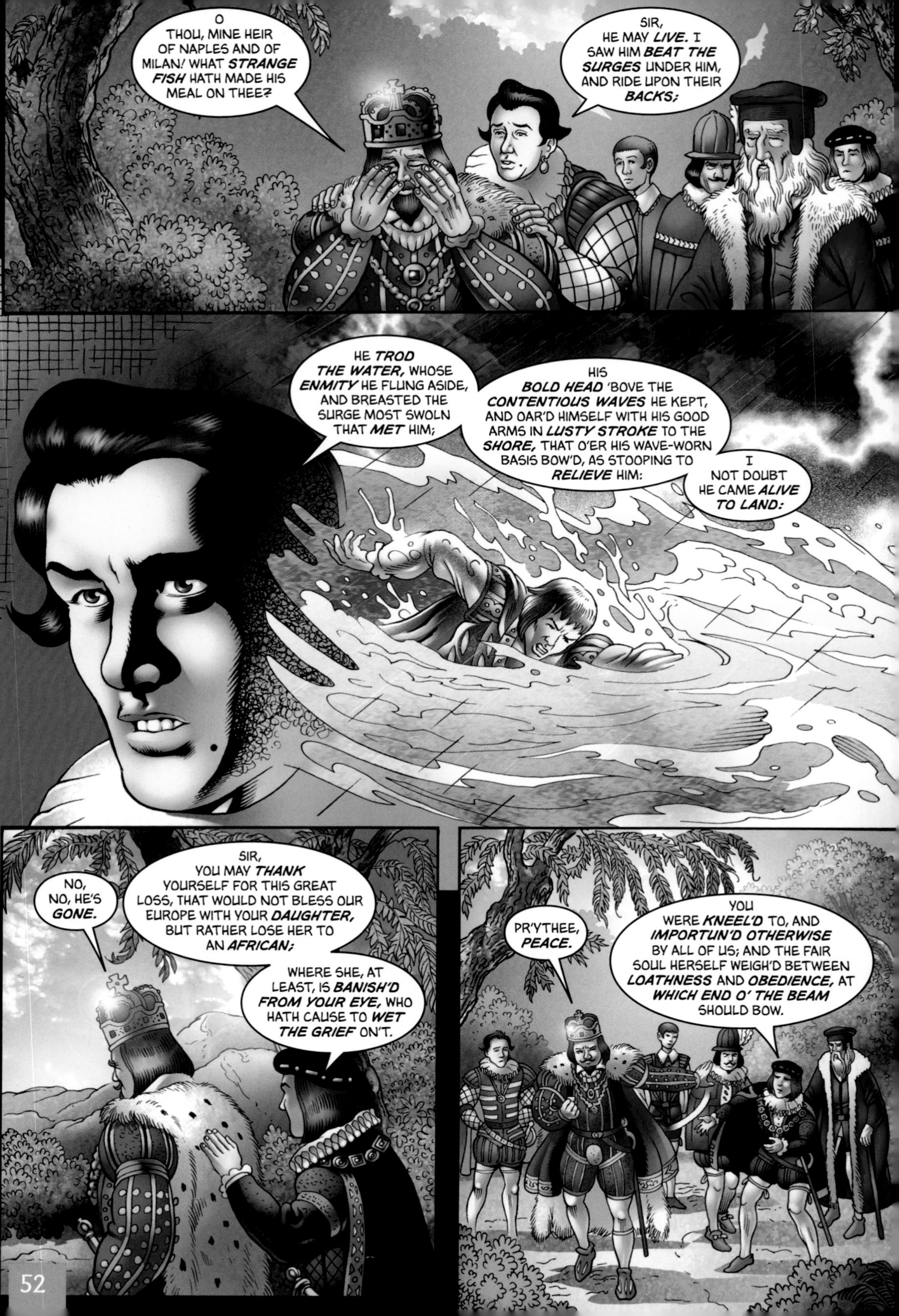
O THOU, MINE HEIR OF NAPLES AND OF MILAN! WHAT STRANGE FISH HATH MADE HIS MEAL ON THEE?
SIR, HE MAY LIVE. I SAW HIM BEAT THE SURGES UNDER HIM, AND RIDE UPON THEIR BACKS;
HE TROD THE WATER, WHOSE ENMITY HE FLUNG ASIDE, AND BREASTED THE SURGE MOST SWOLN THAT MET HIM;
HIS BOLD HEAD 'BOVE THE CONTENTIOUS WAVES HE KEPT, AND OAR'D HIMSELF WITH HIS GOOD ARMS IN LUSTY STROKE TO THE SHORE, THAT O'ER HIS WAVE-WORN BASIS BOW'D, AS STOOPING TO RELIEVE HIM:
I NOT DOUBT HE CAME ALIVE TO LAND:
NO, NO, HE'S GONE.
SIR, YOU MAY THANK YOURSELF FOR THIS GREAT LOSS, THAT WOULD NOT BLESS OUR EUROPE WITH YOUR DAUGHTER, BUT RATHER LOSE HER TO AN AFRICAN;
WHERE SHE, AT LEAST, IS BANISH'D FROM YOUR EYE, WHO HATH CAUSE TO WET THE GRIEF ON'T.
PR'YTHEE, PEACE.
YOU WERE KNEEL'D TO, AND IMPORTUN'D OTHERWISE BY ALL OF US; AND THE FAIR SOUL HERSELF WEIGH'D BETWEEN LOATHNESS AND OBEDIENCE, AT WHICH END O' THE BEAM SHOULD BOW.

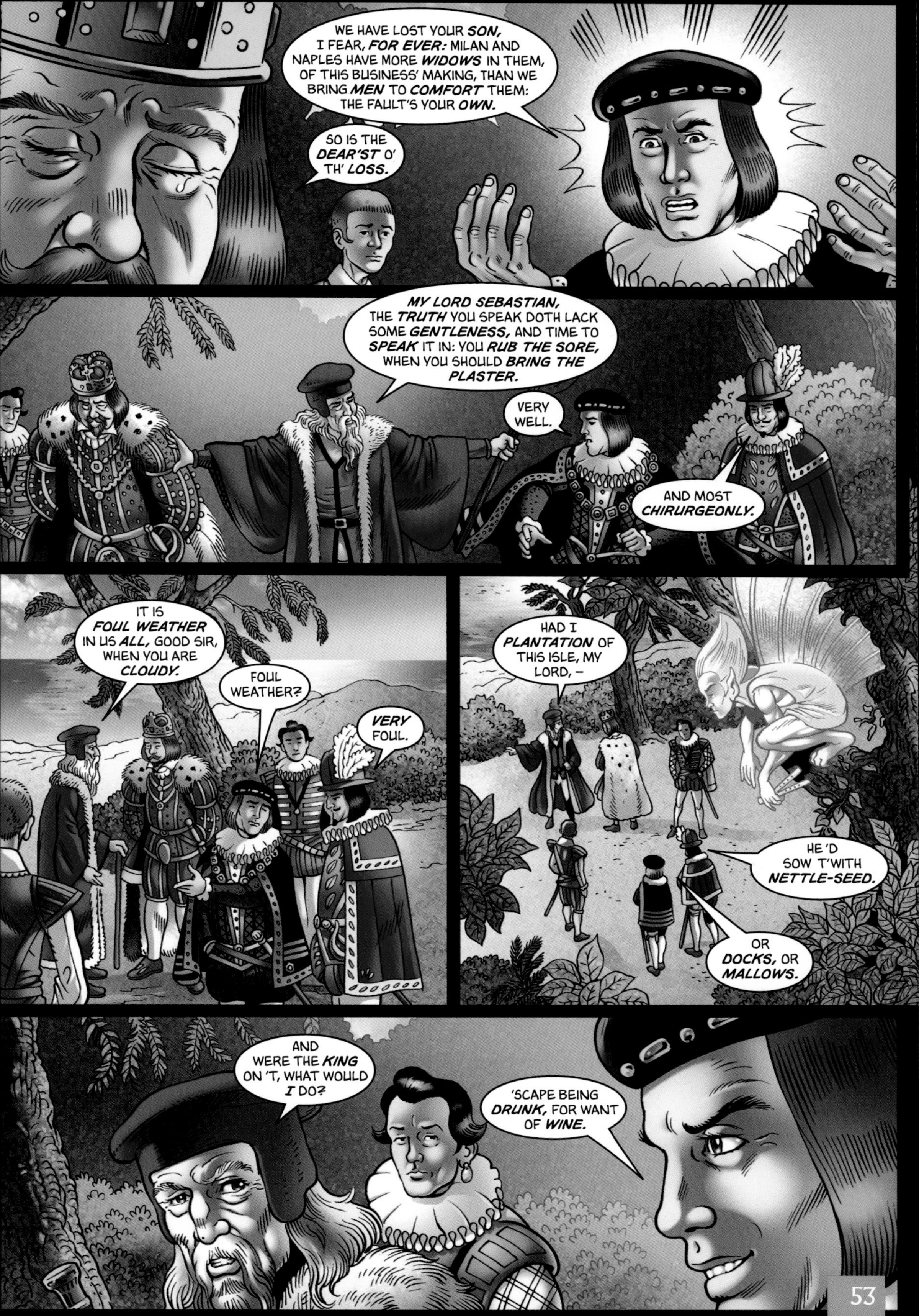
WE HAVE LOST YOUR SON, I FEAR, FOR EVER: MILAN AND NAPLES HAVE MORE WIDOWS IN THEM, OF THIS BUSINESS' MAKING, THAN WE BRING MEN TO COMFORT THEM: THE FAULT'S YOUR OWN.
SO IS THE DEAR'ST O' TH' LOSS.
MY LORD SEBASTIAN, THE TRUTH YOU SPEAK DOTH LACK SOME GENTLENESS, AND TIME TO SPEAK IT IN: YOU RUB THE SORE, WHEN YOU SHOULD BRING THE PLASTER.
VERY WELL.
AND MOST CHIRURGEONLY.
IT IS FOUL WEATHER IN US ALL, GOOD SIR, WHEN YOU ARE CLOUDY.
FOUL WEATHER?
VERY FOUL.
HAD I PLANTATION OF THIS ISLE, MY LORD, –
HE'D SOW T'WITH NETTLE-SEED.
OR DOCKS, OR MALLOWS.
AND WERE THE KING ON 'T, WHAT WOULD I DO?
'SCAPE BEING DRUNK, FOR WANT OF WINE.

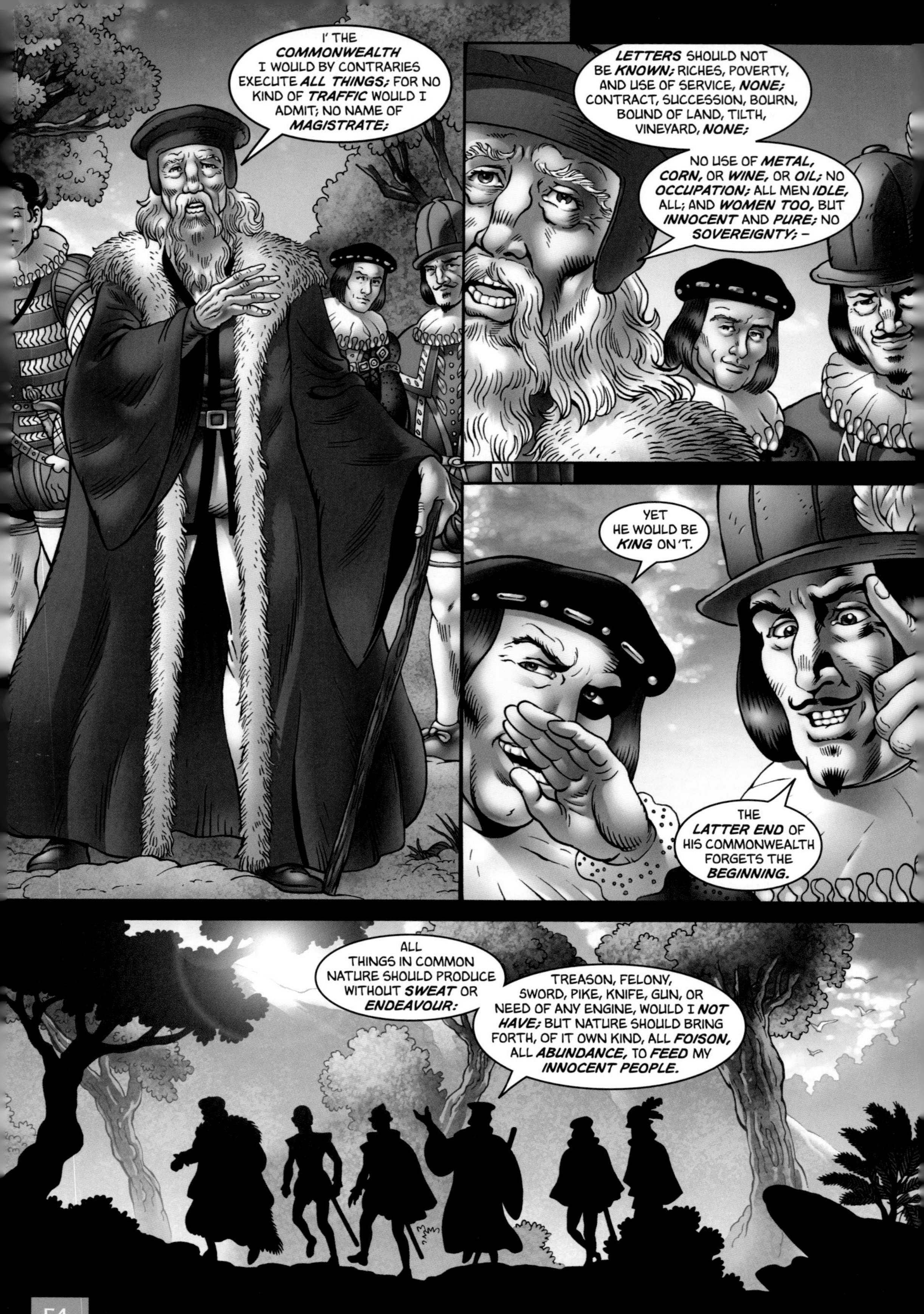

I' THE COMMONWEALTH I WOULD BY CONTRARIES EXECUTE ALL THINGS; FOR NO KIND OF TRAFFIC WOULD I ADMIT; NO NAME OF MAGISTRATE;
LETTERS SHOULD NOT BE KNOWN; RICHES, POVERTY, AND USE OF SERVICE, NONE; CONTRACT, SUCCESSION, BOURN, BOUND OF LAND, TILTH, VINEYARD, NONE;
NO USE OF METAL, CORN, OR WINE, OR OIL; NO OCCUPATION; ALL MEN IDLE, ALL; AND WOMEN TOO, BUT INNOCENT AND PURE; NO SOVEREIGNTY; –
YET HE WOULD BE KING ON'T.
THE LATTER END OF HIS COMMONWEALTH FORGETS THE BEGINNING.
ALL THINGS IN COMMON NATURE SHOULD PRODUCE WITHOUT SWEAT OR ENDEAVOUR:
TREASON, FELONY, SWORD, PIKE, KNIFE, GUN, OR NEED OF ANY ENGINE, WOULD I NOT HAVE; BUT NATURE SHOULD BRING FORTH, OF IT OWN KIND, ALL FOISON, ALL ABUNDANCE, TO FEED MY INNOCENT PEOPLE.

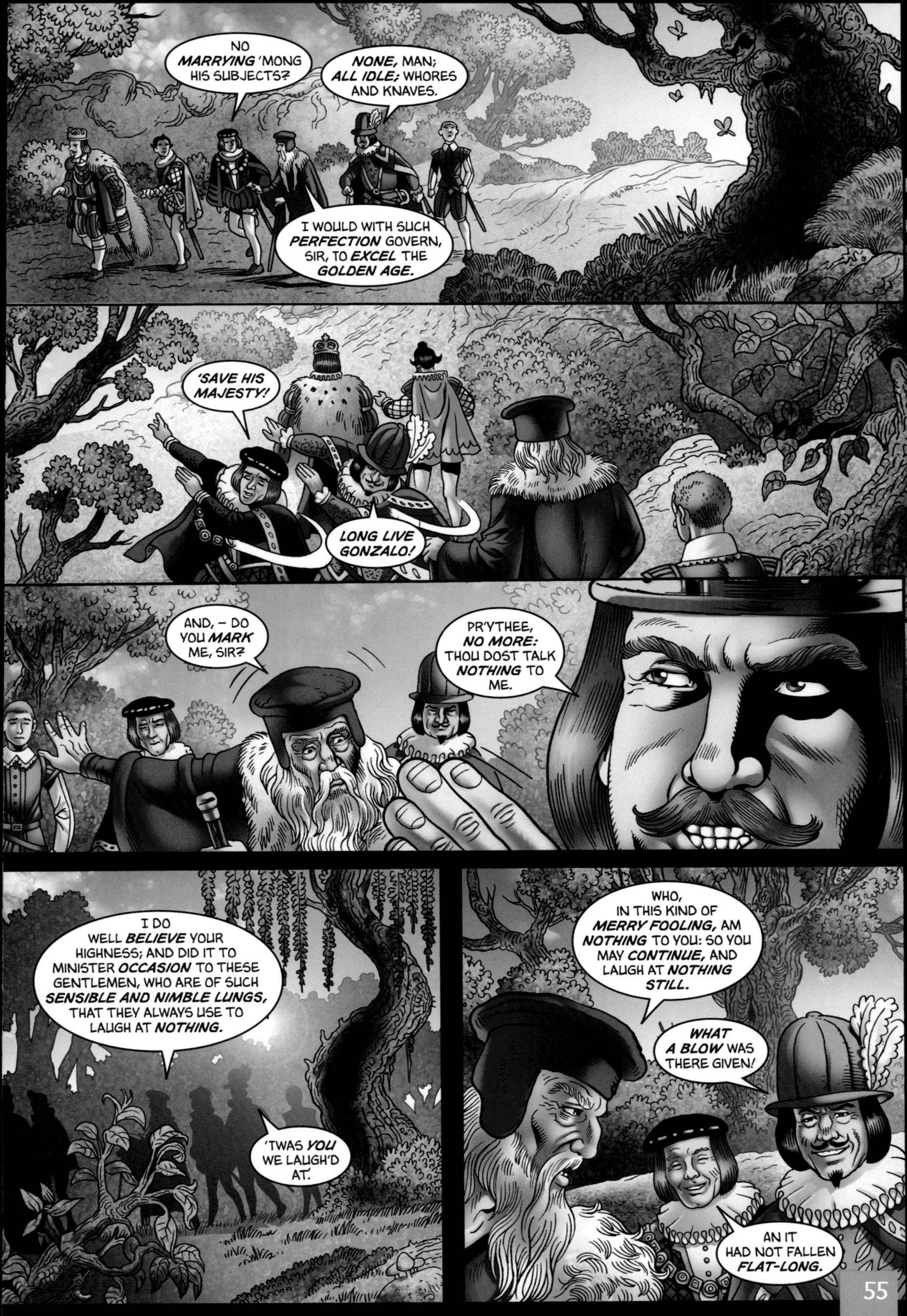
NO MARRYING 'MONG HIS SUBJECTS?
NONE, MAN; ALL IDLE; WHORES AND KNAVES.
I WOULD WITH SUCH PERFECTION GOVERN, SIR, TO EXCEL THE GOLDEN AGE.
'SAVE HIS MAJESTY!
LONG LIVE GONZALO!
AND, – DO YOU MARK ME, SIR?
PR'YTHEE, NO MORE: THOU DOST TALK NOTHING TO ME.
I DO WELL BELIEVE YOUR HIGHNESS; AND DID IT TO MINISTER OCCASION TO THESE GENTLEMEN, WHO ARE OF SUCH SENSIBLE AND NIMBLE LUNGS, THAT THEY ALWAYS USE TO LAUGH AT NOTHING.
'TWAS YOU WE LAUGH'D AT.
WHO, IN THIS KIND OF MERRY FOOLING, AM NOTHING TO YOU: SO YOU MAY CONTINUE, AND LAUGH AT NOTHING STILL.
WHAT A BLOW WAS THERE GIVEN!
AN IT HAD NOT FALLEN FLAT-LONG.

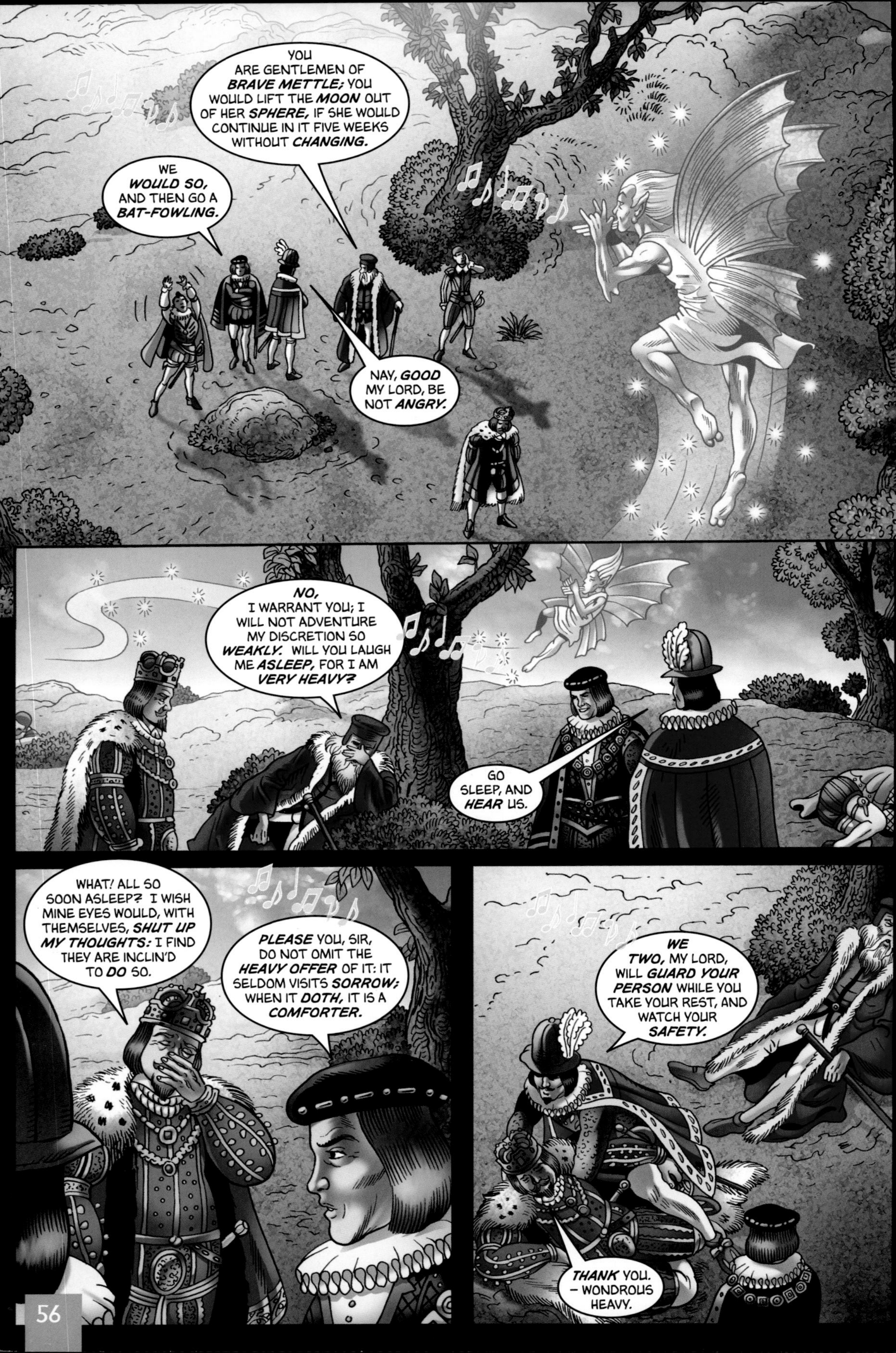
YOU ARE GENTLEMEN OF BRAVE METTLE; YOU WOULD LIFT THE MOON OUT OF HER SPHERE, IF SHE WOULD CONTINUE IN IT FIVE WEEKS WITHOUT CHANGING.
WE WOULD SO, AND THEN GO A BAT-FOWLING.
NAY, GOOD MY LORD, BE NOT ANGRY.
NO, I WARRANT YOU; I WILL NOT ADVENTURE MY DISCRETION SO WEAKLY. WILL YOU LAUGH ME ASLEEP, FOR I AM VERY HEAVY?
GO SLEEP, AND HEAR US.
WHAT! ALL SO SOON ASLEEP? I WISH MINE EYES WOULD, WITH THEMSELVES, SHUT UP MY THOUGHTS: I FIND THEY ARE INCLIN'D TO DO SO.
PLEASE YOU, SIR, DO NOT OMIT THE HEAVY OFFER OF IT: IT SELDOM VISITS SORROW; WHEN IT DOTH, IT IS A COMFORTER.
WE TWO, MY LORD, WILL GUARD YOUR PERSON WHILE YOU TAKE YOUR REST, AND WATCH YOUR SAFETY.
THANK YOU. – WONDROUS HEAVY.

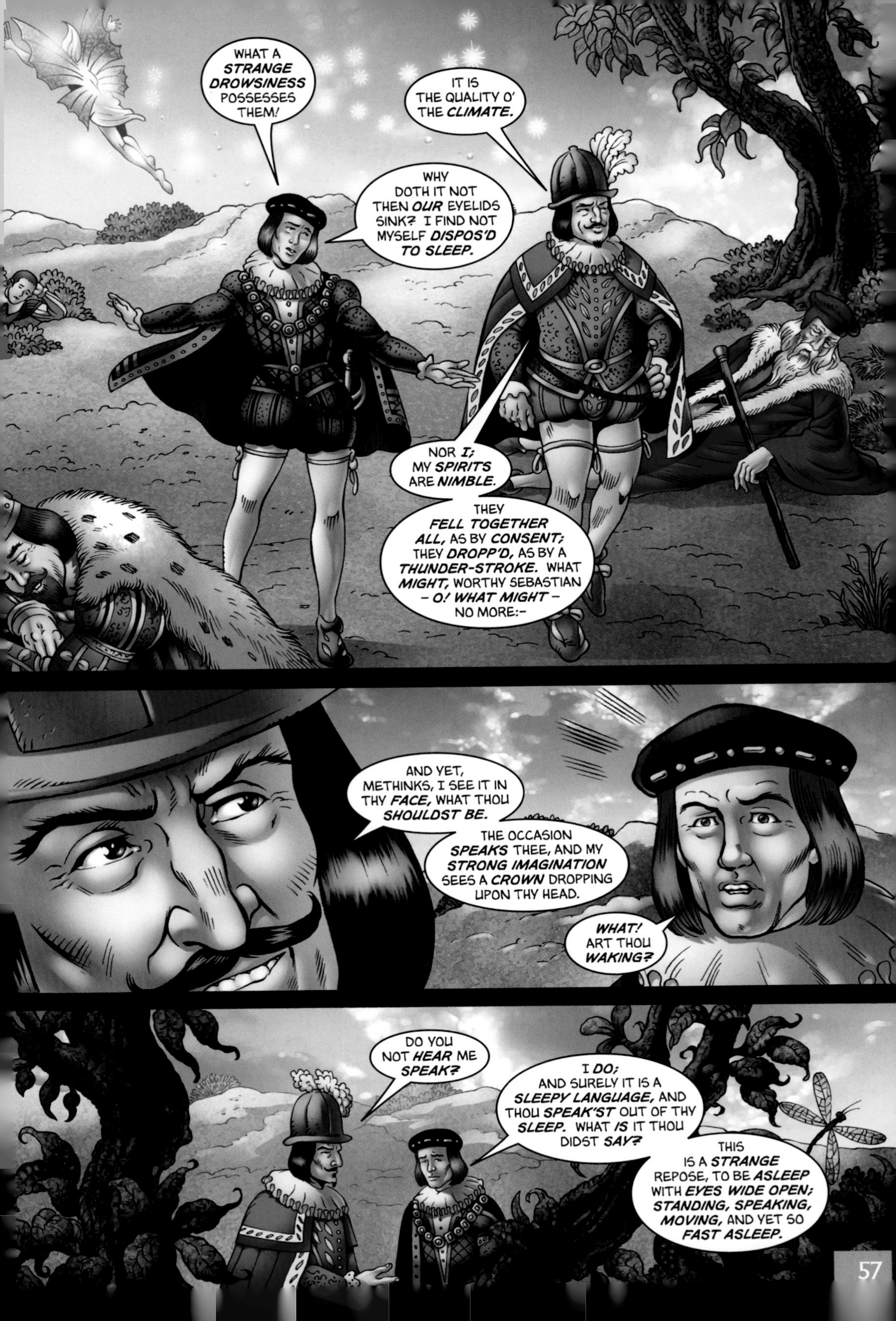
WHAT A STRANGE DROWSINESS POSSESSES THEM!
IT IS THE QUALITY O' THE CLIMATE.
WHY DOTH IT NOT THEN OUR EYELIDS SINK? I FIND NOT MYSELF DISPOS'D TO SLEEP.
NOR I; MY SPIRITS ARE NIMBLE.
THEY FELL TOGETHER ALL, AS BY CONSENT; THEY DROPP'D, AS BY A THUNDER-STROKE. WHAT MIGHT, WORTHY SEBASTIAN – O! WHAT MIGHT – NO MORE:-
AND YET, METHINKS, I SEE IT IN THY FACE, WHAT THOU SHOULDST BE.
THE OCCASION SPEAKS THEE, AND MY STRONG IMAGINATION SEES A CROWN DROPPING UPON THY HEAD.
WHAT! ART THOU WAKING?
DO YOU NOT HEAR ME SPEAK?
I DO; AND SURELY IT IS A SLEEPY LANGUAGE, AND THOU SPEAK'ST OUT OF THY SLEEP. WHAT IS IT THOU DIDST SAY?
THIS IS A STRANGE REPOSE, TO BE ASLEEP WITH EYES WIDE OPEN; STANDING, SPEAKING, MOVING, AND YET SO FAST ASLEEP.

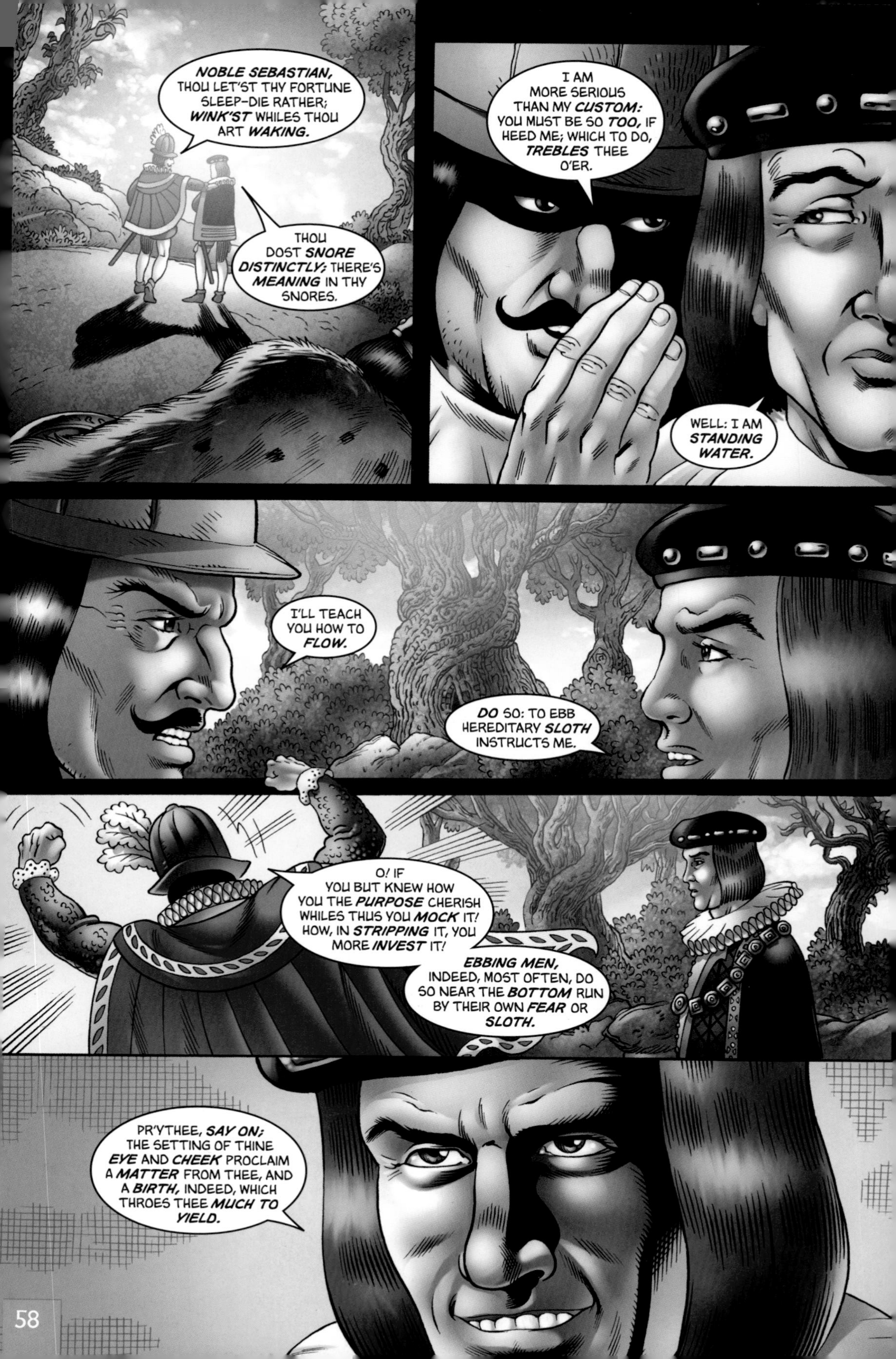
NOBLE SEBASTIAN, THOU LET'ST THY FORTUNE SLEEP–DIE RATHER; WINK'ST WHILES THOU ART WAKING.
THOU DOST SNORE DISTINCTLY; THERE'S MEANING IN THY SNORES.
I AM MORE SERIOUS THAN MY CUSTOM: YOU MUST BE SO TOO, IF HEED ME; WHICH TO DO, TREBLES THEE O'ER.
WELL: I AM STANDING WATER.
I'LL TEACH YOU HOW TO FLOW.
DO SO: TO EBB HEREDITARY SLOTH INSTRUCTS ME.
O! IF YOU BUT KNEW HOW YOU THE PURPOSE CHERISH WHILES THUS YOU MOCK IT! HOW, IN STRIPPING IT, YOU MORE INVEST IT!
EBBING MEN, INDEED, MOST OFTEN, DO SO NEAR THE BOTTOM RUN BY THEIR OWN FEAR OR SLOTH.
PR'YTHEE, SAY ON; THE SETTING OF THINE EYE AND CHEEK PROCLAIM A MATTER FROM THEE, AND A BIRTH, INDEED, WHICH THROES THEE MUCH TO YIELD.

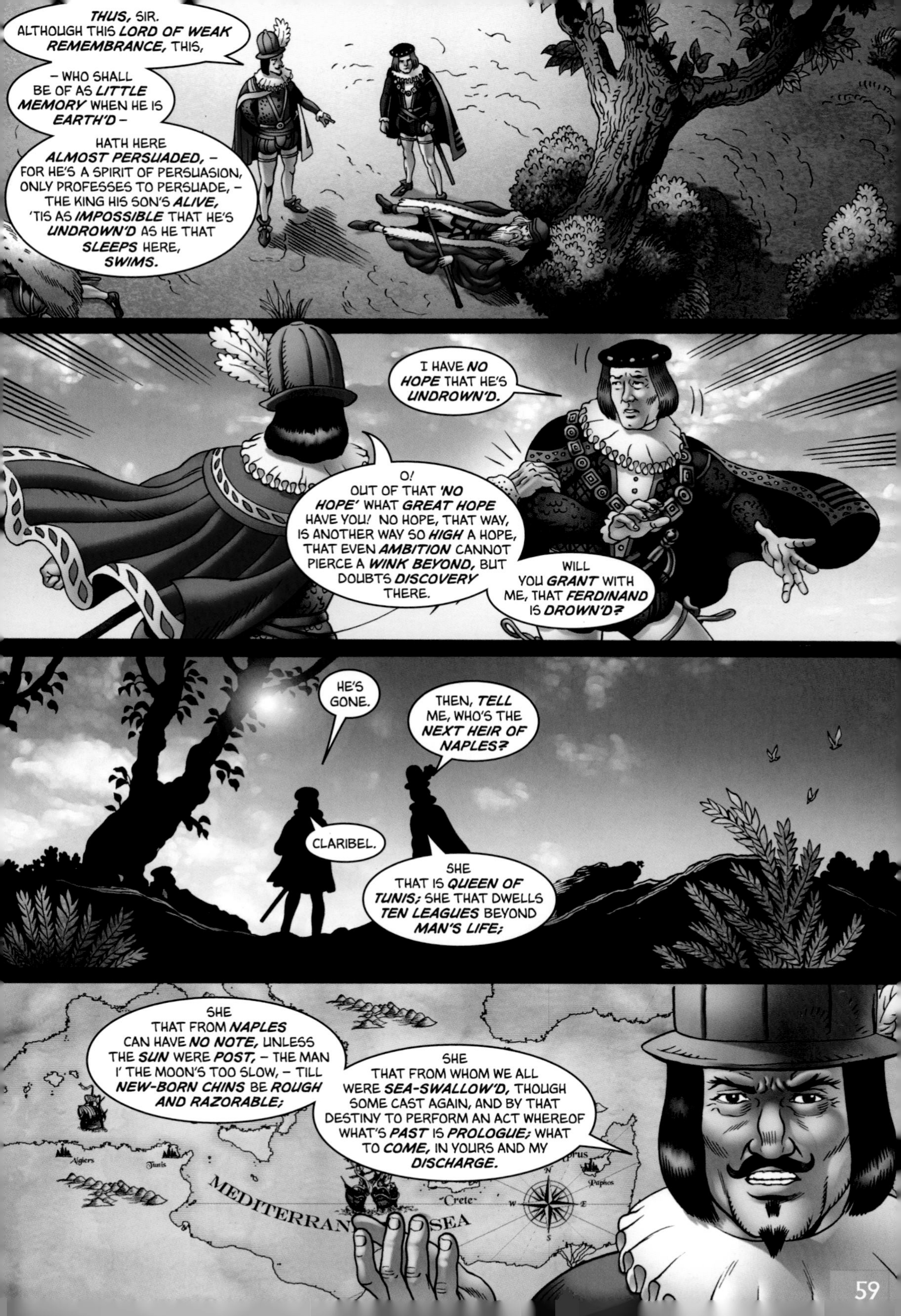
THUS, SIR. ALTHOUGH THIS LORD OF WEAK REMEMBRANCE, THIS,
– WHO SHALL BE OF AS LITTLE MEMORY WHEN HE IS EARTH'D –
HATH HERE ALMOST PERSUADED, – FOR HE'S A SPIRIT OF PERSUASION, ONLY PROFESSES TO PERSUADE, – THE KING HIS SON'S ALIVE, 'TIS AS IMPOSSIBLE THAT HE'S UNDROWN'D AS HE THAT SLEEPS HERE, SWIMS.
I HAVE NO HOPE THAT HE'S UNDROWN'D.
O! OUT OF THAT 'NO HOPE' WHAT GREAT HOPE HAVE YOU! NO HOPE, THAT WAY, IS ANOTHER WAY SO HIGH A HOPE, THAT EVEN AMBITION CANNOT PIERCE A WINK BEYOND, BUT DOUBTS DISCOVERY THERE.
WILL YOU GRANT WITH ME, THAT FERDINAND IS DROWN'D?
HE'S GONE.
THEN, TELL ME, WHO'S THE NEXT HEIR OF NAPLES?
CLARIBEL.
SHE THAT IS QUEEN OF TUNIS; SHE THAT DWELLS TEN LEAGUES BEYOND MAN'S LIFE;
SHE THAT FROM NAPLES CAN HAVE NO NOTE, UNLESS THE SUN WERE POST, – THE MAN I' THE MOON'S TOO SLOW, – TILL NEW-BORN CHINS BE ROUGH AND RAZORABLE;
SHE THAT FROM WHOM WE ALL WERE SEA-SWALLOW'D, THOUGH SOME CAST AGAIN, AND BY THAT DESTINY TO PERFORM AN ACT WHEREOF WHAT'S PAST IS PROLOGUE; WHAT TO COME, IN YOURS AND MY DISCHARGE.
Algiers
Tunis
MEDITERRAN SEA
Crete
Paphos

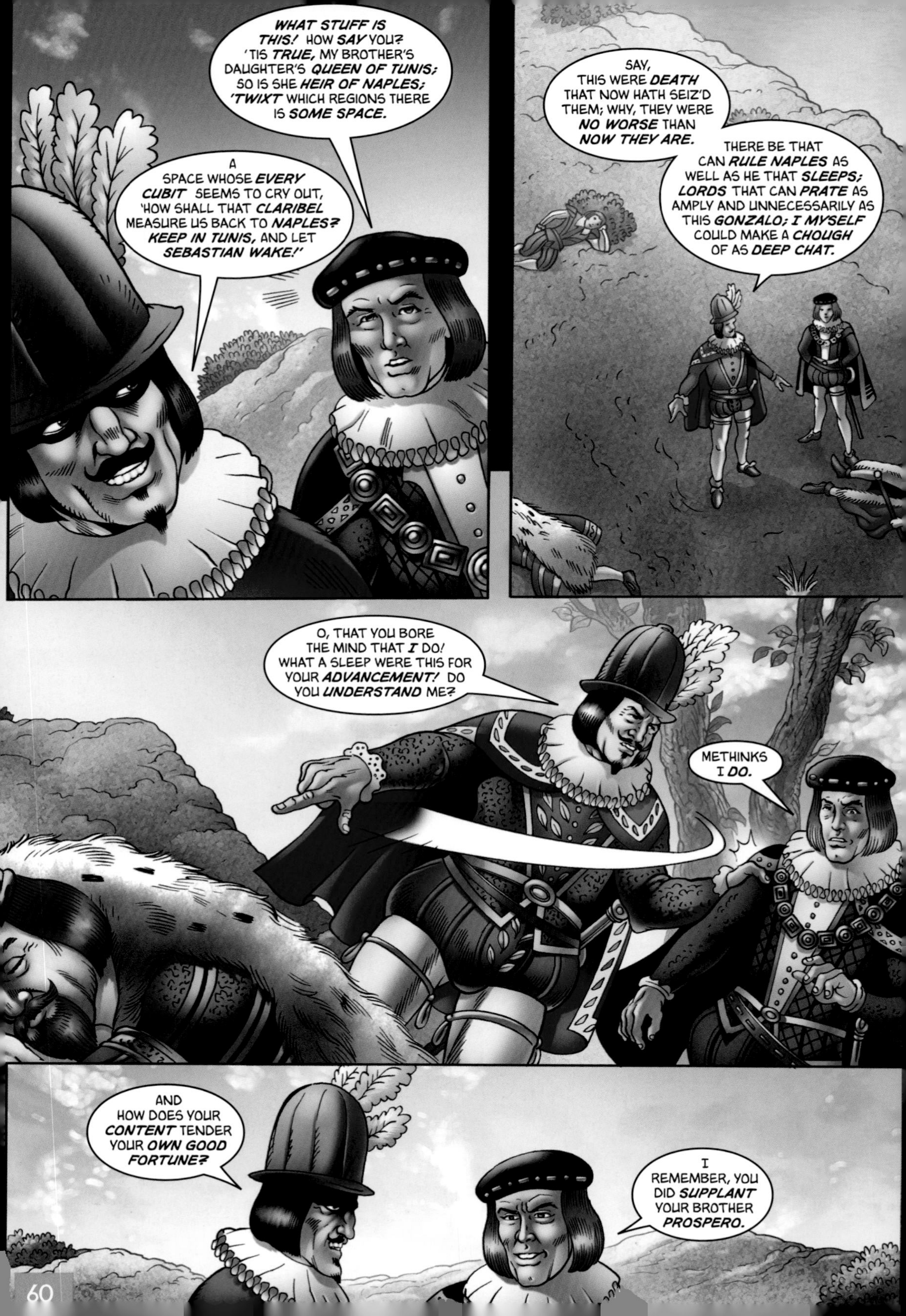
WHAT STUFF IS THIS! HOW SAY YOU? 'TIS TRUE, MY BROTHER'S DAUGHTER'S QUEEN OF TUNIS; SO IS SHE HEIR OF NAPLES; 'TWIXT WHICH REGIONS THERE IS SOME SPACE.
A SPACE WHOSE EVERY CUBIT SEEMS TO CRY OUT, 'HOW SHALL THAT CLARIBEL MEASURE US BACK TO NAPLES? KEEP IN TUNIS, AND LET SEBASTIAN WAKE!'
SAY, THIS WERE DEATH THAT NOW HATH SEIZ'D THEM; WHY, THEY WERE NO WORSE THAN NOW THEY ARE.
THERE BE THAT CAN RULE NAPLES AS WELL AS HE THAT SLEEPS; LORDS THAT CAN PRATE AS AMPLY AND UNNECESSARILY AS THIS GONZALO; I MYSELF COULD MAKE A CHOUGH OF AS DEEP CHAT.
O, THAT YOU BORE THE MIND THAT I DO! WHAT A SLEEP WERE THIS FOR YOUR ADVANCEMENT! DO YOU UNDERSTAND ME?
METHINKS I DO.
AND HOW DOES YOUR CONTENT TENDER YOUR OWN GOOD FORTUNE?
I REMEMBER, YOU DID SUPPLANT YOUR BROTHER PROSPERO.

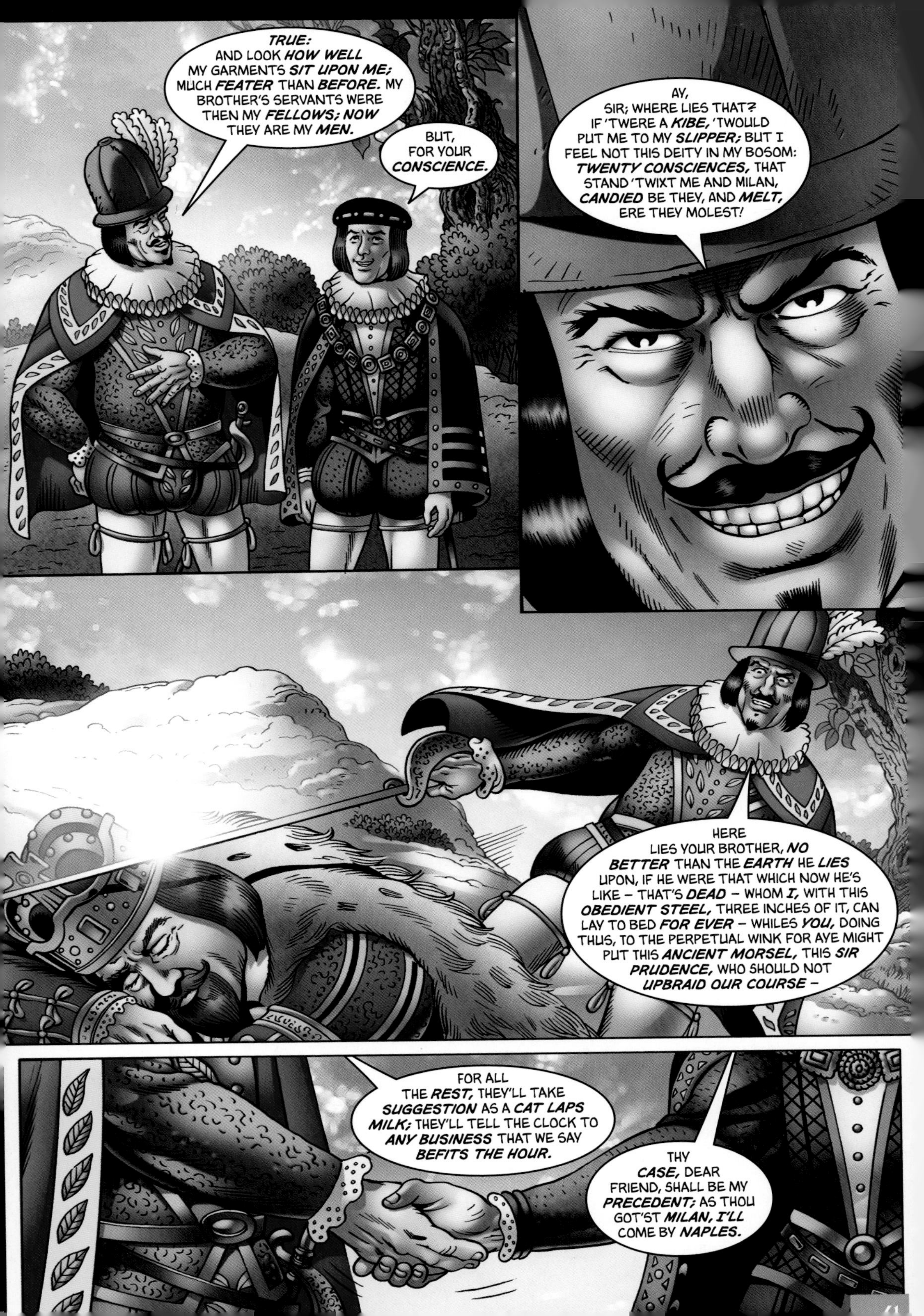
TRUE: AND LOOK HOW WELL MY GARMENTS SIT UPON ME; MUCH FEATER THAN BEFORE. MY BROTHER'S SERVANTS WERE THEN MY FELLOWS; NOW THEY ARE MY MEN.
BUT, FOR YOUR CONSCIENCE.
AY, SIR; WHERE LIES THAT? IF 'TWERE A KIBE, 'TWOULD PUT ME TO MY SLIPPER; BUT I FEEL NOT THIS DEITY IN MY BOSOM: TWENTY CONSCIENCES, THAT STAND 'TWIXT ME AND MILAN, CANDIED BE THEY, AND MELT, ERE THEY MOLEST!
HERE LIES YOUR BROTHER, NO BETTER THAN THE EARTH HE LIES UPON, IF HE WERE THAT WHICH NOW HE'S LIKE – THAT'S DEAD – WHOM I, WITH THIS OBEDIENT STEEL, THREE INCHES OF IT, CAN LAY TO BED FOR EVER – WHILES YOU, DOING THUS, TO THE PERPETUAL WINK FOR AYE MIGHT PUT THIS ANCIENT MORSEL, THIS SIR PRUDENCE, WHO SHOULD NOT UPBRAID OUR COURSE –
FOR ALL THE REST, THEY'LL TAKE SUGGESTION AS A CAT LAPS MILK; THEY'LL TELL THE CLOCK TO ANY BUSINESS THAT WE SAY BEFITS THE HOUR.
THY CASE, DEAR FRIEND, SHALL BE MY PRECEDENT; AS THOU GOT'ST MILAN, I'LL COME BY NAPLES.

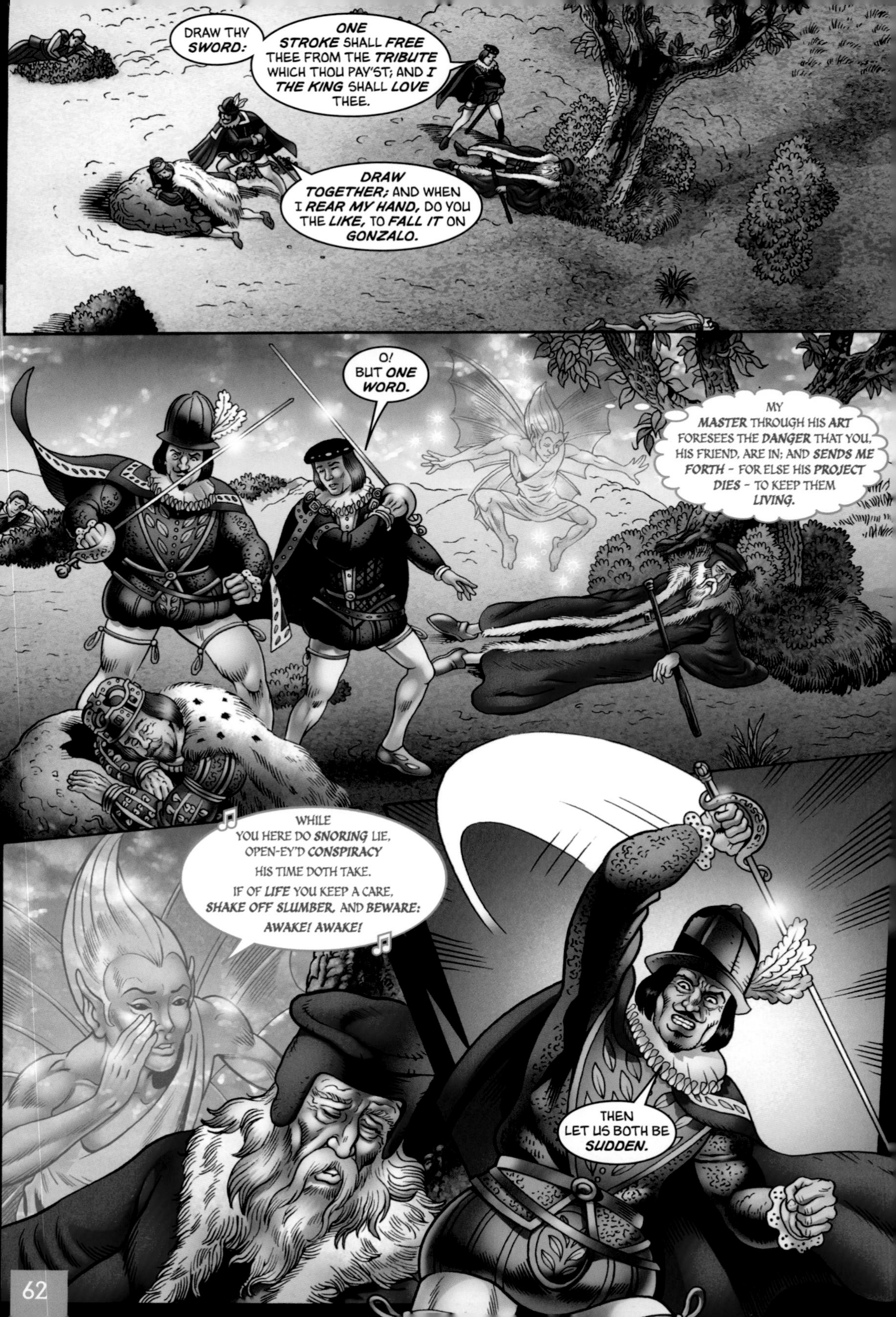
DRAW THY SWORD:
ONE STROKE SHALL FREE THEE FROM THE TRIBUTE WHICH THOU PAY'ST; AND I THE KING SHALL LOVE THEE.
DRAW TOGETHER; AND WHEN I REAR MY HAND, DO YOU THE LIKE, TO FALL IT ON GONZALO.
O! BUT ONE WORD.
MY MASTER THROUGH HIS ART FORESEES THE DANGER THAT YOU, HIS FRIEND, ARE IN; AND SENDS ME FORTH - FOR ELSE HIS PROJECT DIES - TO KEEP THEM LIVING.
WHILE YOU HERE DO SNORING LIE, OPEN-EY'D CONSPIRACY HIS TIME DOTH TAKE.
IF OF LIFE YOU KEEP A CARE, SHAKE OFF SLUMBER, AND BEWARE:
AWAKE! AWAKE!
THEN LET US BOTH BE SUDDEN.

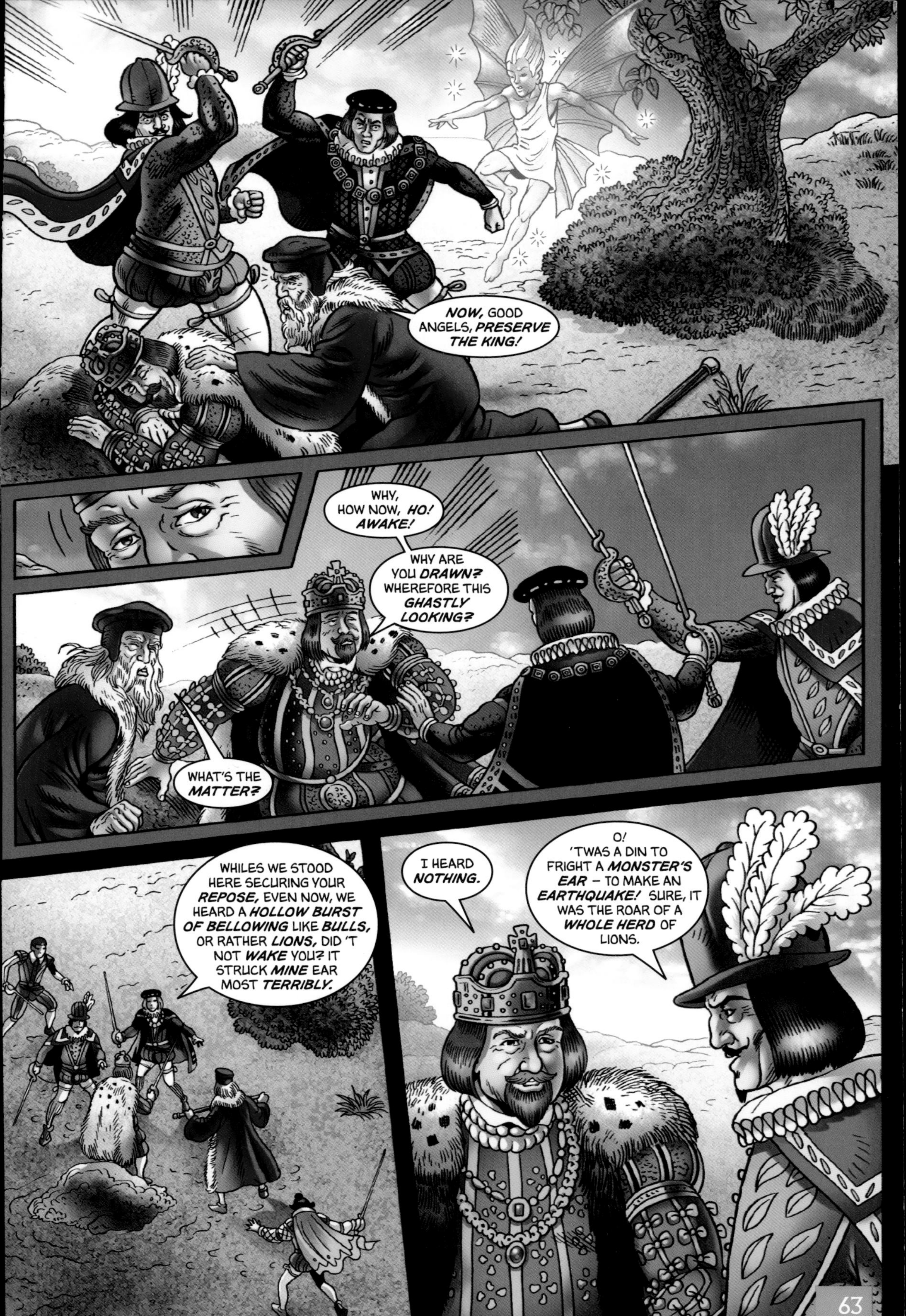
NOW, GOOD ANGELS, PRESERVE THE KING!
WHY, HOW NOW, HO! AWAKE!
WHY ARE YOU DRAWN? WHEREFORE THIS GHASTLY LOOKING?
WHAT'S THE MATTER?
WHILES WE STOOD HERE SECURING YOUR REPOSE, EVEN NOW, WE HEARD A HOLLOW BURST OF BELLOWING LIKE BULLS, OR RATHER LIONS, DID 'T NOT WAKE YOU? IT STRUCK MINE EAR MOST TERRIBLY.
I HEARD NOTHING.
O! 'TWAS A DIN TO FRIGHT A MONSTER'S EAR – TO MAKE AN EARTHQUAKE! SURE, IT WAS THE ROAR OF A WHOLE HERD OF LIONS.

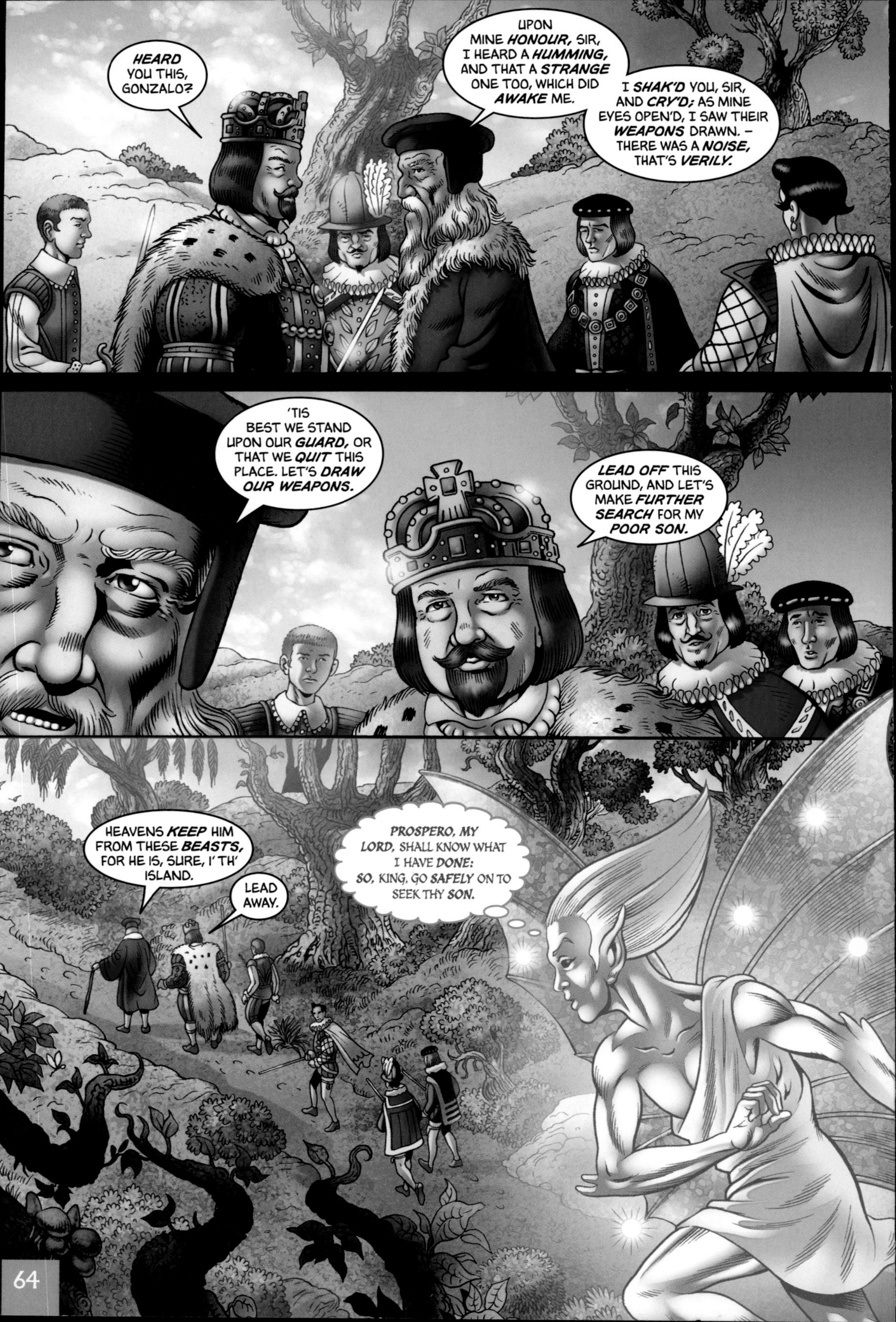
HEARD YOU THIS, GONZALO?
UPON MINE HONOUR, SIR, I HEARD A HUMMING, AND THAT A STRANGE ONE TOO, WHICH DID AWAKE ME.
I SHAK'D YOU, SIR, AND CRY'D; AS MINE EYES OPEN'D, I SAW THEIR WEAPONS DRAWN. – THERE WAS A NOISE, THAT'S VERILY.
'TIS BEST WE STAND UPON OUR GUARD, OR THAT WE QUIT THIS PLACE. LET'S DRAW OUR WEAPONS.
LEAD OFF THIS GROUND, AND LET'S MAKE FURTHER SEARCH FOR MY POOR SON.
HEAVENS KEEP HIM FROM THESE BEASTS, FOR HE IS, SURE, I' TH' ISLAND.
LEAD AWAY.
PROSPERO, MY LORD, SHALL KNOW WHAT I HAVE DONE: SO, KING, GO SAFELY ON TO SEEK THY SON.

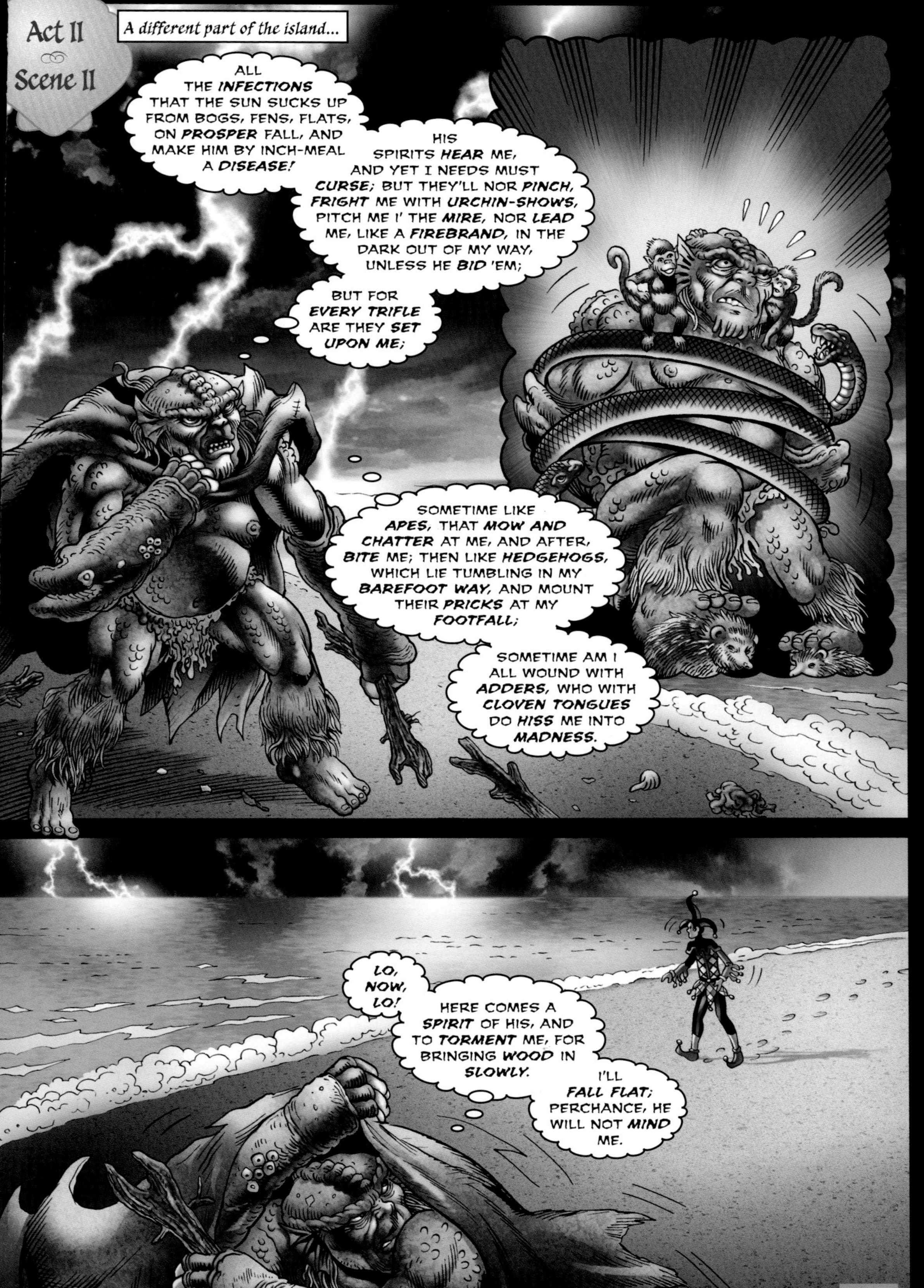
Act II
Scene II
A different part of the island...
ALL THE INFECTIONS THAT THE SUN SUCKS UP FROM BOGS, FENS, FLATS, ON PROSPER FALL, AND MAKE HIM BY INCH-MEAL A DISEASE!
HIS SPIRITS HEAR ME, AND YET I NEEDS MUST CURSE; BUT THEY'LL NOR PINCH, FRIGHT ME WITH URCHIN-SHOWS, PITCH ME I' THE MIRE, NOR LEAD ME, LIKE A FIREBRAND, IN THE DARK OUT OF MY WAY, UNLESS HE BID 'EM;
BUT FOR EVERY TRIFLE ARE THEY SET UPON ME;
SOMETIME LIKE APES, THAT MOW AND CHATTER AT ME, AND AFTER, BITE ME; THEN LIKE HEDGEHOGS, WHICH LIE TUMBLING IN MY BAREFOOT WAY, AND MOUNT THEIR PRICKS AT MY FOOTFALL;
SOMETIME AM I ALL WOUND WITH ADDERS, WHO WITH CLOVEN TONGUES DO HISS ME INTO MADNESS.
LO, NOW, LO!
HERE COMES A SPIRIT OF HIS, AND TO TORMENT ME, FOR BRINGING WOOD IN SLOWLY.
I'LL FALL FLAT; PERCHANCE, HE WILL NOT MIND ME.

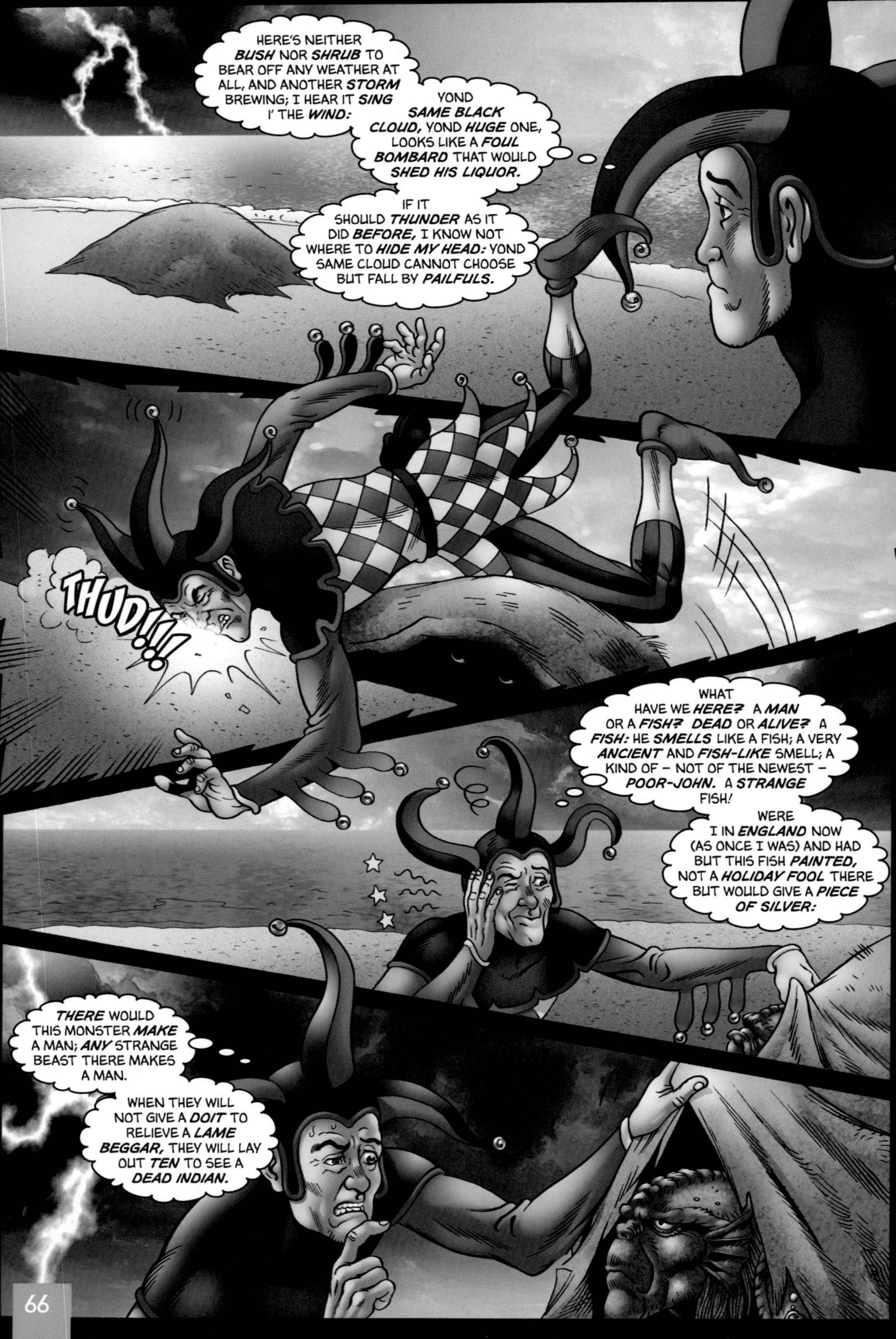
HERE'S NEITHER BUSH NOR SHRUB TO BEAR OFF ANY WEATHER AT ALL, AND ANOTHER STORM BREWING; I HEAR IT SING I' THE WIND:
YOND SAME BLACK CLOUD, YOND HUGE ONE, LOOKS LIKE A FOUL BOMBARD THAT WOULD SHED HIS LIQUOR.
IF IT SHOULD THUNDER AS IT DID BEFORE, I KNOW NOT WHERE TO HIDE MY HEAD: YOND SAME CLOUD CANNOT CHOOSE BUT FALL BY PAILFULS.
THUD!!!
WHAT HAVE WE HERE? A MAN OR A FISH? DEAD OR ALIVE? A FISH: HE SMELLS LIKE A FISH; A VERY ANCIENT AND FISH-LIKE SMELL; A KIND OF – NOT OF THE NEWEST – POOR-JOHN. A STRANGE FISH!
WERE I IN ENGLAND NOW (AS ONCE I WAS) AND HAD BUT THIS FISH PAINTED, NOT A HOLIDAY FOOL THERE BUT WOULD GIVE A PIECE OF SILVER:
THERE WOULD THIS MONSTER MAKE A MAN; ANY STRANGE BEAST THERE MAKES A MAN.
WHEN THEY WILL NOT GIVE A DOIT TO RELIEVE A LAME BEGGAR, THEY WILL LAY OUT TEN TO SEE A DEAD INDIAN.

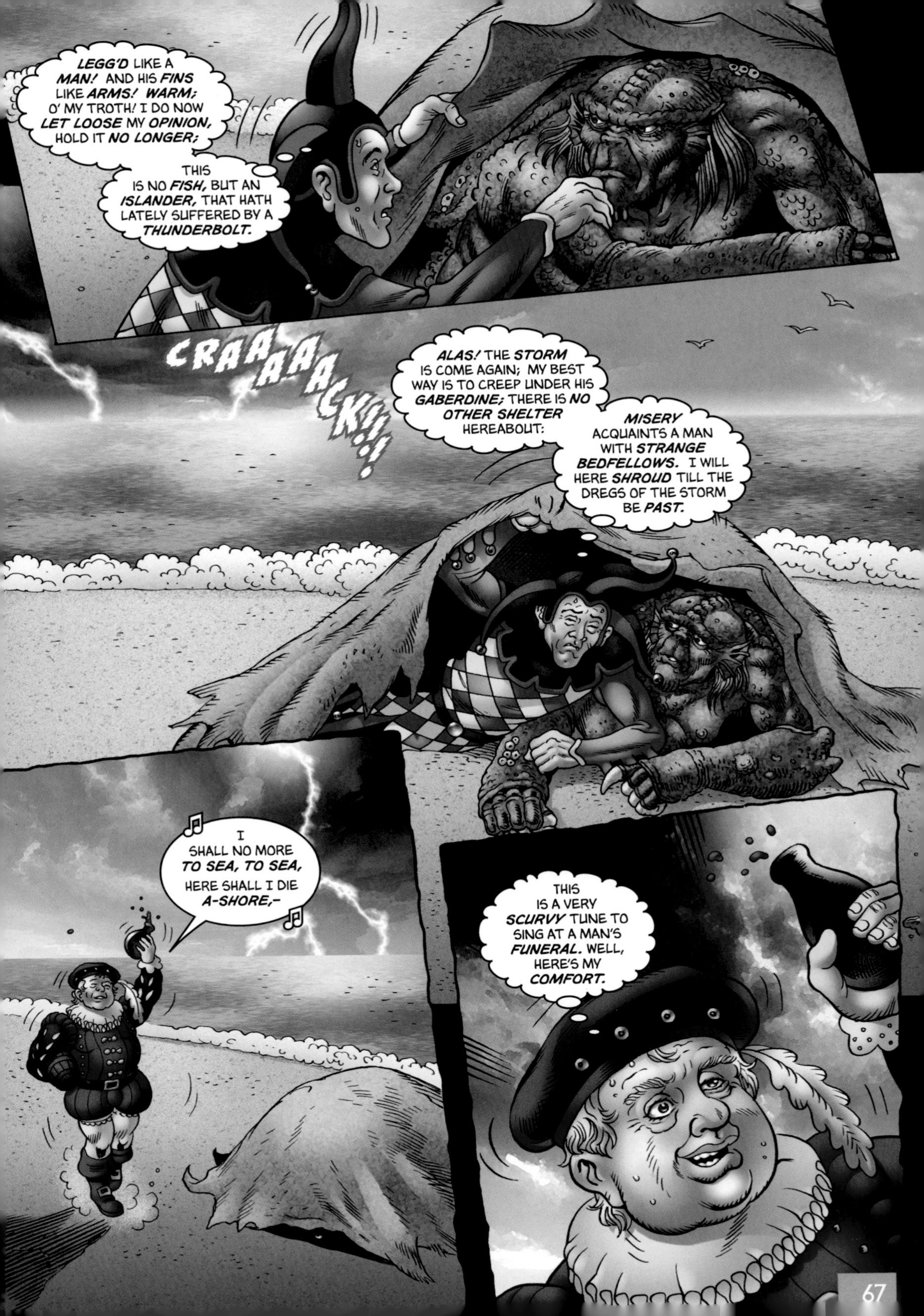
LEGG'D LIKE A MAN! AND HIS FINS LIKE ARMS! WARM; O' MY TROTH! I DO NOW LET LOOSE MY OPINION, HOLD IT NO LONGER;
THIS IS NO FISH, BUT AN ISLANDER, THAT HATH LATELY SUFFERED BY A THUNDERBOLT.
CRAAAAACK!!!
ALAS! THE STORM IS COME AGAIN; MY BEST WAY IS TO CREEP UNDER HIS GABERDINE; THERE IS NO OTHER SHELTER HEREABOUT:
MISERY ACQUAINTS A MAN WITH STRANGE BEDFELLOWS. I WILL HERE SHROUD TILL THE DREGS OF THE STORM BE PAST.
I SHALL NO MORE TO SEA, TO SEA, HERE SHALL I DIE A-SHORE,–
THIS IS A VERY SCURVY TUNE TO SING AT A MAN'S FUNERAL. WELL, HERE'S MY COMFORT.

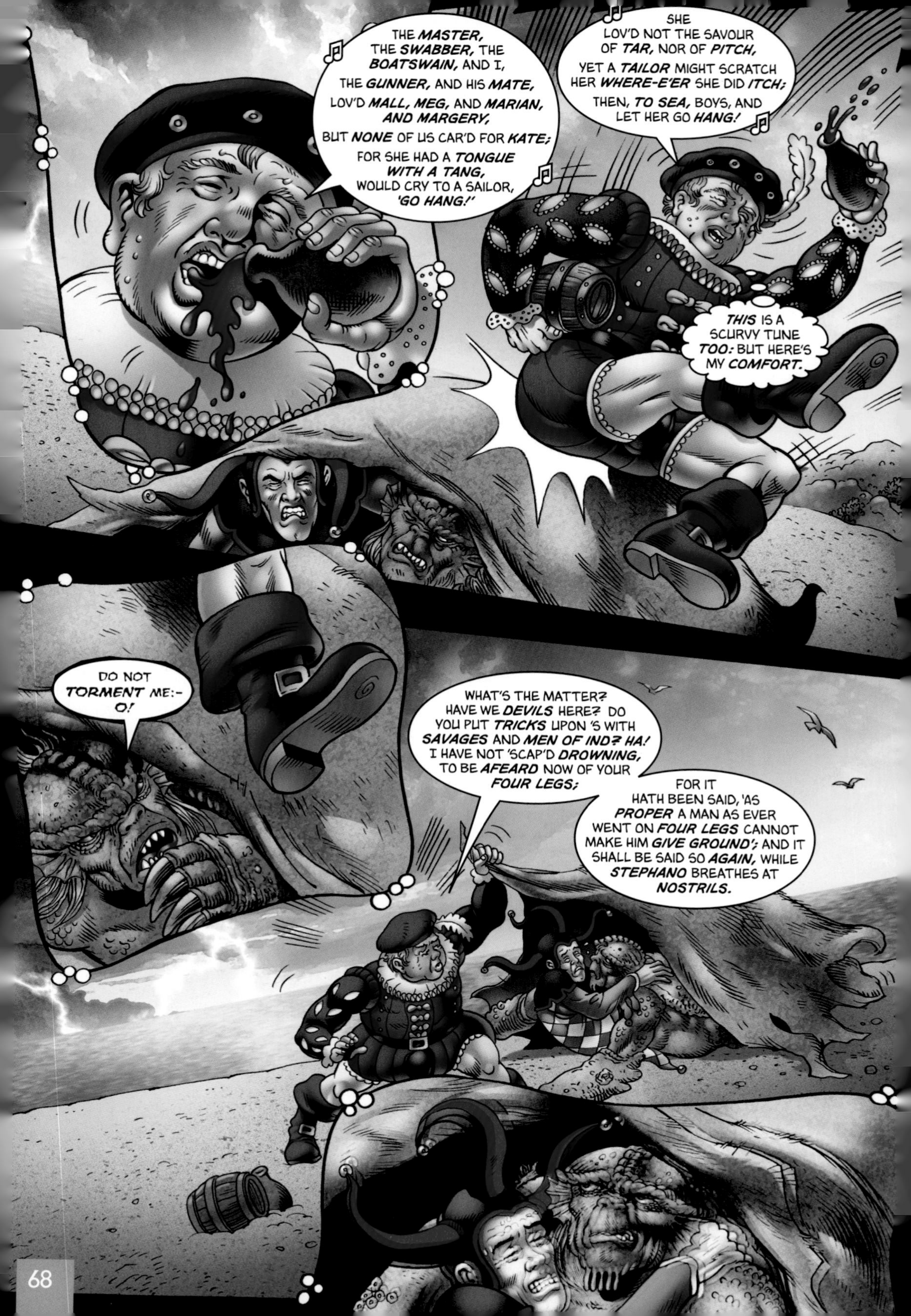

THE MASTER, THE SWABBER, THE BOATSWAIN, AND I, THE GUNNER, AND HIS MATE, LOV'D MALL, MEG, AND MARIAN, AND MARGERY, BUT NONE OF US CAR'D FOR KATE; FOR SHE HAD A TONGUE WITH A TANG, WOULD CRY TO A SAILOR, 'GO HANG!'
SHE LOV'D NOT THE SAVOUR OF TAR, NOR OF PITCH, YET A TAILOR MIGHT SCRATCH HER WHERE-E'ER SHE DID ITCH; THEN, TO SEA, BOYS, AND LET HER GO HANG!
THIS IS A SCURVY TUNE TOO: BUT HERE'S MY COMFORT.
DO NOT TORMENT ME:- O!
WHAT'S THE MATTER? HAVE WE DEVILS HERE? DO YOU PUT TRICKS UPON 'S WITH SAVAGES AND MEN OF IND? HA! I HAVE NOT 'SCAP'D DROWNING, TO BE AFEARD NOW OF YOUR FOUR LEGS;
FOR IT HATH BEEN SAID, 'AS PROPER A MAN AS EVER WENT ON FOUR LEGS CANNOT MAKE HIM GIVE GROUND'; AND IT SHALL BE SAID SO AGAIN, WHILE STEPHANO BREATHES AT NOSTRILS.

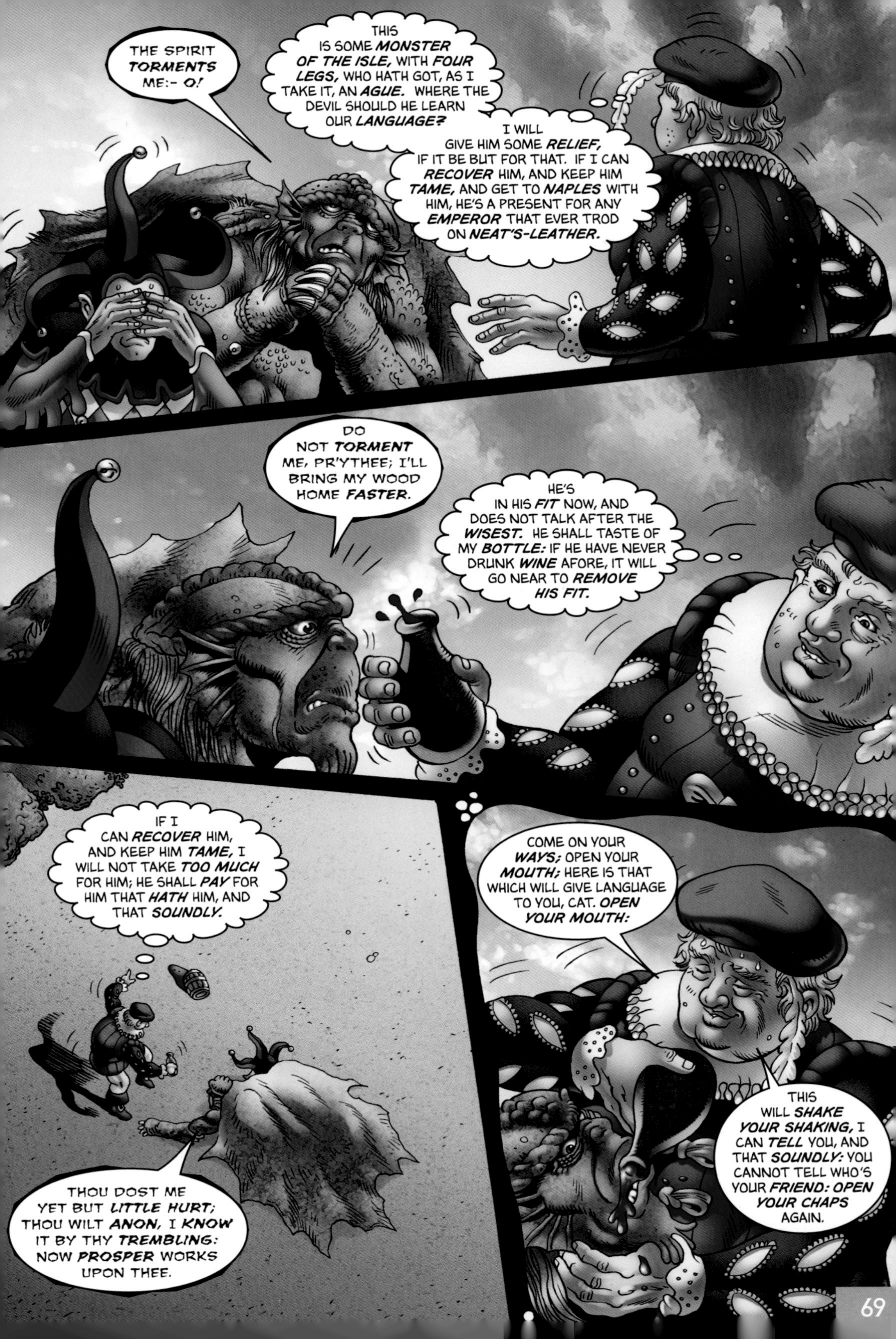
THE SPIRIT TORMENTS ME:- O!
THIS IS SOME MONSTER OF THE ISLE, WITH FOUR LEGS, WHO HATH GOT, AS I TAKE IT, AN AGUE. WHERE THE DEVIL SHOULD HE LEARN OUR LANGUAGE?
I WILL GIVE HIM SOME RELIEF, IF IT BE BUT FOR THAT. IF I CAN RECOVER HIM, AND KEEP HIM TAME, AND GET TO NAPLES WITH HIM, HE'S A PRESENT FOR ANY EMPEROR THAT EVER TROD ON NEAT'S-LEATHER.
DO NOT TORMENT ME, PR'YTHEE; I'LL BRING MY WOOD HOME FASTER.
HE'S IN HIS FIT NOW, AND DOES NOT TALK AFTER THE WISEST. HE SHALL TASTE OF MY BOTTLE: IF HE HAVE NEVER DRUNK WINE AFORE, IT WILL GO NEAR TO REMOVE HIS FIT.
IF I CAN RECOVER HIM, AND KEEP HIM TAME, I WILL NOT TAKE TOO MUCH FOR HIM; HE SHALL PAY FOR HIM THAT HATH HIM, AND THAT SOUNDLY.
THOU DOST ME YET BUT LITTLE HURT; THOU WILT ANON, I KNOW IT BY THY TREMBLING: NOW PROSPER WORKS UPON THEE.
COME ON YOUR WAYS; OPEN YOUR MOUTH; HERE IS THAT WHICH WILL GIVE LANGUAGE TO YOU, CAT. OPEN YOUR MOUTH:
THIS WILL SHAKE YOUR SHAKING, I CAN TELL YOU, AND THAT SOUNDLY: YOU CANNOT TELL WHO'S YOUR FRIEND: OPEN YOUR CHAPS AGAIN.

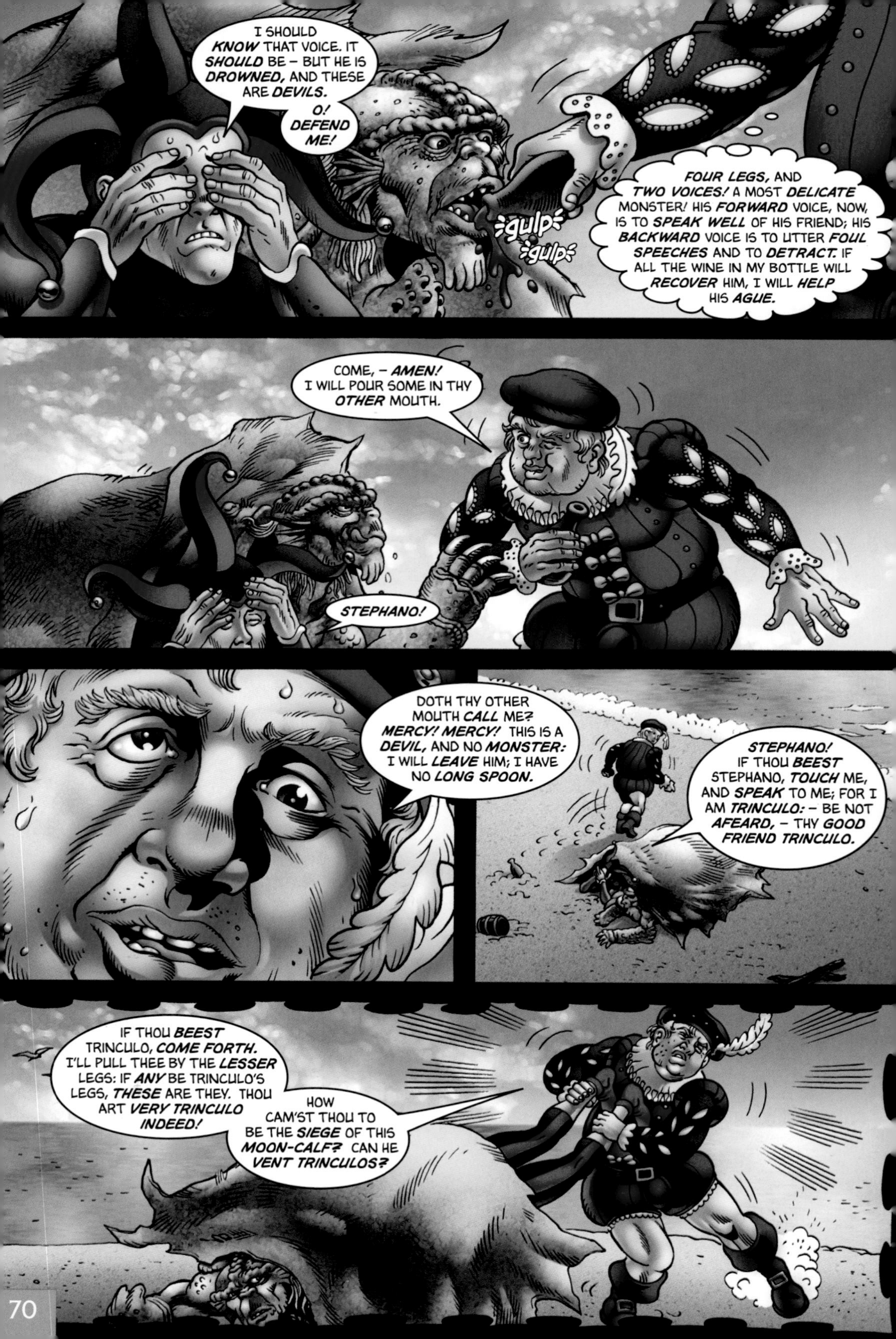
I SHOULD KNOW THAT VOICE. IT SHOULD BE – BUT HE IS DROWNED, AND THESE ARE DEVILS.
O! DEFEND ME!
FOUR LEGS, AND TWO VOICES! A MOST DELICATE MONSTER! HIS FORWARD VOICE, NOW, IS TO SPEAK WELL OF HIS FRIEND; HIS BACKWARD VOICE IS TO UTTER FOUL SPEECHES AND TO DETRACT. IF ALL THE WINE IN MY BOTTLE WILL RECOVER HIM, I WILL HELP HIS AGUE.
gulp
gulp
COME, – AMEN! I WILL POUR SOME IN THY OTHER MOUTH.
STEPHANO!
DOTH THY OTHER MOUTH CALL ME? MERCY! MERCY! THIS IS A DEVIL, AND NO MONSTER: I WILL LEAVE HIM; I HAVE NO LONG SPOON.
STEPHANO! IF THOU BEEST STEPHANO, TOUCH ME, AND SPEAK TO ME; FOR I AM TRINCULO: – BE NOT AFEARD, – THY GOOD FRIEND TRINCULO.
IF THOU BEEST TRINCULO, COME FORTH. I'LL PULL THEE BY THE LESSER LEGS: IF ANY BE TRINCULO'S LEGS, THESE ARE THEY. THOU ART VERY TRINCULO INDEED!
HOW CAM'ST THOU TO BE THE SIEGE OF THIS MOON-CALF? CAN HE VENT TRINCULOS?

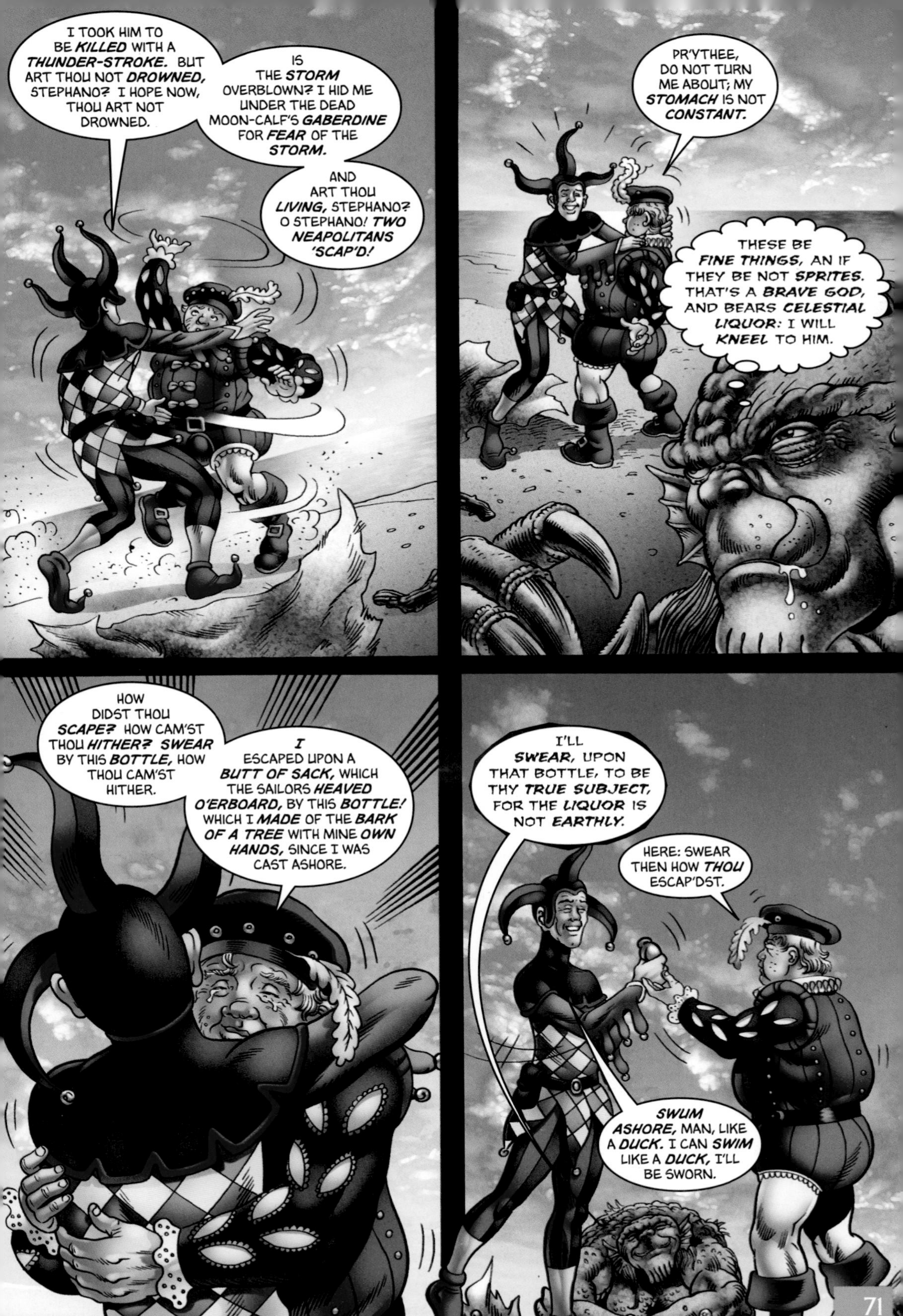
I TOOK HIM TO BE KILLED WITH A THUNDER-STROKE. BUT ART THOU NOT DROWNED, STEPHANO? I HOPE NOW, THOU ART NOT DROWNED.
IS THE STORM OVERBLOWN? I HID ME UNDER THE DEAD MOON-CALF'S GABERDINE FOR FEAR OF THE STORM.
AND ART THOU LIVING, STEPHANO? O STEPHANO! TWO NEAPOLITANS 'SCAP'D!
PR'YTHEE, DO NOT TURN ME ABOUT; MY STOMACH IS NOT CONSTANT.
THESE BE FINE THINGS, AN IF THEY BE NOT SPRITES. THAT'S A BRAVE GOD, AND BEARS CELESTIAL LIQUOR: I WILL KNEEL TO HIM.
HOW DIDST THOU SCAPE? HOW CAM'ST THOU HITHER? SWEAR BY THIS BOTTLE, HOW THOU CAM'ST HITHER.
I ESCAPED UPON A BUTT OF SACK, WHICH THE SAILORS HEAVED O'ERBOARD, BY THIS BOTTLE! WHICH I MADE OF THE BARK OF A TREE WITH MINE OWN HANDS, SINCE I WAS CAST ASHORE.
I'LL SWEAR, UPON THAT BOTTLE, TO BE THY TRUE SUBJECT, FOR THE LIQUOR IS NOT EARTHLY.
HERE: SWEAR THEN HOW THOU ESCAP'DST.
SWUM ASHORE, MAN, LIKE A DUCK. I CAN SWIM LIKE A DUCK, I'LL BE SWORN.

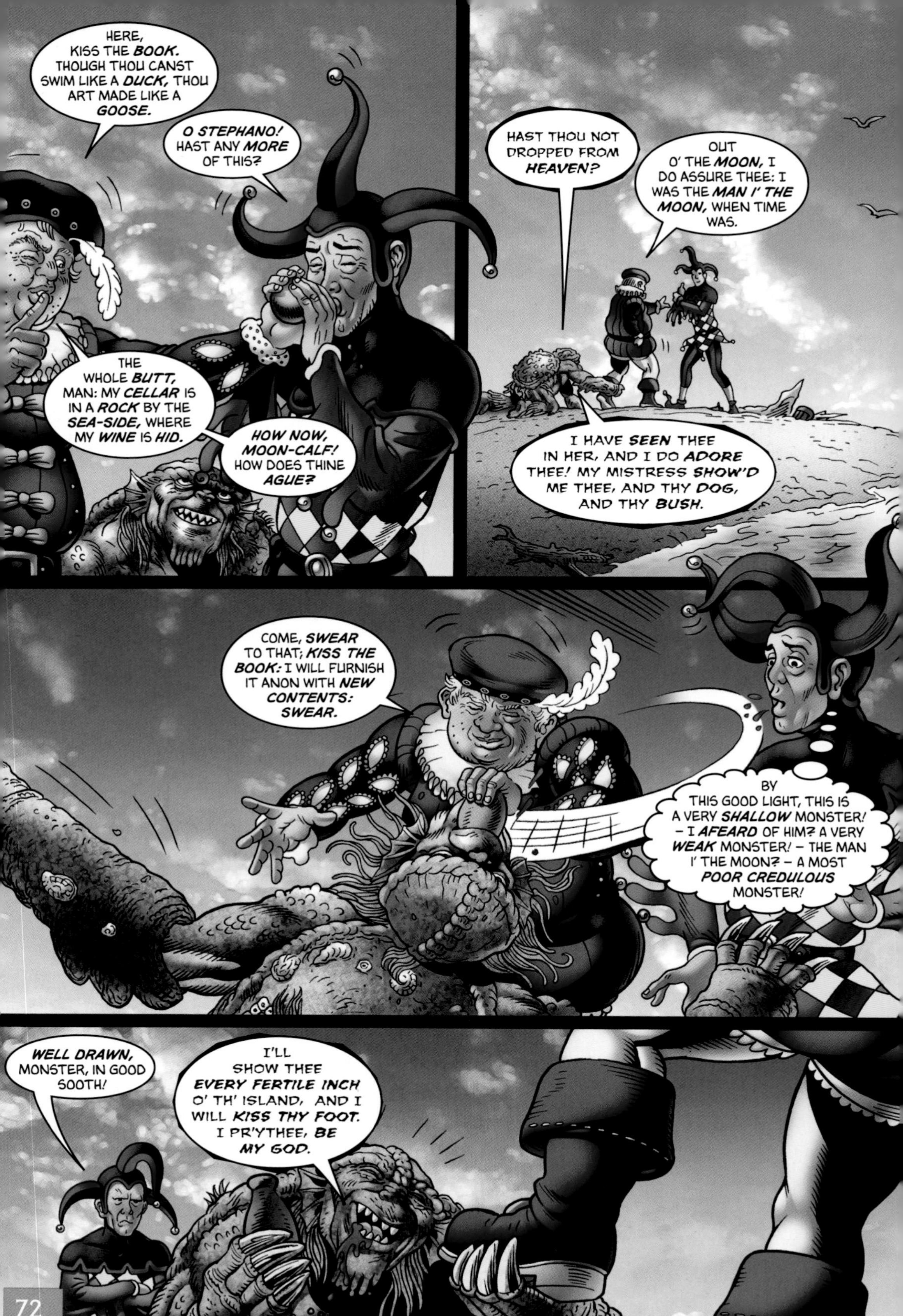

HERE, KISS THE BOOK. THOUGH THOU CANST SWIM LIKE A DUCK, THOU ART MADE LIKE A GOOSE.
O STEPHANO! HAST ANY MORE OF THIS?
THE WHOLE BUTT, MAN: MY CELLAR IS IN A ROCK BY THE SEA-SIDE, WHERE MY WINE IS HID.
HOW NOW, MOON-CALF! HOW DOES THINE AGUE?
HAST THOU NOT DROPPED FROM HEAVEN?
OUT O' THE MOON, I DO ASSURE THEE: I WAS THE MAN I' THE MOON, WHEN TIME WAS.
I HAVE SEEN THEE IN HER, AND I DO ADORE THEE! MY MISTRESS SHOW'D ME THEE, AND THY DOG, AND THY BUSH.
COME, SWEAR TO THAT; KISS THE BOOK: I WILL FURNISH IT ANON WITH NEW CONTENTS: SWEAR.
BY THIS GOOD LIGHT, THIS IS A VERY SHALLOW MONSTER! – I AFEARD OF HIM? A VERY WEAK MONSTER! – THE MAN I' THE MOON? – A MOST POOR CREDULOUS MONSTER!
WELL DRAWN, MONSTER, IN GOOD SOOTH!
I'LL SHOW THEE EVERY FERTILE INCH O' TH' ISLAND, AND I WILL KISS THY FOOT. I PR'YTHEE, BE MY GOD.

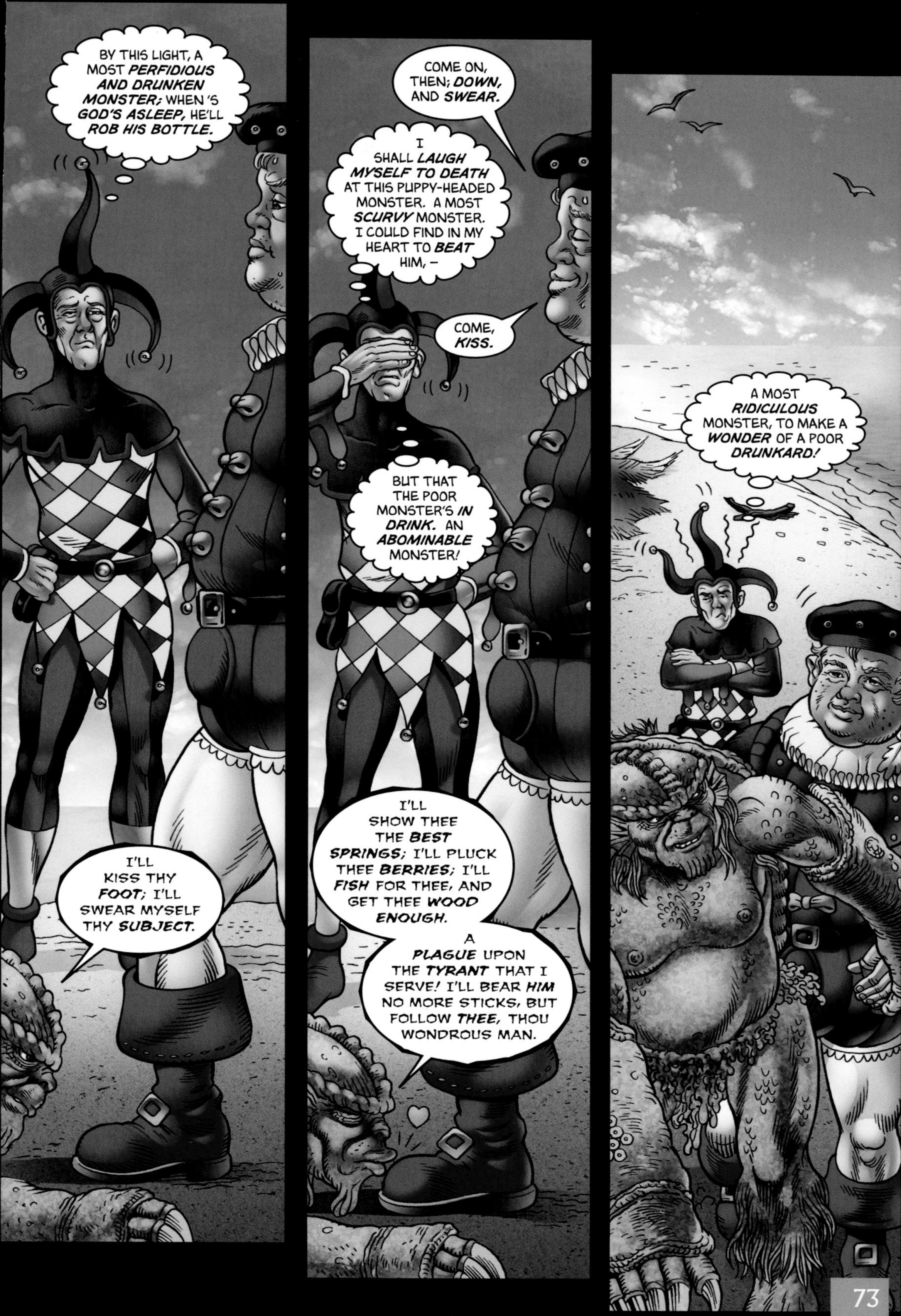
BY THIS LIGHT, A MOST PERFIDIOUS AND DRUNKEN MONSTER; WHEN 'S GOD'S ASLEEP, HE'LL ROB HIS BOTTLE.
I'LL KISS THY FOOT; I'LL SWEAR MYSELF THY SUBJECT.
COME ON, THEN; DOWN, AND SWEAR.
I SHALL LAUGH MYSELF TO DEATH AT THIS PUPPY-HEADED MONSTER. A MOST SCURVY MONSTER. I COULD FIND IN MY HEART TO BEAT HIM, –
COME, KISS.
BUT THAT THE POOR MONSTER'S IN DRINK. AN ABOMINABLE MONSTER!
I'LL SHOW THEE THE BEST SPRINGS; I'LL PLUCK THEE BERRIES; I'LL FISH FOR THEE, AND GET THEE WOOD ENOUGH.
A PLAGUE UPON THE TYRANT THAT I SERVE! I'LL BEAR HIM NO MORE STICKS, BUT FOLLOW THEE, THOU WONDROUS MAN.
A MOST RIDICULOUS MONSTER, TO MAKE A WONDER OF A POOR DRUNKARD!

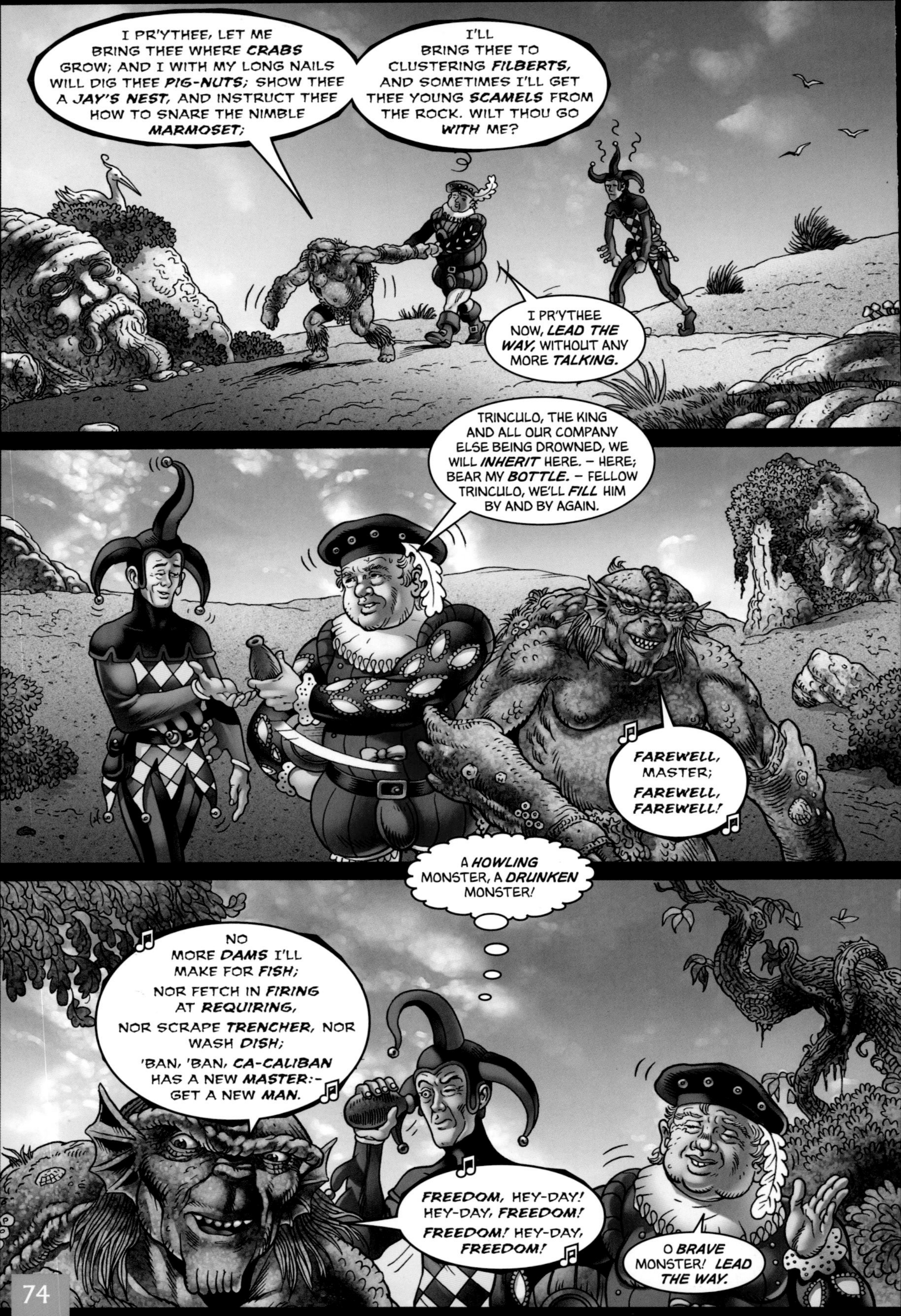
I PR'YTHEE, LET ME BRING THEE WHERE CRABS GROW; AND I WITH MY LONG NAILS WILL DIG THEE PIG-NUTS; SHOW THEE A JAY'S NEST, AND INSTRUCT THEE HOW TO SNARE THE NIMBLE MARMOSET;
I'LL BRING THEE TO CLUSTERING FILBERTS, AND SOMETIMES I'LL GET THEE YOUNG SCAMELS FROM THE ROCK. WILT THOU GO WITH ME?
I PR'YTHEE NOW, LEAD THE WAY, WITHOUT ANY MORE TALKING.
TRINCULO, THE KING AND ALL OUR COMPANY ELSE BEING DROWNED, WE WILL INHERIT HERE. – HERE; BEAR MY BOTTLE. – FELLOW TRINCULO, WE'LL FILL HIM BY AND BY AGAIN.
FAREWELL, MASTER; FAREWELL, FAREWELL!
A HOWLING MONSTER, A DRUNKEN MONSTER!
NO MORE DAMS I'LL MAKE FOR FISH; NOR FETCH IN FIRING AT REQUIRING, NOR SCRAPE TRENCHER, NOR WASH DISH; 'BAN, 'BAN, CA-CALIBAN HAS A NEW MASTER:- GET A NEW MAN.
FREEDOM, HEY-DAY! HEY-DAY, FREEDOM! FREEDOM! HEY-DAY, FREEDOM!
O BRAVE MONSTER! LEAD THE WAY.

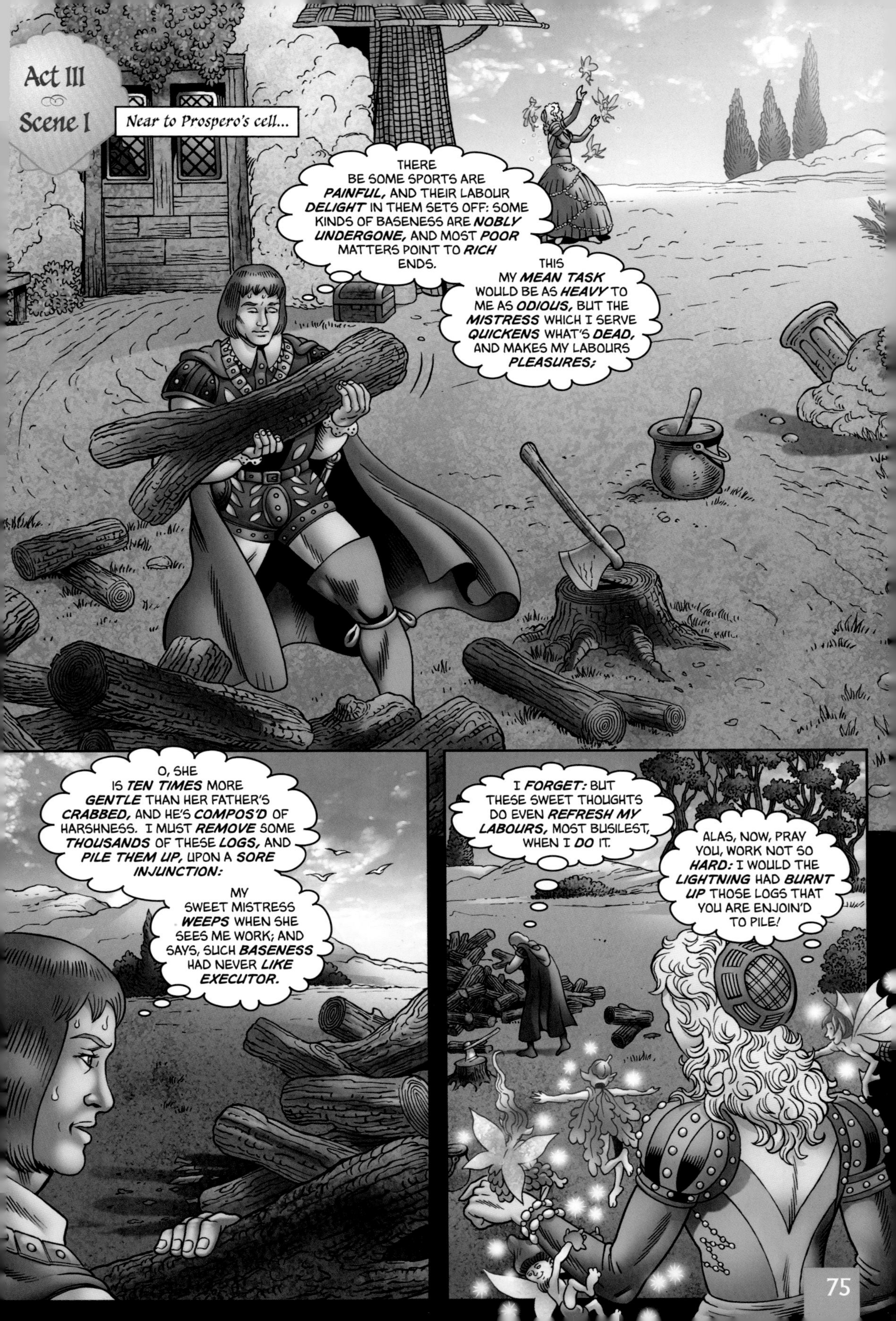
Act III
Scene I
Near to Prospero's cell...
THERE BE SOME SPORTS ARE PAINFUL, AND THEIR LABOUR DELIGHT IN THEM SETS OFF: SOME KINDS OF BASENESS ARE NOBLY UNDERGONE, AND MOST POOR MATTERS POINT TO RICH ENDS.
THIS MY MEAN TASK WOULD BE AS HEAVY TO ME AS ODIOUS, BUT THE MISTRESS WHICH I SERVE QUICKENS WHAT'S DEAD, AND MAKES MY LABOURS PLEASURES;
O, SHE IS TEN TIMES MORE GENTLE THAN HER FATHER'S CRABBED, AND HE'S COMPOS'D OF HARSHNESS. I MUST REMOVE SOME THOUSANDS OF THESE LOGS, AND PILE THEM UP, UPON A SORE INJUNCTION:
MY SWEET MISTRESS WEEPS WHEN SHE SEES ME WORK; AND SAYS, SUCH BASENESS HAD NEVER LIKE EXECUTOR.
I FORGET: BUT THESE SWEET THOUGHTS DO EVEN REFRESH MY LABOURS, MOST BUSILEST, WHEN I DO IT.
ALAS, NOW, PRAY YOU, WORK NOT SO HARD: I WOULD THE LIGHTNING HAD BURNT UP THOSE LOGS THAT YOU ARE ENJOIN'D TO PILE!

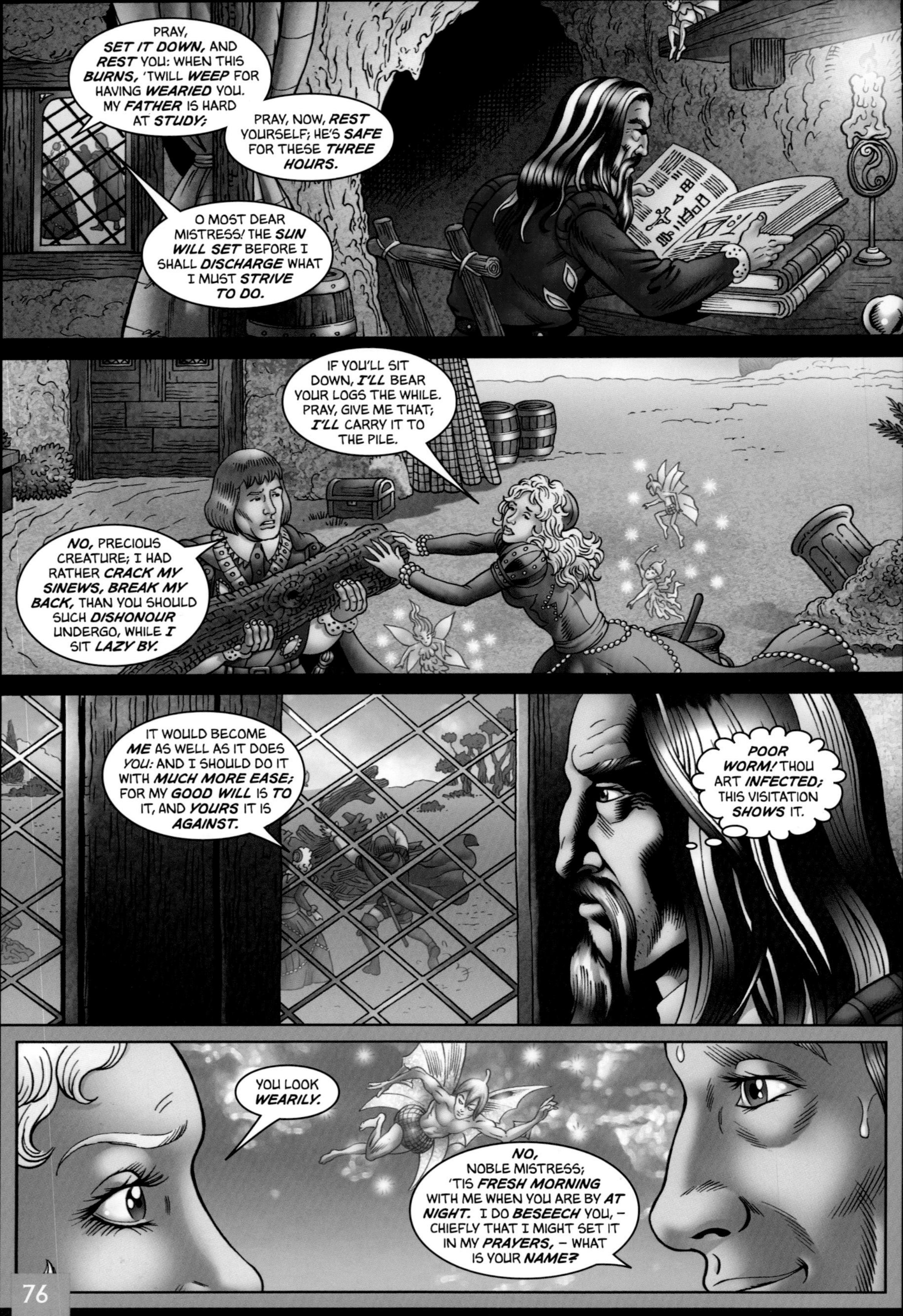
PRAY, SET IT DOWN, AND REST YOU: WHEN THIS BURNS, 'TWILL WEEP FOR HAVING WEARIED YOU. MY FATHER IS HARD AT STUDY;
PRAY, NOW, REST YOURSELF; HE'S SAFE FOR THESE THREE HOURS.
O MOST DEAR MISTRESS! THE SUN WILL SET BEFORE I SHALL DISCHARGE WHAT I MUST STRIVE TO DO.
IF YOU'LL SIT DOWN, I'LL BEAR YOUR LOGS THE WHILE. PRAY, GIVE ME THAT; I'LL CARRY IT TO THE PILE.
NO, PRECIOUS CREATURE; I HAD RATHER CRACK MY SINEWS, BREAK MY BACK, THAN YOU SHOULD SUCH DISHONOUR UNDERGO, WHILE I SIT LAZY BY.
IT WOULD BECOME ME AS WELL AS IT DOES YOU: AND I SHOULD DO IT WITH MUCH MORE EASE; FOR MY GOOD WILL IS TO IT, AND YOURS IT IS AGAINST.
POOR WORM! THOU ART INFECTED; THIS VISITATION SHOWS IT.
YOU LOOK WEARILY.
NO, NOBLE MISTRESS; 'TIS FRESH MORNING WITH ME WHEN YOU ARE BY AT NIGHT. I DO BESEECH YOU, – CHIEFLY THAT I MIGHT SET IT IN MY PRAYERS, – WHAT IS YOUR NAME?

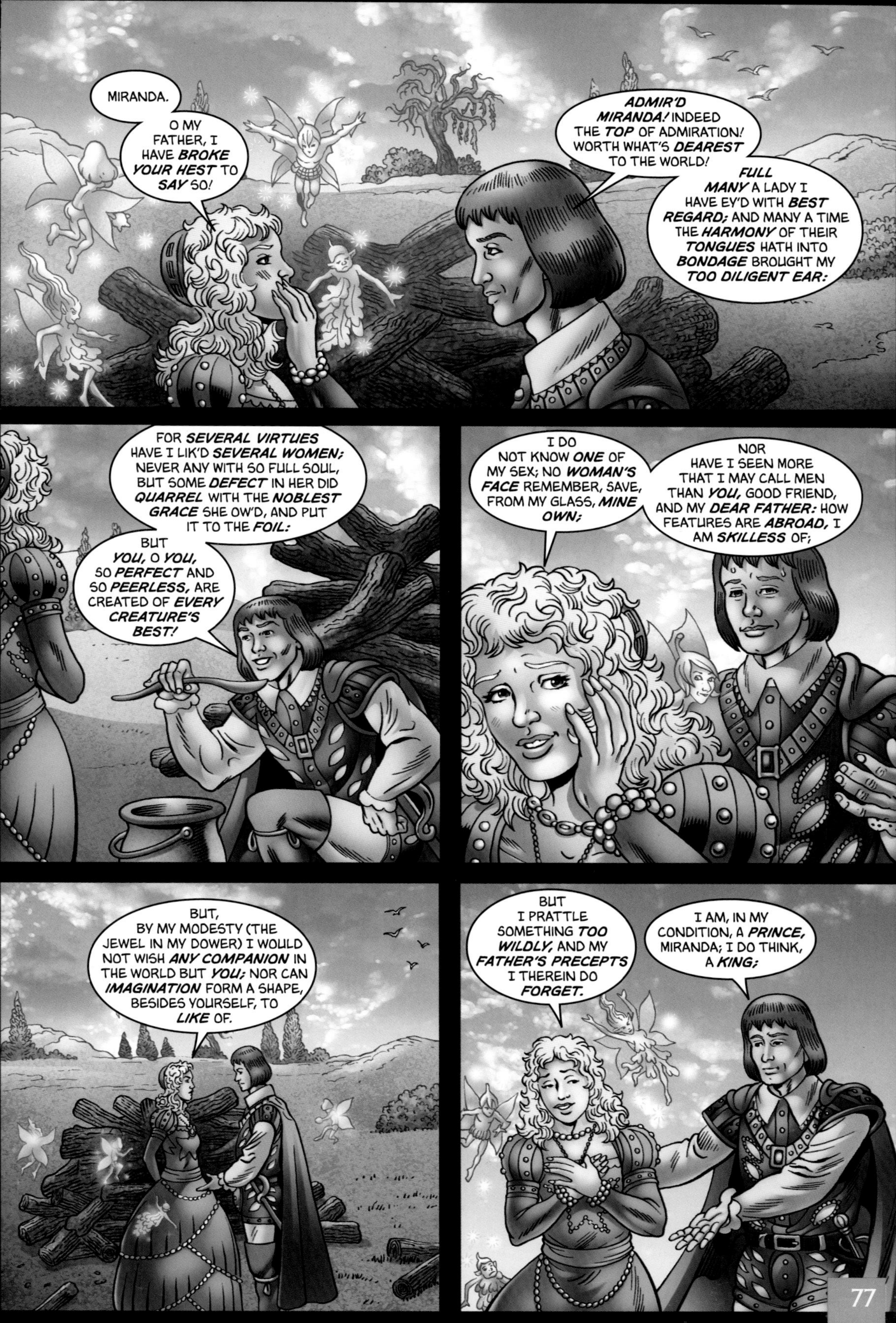
MIRANDA.
O MY FATHER, I HAVE BROKE YOUR HEST TO SAY SO!
ADMIR'D MIRANDA! INDEED THE TOP OF ADMIRATION! WORTH WHAT'S DEAREST TO THE WORLD!
FULL MANY A LADY I HAVE EY'D WITH BEST REGARD; AND MANY A TIME THE HARMONY OF THEIR TONGUES HATH INTO BONDAGE BROUGHT MY TOO DILIGENT EAR:
FOR SEVERAL VIRTUES HAVE I LIK'D SEVERAL WOMEN; NEVER ANY WITH SO FULL SOUL, BUT SOME DEFECT IN HER DID QUARREL WITH THE NOBLEST GRACE SHE OW'D, AND PUT IT TO THE FOIL:
BUT YOU, O YOU, SO PERFECT AND SO PEERLESS, ARE CREATED OF EVERY CREATURE'S BEST!
I DO NOT KNOW ONE OF MY SEX; NO WOMAN'S FACE REMEMBER, SAVE, FROM MY GLASS, MINE OWN;
NOR HAVE I SEEN MORE THAT I MAY CALL MEN THAN YOU, GOOD FRIEND, AND MY DEAR FATHER: HOW FEATURES ARE ABROAD, I AM SKILLESS OF;
BUT, BY MY MODESTY (THE JEWEL IN MY DOWER) I WOULD NOT WISH ANY COMPANION IN THE WORLD BUT YOU; NOR CAN IMAGINATION FORM A SHAPE, BESIDES YOURSELF, TO LIKE OF.
BUT I PRATTLE SOMETHING TOO WILDLY, AND MY FATHER'S PRECEPTS I THEREIN DO FORGET.
I AM, IN MY CONDITION, A PRINCE, MIRANDA; I DO THINK, A KING;

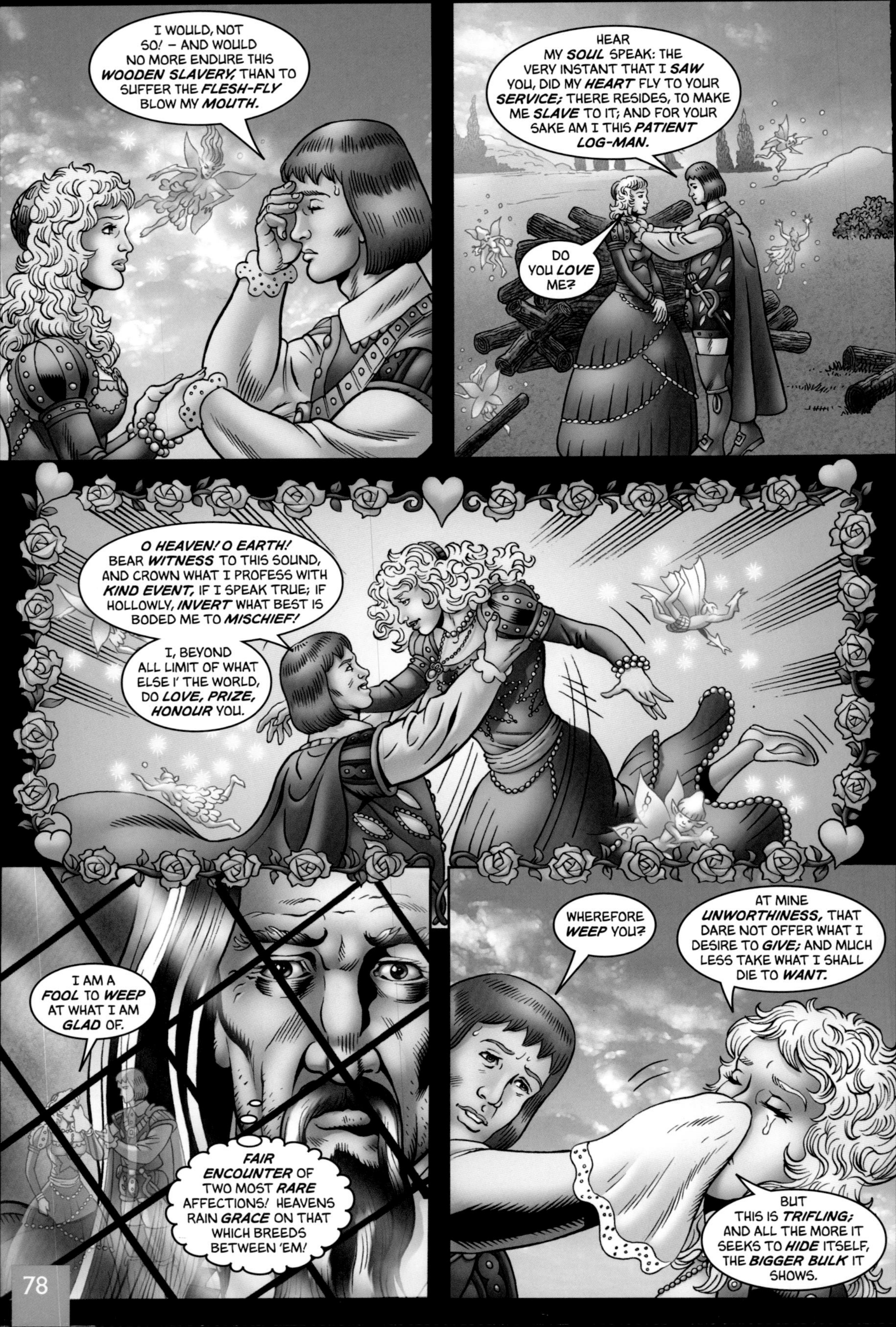

I WOULD, NOT SO! – AND WOULD NO MORE ENDURE THIS WOODEN SLAVERY, THAN TO SUFFER THE FLESH-FLY BLOW MY MOUTH.
HEAR MY SOUL SPEAK: THE VERY INSTANT THAT I SAW YOU, DID MY HEART FLY TO YOUR SERVICE; THERE RESIDES, TO MAKE ME SLAVE TO IT; AND FOR YOUR SAKE AM I THIS PATIENT LOG-MAN.
DO YOU LOVE ME?
O HEAVEN! O EARTH! BEAR WITNESS TO THIS SOUND, AND CROWN WHAT I PROFESS WITH KIND EVENT, IF I SPEAK TRUE; IF HOLLOWLY, INVERT WHAT BEST IS BODED ME TO MISCHIEF!
I, BEYOND ALL LIMIT OF WHAT ELSE I' THE WORLD, DO LOVE, PRIZE, HONOUR YOU.
I AM A FOOL TO WEEP AT WHAT I AM GLAD OF.
FAIR ENCOUNTER OF TWO MOST RARE AFFECTIONS! HEAVENS RAIN GRACE ON THAT WHICH BREEDS BETWEEN 'EM!
WHEREFORE WEEP YOU?
AT MINE UNWORTHINESS, THAT DARE NOT OFFER WHAT I DESIRE TO GIVE; AND MUCH LESS TAKE WHAT I SHALL DIE TO WANT.
BUT THIS IS TRIFLING; AND ALL THE MORE IT SEEKS TO HIDE ITSELF, THE BIGGER BULK IT SHOWS.

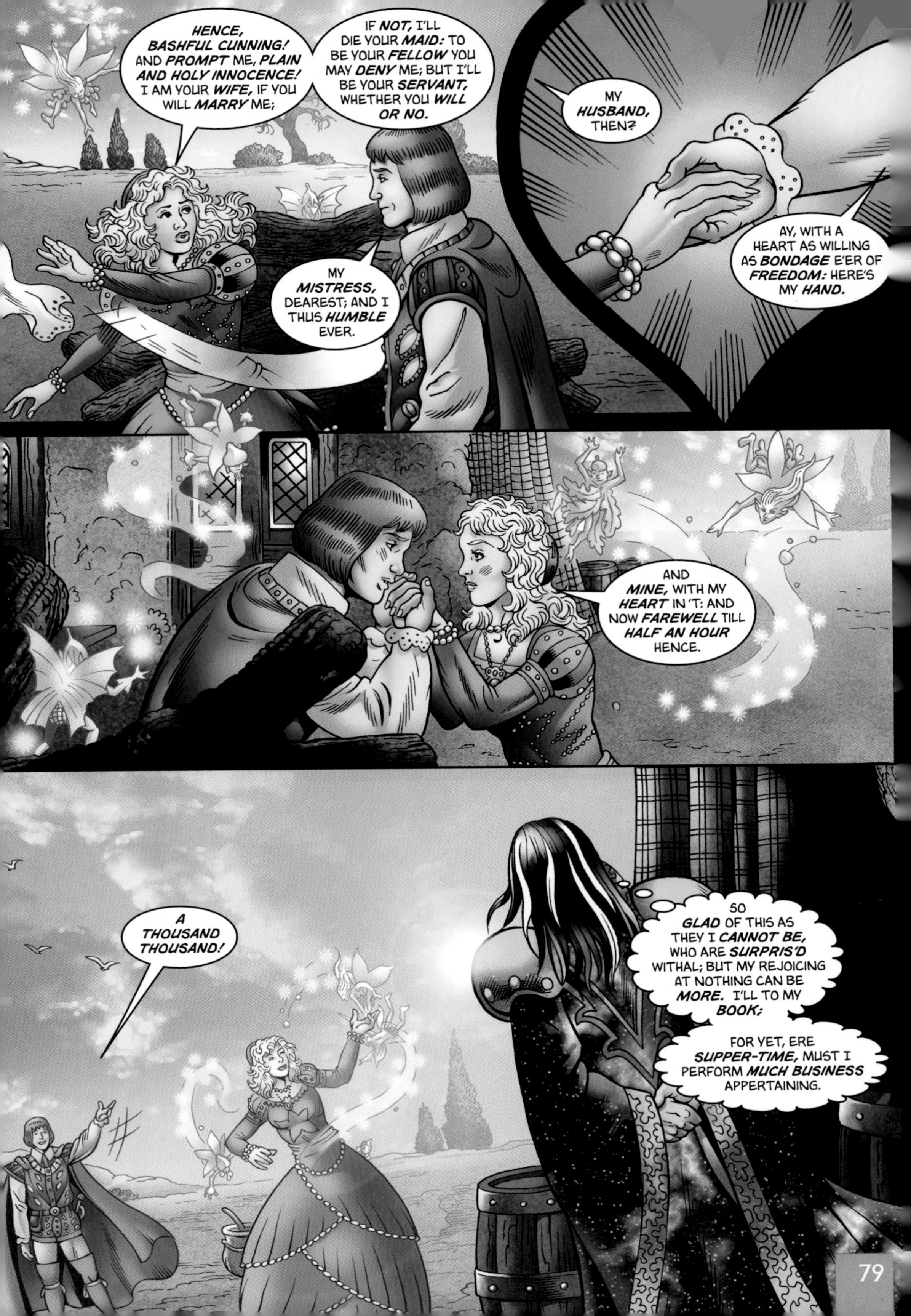
HENCE, BASHFUL CUNNING! AND PROMPT ME, PLAIN AND HOLY INNOCENCE! I AM YOUR WIFE, IF YOU WILL MARRY ME;
IF NOT, I'LL DIE YOUR MAID: TO BE YOUR FELLOW YOU MAY DENY ME; BUT I'LL BE YOUR SERVANT, WHETHER YOU WILL OR NO.
MY MISTRESS, DEAREST; AND I THUS HUMBLE EVER.
MY HUSBAND, THEN?
AY, WITH A HEART AS WILLING AS BONDAGE E'ER OF FREEDOM: HERE'S MY HAND.
AND MINE, WITH MY HEART IN 'T: AND NOW FAREWELL TILL HALF AN HOUR HENCE.
A THOUSAND THOUSAND!
SO GLAD OF THIS AS THEY I CANNOT BE, WHO ARE SURPRIS'D WITHAL; BUT MY REJOICING AT NOTHING CAN BE MORE. I'LL TO MY BOOK;
FOR YET, ERE SUPPER-TIME, MUST I PERFORM MUCH BUSINESS APPERTAINING.

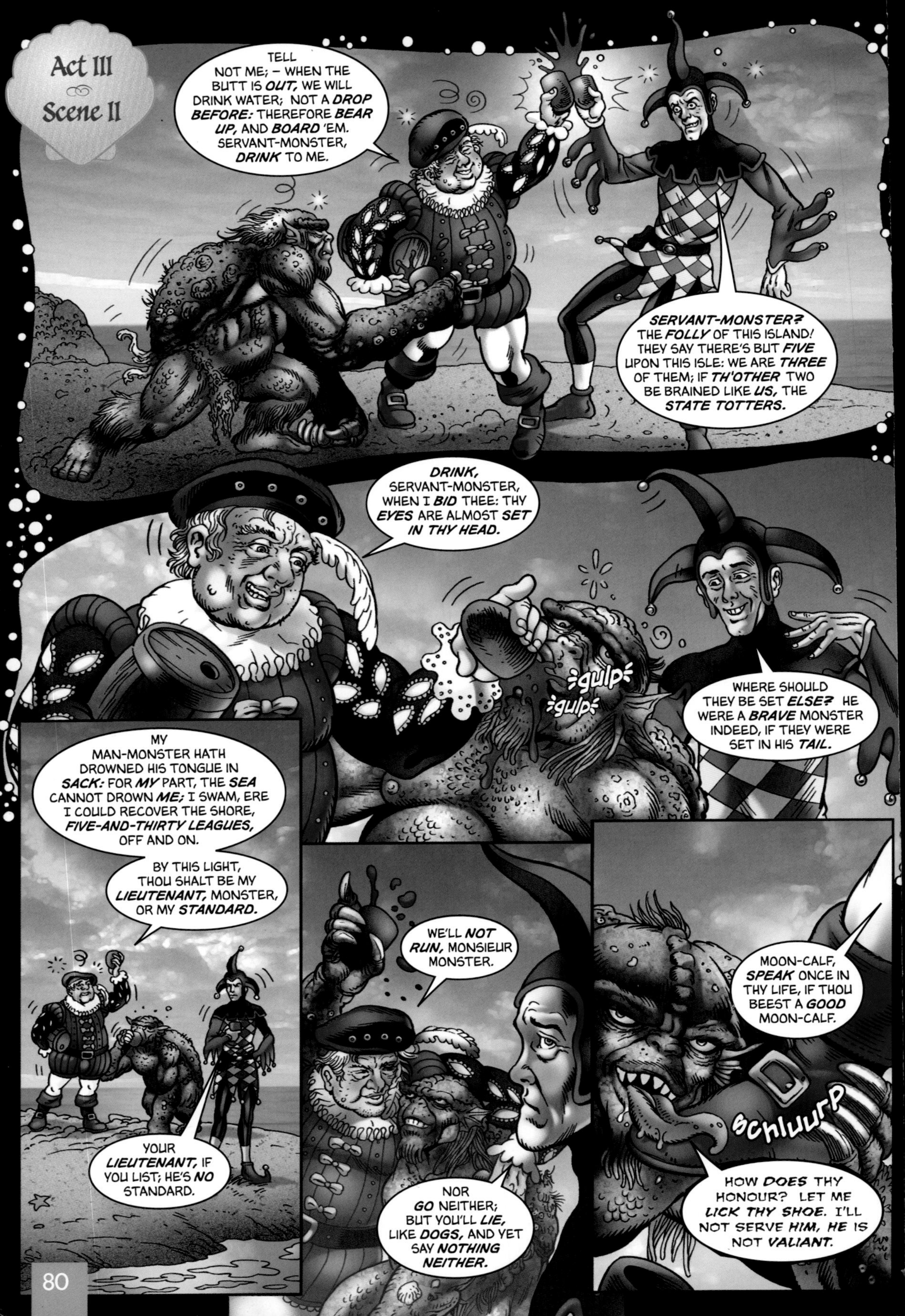
Act III Scene II
TELL NOT ME; – WHEN THE BUTT IS OUT, WE WILL DRINK WATER; NOT A DROP BEFORE: THEREFORE BEAR UP, AND BOARD 'EM. SERVANT-MONSTER, DRINK TO ME.
SERVANT-MONSTER? THE FOLLY OF THIS ISLAND! THEY SAY THERE'S BUT FIVE UPON THIS ISLE: WE ARE THREE OF THEM; IF TH'OTHER TWO BE BRAINED LIKE US, THE STATE TOTTERS.
DRINK, SERVANT-MONSTER, WHEN I BID THEE: THY EYES ARE ALMOST SET IN THY HEAD.
gulp
gulp
WHERE SHOULD THEY BE SET ELSE? HE WERE A BRAVE MONSTER INDEED, IF THEY WERE SET IN HIS TAIL.
MY MAN-MONSTER HATH DROWNED HIS TONGUE IN SACK: FOR MY PART, THE SEA CANNOT DROWN ME; I SWAM, ERE I COULD RECOVER THE SHORE, FIVE-AND-THIRTY LEAGUES, OFF AND ON.
BY THIS LIGHT, THOU SHALT BE MY LIEUTENANT, MONSTER, OR MY STANDARD.
YOUR LIEUTENANT, IF YOU LIST; HE'S NO STANDARD.
WE'LL NOT RUN, MONSIEUR MONSTER.
NOR GO NEITHER; BUT YOU'LL LIE, LIKE DOGS, AND YET SAY NOTHING NEITHER.
MOON-CALF, SPEAK ONCE IN THY LIFE, IF THOU BEEST A GOOD MOON-CALF.
schluurp
HOW DOES THY HONOUR? LET ME LICK THY SHOE. I'LL NOT SERVE HIM, HE IS NOT VALIANT.

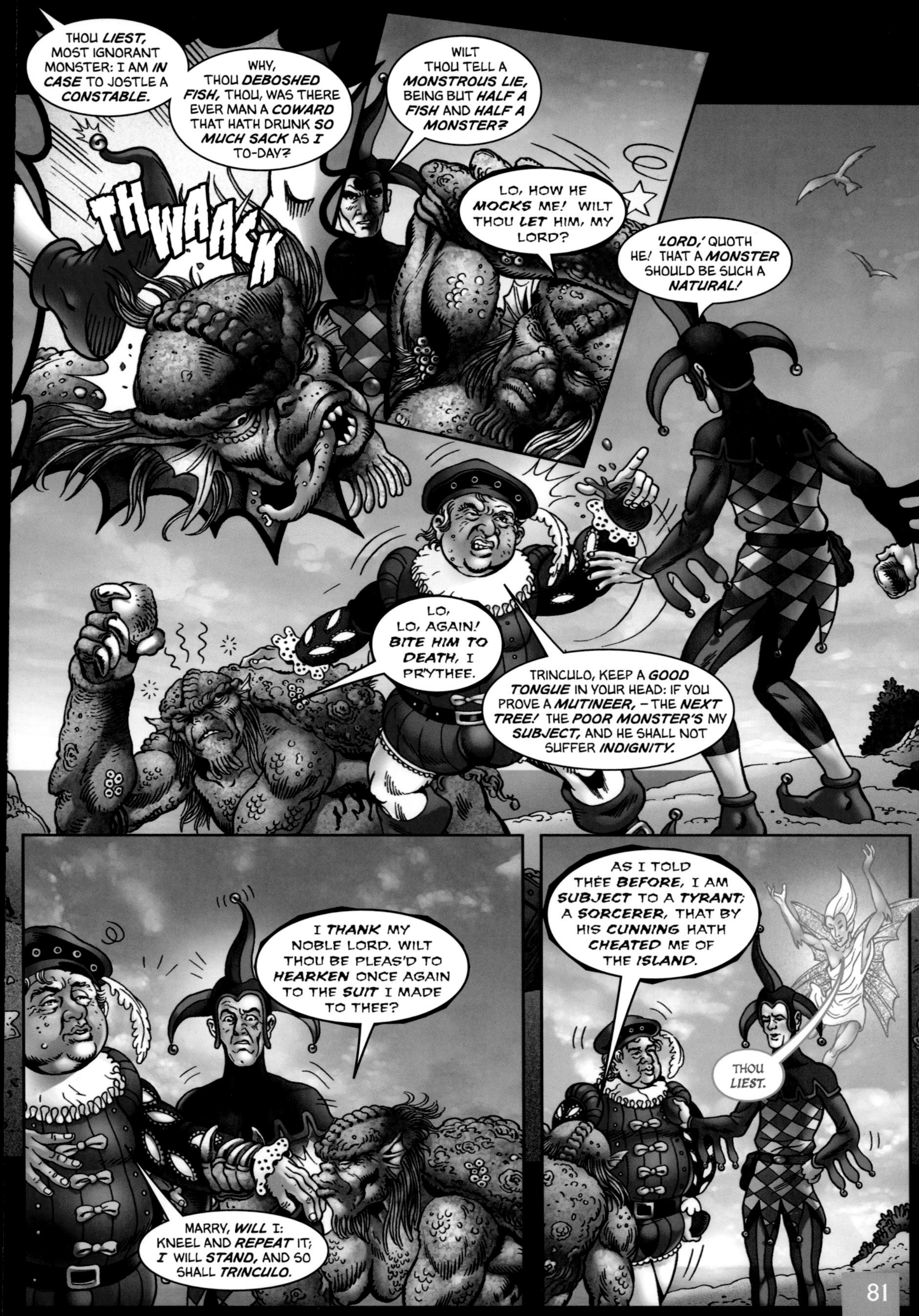
THOU LIEST, MOST IGNORANT MONSTER: I AM IN CASE TO JOSTLE A CONSTABLE.
WHY, THOU DEBOSHED FISH, THOU, WAS THERE EVER MAN A COWARD THAT HATH DRUNK SO MUCH SACK AS I TO-DAY?
WILT THOU TELL A MONSTROUS LIE, BEING BUT HALF A FISH AND HALF A MONSTER?
THWAACK
LO, HOW HE MOCKS ME! WILT THOU LET HIM, MY LORD?
'LORD,' QUOTH HE! THAT A MONSTER SHOULD BE SUCH A NATURAL!
LO, LO, AGAIN! BITE HIM TO DEATH, I PRY'THEE.
TRINCULO, KEEP A GOOD TONGUE IN YOUR HEAD: IF YOU PROVE A MUTINEER, – THE NEXT TREE! THE POOR MONSTER'S MY SUBJECT, AND HE SHALL NOT SUFFER INDIGNITY.
I THANK MY NOBLE LORD. WILT THOU BE PLEAS'D TO HEARKEN ONCE AGAIN TO THE SUIT I MADE TO THEE?
MARRY, WILL I: KNEEL AND REPEAT IT; I WILL STAND, AND SO SHALL TRINCULO.
AS I TOLD THEE BEFORE, I AM SUBJECT TO A TYRANT; A SORCERER, THAT BY HIS CUNNING HATH CHEATED ME OF THE ISLAND.
THOU LIEST.

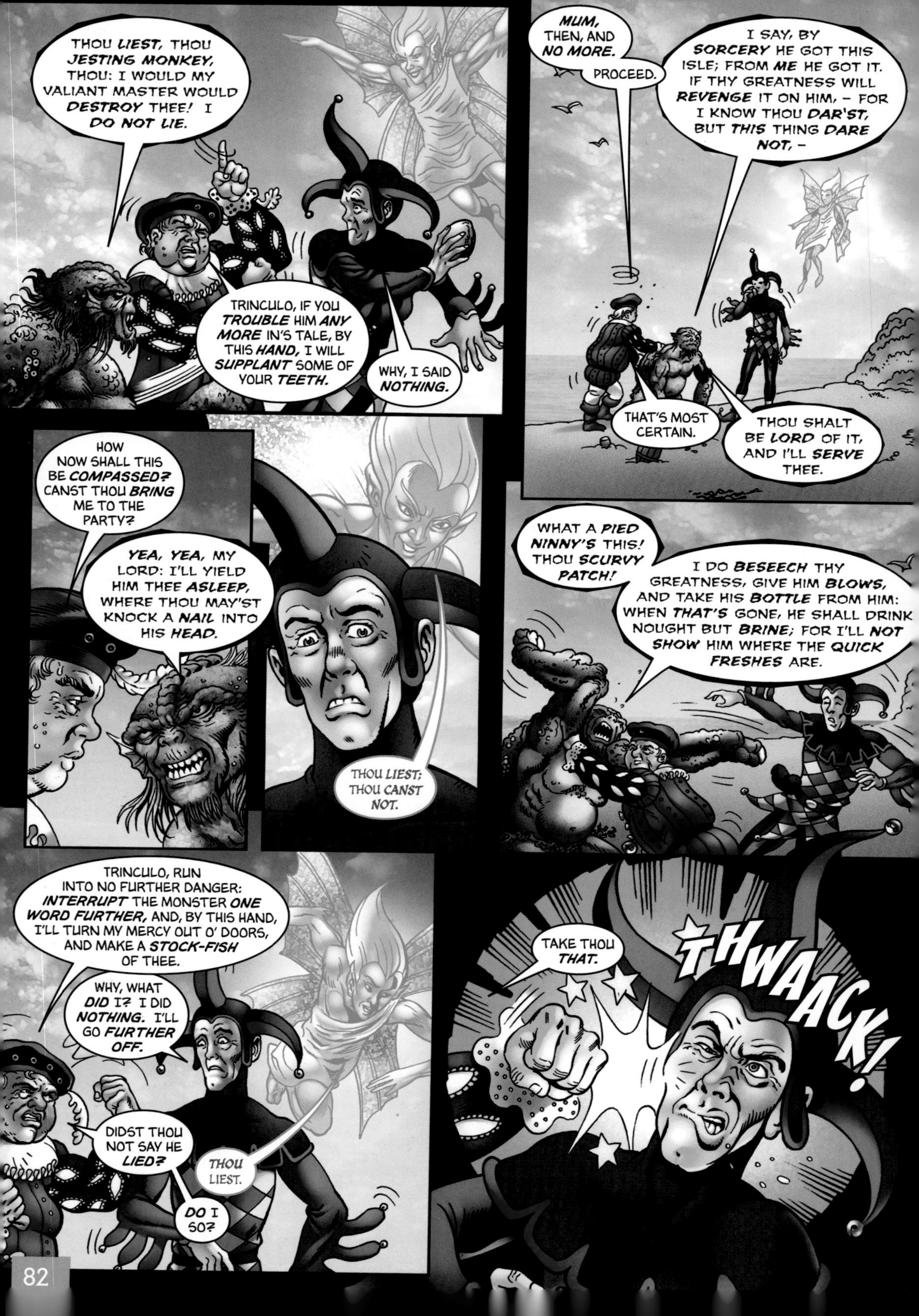
THOU LIEST, THOU JESTING MONKEY, THOU: I WOULD MY VALIANT MASTER WOULD DESTROY THEE! I DO NOT LIE.
TRINCULO, IF YOU TROUBLE HIM ANY MORE IN'S TALE, BY THIS HAND, I WILL SUPPLANT SOME OF YOUR TEETH.
WHY, I SAID NOTHING.
MUM, THEN, AND NO MORE.
PROCEED.
I SAY, BY SORCERY HE GOT THIS ISLE; FROM ME HE GOT IT. IF THY GREATNESS WILL REVENGE IT ON HIM, – FOR I KNOW THOU DAR'ST, BUT THIS THING DARE NOT, –
THAT'S MOST CERTAIN.
THOU SHALT BE LORD OF IT, AND I'LL SERVE THEE.
HOW NOW SHALL THIS BE COMPASSED? CANST THOU BRING ME TO THE PARTY?
YEA, YEA, MY LORD: I'LL YIELD HIM THEE ASLEEP, WHERE THOU MAY'ST KNOCK A NAIL INTO HIS HEAD.
THOU LIEST; THOU CANST NOT.
WHAT A PIED NINNY'S THIS! THOU SCURVY PATCH!
I DO BESEECH THY GREATNESS, GIVE HIM BLOWS, AND TAKE HIS BOTTLE FROM HIM: WHEN THAT'S GONE, HE SHALL DRINK NOUGHT BUT BRINE; FOR I'LL NOT SHOW HIM WHERE THE QUICK FRESHES ARE.
TRINCULO, RUN INTO NO FURTHER DANGER: INTERRUPT THE MONSTER ONE WORD FURTHER, AND, BY THIS HAND, I'LL TURN MY MERCY OUT O' DOORS, AND MAKE A STOCK-FISH OF THEE.
WHY, WHAT DID I? I DID NOTHING. I'LL GO FURTHER OFF.
DIDST THOU NOT SAY HE LIED?
THOU LIEST.
DO I SO?
TAKE THOU THAT.
THWAACK!

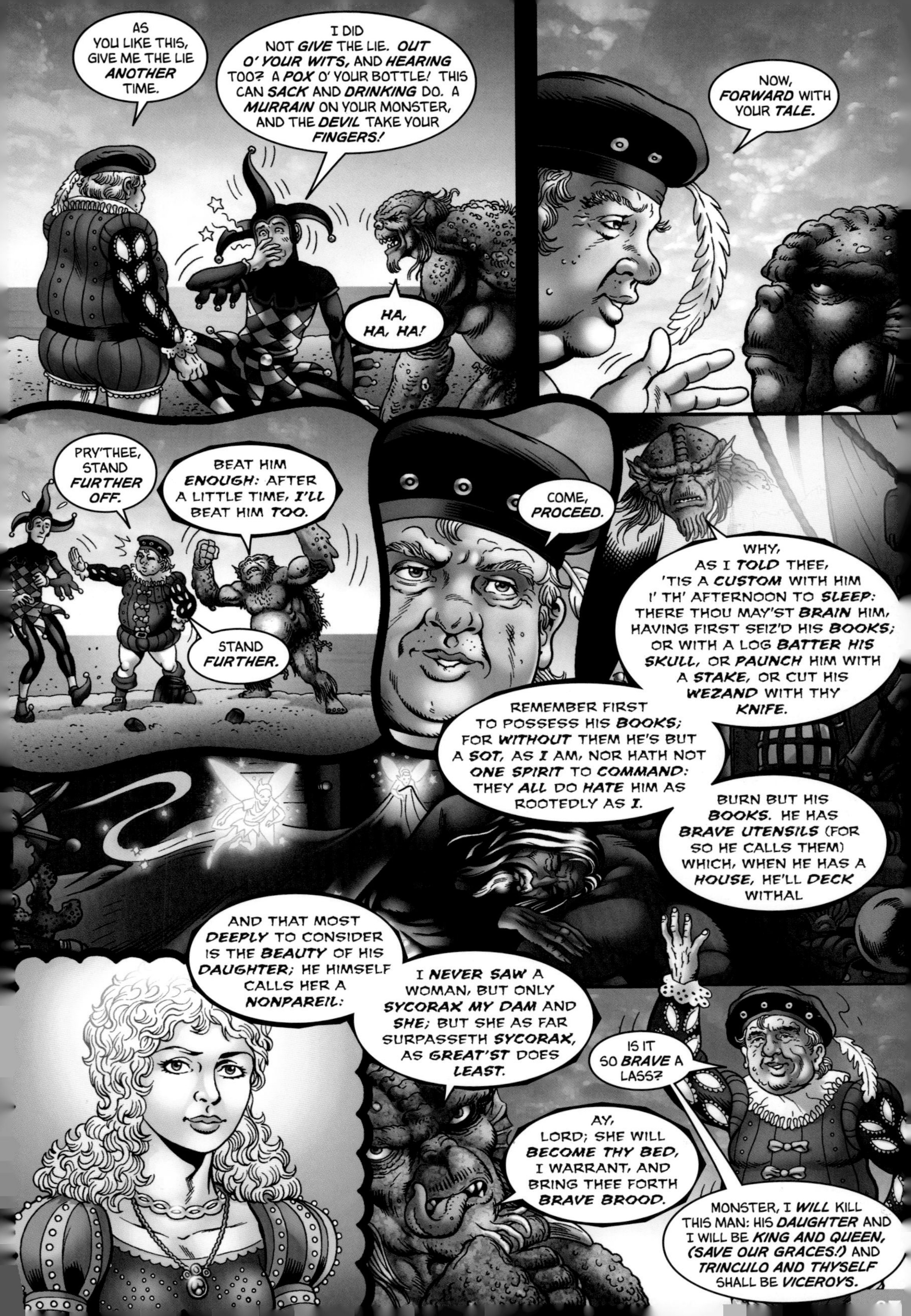
AS YOU LIKE THIS, GIVE ME THE LIE ANOTHER TIME.
I DID NOT GIVE THE LIE. OUT O' YOUR WITS, AND HEARING TOO? A POX O' YOUR BOTTLE! THIS CAN SACK AND DRINKING DO. A MURRAIN ON YOUR MONSTER, AND THE DEVIL TAKE YOUR FINGERS!
HA, HA, HA!
NOW, FORWARD WITH YOUR TALE.
PRY'THEE, STAND FURTHER OFF.
BEAT HIM ENOUGH: AFTER A LITTLE TIME, I'LL BEAT HIM TOO.
STAND FURTHER.
COME, PROCEED.
WHY, AS I TOLD THEE, 'TIS A CUSTOM WITH HIM I' TH' AFTERNOON TO SLEEP: THERE THOU MAY'ST BRAIN HIM, HAVING FIRST SEIZ'D HIS BOOKS; OR WITH A LOG BATTER HIS SKULL, OR PAUNCH HIM WITH A STAKE, OR CUT HIS WEZAND WITH THY KNIFE.
REMEMBER FIRST TO POSSESS HIS BOOKS; FOR WITHOUT THEM HE'S BUT A SOT, AS I AM, NOR HATH NOT ONE SPIRIT TO COMMAND: THEY ALL DO HATE HIM AS ROOTEDLY AS I.
BURN BUT HIS BOOKS. HE HAS BRAVE UTENSILS (FOR SO HE CALLS THEM) WHICH, WHEN HE HAS A HOUSE, HE'LL DECK WITHAL
AND THAT MOST DEEPLY TO CONSIDER IS THE BEAUTY OF HIS DAUGHTER; HE HIMSELF CALLS HER A NONPAREIL:
I NEVER SAW A WOMAN, BUT ONLY SYCORAX MY DAM AND SHE; BUT SHE AS FAR SURPASSETH SYCORAX, AS GREAT'ST DOES LEAST.
IS IT SO BRAVE A LASS?
AY, LORD; SHE WILL BECOME THY BED, I WARRANT, AND BRING THEE FORTH BRAVE BROOD.
MONSTER, I WILL KILL THIS MAN: HIS DAUGHTER AND I WILL BE KING AND QUEEN, (SAVE OUR GRACES!) AND TRINCULO AND THYSELF SHALL BE VICEROYS.

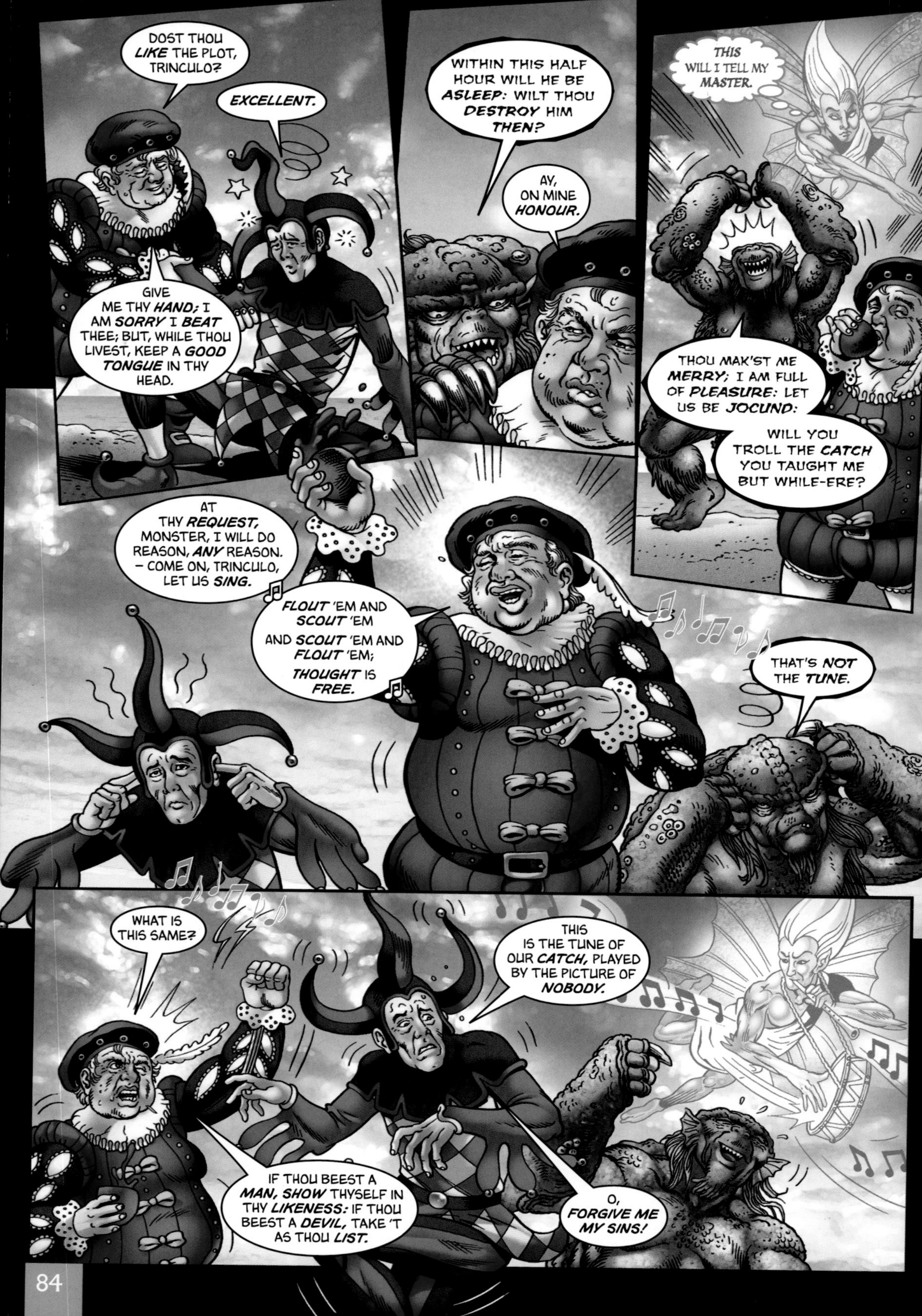
DOST THOU LIKE THE PLOT, TRINCULO?
EXCELLENT.
GIVE ME THY HAND; I AM SORRY I BEAT THEE; BUT, WHILE THOU LIVEST, KEEP A GOOD TONGUE IN THY HEAD.
WITHIN THIS HALF HOUR WILL HE BE ASLEEP: WILT THOU DESTROY HIM THEN?
AY, ON MINE HONOUR.
THIS WILL I TELL MY MASTER.
THOU MAK'ST ME MERRY; I AM FULL OF PLEASURE: LET US BE JOCUND:
WILL YOU TROLL THE CATCH YOU TAUGHT ME BUT WHILE-ERE?
AT THY REQUEST, MONSTER, I WILL DO REASON, ANY REASON. – COME ON, TRINCULO, LET US SING.
FLOUT 'EM AND SCOUT 'EM AND SCOUT 'EM AND FLOUT 'EM; THOUGHT IS FREE.
THAT'S NOT THE TUNE.
WHAT IS THIS SAME?
THIS IS THE TUNE OF OUR CATCH, PLAYED BY THE PICTURE OF NOBODY.
IF THOU BEEST A MAN, SHOW THYSELF IN THY LIKENESS: IF THOU BEEST A DEVIL, TAKE 'T AS THOU LIST.
O, FORGIVE ME MY SINS!

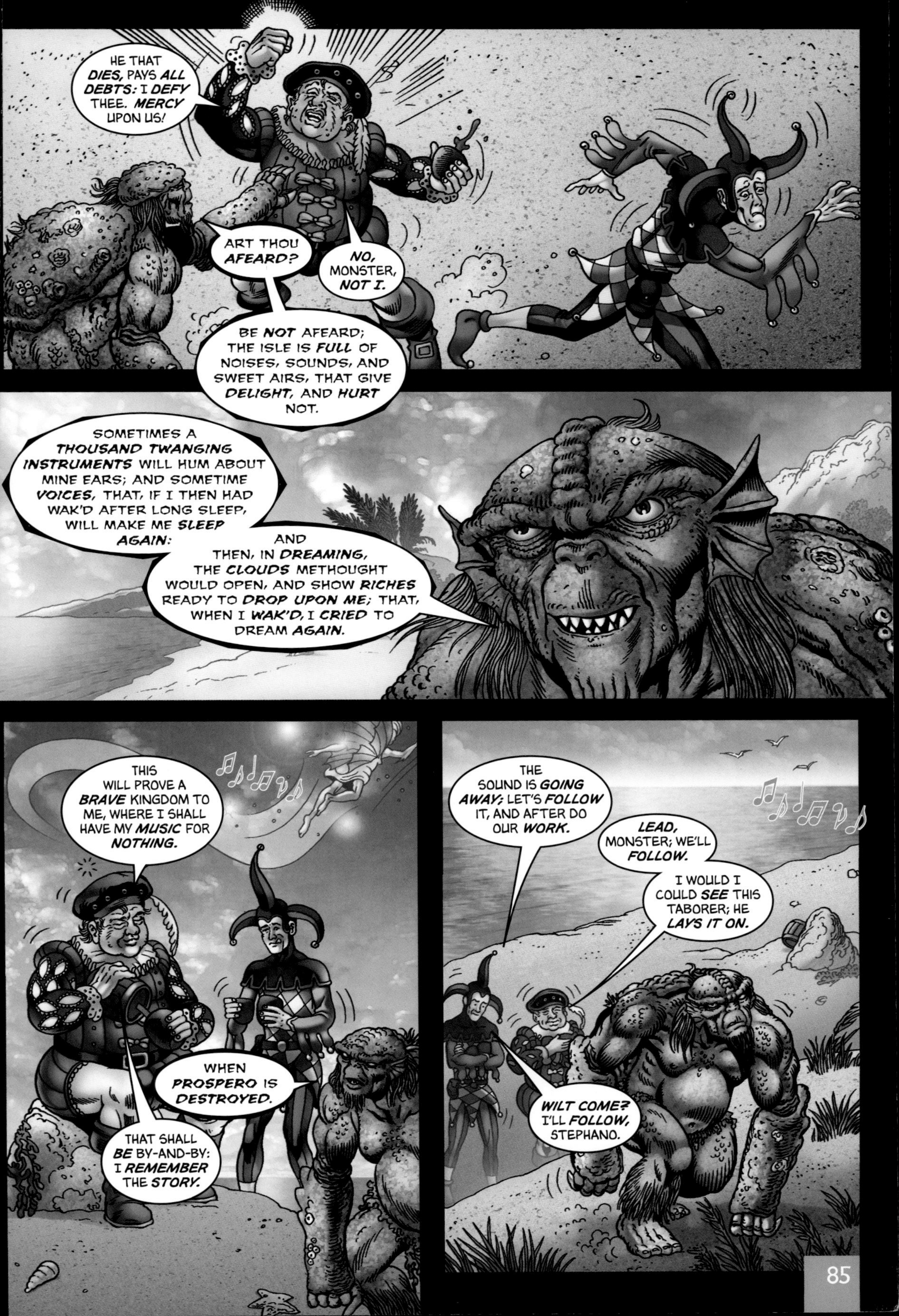
HE THAT DIES, PAYS ALL DEBTS: I DEFY THEE. MERCY UPON US!
ART THOU AFEARD?
NO, MONSTER, NOT I.
BE NOT AFEARD; THE ISLE IS FULL OF NOISES, SOUNDS, AND SWEET AIRS, THAT GIVE DELIGHT, AND HURT NOT.
SOMETIMES A THOUSAND TWANGING INSTRUMENTS WILL HUM ABOUT MINE EARS; AND SOMETIME VOICES, THAT, IF I THEN HAD WAK'D AFTER LONG SLEEP, WILL MAKE ME SLEEP AGAIN:
AND THEN, IN DREAMING, THE CLOUDS METHOUGHT WOULD OPEN, AND SHOW RICHES READY TO DROP UPON ME; THAT, WHEN I WAK'D, I CRIED TO DREAM AGAIN.
THIS WILL PROVE A BRAVE KINGDOM TO ME, WHERE I SHALL HAVE MY MUSIC FOR NOTHING.
WHEN PROSPERO IS DESTROYED.
THAT SHALL BE BY-AND-BY: I REMEMBER THE STORY.
THE SOUND IS GOING AWAY; LET'S FOLLOW IT, AND AFTER DO OUR WORK.
LEAD, MONSTER; WE'LL FOLLOW.
I WOULD I COULD SEE THIS TABORER; HE LAYS IT ON.
WILT COME? I'LL FOLLOW, STEPHANO.

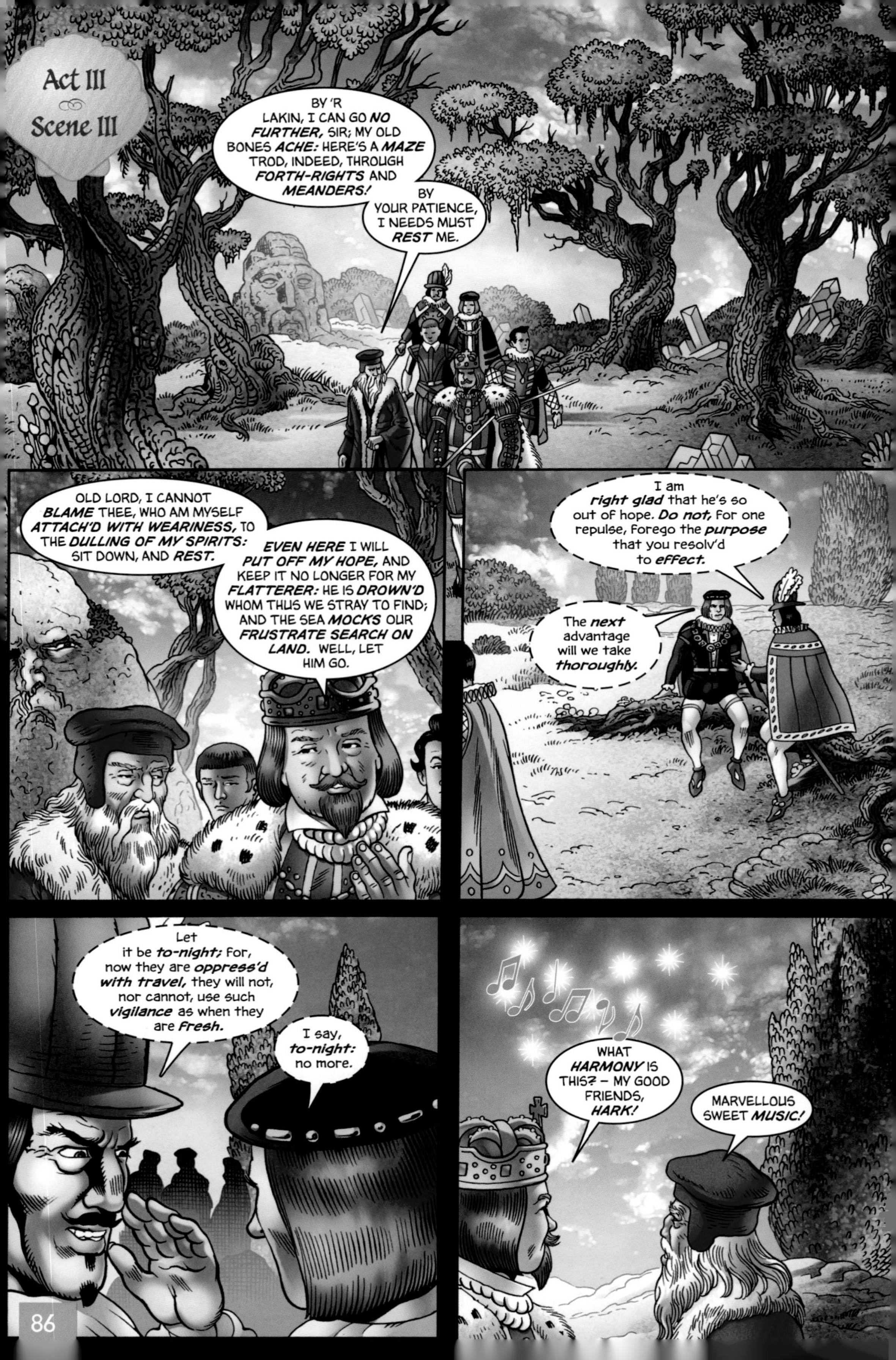
Act III
Scene III
BY 'R LAKIN, I CAN GO NO FURTHER, SIR; MY OLD BONES ACHE: HERE'S A MAZE TROD, INDEED, THROUGH FORTH-RIGHTS AND MEANDERS!
BY YOUR PATIENCE, I NEEDS MUST REST ME.
OLD LORD, I CANNOT BLAME THEE, WHO AM MYSELF ATTACH'D WITH WEARINESS, TO THE DULLING OF MY SPIRITS: SIT DOWN, AND REST.
EVEN HERE I WILL PUT OFF MY HOPE, AND KEEP IT NO LONGER FOR MY FLATTERER: HE IS DROWN'D WHOM THUS WE STRAY TO FIND; AND THE SEA MOCKS OUR FRUSTRATE SEARCH ON LAND. WELL, LET HIM GO.
I am right glad that he's so out of hope. Do not, for one repulse, forego the purpose that you resolv'd to effect.
The next advantage will we take thoroughly.
Let it be to-night; For, now they are oppress'd with travel, they will not, nor cannot, use such vigilance as when they are fresh.
I say, to-night: no more.
WHAT HARMONY IS THIS? – MY GOOD FRIENDS, HARK!
MARVELLOUS SWEET MUSIC!

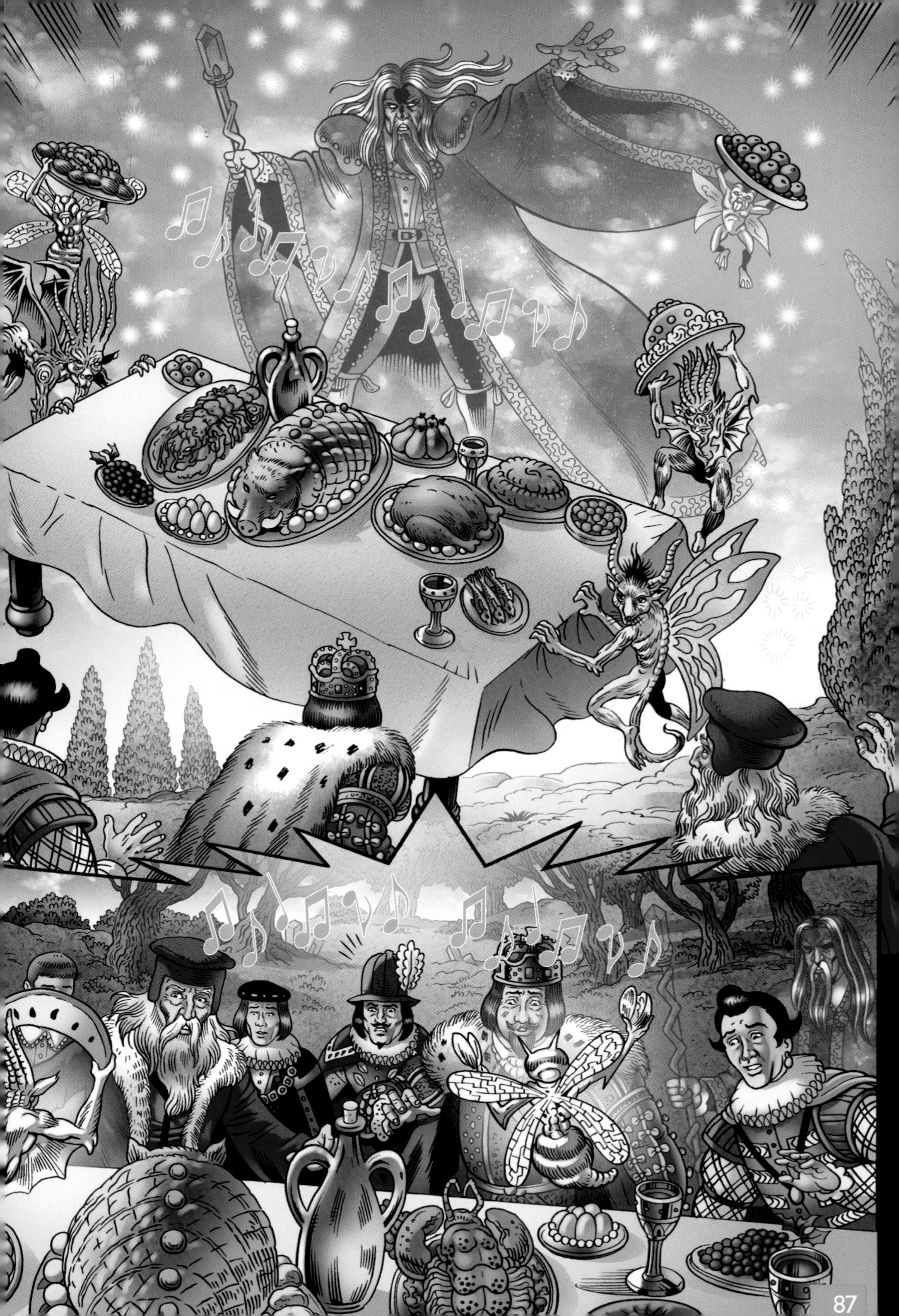

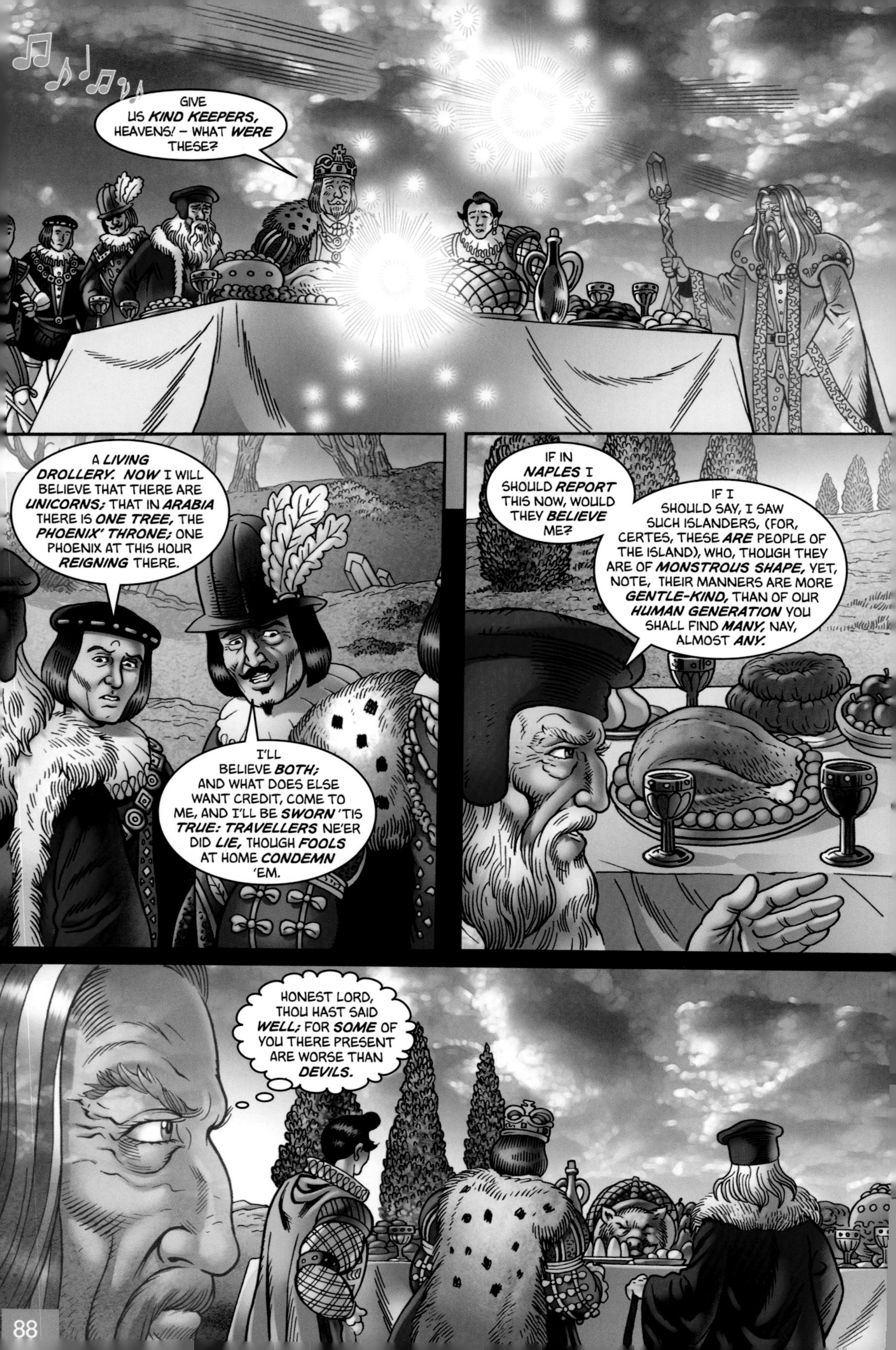
GIVE US KIND KEEPERS, HEAVENS! – WHAT WERE THESE?
A LIVING DROLLERY. NOW I WILL BELIEVE THAT THERE ARE UNICORNS; THAT IN ARABIA THERE IS ONE TREE, THE PHOENIX' THRONE; ONE PHOENIX AT THIS HOUR REIGNING THERE.
I'LL BELIEVE BOTH; AND WHAT DOES ELSE WANT CREDIT, COME TO ME, AND I'LL BE SWORN 'TIS TRUE: TRAVELLERS NE'ER DID LIE, THOUGH FOOLS AT HOME CONDEMN 'EM.
IF IN NAPLES I SHOULD REPORT THIS NOW, WOULD THEY BELIEVE ME?
IF I SHOULD SAY, I SAW SUCH ISLANDERS, (FOR, CERTES, THESE ARE PEOPLE OF THE ISLAND), WHO, THOUGH THEY ARE OF MONSTROUS SHAPE, YET, NOTE, THEIR MANNERS ARE MORE GENTLE-KIND, THAN OF OUR HUMAN GENERATION YOU SHALL FIND MANY, NAY, ALMOST ANY.
HONEST LORD, THOU HAST SAID WELL; FOR SOME OF YOU THERE PRESENT ARE WORSE THAN DEVILS.

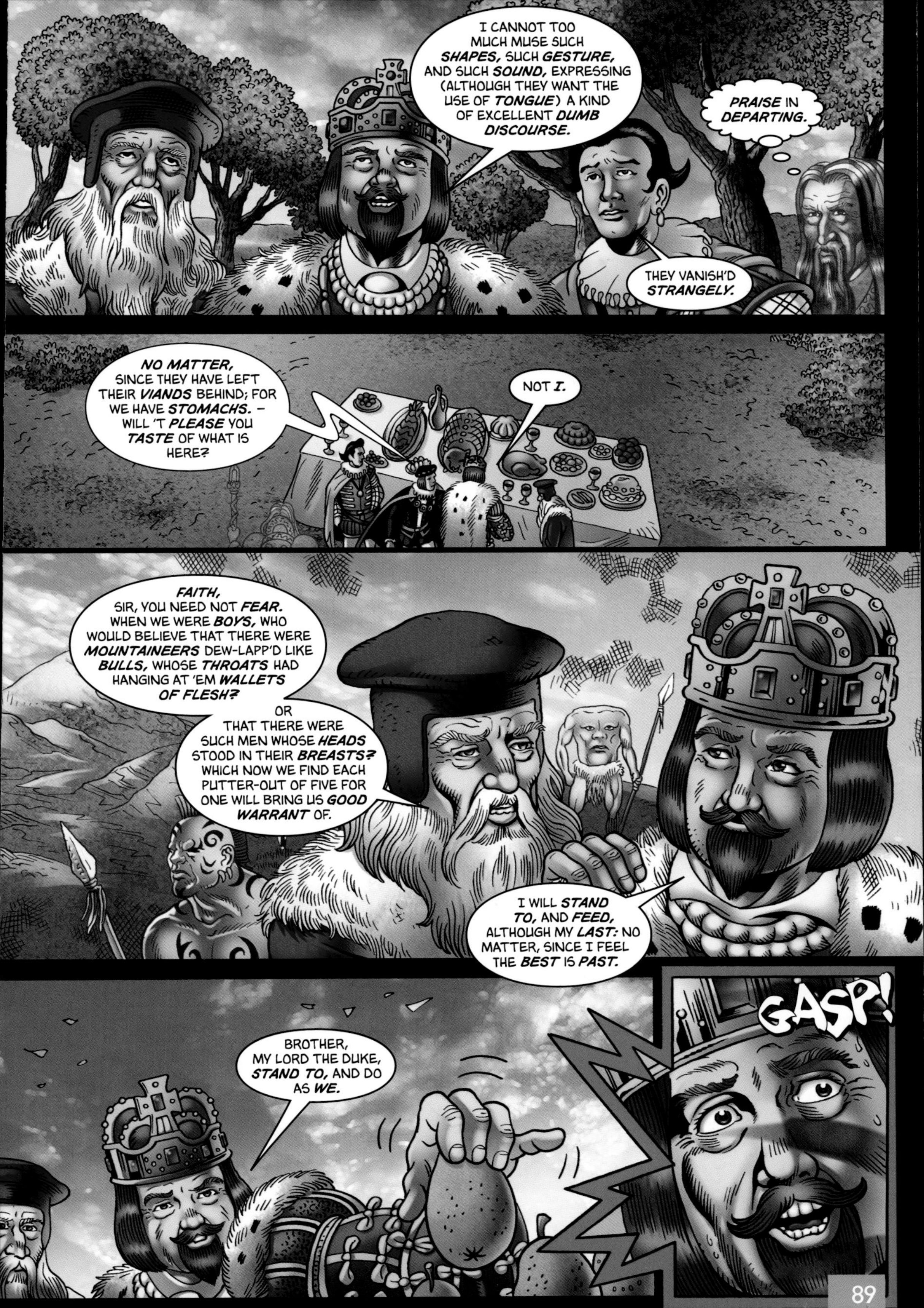

I CANNOT TOO MUCH MUSE SUCH SHAPES, SUCH GESTURE, AND SUCH SOUND, EXPRESSING (ALTHOUGH THEY WANT THE USE OF TONGUE) A KIND OF EXCELLENT DUMB DISCOURSE.
PRAISE IN DEPARTING.
THEY VANISH'D STRANGELY.
NO MATTER, SINCE THEY HAVE LEFT THEIR VIANDS BEHIND; FOR WE HAVE STOMACHS. – WILL 'T PLEASE YOU TASTE OF WHAT IS HERE?
NOT I.
FAITH, SIR, YOU NEED NOT FEAR. WHEN WE WERE BOYS, WHO WOULD BELIEVE THAT THERE WERE MOUNTAINEERS DEW-LAPP'D LIKE BULLS, WHOSE THROATS HAD HANGING AT 'EM WALLETS OF FLESH?
OR THAT THERE WERE SUCH MEN WHOSE HEADS STOOD IN THEIR BREASTS? WHICH NOW WE FIND EACH PUTTER-OUT OF FIVE FOR ONE WILL BRING US GOOD WARRANT OF.
I WILL STAND TO, AND FEED, ALTHOUGH MY LAST: NO MATTER, SINCE I FEEL THE BEST IS PAST.
BROTHER, MY LORD THE DUKE, STAND TO, AND DO AS WE.
GASP!

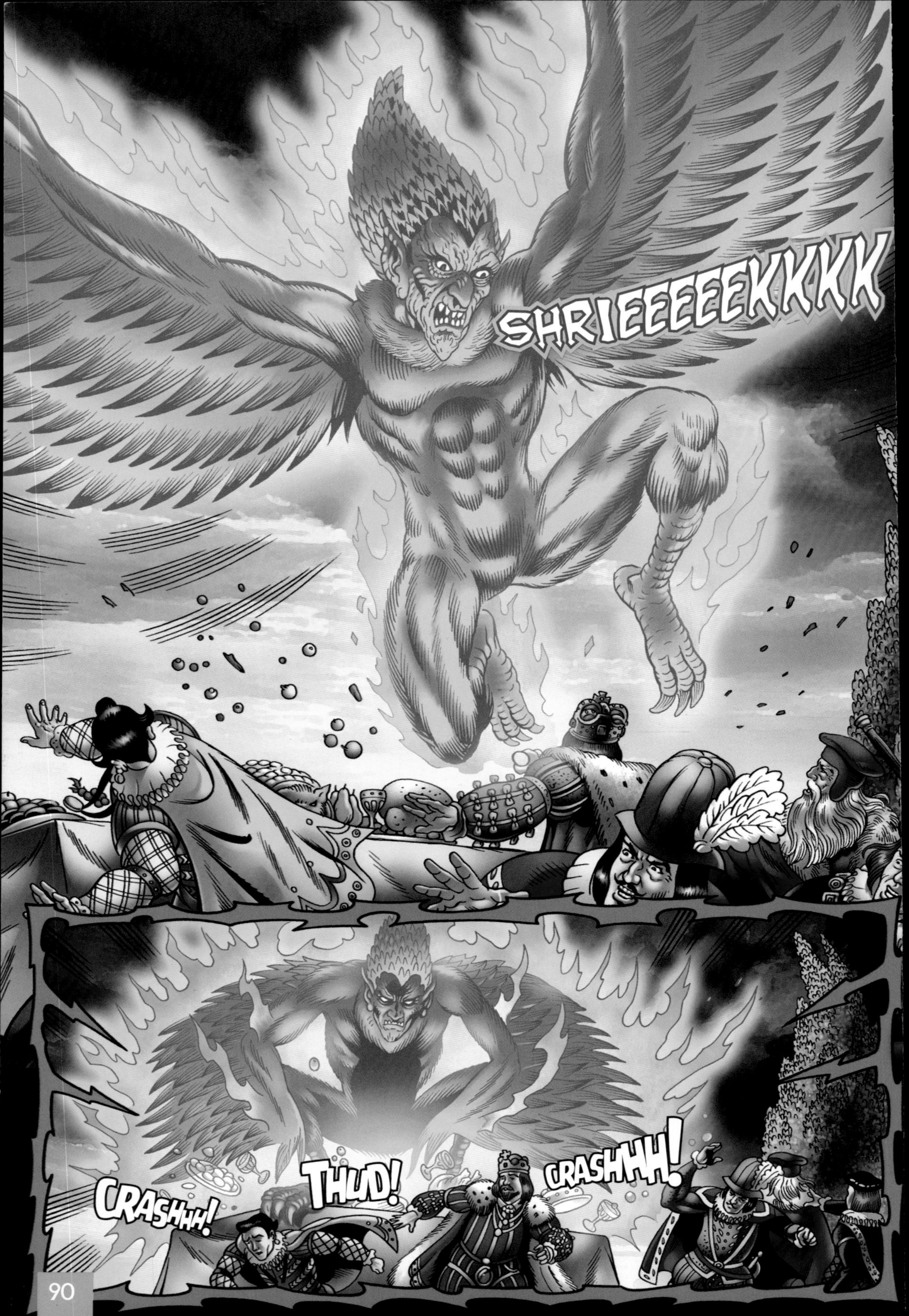
SHRIEEEEEEKKKK
CRASHHH!
THUD!
CRASHHHH!

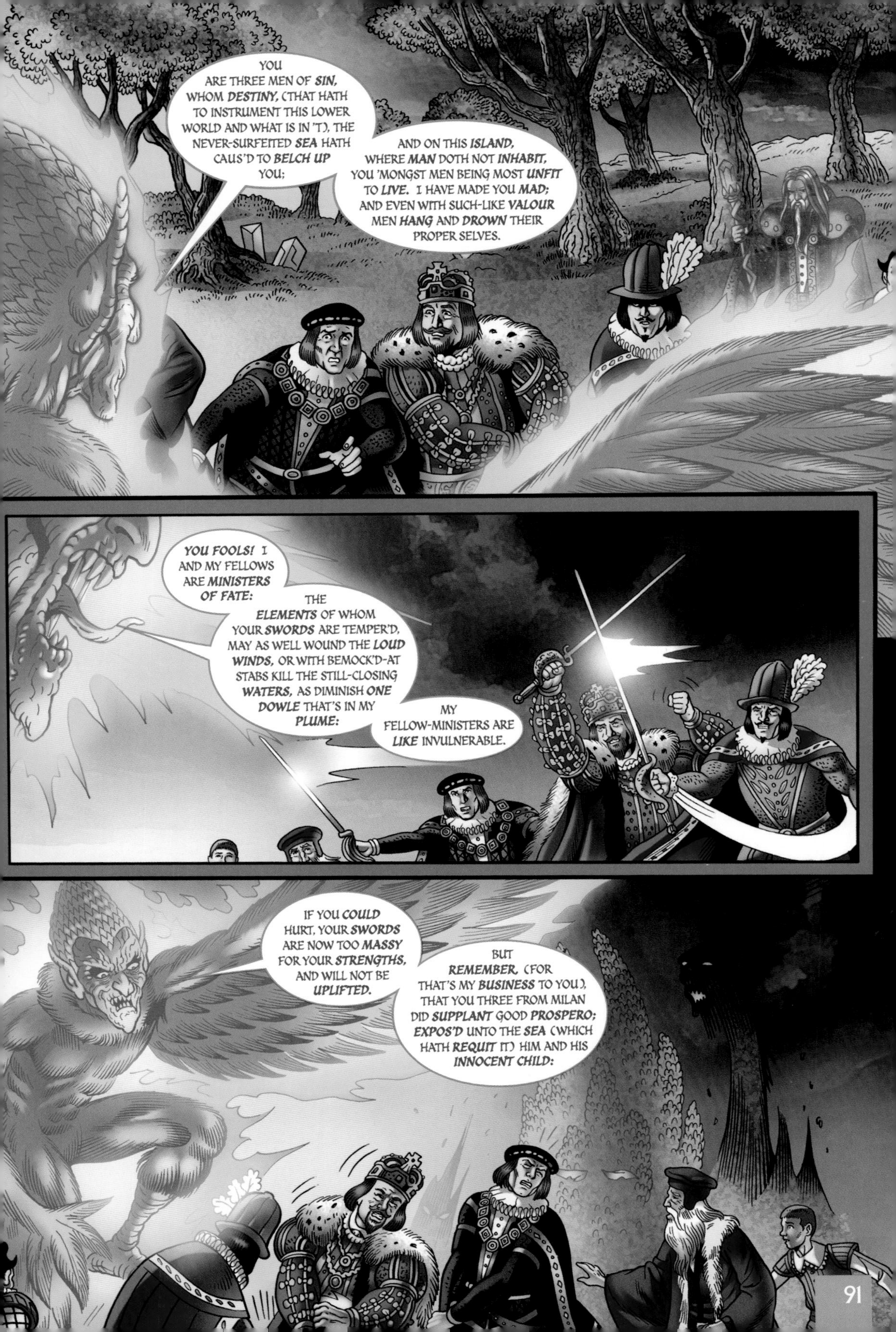
YOU ARE THREE MEN OF SIN, WHOM DESTINY, (THAT HATH TO INSTRUMENT THIS LOWER WORLD AND WHAT IS IN 'T), THE NEVER-SURFEITED SEA HATH CAUS'D TO BELCH UP YOU;
AND ON THIS ISLAND, WHERE MAN DOTH NOT INHABIT, YOU 'MONGST MEN BEING MOST UNFIT TO LIVE. I HAVE MADE YOU MAD; AND EVEN WITH SUCH-LIKE VALOUR MEN HANG AND DROWN THEIR PROPER SELVES.
YOU FOOLS! I AND MY FELLOWS ARE MINISTERS OF FATE:
THE ELEMENTS OF WHOM YOUR SWORDS ARE TEMPER'D, MAY AS WELL WOUND THE LOUD WINDS, OR WITH BEMOCK'D-AT STABS KILL THE STILL-CLOSING WATERS, AS DIMINISH ONE DOWLE THAT'S IN MY PLUME:
MY FELLOW-MINISTERS ARE LIKE INVULNERABLE.
IF YOU COULD HURT, YOUR SWORDS ARE NOW TOO MASSY FOR YOUR STRENGTHS, AND WILL NOT BE UPLIFTED.
BUT REMEMBER, (FOR THAT'S MY BUSINESS TO YOU), THAT YOU THREE FROM MILAN DID SUPPLANT GOOD PROSPERO; EXPOS'D UNTO THE SEA (WHICH HATH REQUIT IT) HIM AND HIS INNOCENT CHILD:

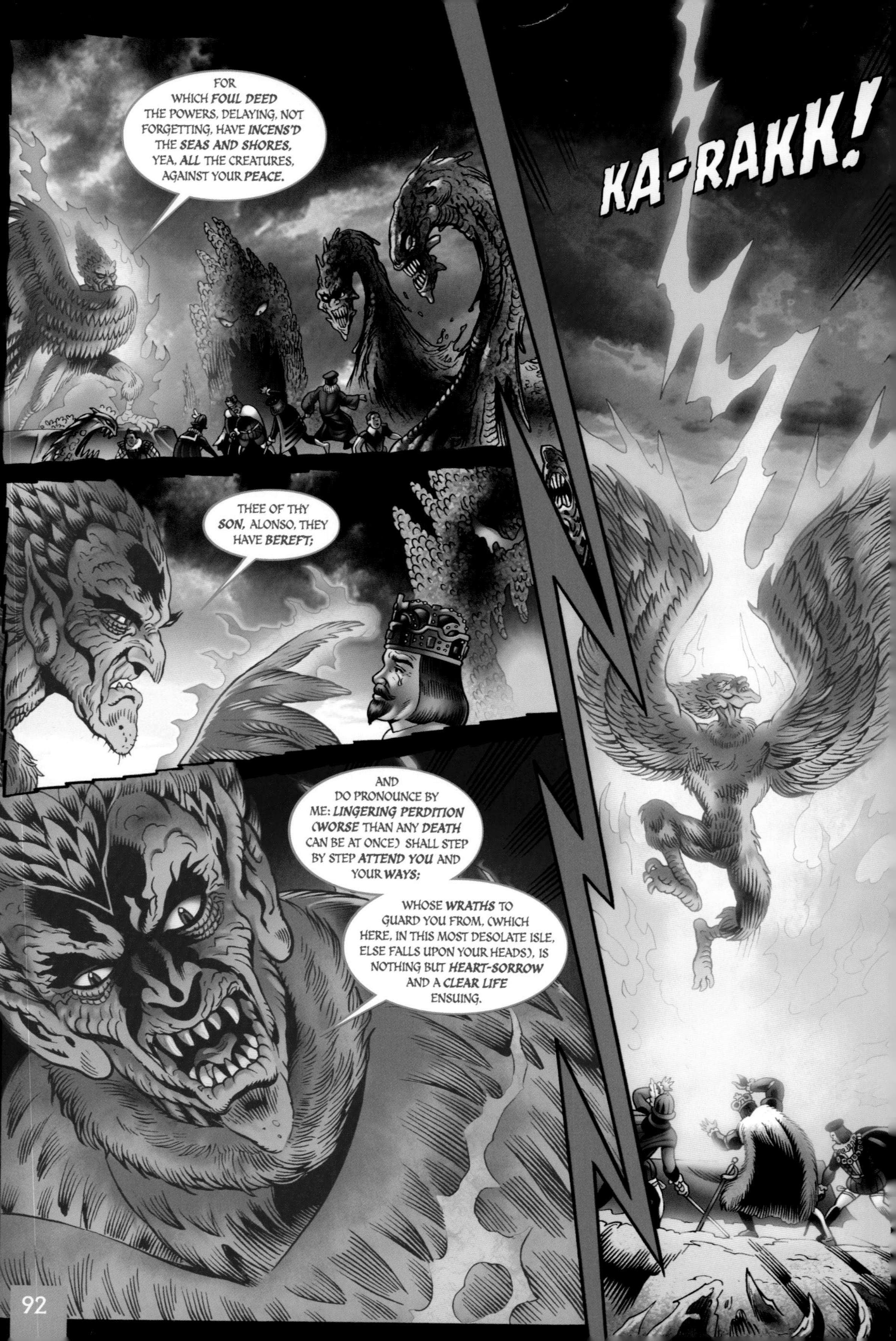
FOR WHICH FOUL DEED THE POWERS, DELAYING, NOT FORGETTING, HAVE INCENS'D THE SEAS AND SHORES, YEA, ALL THE CREATURES, AGAINST YOUR PEACE.
KA-RAKK!
THEE OF THY SON, ALONSO, THEY HAVE BEREFT;
AND DO PRONOUNCE BY ME: LINGERING PERDITION (WORSE THAN ANY DEATH CAN BE AT ONCE) SHALL STEP BY STEP ATTEND YOU AND YOUR WAYS;
WHOSE WRATHS TO GUARD YOU FROM, (WHICH HERE, IN THIS MOST DESOLATE ISLE, ELSE FALLS UPON YOUR HEADS), IS NOTHING BUT HEART-SORROW AND A CLEAR LIFE ENSUING.

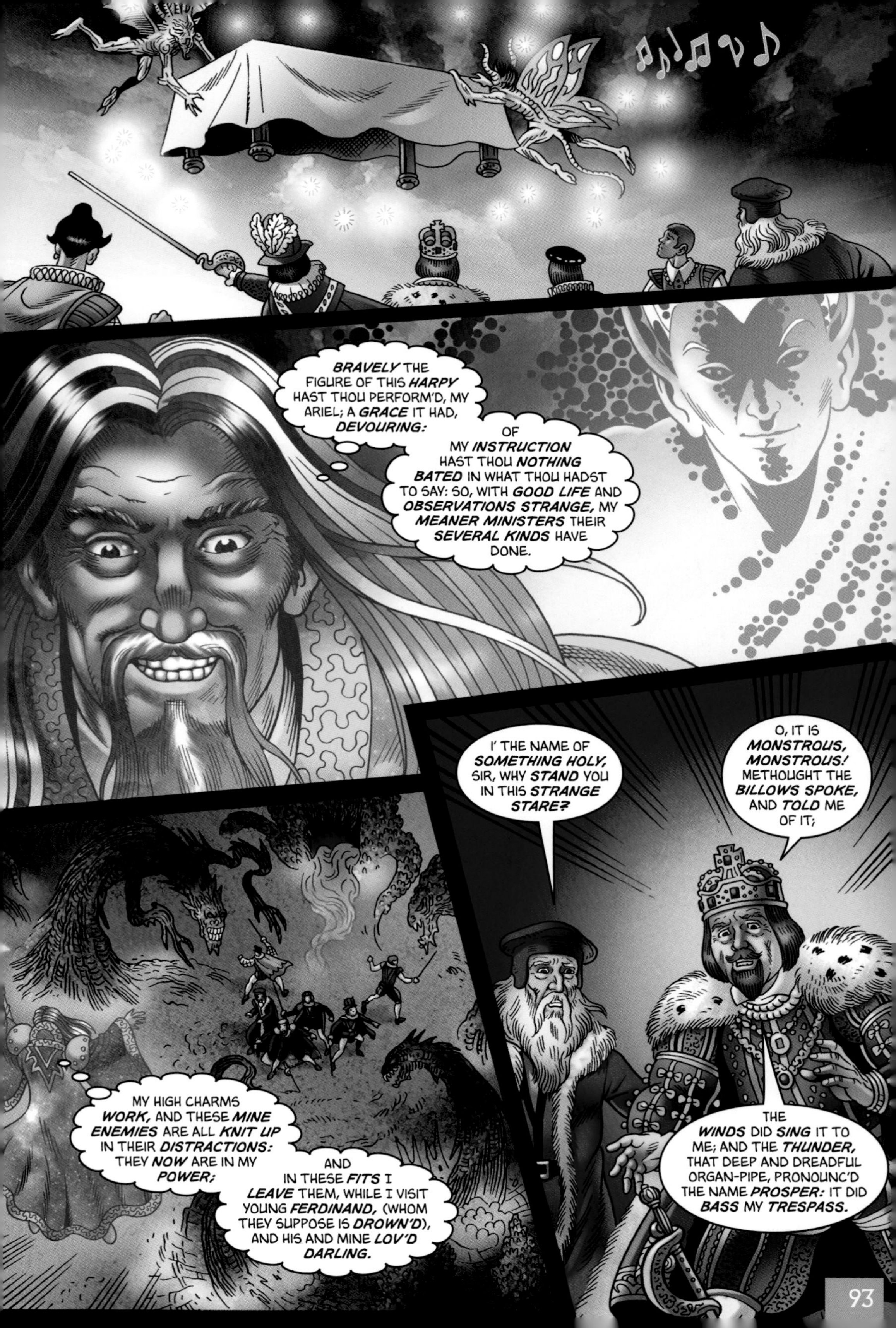
BRAVELY THE FIGURE OF THIS HARPY HAST THOU PERFORM'D, MY ARIEL; A GRACE IT HAD, DEVOURING:
OF MY INSTRUCTION HAST THOU NOTHING BATED IN WHAT THOU HADST TO SAY: SO, WITH GOOD LIFE AND OBSERVATIONS STRANGE, MY MEANER MINISTERS THEIR SEVERAL KINDS HAVE DONE.
MY HIGH CHARMS WORK, AND THESE MINE ENEMIES ARE ALL KNIT UP IN THEIR DISTRACTIONS: THEY NOW ARE IN MY POWER;
AND IN THESE FITS I LEAVE THEM, WHILE I VISIT YOUNG FERDINAND, (WHOM THEY SUPPOSE IS DROWN'D), AND HIS AND MINE LOV'D DARLING.
I' THE NAME OF SOMETHING HOLY, SIR, WHY STAND YOU IN THIS STRANGE STARE?
O, IT IS MONSTROUS, MONSTROUS! METHOUGHT THE BILLOWS SPOKE, AND TOLD ME OF IT;
THE WINDS DID SING IT TO ME; AND THE THUNDER, THAT DEEP AND DREADFUL ORGAN-PIPE, PRONOUNC'D THE NAME PROSPER: IT DID BASS MY TRESPASS.

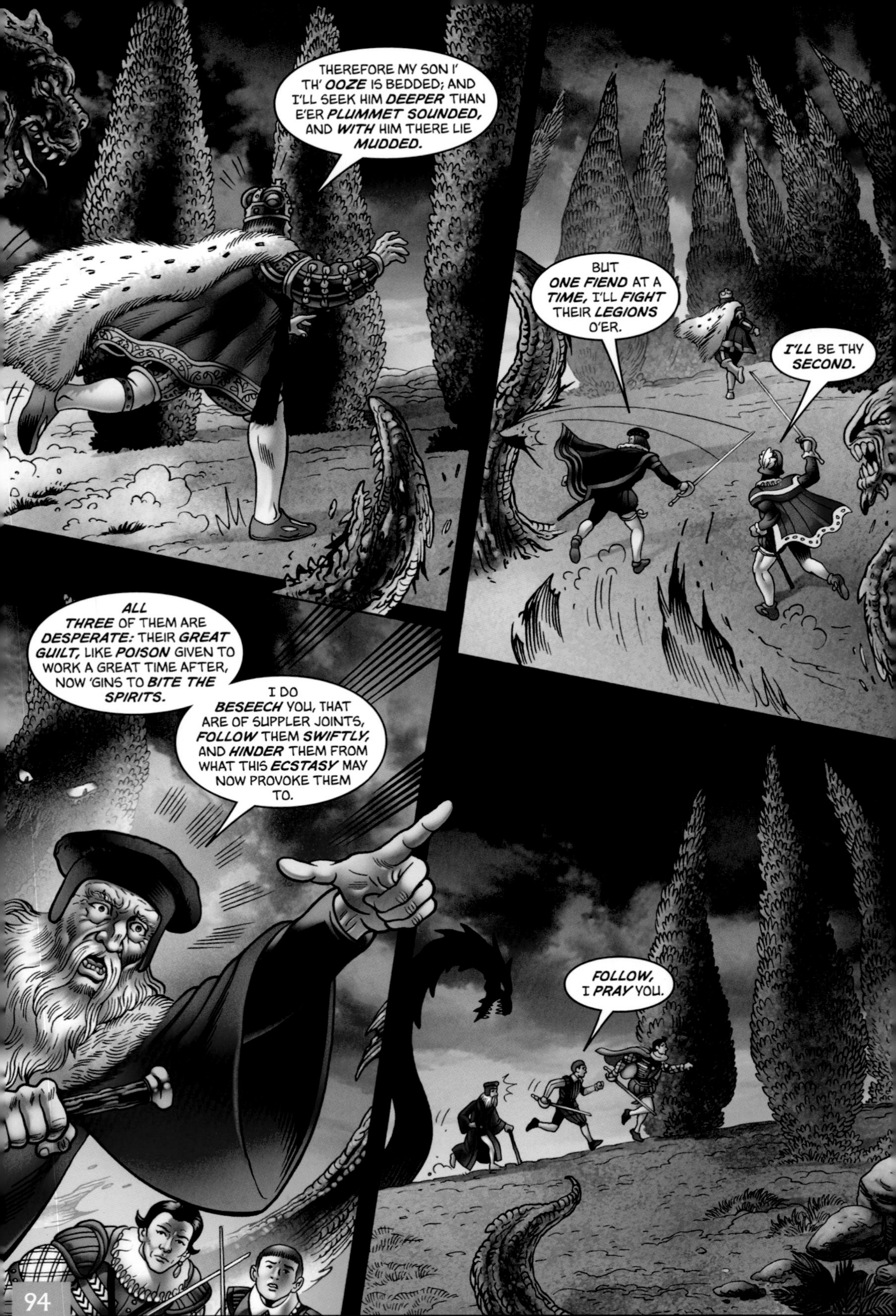

THEREFORE MY SON I' TH' OOZE IS BEDDED; AND I'LL SEEK HIM DEEPER THAN E'ER PLUMMET SOUNDED, AND WITH HIM THERE LIE MUDDED.
BUT ONE FIEND AT A TIME, I'LL FIGHT THEIR LEGIONS O'ER.
I'LL BE THY SECOND.
ALL THREE OF THEM ARE DESPERATE: THEIR GREAT GUILT, LIKE POISON GIVEN TO WORK A GREAT TIME AFTER, NOW 'GINS TO BITE THE SPIRITS.
I DO BESEECH YOU, THAT ARE OF SUPPLER JOINTS, FOLLOW THEM SWIFTLY, AND HINDER THEM FROM WHAT THIS ECSTASY MAY NOW PROVOKE THEM TO.
FOLLOW, I PRAY YOU.

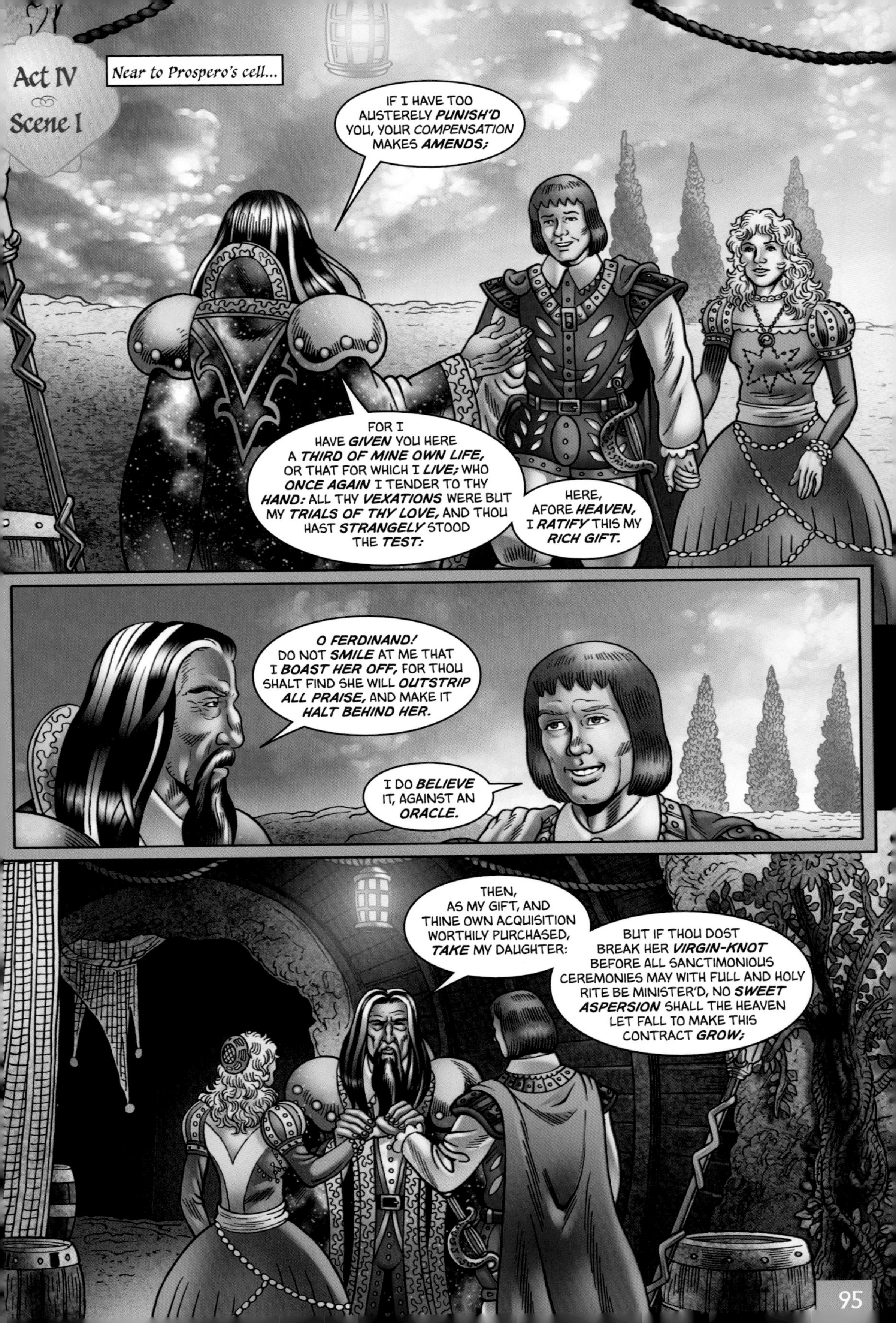
Act IV
Scene I
Near to Prospero's cell...
IF I HAVE TOO AUSTERELY PUNISH'D YOU, YOUR COMPENSATION MAKES AMENDS;
FOR I HAVE GIVEN YOU HERE A THIRD OF MINE OWN LIFE, OR THAT FOR WHICH I LIVE; WHO ONCE AGAIN I TENDER TO THY HAND: ALL THY VEXATIONS WERE BUT MY TRIALS OF THY LOVE, AND THOU HAST STRANGELY STOOD THE TEST:
HERE, AFORE HEAVEN, I RATIFY THIS MY RICH GIFT.
O FERDINAND! DO NOT SMILE AT ME THAT I BOAST HER OFF, FOR THOU SHALT FIND SHE WILL OUTSTRIP ALL PRAISE, AND MAKE IT HALT BEHIND HER.
I DO BELIEVE IT, AGAINST AN ORACLE.
THEN, AS MY GIFT, AND THINE OWN ACQUISITION WORTHILY PURCHASED, TAKE MY DAUGHTER:
BUT IF THOU DOST BREAK HER VIRGIN-KNOT BEFORE ALL SANCTIMONIOUS CEREMONIES MAY WITH FULL AND HOLY RITE BE MINISTER'D, NO SWEET ASPERSION SHALL THE HEAVEN LET FALL TO MAKE THIS CONTRACT GROW;

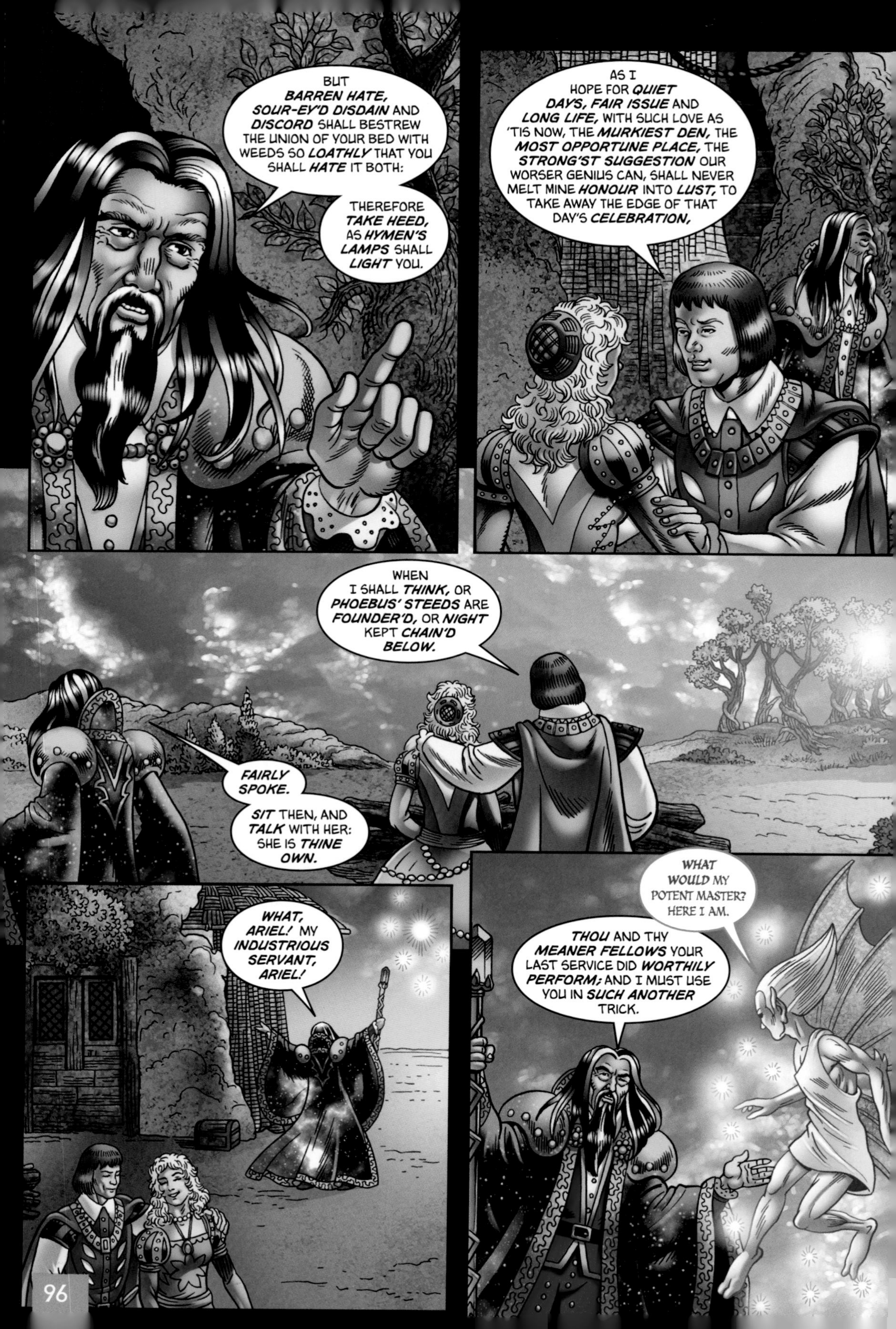

BUT BARREN HATE, SOUR-EY'D DISDAIN AND DISCORD SHALL BESTREW THE UNION OF YOUR BED WITH WEEDS SO LOATHLY THAT YOU SHALL HATE IT BOTH:
THEREFORE TAKE HEED, AS HYMEN'S LAMPS SHALL LIGHT YOU.
AS I HOPE FOR QUIET DAYS, FAIR ISSUE AND LONG LIFE, WITH SUCH LOVE AS 'TIS NOW, THE MURKIEST DEN, THE MOST OPPORTUNE PLACE, THE STRONG'ST SUGGESTION OUR WORSER GENIUS CAN, SHALL NEVER MELT MINE HONOUR INTO LUST, TO TAKE AWAY THE EDGE OF THAT DAY'S CELEBRATION,
WHEN I SHALL THINK, OR PHOEBUS' STEEDS ARE FOUNDER'D, OR NIGHT KEPT CHAIN'D BELOW.
FAIRLY SPOKE.
SIT THEN, AND TALK WITH HER: SHE IS THINE OWN.
WHAT, ARIEL! MY INDUSTRIOUS SERVANT, ARIEL!
WHAT WOULD MY POTENT MASTER? HERE I AM.
THOU AND THY MEANER FELLOWS YOUR LAST SERVICE DID WORTHILY PERFORM; AND I MUST USE YOU IN SUCH ANOTHER TRICK.

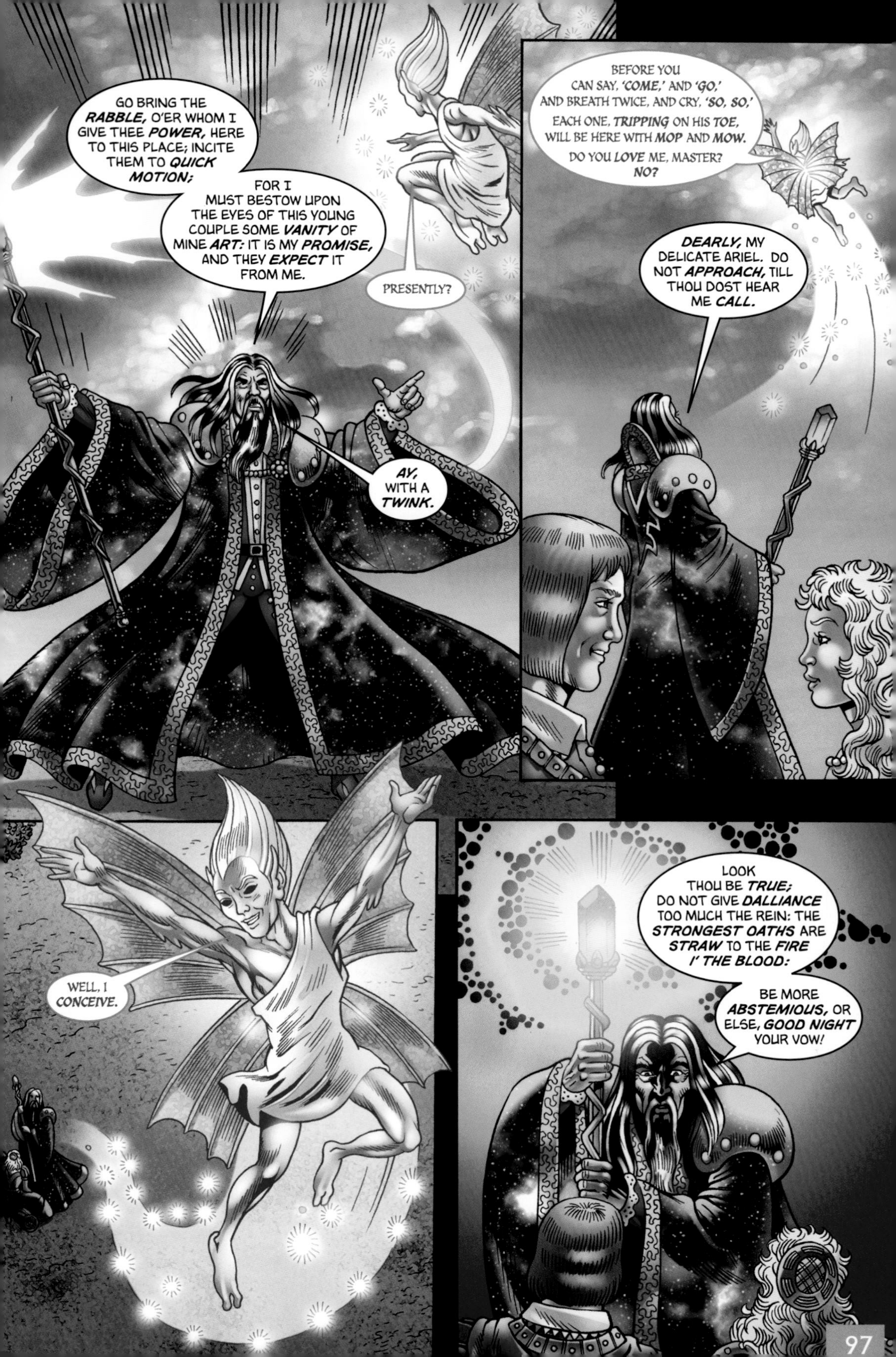
GO BRING THE RABBLE, O'ER WHOM I GIVE THEE POWER, HERE TO THIS PLACE; INCITE THEM TO QUICK MOTION;
FOR I MUST BESTOW UPON THE EYES OF THIS YOUNG COUPLE SOME VANITY OF MINE ART: IT IS MY PROMISE, AND THEY EXPECT IT FROM ME.
PRESENTLY?
AY, WITH A TWINK.
BEFORE YOU CAN SAY, 'COME,' AND 'GO,' AND BREATH TWICE, AND CRY, 'SO, SO,' EACH ONE, TRIPPING ON HIS TOE, WILL BE HERE WITH MOP AND MOW. DO YOU LOVE ME, MASTER? NO?
DEARLY, MY DELICATE ARIEL. DO NOT APPROACH, TILL THOU DOST HEAR ME CALL.
WELL, I CONCEIVE.
LOOK THOU BE TRUE; DO NOT GIVE DALLIANCE TOO MUCH THE REIN: THE STRONGEST OATHS ARE STRAW TO THE FIRE I' THE BLOOD:
BE MORE ABSTEMIOUS, OR ELSE, GOOD NIGHT YOUR VOW!

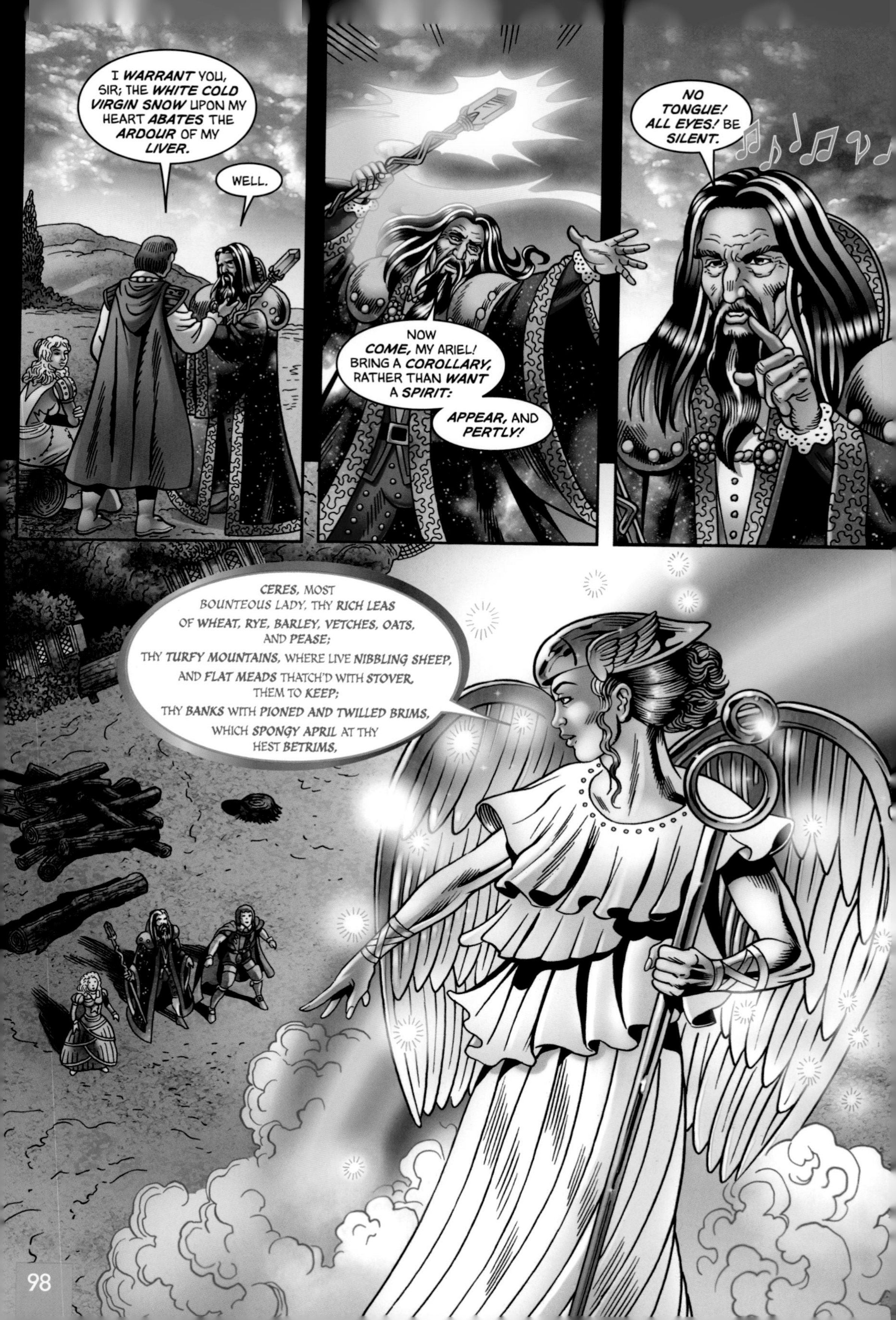

I WARRANT YOU, SIR; THE WHITE COLD VIRGIN SNOW UPON MY HEART ABATES THE ARDOUR OF MY LIVER.
WELL.
NOW COME, MY ARIEL! BRING A COROLLARY, RATHER THAN WANT A SPIRIT:
APPEAR, AND PERTLY!
NO TONGUE! ALL EYES! BE SILENT.
CERES, MOST BOUNTEOUS LADY, THY RICH LEAS OF WHEAT, RYE, BARLEY, VETCHES, OATS, AND PEASE; THY TURFY MOUNTAINS, WHERE LIVE NIBBLING SHEEP, AND FLAT MEADS THATCH'D WITH STOVER, THEM TO KEEP; THY BANKS WITH PIONED AND TWILLED BRIMS, WHICH SPONGY APRIL AT THY HEST BETRIMS,

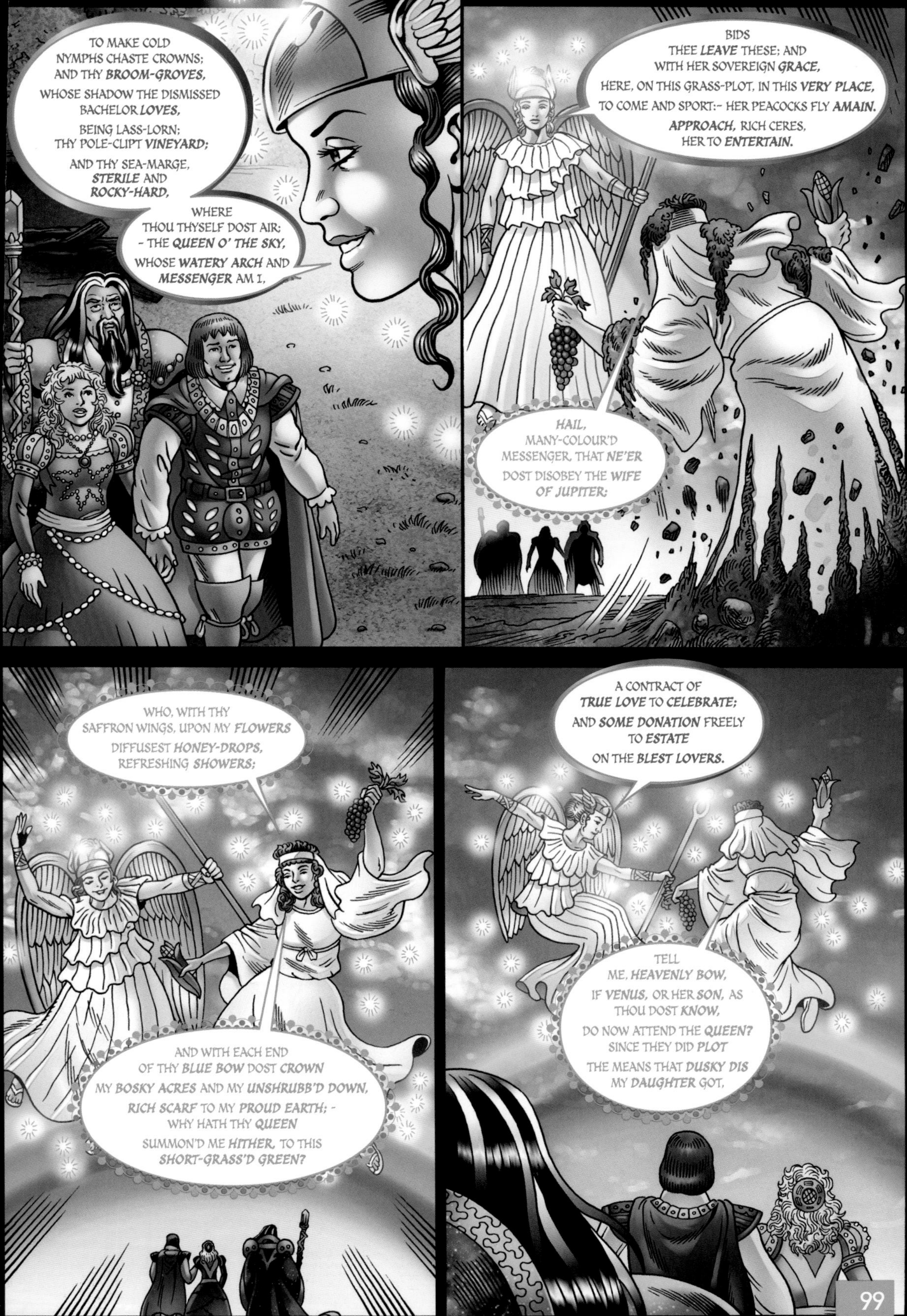
TO MAKE COLD NYMPHS CHASTE CROWNS; AND THY BROOM-GROVES, WHOSE SHADOW THE DISMISSED BACHELOR LOVES, BEING LASS-LORN; THY POLE-CLIPT VINEYARD; AND THY SEA-MARGE, STERILE AND ROCKY-HARD,
WHERE THOU THYSELF DOST AIR: - THE QUEEN O' THE SKY, WHOSE WATERY ARCH AND MESSENGER AM I,
BIDS THEE LEAVE THESE; AND WITH HER SOVEREIGN GRACE, HERE, ON THIS GRASS-PLOT, IN THIS VERY PLACE, TO COME AND SPORT:- HER PEACOCKS FLY AMAIN. APPROACH, RICH CERES, HER TO ENTERTAIN.
HAIL, MANY-COLOUR'D MESSENGER, THAT NE'ER DOST DISOBEY THE WIFE OF JUPITER;
WHO, WITH THY SAFFRON WINGS, UPON MY FLOWERS DIFFUSEST HONEY-DROPS, REFRESHING SHOWERS;
AND WITH EACH END OF THY BLUE BOW DOST CROWN MY BOSKY ACRES AND MY UNSHRUBB'D DOWN, RICH SCARF TO MY PROUD EARTH; - WHY HATH THY QUEEN SUMMON'D ME HITHER, TO THIS SHORT-GRASS'D GREEN?
A CONTRACT OF TRUE LOVE TO CELEBRATE; AND SOME DONATION FREELY TO ESTATE ON THE BLEST LOVERS.
TELL ME, HEAVENLY BOW, IF VENUS, OR HER SON, AS THOU DOST KNOW, DO NOW ATTEND THE QUEEN? SINCE THEY DID PLOT THE MEANS THAT DUSKY DIS MY DAUGHTER GOT,

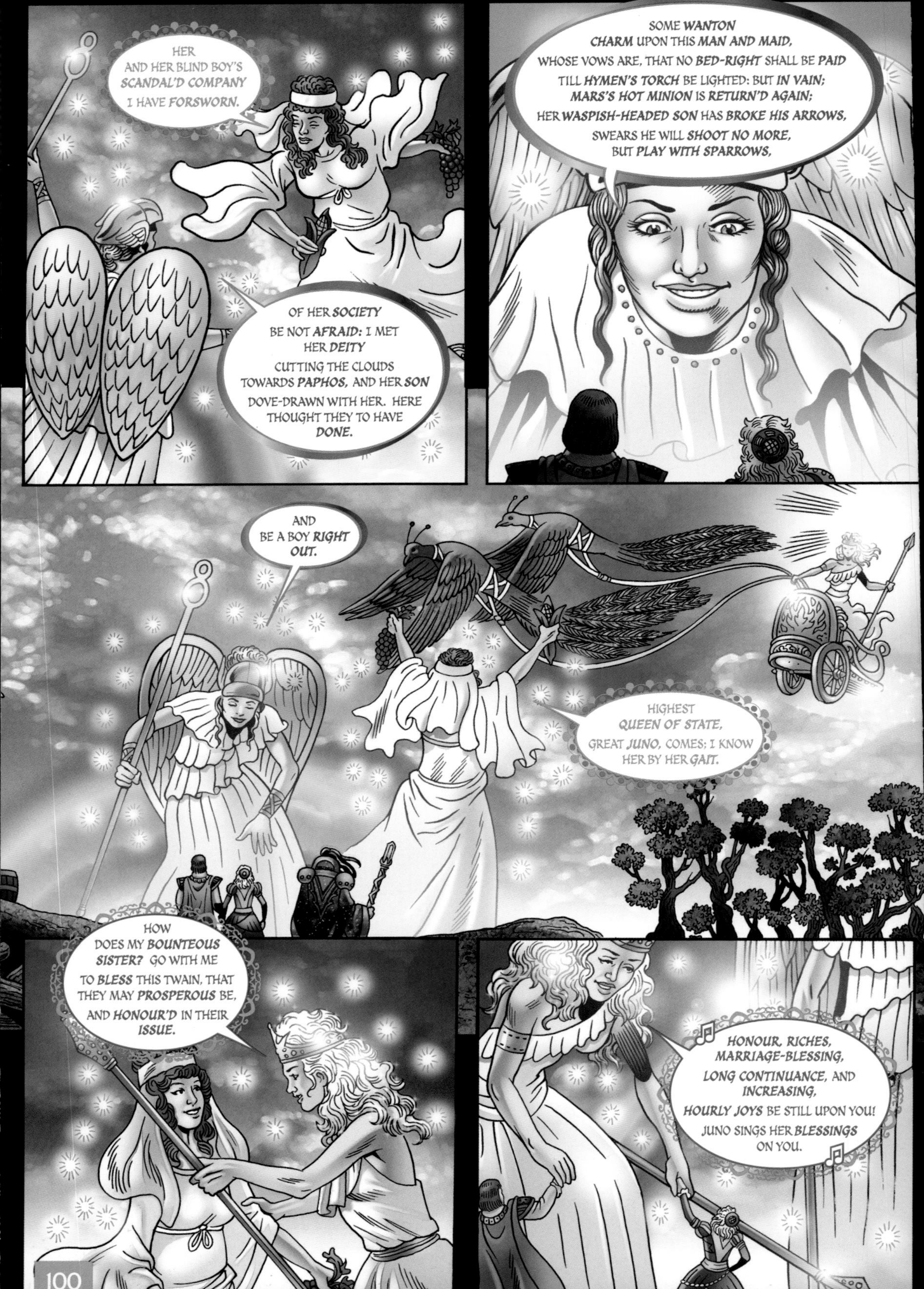
HER AND HER BLIND BOY'S SCANDAL'D COMPANY I HAVE FORSWORN.
OF HER SOCIETY BE NOT AFRAID: I MET HER DEITY CUTTING THE CLOUDS TOWARDS PAPHOS, AND HER SON DOVE-DRAWN WITH HER. HERE THOUGHT THEY TO HAVE DONE.
SOME WANTON CHARM UPON THIS MAN AND MAID, WHOSE VOWS ARE, THAT NO BED-RIGHT SHALL BE PAID TILL HYMEN'S TORCH BE LIGHTED: BUT IN VAIN; MARS'S HOT MINION IS RETURN'D AGAIN; HER WASPISH-HEADED SON HAS BROKE HIS ARROWS, SWEARS HE WILL SHOOT NO MORE, BUT PLAY WITH SPARROWS,
AND BE A BOY RIGHT OUT.
HIGHEST QUEEN OF STATE, GREAT JUNO, COMES; I KNOW HER BY HER GAIT.
HOW DOES MY BOUNTEOUS SISTER? GO WITH ME TO BLESS THIS TWAIN, THAT THEY MAY PROSPEROUS BE, AND HONOUR'D IN THEIR ISSUE.
HONOUR, RICHES, MARRIAGE-BLESSING, LONG CONTINUANCE, AND INCREASING, HOURLY JOYS BE STILL UPON YOU! JUNO SINGS HER BLESSINGS ON YOU.

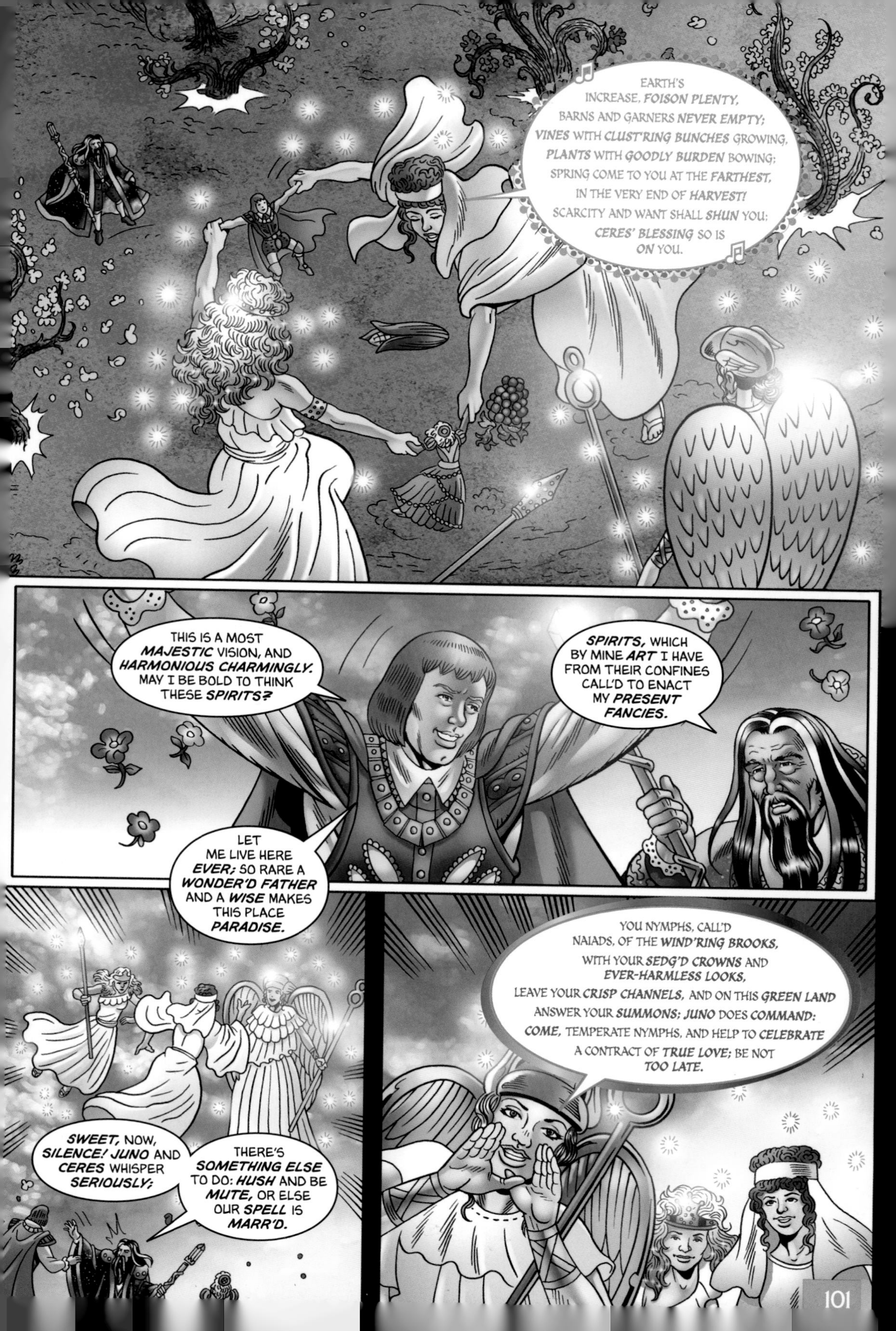
EARTH'S INCREASE, FOISON PLENTY, BARNS AND GARNERS NEVER EMPTY; VINES WITH CLUST'RING BUNCHES GROWING, PLANTS WITH GOODLY BURDEN BOWING; SPRING COME TO YOU AT THE FARTHEST, IN THE VERY END OF HARVEST! SCARCITY AND WANT SHALL SHUN YOU; CERES' BLESSING SO IS ON YOU.
THIS IS A MOST MAJESTIC VISION, AND HARMONIOUS CHARMINGLY. MAY I BE BOLD TO THINK THESE SPIRITS?
SPIRITS, WHICH BY MINE ART I HAVE FROM THEIR CONFINES CALL'D TO ENACT MY PRESENT FANCIES.
LET ME LIVE HERE EVER; SO RARE A WONDER'D FATHER AND A WISE MAKES THIS PLACE PARADISE.
SWEET, NOW, SILENCE! JUNO AND CERES WHISPER SERIOUSLY;
THERE'S SOMETHING ELSE TO DO: HUSH AND BE MUTE, OR ELSE OUR SPELL IS MARR'D.
YOU NYMPHS, CALL'D NAIADS, OF THE WIND'RING BROOKS, WITH YOUR SEDG'D CROWNS AND EVER-HARMLESS LOOKS, LEAVE YOUR CRISP CHANNELS, AND ON THIS GREEN LAND ANSWER YOUR SUMMONS; JUNO DOES COMMAND: COME, TEMPERATE NYMPHS, AND HELP TO CELEBRATE A CONTRACT OF TRUE LOVE; BE NOT TOO LATE.

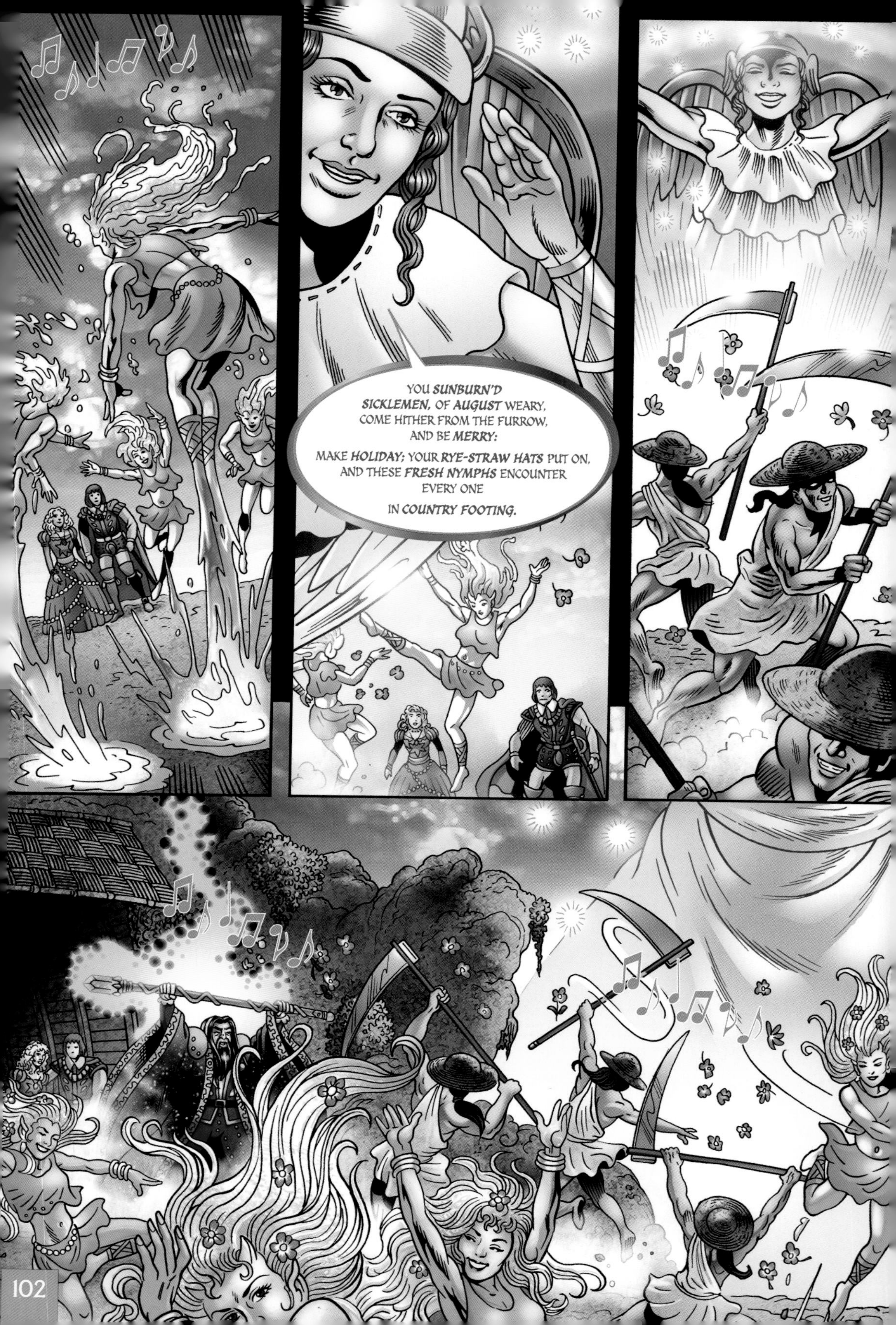
YOU SUNBURN'D SICKLEMEN, OF AUGUST WEARY,
COME HITHER FROM THE FURROW,
AND BE MERRY:
MAKE HOLIDAY: YOUR RYE-STRAW HATS PUT ON,
AND THESE FRESH NYMPHS ENCOUNTER
EVERY ONE
IN COUNTRY FOOTING.

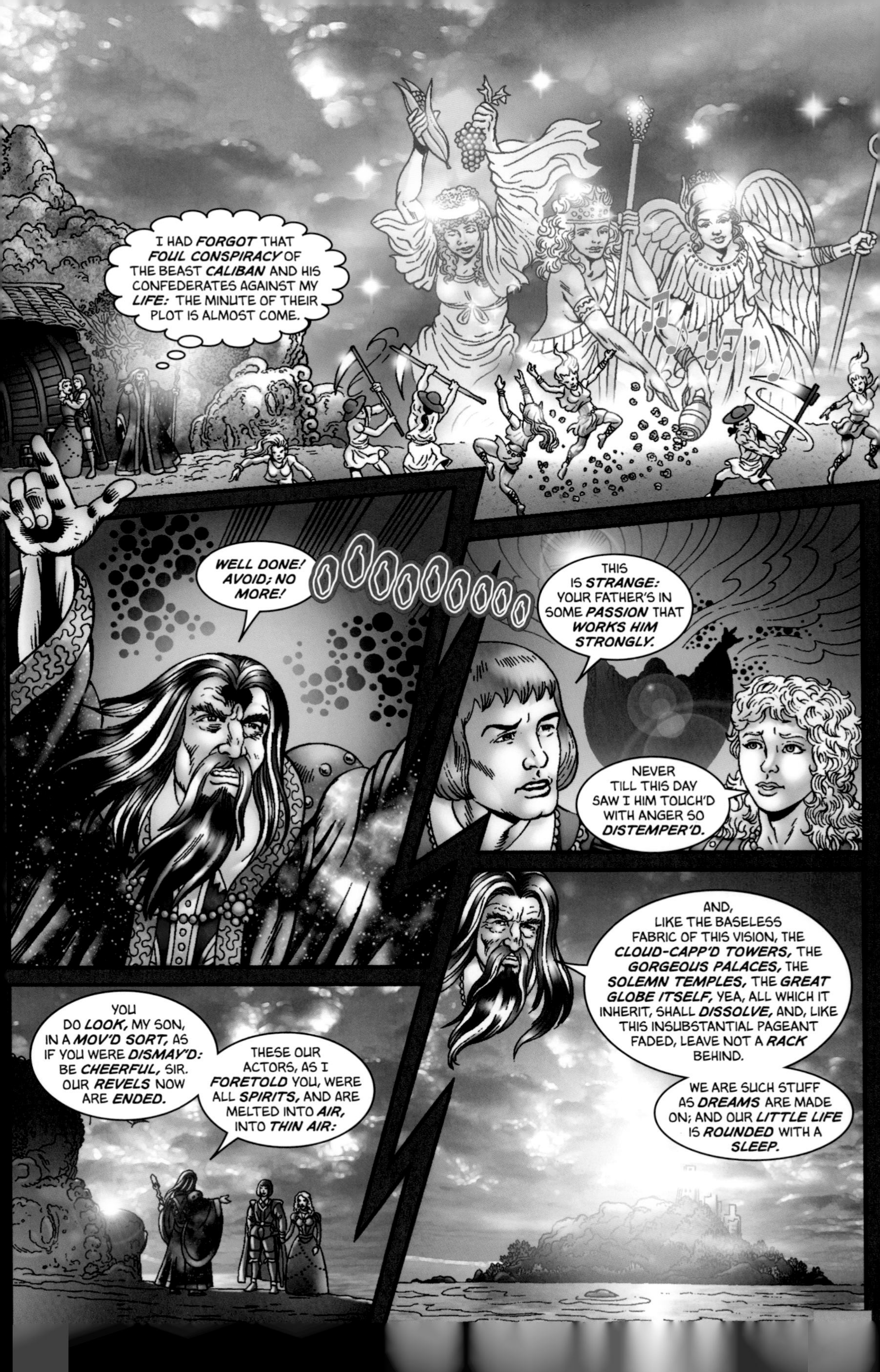
I HAD FORGOT THAT FOUL CONSPIRACY OF THE BEAST CALIBAN AND HIS CONFEDERATES AGAINST MY LIFE: THE MINUTE OF THEIR PLOT IS ALMOST COME.
WELL DONE! AVOID; NO MORE!
THIS IS STRANGE: YOUR FATHER'S IN SOME PASSION THAT WORKS HIM STRONGLY.
NEVER TILL THIS DAY SAW I HIM TOUCH'D WITH ANGER SO DISTEMPER'D.
YOU DO LOOK, MY SON, IN A MOV'D SORT, AS IF YOU WERE DISMAY'D: BE CHEERFUL, SIR. OUR REVELS NOW ARE ENDED.
THESE OUR ACTORS, AS I FORETOLD YOU, WERE ALL SPIRITS, AND ARE MELTED INTO AIR, INTO THIN AIR:
AND, LIKE THE BASELESS FABRIC OF THIS VISION, THE CLOUD-CAPP'D TOWERS, THE GORGEOUS PALACES, THE SOLEMN TEMPLES, THE GREAT GLOBE ITSELF, YEA, ALL WHICH IT INHERIT, SHALL DISSOLVE, AND, LIKE THIS INSUBSTANTIAL PAGEANT FADED, LEAVE NOT A RACK BEHIND.
WE ARE SUCH STUFF AS DREAMS ARE MADE ON; AND OUR LITTLE LIFE IS ROUNDED WITH A SLEEP.

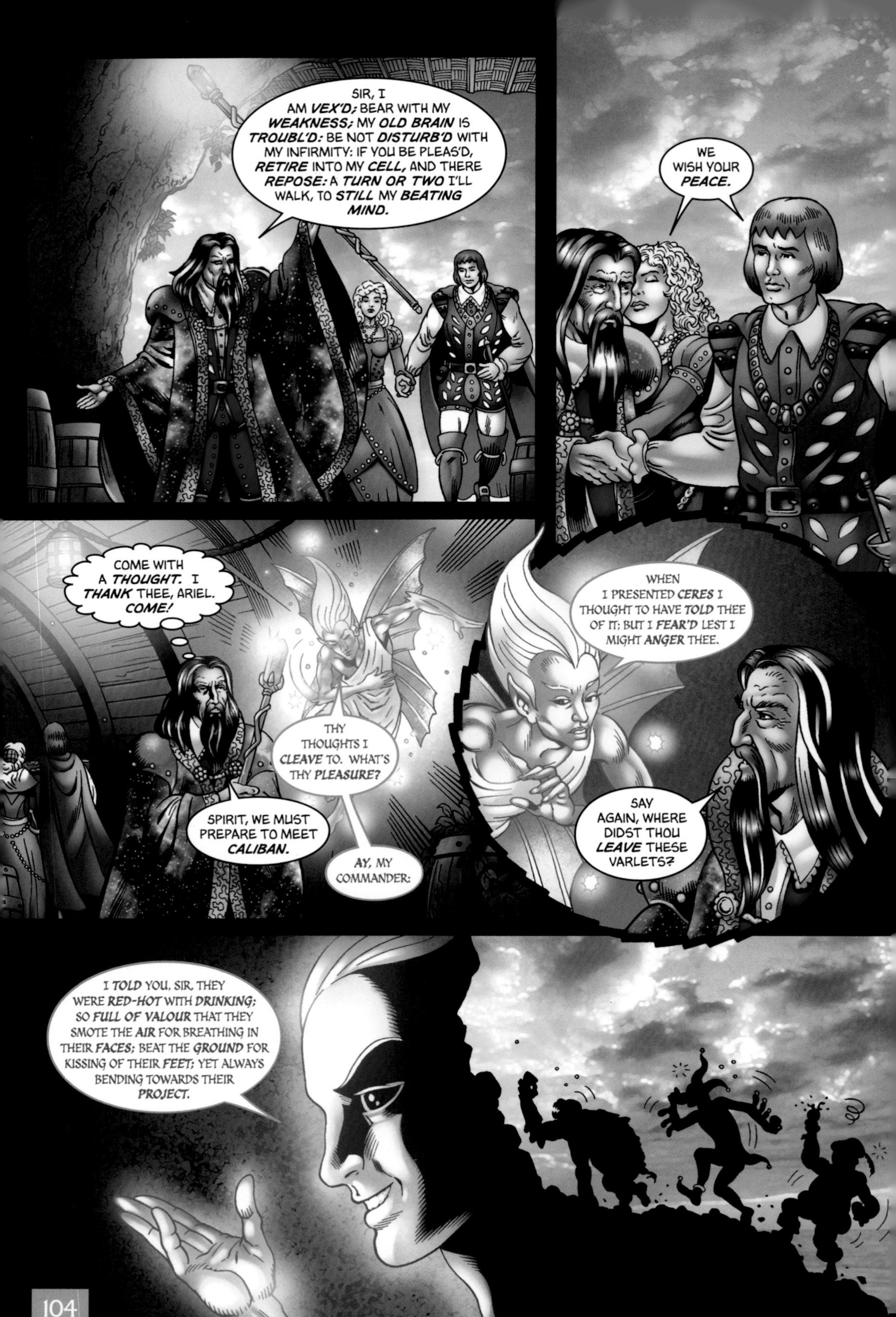
SIR, I AM VEX'D; BEAR WITH MY WEAKNESS; MY OLD BRAIN IS TROUBL'D: BE NOT DISTURB'D WITH MY INFIRMITY: IF YOU BE PLEAS'D, RETIRE INTO MY CELL, AND THERE REPOSE: A TURN OR TWO I'LL WALK, TO STILL MY BEATING MIND.
WE WISH YOUR PEACE.
COME WITH A THOUGHT. I THANK THEE, ARIEL. COME!
THY THOUGHTS I CLEAVE TO. WHAT'S THY PLEASURE?
SPIRIT, WE MUST PREPARE TO MEET CALIBAN.
AY, MY COMMANDER:
WHEN I PRESENTED CERES I THOUGHT TO HAVE TOLD THEE OF IT; BUT I FEAR'D LEST I MIGHT ANGER THEE.
SAY AGAIN, WHERE DIDST THOU LEAVE THESE VARLETS?
I TOLD YOU, SIR, THEY WERE RED-HOT WITH DRINKING; SO FULL OF VALOUR THAT THEY SMOTE THE AIR FOR BREATHING IN THEIR FACES; BEAT THE GROUND FOR KISSING OF THEIR FEET; YET ALWAYS BENDING TOWARDS THEIR PROJECT.

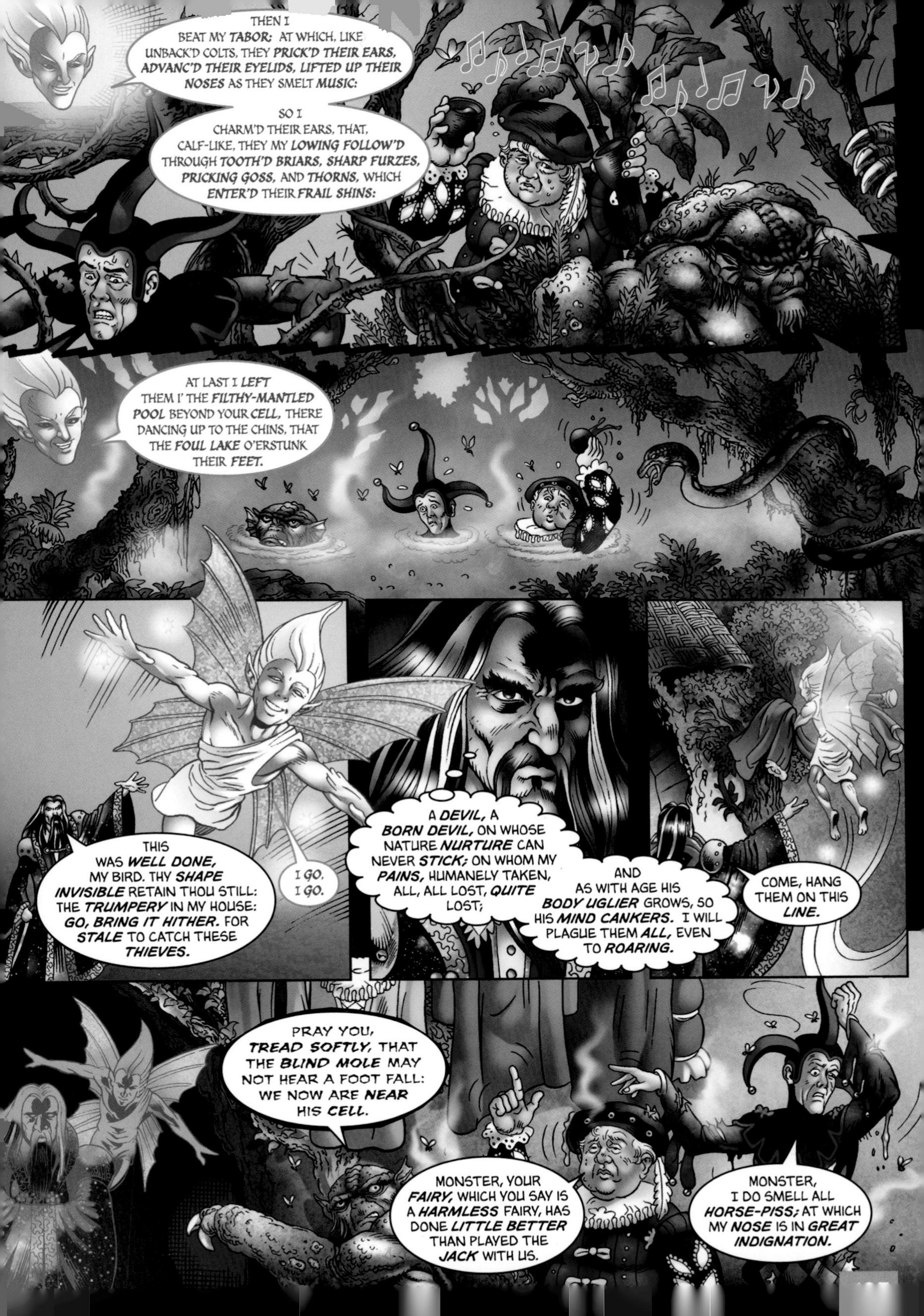

THEN I BEAT MY TABOR: AT WHICH, LIKE UNBACK'D COLTS, THEY PRICK'D THEIR EARS, ADVANC'D THEIR EYELIDS, LIFTED UP THEIR NOSES AS THEY SMELT MUSIC:
SO I CHARM'D THEIR EARS, THAT, CALF-LIKE, THEY MY LOWING FOLLOW'D THROUGH TOOTH'D BRIARS, SHARP FURZES, PRICKING GOSS, AND THORNS, WHICH ENTER'D THEIR FRAIL SHINS:
AT LAST I LEFT THEM I' THE FILTHY-MANTLED POOL BEYOND YOUR CELL, THERE DANCING UP TO THE CHINS, THAT THE FOUL LAKE O'ERSTUNK THEIR FEET.
THIS WAS WELL DONE, MY BIRD. THY SHAPE INVISIBLE RETAIN THOU STILL: THE TRUMPERY IN MY HOUSE: GO, BRING IT HITHER. FOR STALE TO CATCH THESE THIEVES.
I GO, I GO.
A DEVIL, A BORN DEVIL, ON WHOSE NATURE NURTURE CAN NEVER STICK; ON WHOM MY PAINS, HUMANELY TAKEN, ALL, ALL LOST, QUITE LOST;
AND AS WITH AGE HIS BODY UGLIER GROWS, SO HIS MIND CANKERS. I WILL PLAGUE THEM ALL, EVEN TO ROARING.
COME, HANG THEM ON THIS LINE.
PRAY YOU, TREAD SOFTLY, THAT THE BLIND MOLE MAY NOT HEAR A FOOT FALL: WE NOW ARE NEAR HIS CELL.
MONSTER, YOUR FAIRY, WHICH YOU SAY IS A HARMLESS FAIRY, HAS DONE LITTLE BETTER THAN PLAYED THE JACK WITH US.
MONSTER, I DO SMELL ALL HORSE-PISS; AT WHICH MY NOSE IS IN GREAT INDIGNATION.

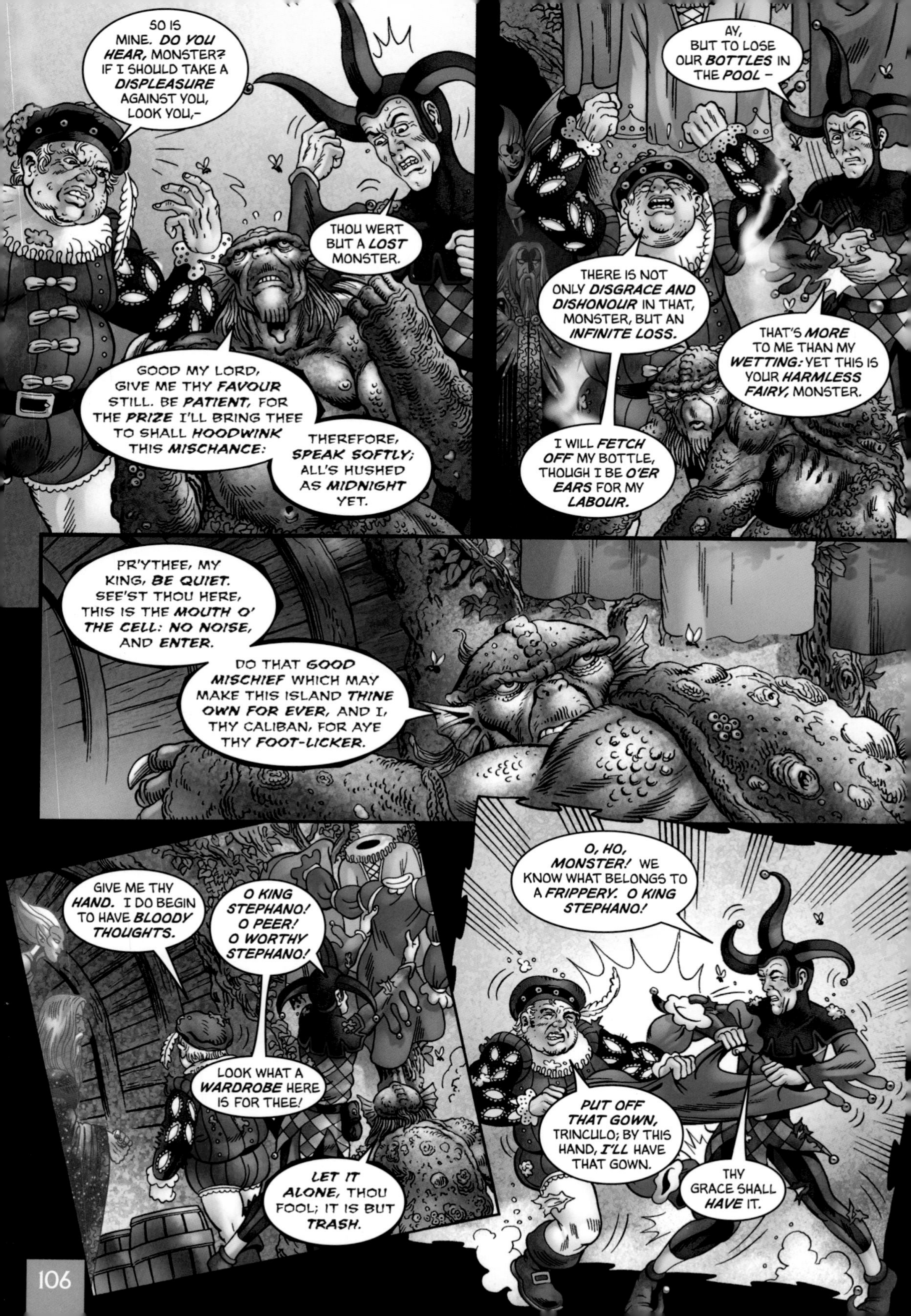
SO IS MINE. DO YOU HEAR, MONSTER? IF I SHOULD TAKE A DISPLEASURE AGAINST YOU, LOOK YOU,-
THOU WERT BUT A LOST MONSTER.
GOOD MY LORD, GIVE ME THY FAVOUR STILL. BE PATIENT, FOR THE PRIZE I'LL BRING THEE TO SHALL HOODWINK THIS MISCHANCE:
THEREFORE, SPEAK SOFTLY; ALL'S HUSHED AS MIDNIGHT YET.
AY, BUT TO LOSE OUR BOTTLES IN THE POOL –
THERE IS NOT ONLY DISGRACE AND DISHONOUR IN THAT, MONSTER, BUT AN INFINITE LOSS.
THAT'S MORE TO ME THAN MY WETTING: YET THIS IS YOUR HARMLESS FAIRY, MONSTER.
I WILL FETCH OFF MY BOTTLE, THOUGH I BE O'ER EARS FOR MY LABOUR.
PR'YTHEE, MY KING, BE QUIET. SEE'ST THOU HERE, THIS IS THE MOUTH O' THE CELL: NO NOISE, AND ENTER.
DO THAT GOOD MISCHIEF WHICH MAY MAKE THIS ISLAND THINE OWN FOR EVER, AND I, THY CALIBAN, FOR AYE THY FOOT-LICKER.
GIVE ME THY HAND. I DO BEGIN TO HAVE BLOODY THOUGHTS.
O KING STEPHANO! O PEER! O WORTHY STEPHANO!
LOOK WHAT A WARDROBE HERE IS FOR THEE!
LET IT ALONE, THOU FOOL; IT IS BUT TRASH.
O, HO, MONSTER! WE KNOW WHAT BELONGS TO A FRIPPERY. O KING STEPHANO!
PUT OFF THAT GOWN, TRINCULO; BY THIS HAND, I'LL HAVE THAT GOWN.
THY GRACE SHALL HAVE IT.

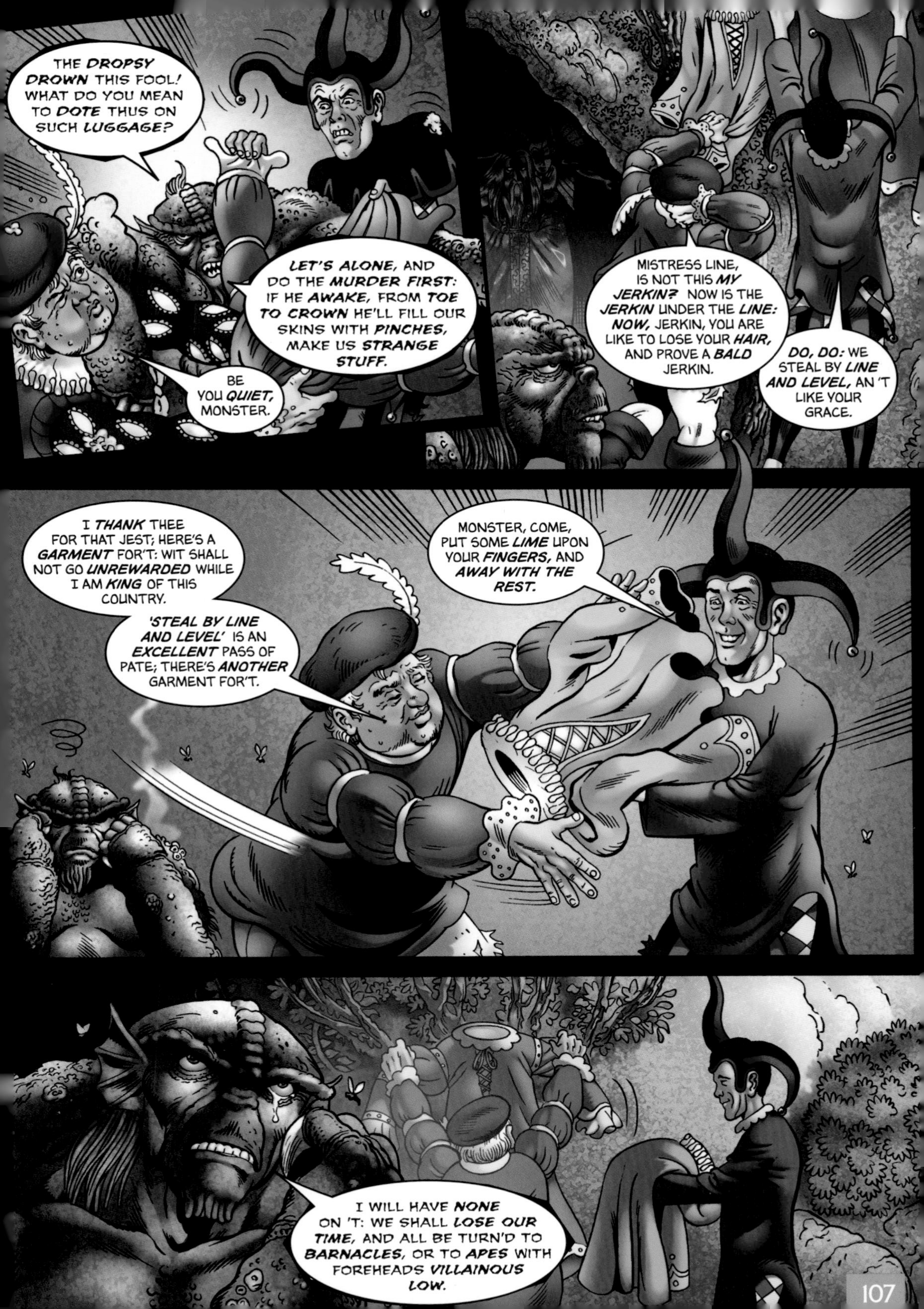
THE DROPSY DROWN THIS FOOL! WHAT DO YOU MEAN TO DOTE THUS ON SUCH LUGGAGE?
LET'S ALONE, AND DO THE MURDER FIRST: IF HE AWAKE, FROM TOE TO CROWN HE'LL FILL OUR SKINS WITH PINCHES, MAKE US STRANGE STUFF.
BE YOU QUIET, MONSTER.
MISTRESS LINE, IS NOT THIS MY JERKIN? NOW IS THE JERKIN UNDER THE LINE: NOW, JERKIN, YOU ARE LIKE TO LOSE YOUR HAIR, AND PROVE A BALD JERKIN.
DO, DO: WE STEAL BY LINE AND LEVEL, AN 'T LIKE YOUR GRACE.
I THANK THEE FOR THAT JEST; HERE'S A GARMENT FOR'T: WIT SHALL NOT GO UNREWARDED WHILE I AM KING OF THIS COUNTRY.
'STEAL BY LINE AND LEVEL' IS AN EXCELLENT PASS OF PATE; THERE'S ANOTHER GARMENT FOR'T.
MONSTER, COME, PUT SOME LIME UPON YOUR FINGERS, AND AWAY WITH THE REST.
I WILL HAVE NONE ON 'T: WE SHALL LOSE OUR TIME, AND ALL BE TURN'D TO BARNACLES, OR TO APES WITH FOREHEADS VILLAINOUS LOW.

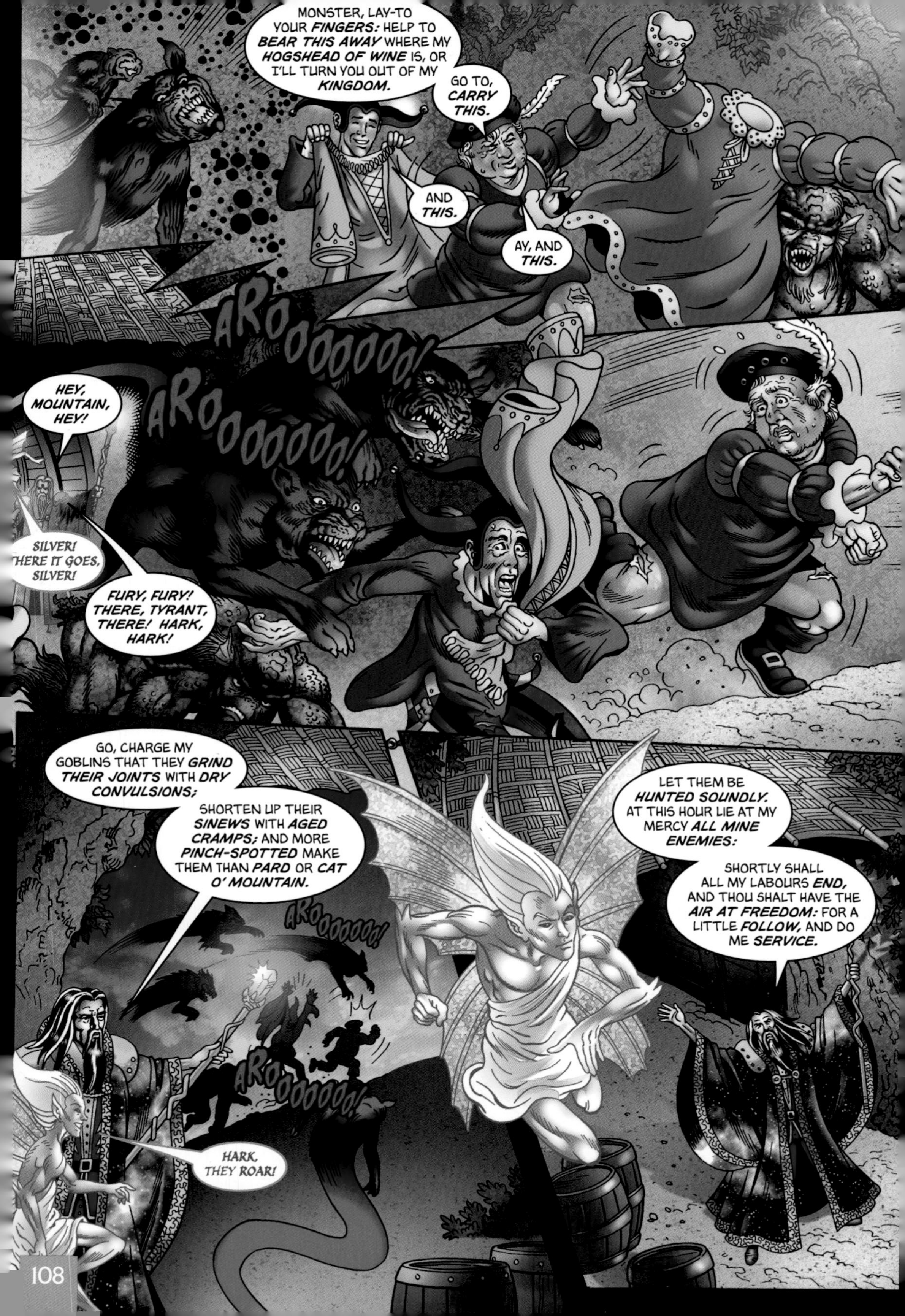

MONSTER, LAY-TO YOUR FINGERS: HELP TO BEAR THIS AWAY WHERE MY HOGSHEAD OF WINE IS, OR I'LL TURN YOU OUT OF MY KINGDOM.
GO TO, CARRY THIS.
AND THIS.
AY, AND THIS.
AROOOOOOOO!
AROOOOOOOO!
HEY, MOUNTAIN, HEY!
SILVER! THERE IT GOES, SILVER!
FURY, FURY! THERE, TYRANT, THERE! HARK, HARK!
GO, CHARGE MY GOBLINS THAT THEY GRIND THEIR JOINTS WITH DRY CONVULSIONS;
SHORTEN UP THEIR SINEWS WITH AGED CRAMPS; AND MORE PINCH-SPOTTED MAKE THEM THAN PARD OR CAT O' MOUNTAIN.
AROOOOOOO!
AROOOOOOO!
HARK, THEY ROAR!
LET THEM BE HUNTED SOUNDLY. AT THIS HOUR LIE AT MY MERCY ALL MINE ENEMIES:
SHORTLY SHALL ALL MY LABOURS END, AND THOU SHALT HAVE THE AIR AT FREEDOM: FOR A LITTLE FOLLOW, AND DO ME SERVICE.

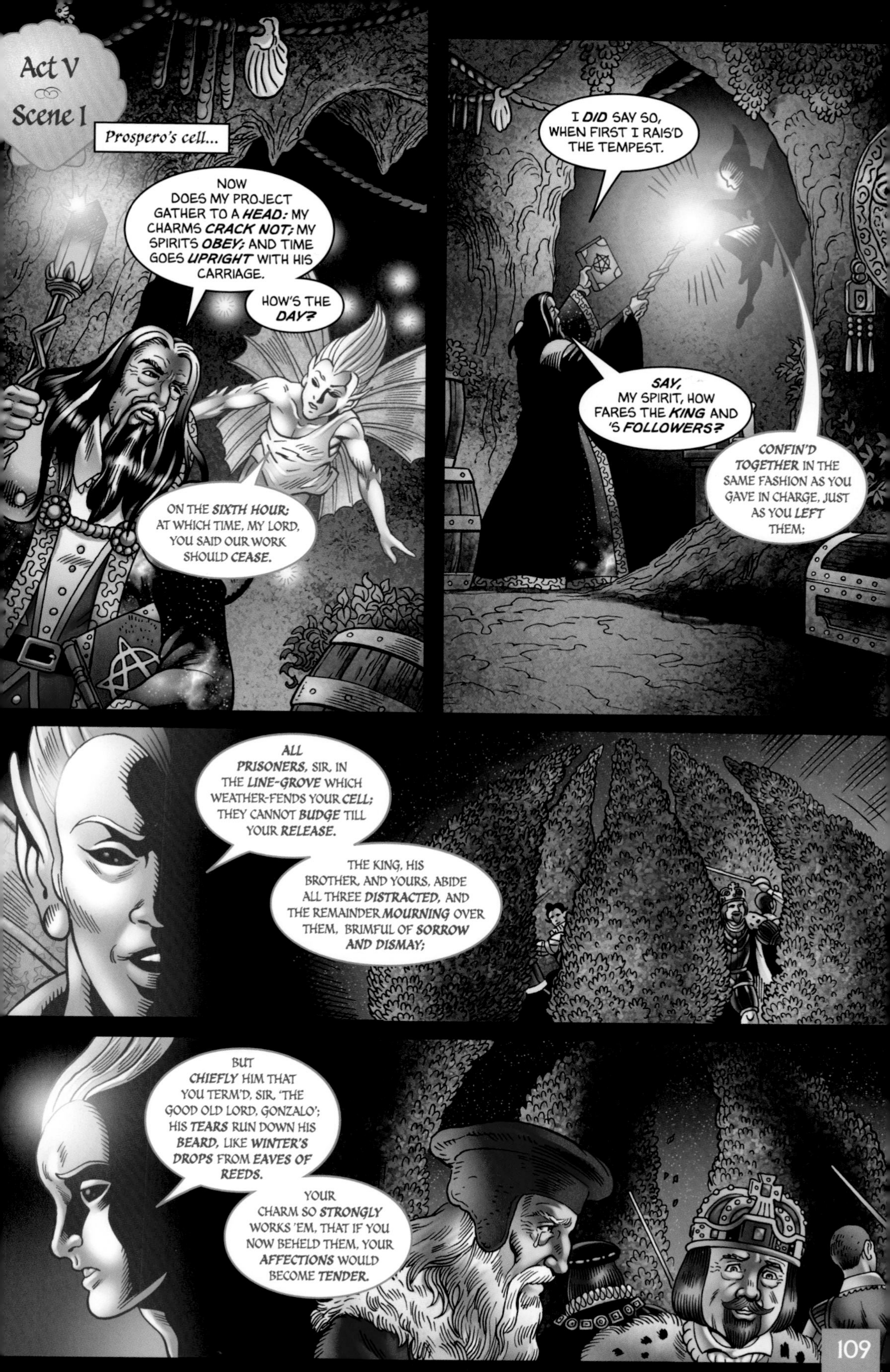
Act V
Scene I
Prospero's cell...
NOW DOES MY PROJECT GATHER TO A HEAD: MY CHARMS CRACK NOT; MY SPIRITS OBEY; AND TIME GOES UPRIGHT WITH HIS CARRIAGE.
HOW'S THE DAY?
ON THE SIXTH HOUR: AT WHICH TIME, MY LORD, YOU SAID OUR WORK SHOULD CEASE.
I DID SAY SO, WHEN FIRST I RAIS'D THE TEMPEST.
SAY, MY SPIRIT, HOW FARES THE KING AND 'S FOLLOWERS?
CONFIN'D TOGETHER IN THE SAME FASHION AS YOU GAVE IN CHARGE, JUST AS YOU LEFT THEM;
ALL PRISONERS, SIR, IN THE LINE-GROVE WHICH WEATHER-FENDS YOUR CELL; THEY CANNOT BUDGE TILL YOUR RELEASE.
THE KING, HIS BROTHER, AND YOURS, ABIDE ALL THREE DISTRACTED, AND THE REMAINDER MOURNING OVER THEM, BRIMFUL OF SORROW AND DISMAY;
BUT CHIEFLY HIM THAT YOU TERM'D, SIR, 'THE GOOD OLD LORD, GONZALO'; HIS TEARS RUN DOWN HIS BEARD, LIKE WINTER'S DROPS FROM EAVES OF REEDS.
YOUR CHARM SO STRONGLY WORKS 'EM, THAT IF YOU NOW BEHELD THEM, YOUR AFFECTIONS WOULD BECOME TENDER.

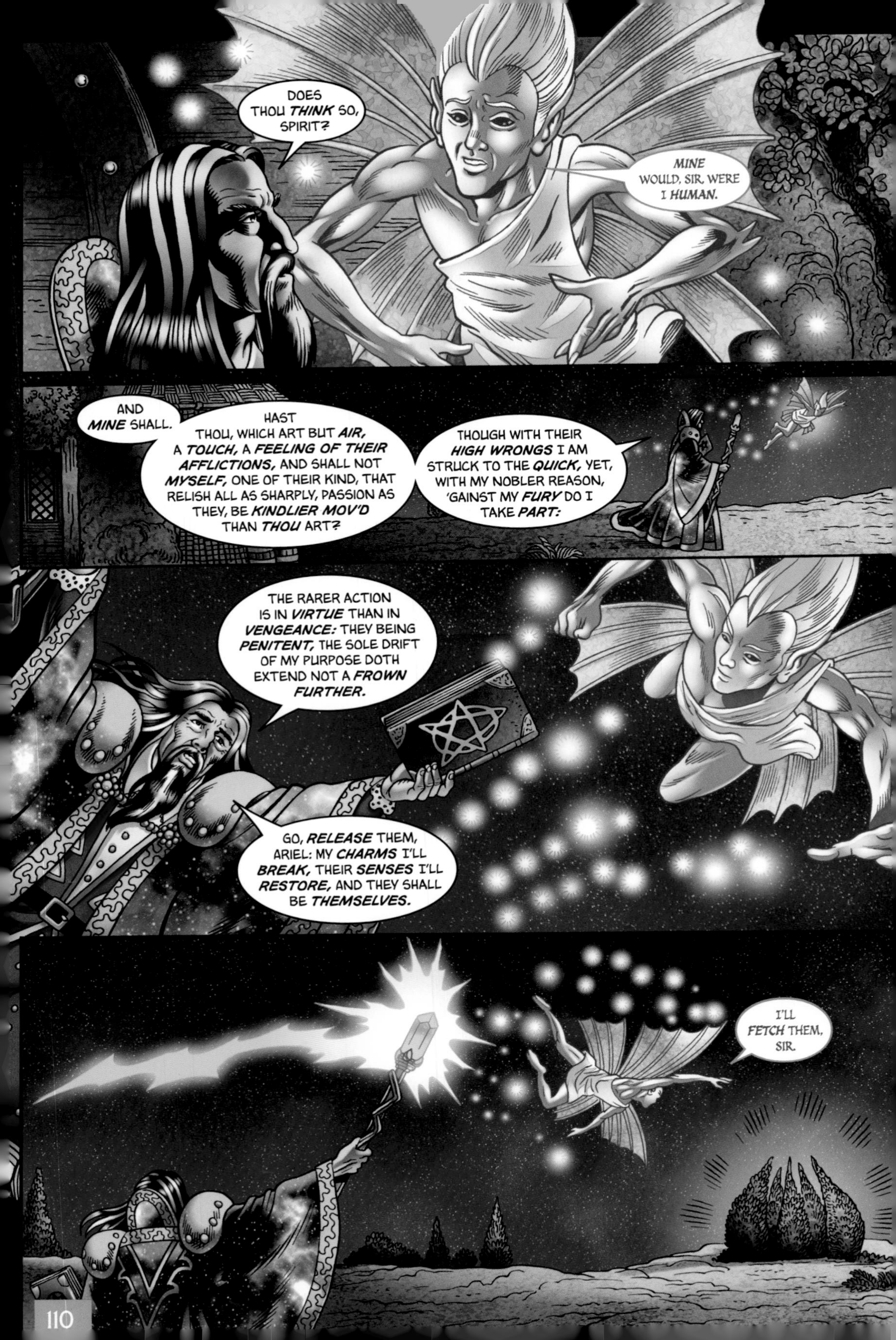

DOES THOU THINK SO, SPIRIT?
MINE WOULD, SIR, WERE I HUMAN.
AND MINE SHALL.
HAST THOU, WHICH ART BUT AIR, A TOUCH, A FEELING OF THEIR AFFLICTIONS, AND SHALL NOT MYSELF, ONE OF THEIR KIND, THAT RELISH ALL AS SHARPLY, PASSION AS THEY, BE KINDLIER MOV'D THAN THOU ART?
THOUGH WITH THEIR HIGH WRONGS I AM STRUCK TO THE QUICK, YET, WITH MY NOBLER REASON, 'GAINST MY FURY DO I TAKE PART:
THE RARER ACTION IS IN VIRTUE THAN IN VENGEANCE: THEY BEING PENITENT, THE SOLE DRIFT OF MY PURPOSE DOTH EXTEND NOT A FROWN FURTHER.
GO, RELEASE THEM, ARIEL: MY CHARMS I'LL BREAK, THEIR SENSES I'LL RESTORE, AND THEY SHALL BE THEMSELVES.
I'LL FETCH THEM, SIR.

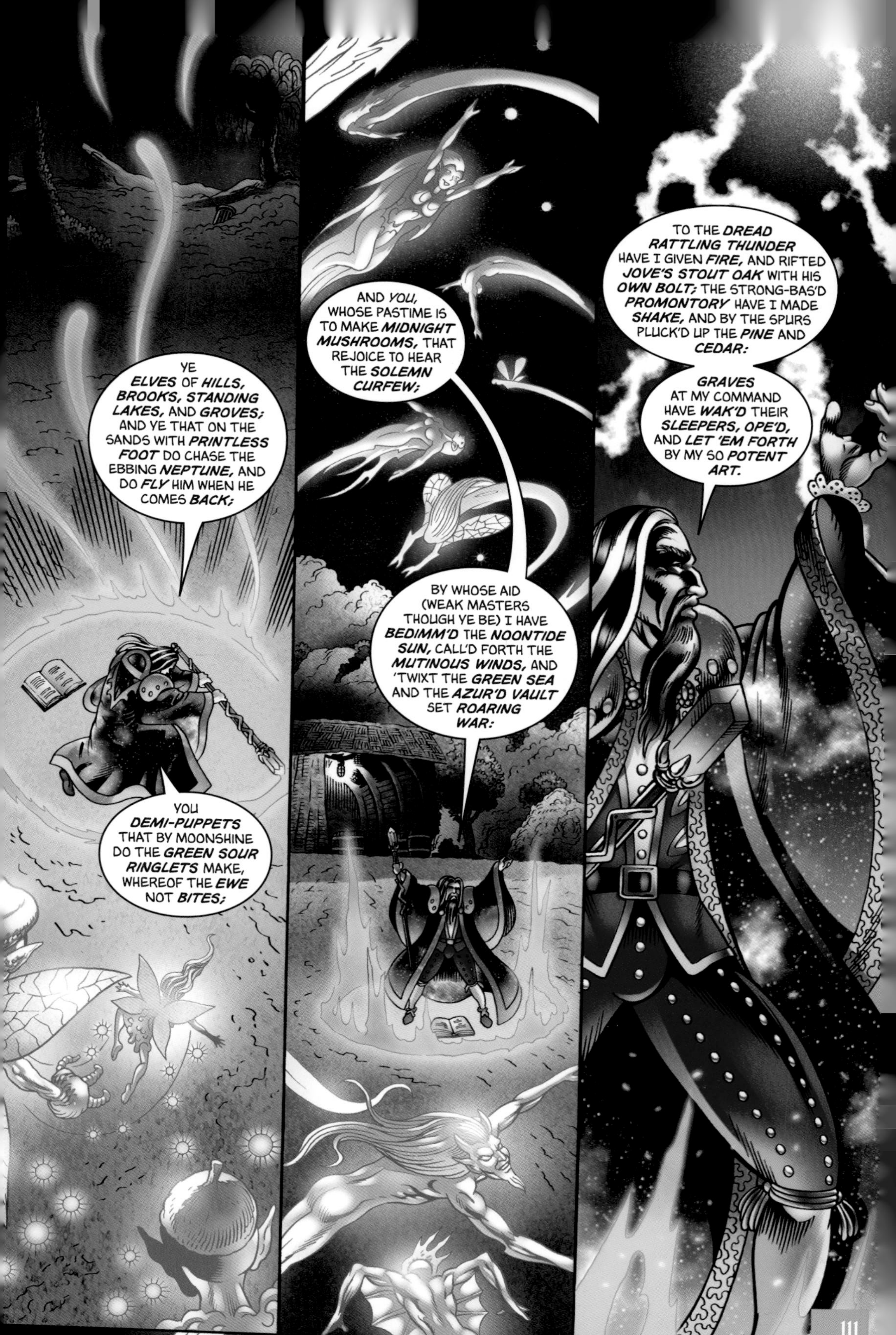
YE ELVES OF HILLS, BROOKS, STANDING LAKES, AND GROVES; AND YE THAT ON THE SANDS WITH PRINTLESS FOOT DO CHASE THE EBBING NEPTUNE, AND DO FLY HIM WHEN HE COMES BACK;
YOU DEMI-PUPPETS THAT BY MOONSHINE DO THE GREEN SOUR RINGLETS MAKE, WHEREOF THE EWE NOT BITES;
AND YOU, WHOSE PASTIME IS TO MAKE MIDNIGHT MUSHROOMS, THAT REJOICE TO HEAR THE SOLEMN CURFEW;
BY WHOSE AID (WEAK MASTERS THOUGH YE BE) I HAVE BEDIMM'D THE NOONTIDE SUN, CALL'D FORTH THE MUTINOUS WINDS, AND 'TWIXT THE GREEN SEA AND THE AZUR'D VAULT SET ROARING WAR:
TO THE DREAD RATTLING THUNDER HAVE I GIVEN FIRE, AND RIFTED JOVE'S STOUT OAK WITH HIS OWN BOLT; THE STRONG-BAS'D PROMONTORY HAVE I MADE SHAKE, AND BY THE SPURS PLUCK'D UP THE PINE AND CEDAR:
GRAVES AT MY COMMAND HAVE WAK'D THEIR SLEEPERS, OPE'D, AND LET 'EM FORTH BY MY SO POTENT ART.

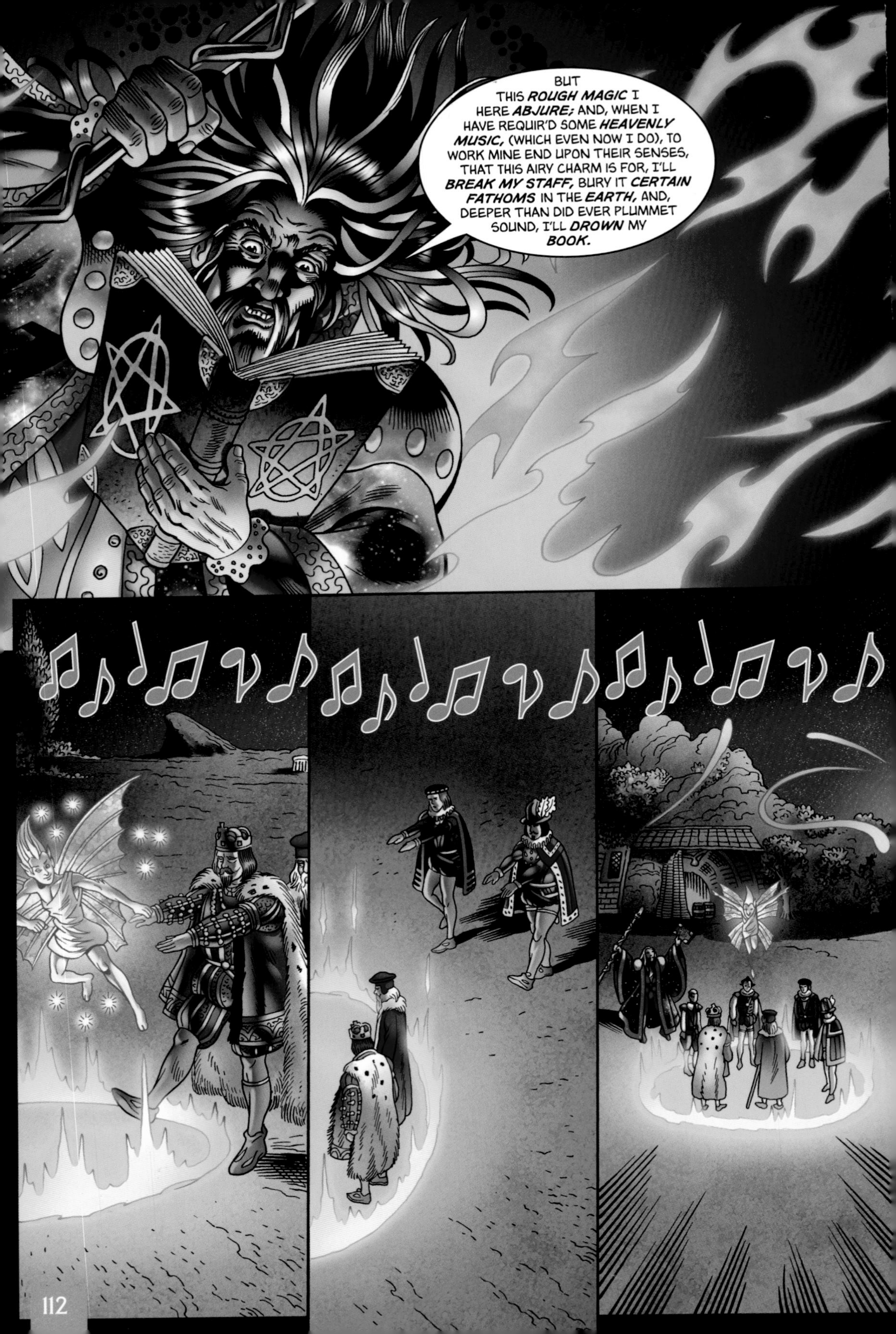
BUT THIS ROUGH MAGIC I HERE ABJURE; AND, WHEN I HAVE REQUIR'D SOME HEAVENLY MUSIC, (WHICH EVEN NOW I DO), TO WORK MINE END UPON THEIR SENSES, THAT THIS AIRY CHARM IS FOR, I'LL BREAK MY STAFF, BURY IT CERTAIN FATHOMS IN THE EARTH, AND, DEEPER THAN DID EVER PLUMMET SOUND, I'LL DROWN MY BOOK.

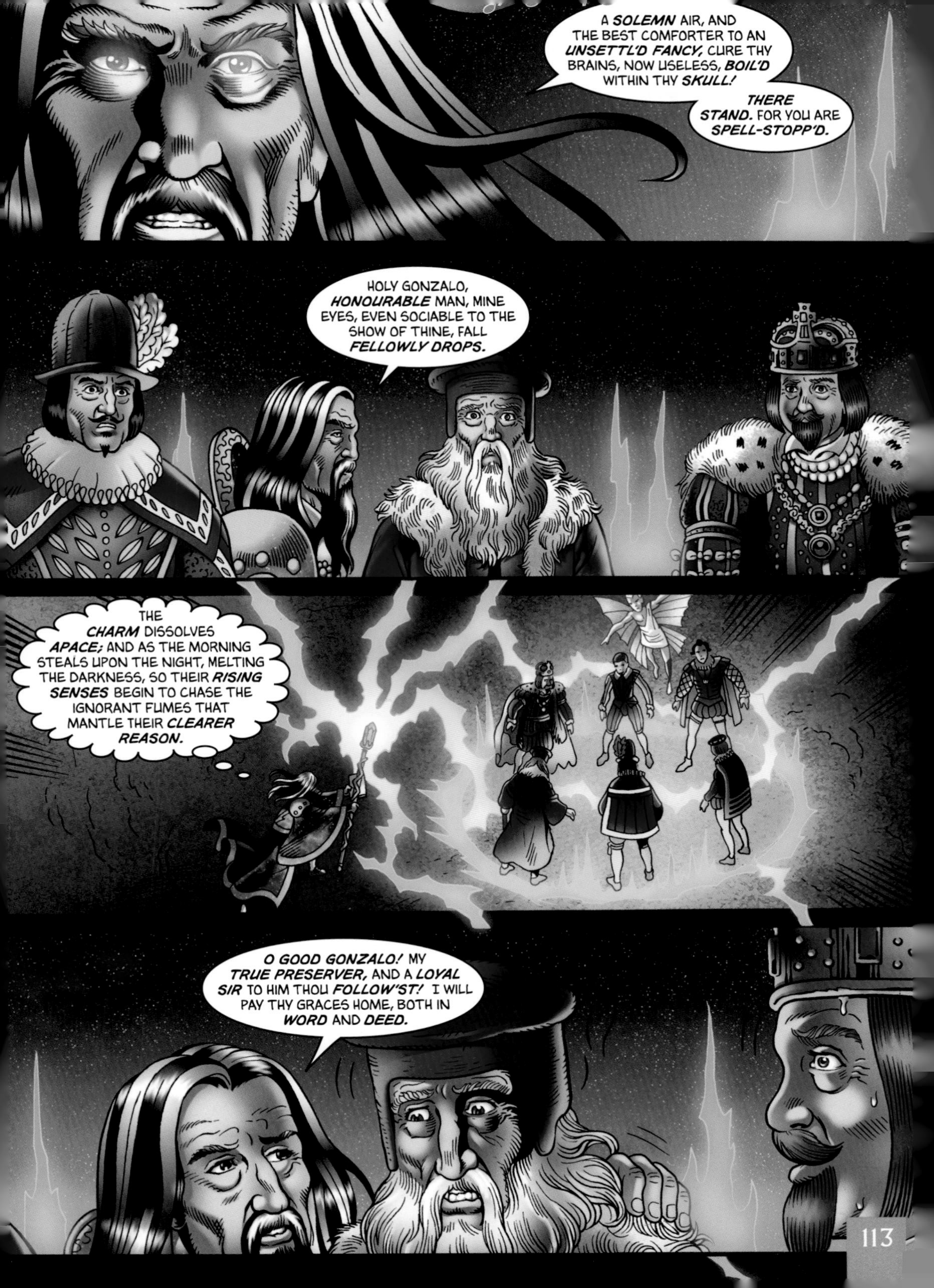
A SOLEMN AIR, AND THE BEST COMFORTER TO AN UNSETTL'D FANCY, CURE THY BRAINS, NOW USELESS, BOIL'D WITHIN THY SKULL!
THERE STAND. FOR YOU ARE SPELL-STOPP'D.
HOLY GONZALO, HONOURABLE MAN, MINE EYES, EVEN SOCIABLE TO THE SHOW OF THINE, FALL FELLOWLY DROPS.
THE CHARM DISSOLVES APACE; AND AS THE MORNING STEALS UPON THE NIGHT, MELTING THE DARKNESS, SO THEIR RISING SENSES BEGIN TO CHASE THE IGNORANT FUMES THAT MANTLE THEIR CLEARER REASON.
O GOOD GONZALO! MY TRUE PRESERVER, AND A LOYAL SIR TO HIM THOU FOLLOW'ST! I WILL PAY THY GRACES HOME, BOTH IN WORD AND DEED.

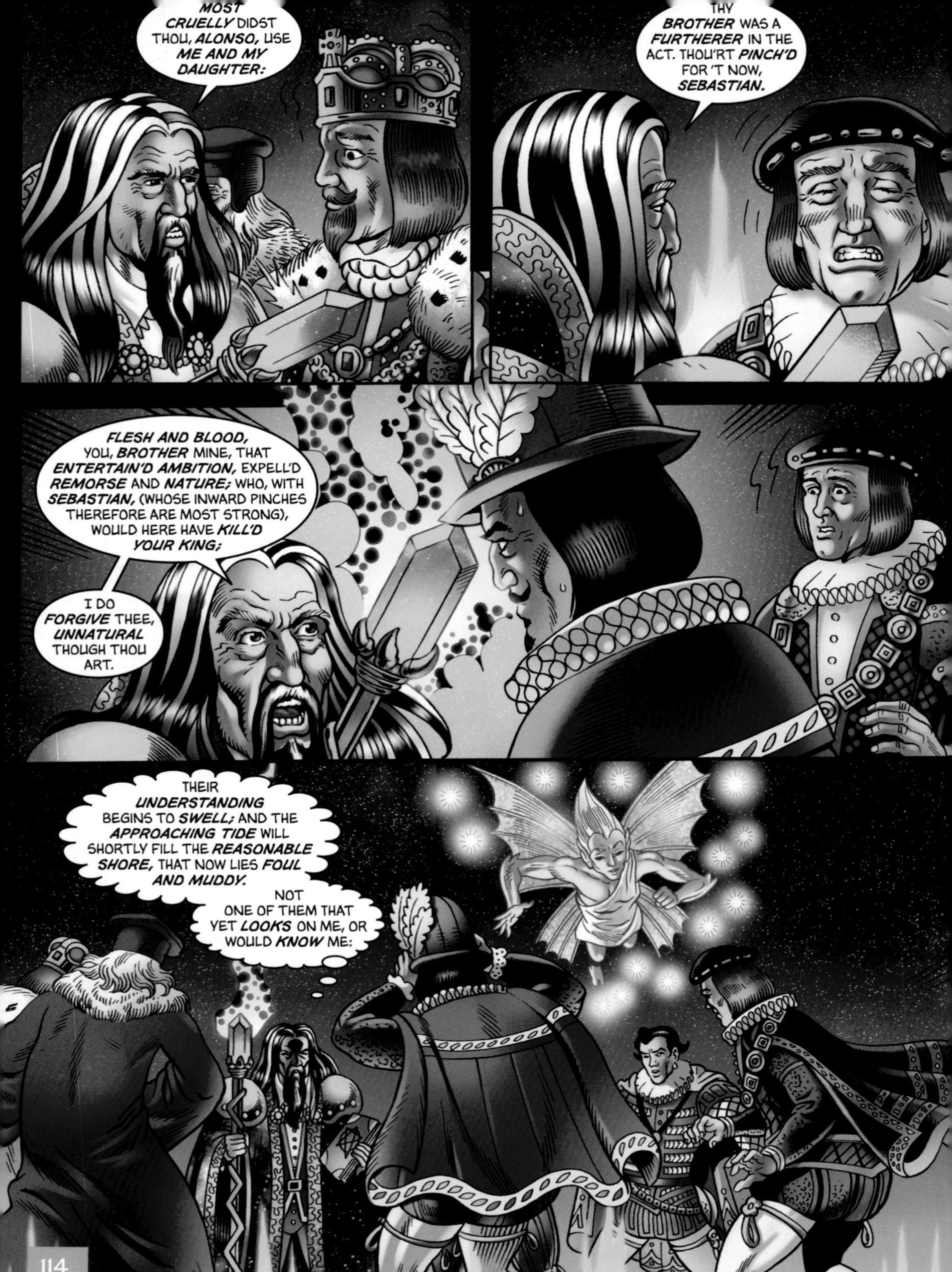

MOST CRUELLY DIDST THOU, ALONSO, USE ME AND MY DAUGHTER:
THY BROTHER WAS A FURTHERER IN THE ACT. THOU'RT PINCH'D FOR 'T NOW, SEBASTIAN.
FLESH AND BLOOD, YOU, BROTHER MINE, THAT ENTERTAIN'D AMBITION, EXPELL'D REMORSE AND NATURE; WHO, WITH SEBASTIAN, (WHOSE INWARD PINCHES THEREFORE ARE MOST STRONG), WOULD HERE HAVE KILL'D YOUR KING;
I DO FORGIVE THEE, UNNATURAL THOUGH THOU ART.
THEIR UNDERSTANDING BEGINS TO SWELL; AND THE APPROACHING TIDE WILL SHORTLY FILL THE REASONABLE SHORE, THAT NOW LIES FOUL AND MUDDY.
NOT ONE OF THEM THAT YET LOOKS ON ME, OR WOULD KNOW ME:

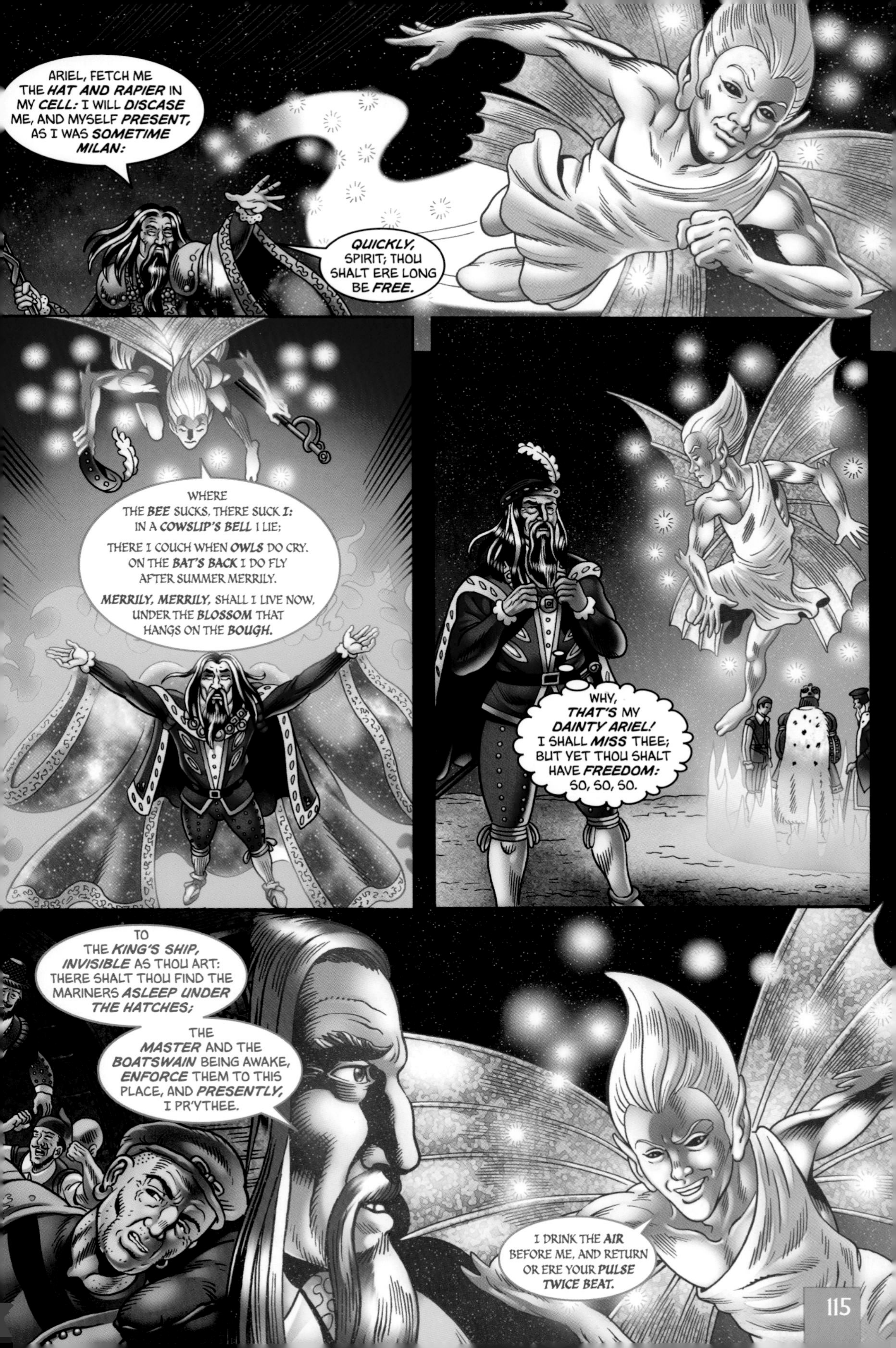
ARIEL, FETCH ME THE HAT AND RAPIER IN MY CELL: I WILL DISCASE ME, AND MYSELF PRESENT, AS I WAS SOMETIME MILAN:
QUICKLY, SPIRIT; THOU SHALT ERE LONG BE FREE.
WHERE THE BEE SUCKS, THERE SUCK I: IN A COWSLIP'S BELL I LIE; THERE I COUCH WHEN OWLS DO CRY. ON THE BAT'S BACK I DO FLY AFTER SUMMER MERRILY. MERRILY, MERRILY, SHALL I LIVE NOW, UNDER THE BLOSSOM THAT HANGS ON THE BOUGH.
WHY, THAT'S MY DAINTY ARIEL! I SHALL MISS THEE; BUT YET THOU SHALT HAVE FREEDOM: SO, SO, SO.
TO THE KING'S SHIP, INVISIBLE AS THOU ART: THERE SHALT THOU FIND THE MARINERS ASLEEP UNDER THE HATCHES;
THE MASTER AND THE BOATSWAIN BEING AWAKE, ENFORCE THEM TO THIS PLACE, AND PRESENTLY, I PR'YTHEE.
I DRINK THE AIR BEFORE ME, AND RETURN OR ERE YOUR PULSE TWICE BEAT.

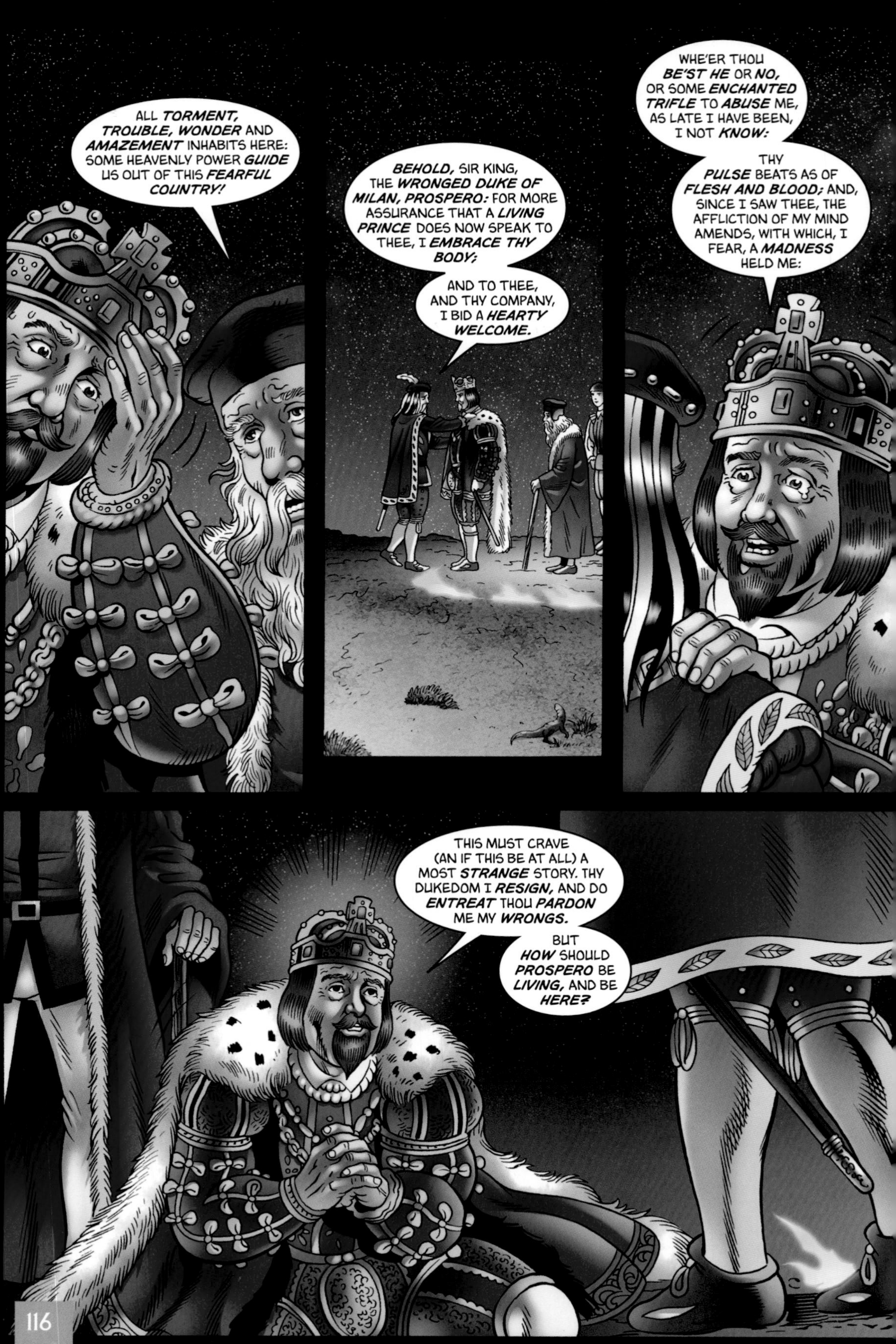
ALL TORMENT, TROUBLE, WONDER AND AMAZEMENT INHABITS HERE: SOME HEAVENLY POWER GUIDE US OUT OF THIS FEARFUL COUNTRY!
BEHOLD, SIR KING, THE WRONGED DUKE OF MILAN, PROSPERO: FOR MORE ASSURANCE THAT A LIVING PRINCE DOES NOW SPEAK TO THEE, I EMBRACE THY BODY;
AND TO THEE, AND THY COMPANY, I BID A HEARTY WELCOME.
WHE'ER THOU BE'ST HE OR NO, OR SOME ENCHANTED TRIFLE TO ABUSE ME, AS LATE I HAVE BEEN, I NOT KNOW:
THY PULSE BEATS AS OF FLESH AND BLOOD; AND, SINCE I SAW THEE, THE AFFLICTION OF MY MIND AMENDS, WITH WHICH, I FEAR, A MADNESS HELD ME:
THIS MUST CRAVE (AN IF THIS BE AT ALL) A MOST STRANGE STORY. THY DUKEDOM I RESIGN, AND DO ENTREAT THOU PARDON ME MY WRONGS.
BUT HOW SHOULD PROSPERO BE LIVING, AND BE HERE?

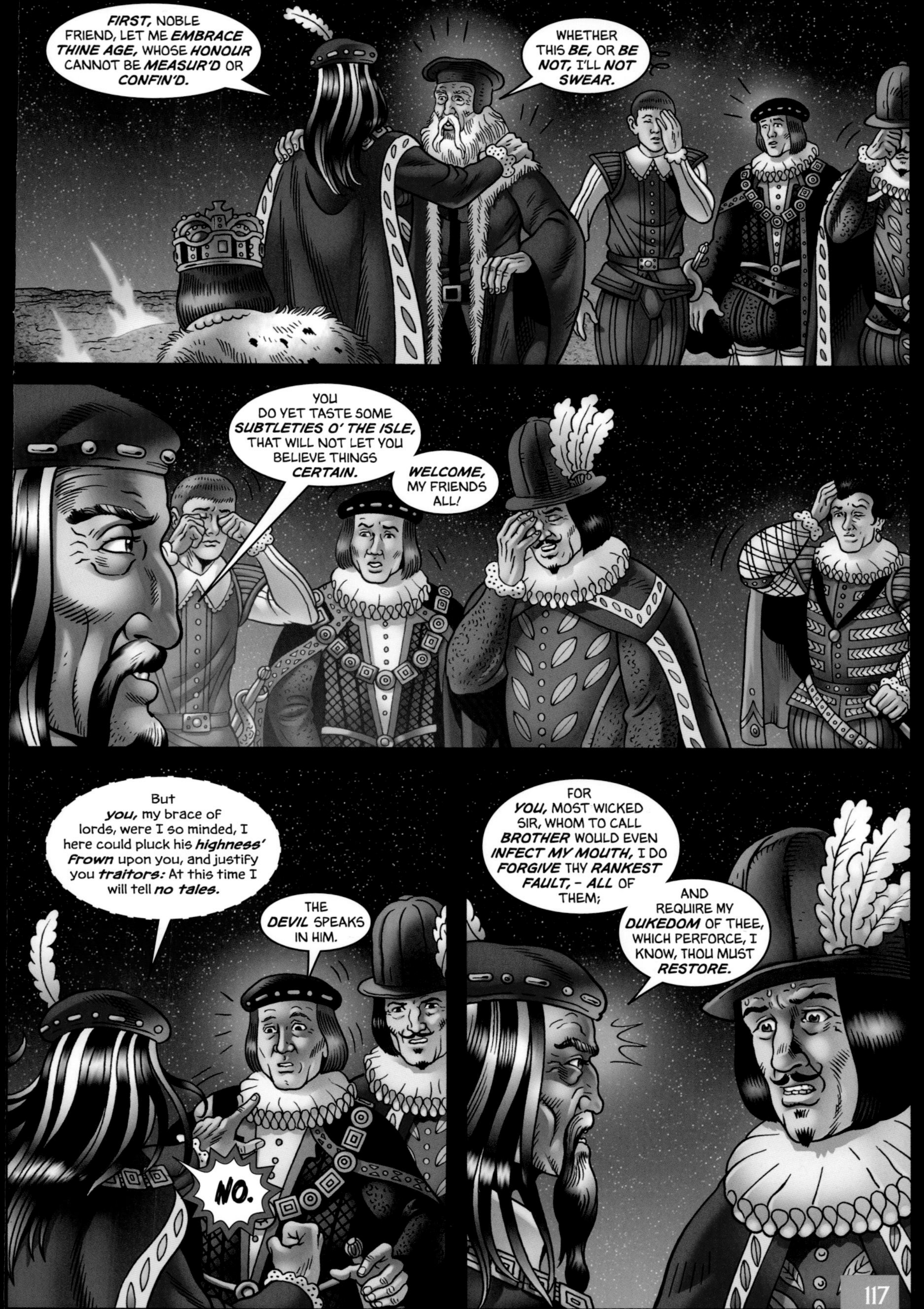
FIRST, NOBLE FRIEND, LET ME EMBRACE THINE AGE, WHOSE HONOUR CANNOT BE MEASUR'D OR CONFIN'D.
WHETHER THIS BE, OR BE NOT, I'LL NOT SWEAR.
YOU DO YET TASTE SOME SUBTLETIES O' THE ISLE, THAT WILL NOT LET YOU BELIEVE THINGS CERTAIN.
WELCOME, MY FRIENDS ALL!
But you, my brace of lords, were I so minded, I here could pluck his highness' frown upon you, and justify you traitors: At this time I will tell no tales.
THE DEVIL SPEAKS IN HIM.
NO.
FOR YOU, MOST WICKED SIR, WHOM TO CALL BROTHER WOULD EVEN INFECT MY MOUTH, I DO FORGIVE THY RANKEST FAULT, - ALL OF THEM;
AND REQUIRE MY DUKEDOM OF THEE, WHICH PERFORCE, I KNOW, THOU MUST RESTORE.

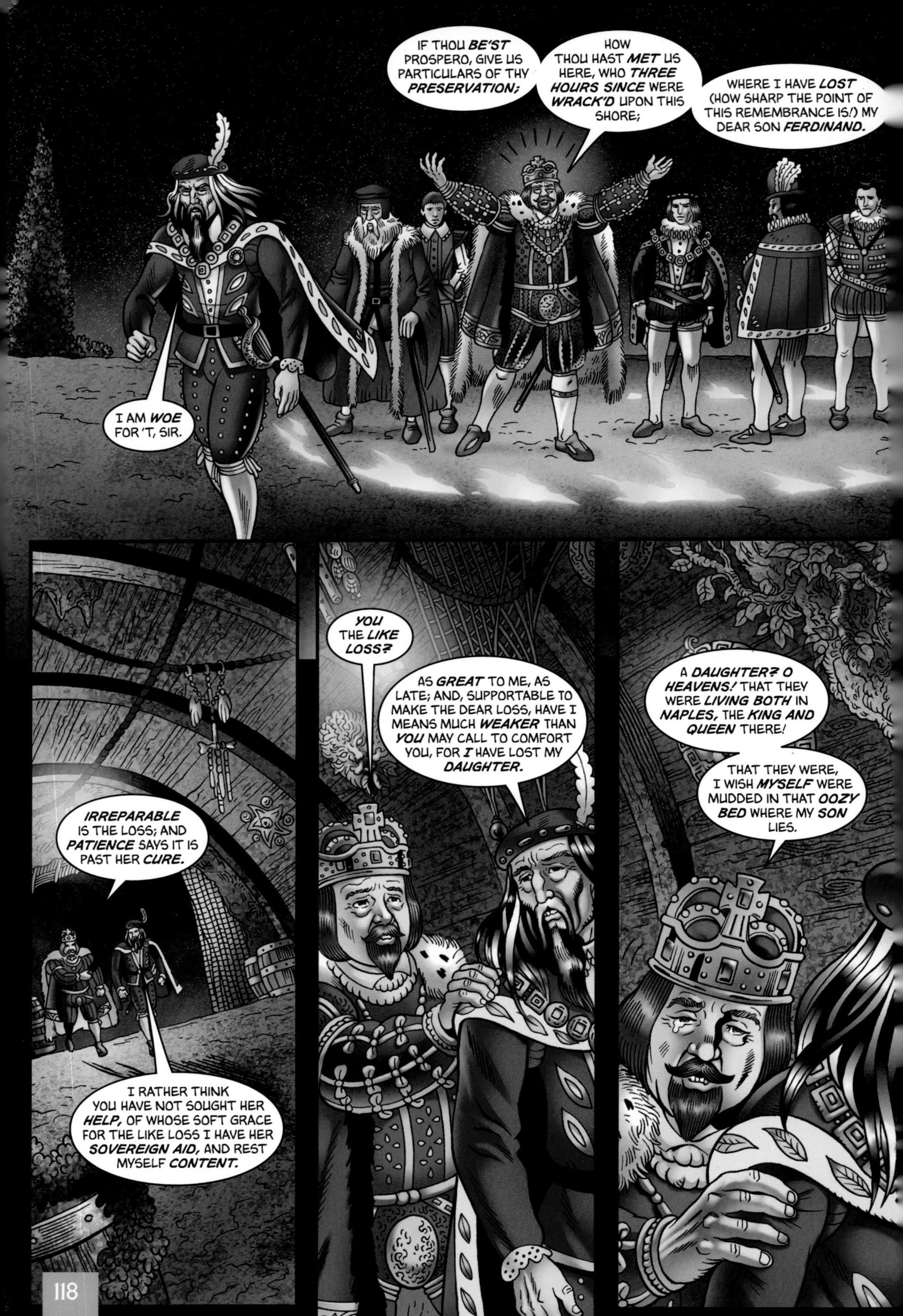
IF THOU BE'ST PROSPERO, GIVE US PARTICULARS OF THY PRESERVATION;
HOW THOU HAST MET US HERE, WHO THREE HOURS SINCE WERE WRACK'D UPON THIS SHORE;
WHERE I HAVE LOST (HOW SHARP THE POINT OF THIS REMEMBRANCE IS!) MY DEAR SON FERDINAND.
I AM WOE FOR 'T, SIR.
IRREPARABLE IS THE LOSS; AND PATIENCE SAYS IT IS PAST HER CURE.
I RATHER THINK YOU HAVE NOT SOUGHT HER HELP, OF WHOSE SOFT GRACE FOR THE LIKE LOSS I HAVE HER SOVEREIGN AID, AND REST MYSELF CONTENT.
YOU THE LIKE LOSS?
AS GREAT TO ME, AS LATE; AND, SUPPORTABLE TO MAKE THE DEAR LOSS, HAVE I MEANS MUCH WEAKER THAN YOU MAY CALL TO COMFORT YOU, FOR I HAVE LOST MY DAUGHTER.
A DAUGHTER? O HEAVENS! THAT THEY WERE LIVING BOTH IN NAPLES, THE KING AND QUEEN THERE!
THAT THEY WERE, I WISH MYSELF WERE MUDDED IN THAT OOZY BED WHERE MY SON LIES.

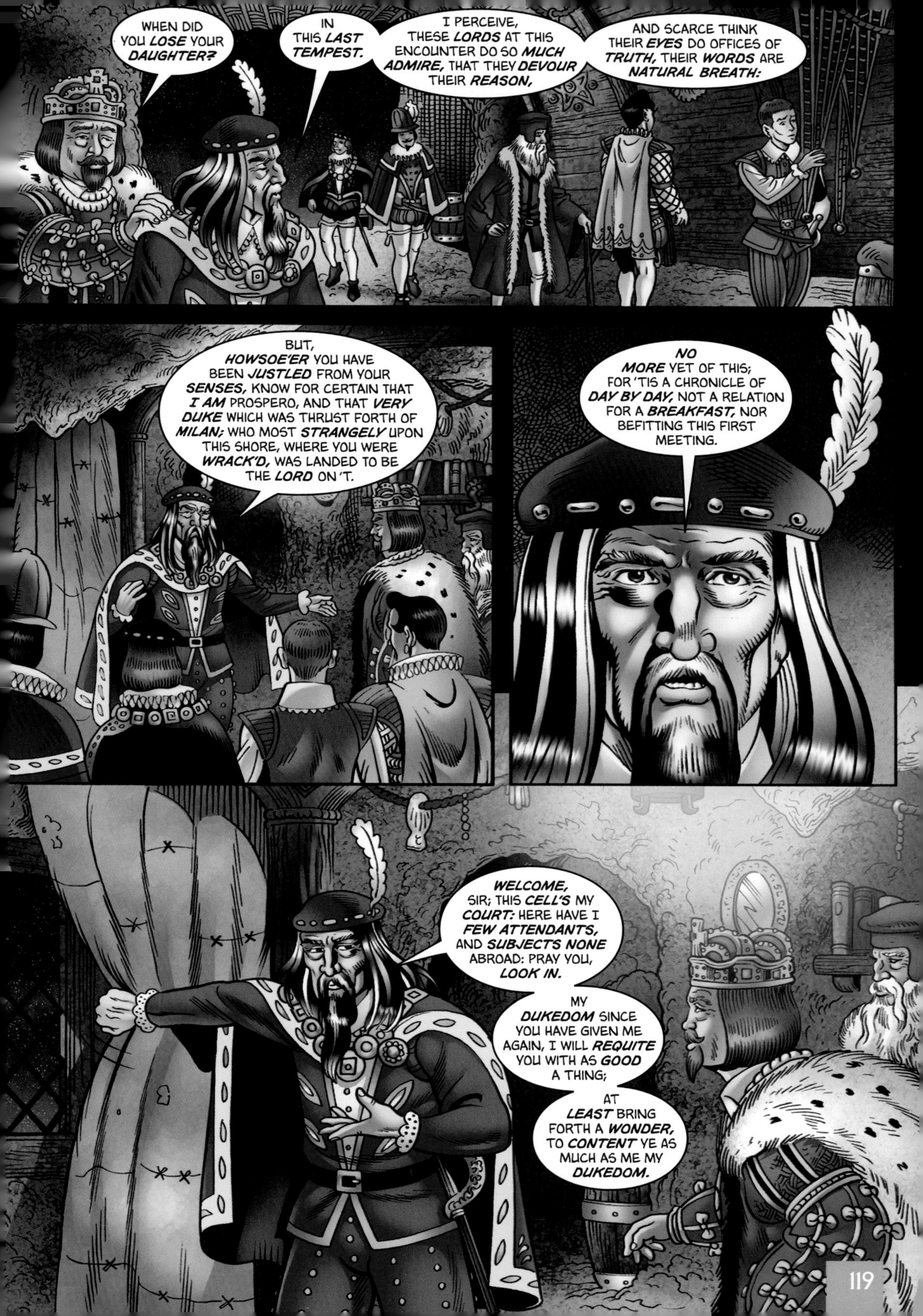
WHEN DID YOU *LOSE* YOUR *DAUGHTER?*
IN THIS *LAST TEMPEST.*
I PERCEIVE, THESE *LORDS* AT THIS ENCOUNTER DO SO *MUCH ADMIRE,* THAT THEY *DEVOUR* THEIR *REASON,*
AND SCARCE THINK THEIR *EYES* DO OFFICES OF *TRUTH,* THEIR *WORDS* ARE *NATURAL BREATH:*
BUT, *HOWSOE'ER* YOU HAVE BEEN *JUSTLED* FROM YOUR *SENSES,* KNOW FOR CERTAIN THAT *I AM* PROSPERO, AND THAT *VERY DUKE* WHICH WAS THRUST FORTH OF *MILAN;* WHO MOST *STRANGELY* UPON THIS SHORE, WHERE YOU WERE *WRACK'D,* WAS LANDED TO BE THE *LORD* ON 'T.
NO MORE YET OF THIS; FOR 'TIS A CHRONICLE OF *DAY BY DAY,* NOT A RELATION FOR A *BREAKFAST,* NOR BEFITTING THIS FIRST MEETING.
WELCOME, SIR; THIS *CELL'S* MY *COURT:* HERE HAVE I *FEW ATTENDANTS,* AND *SUBJECTS NONE* ABROAD: PRAY YOU, *LOOK IN.*
MY *DUKEDOM* SINCE YOU HAVE GIVEN ME AGAIN, I WILL *REQUITE* YOU WITH AS *GOOD* A THING;
AT *LEAST* BRING FORTH A *WONDER,* TO *CONTENT* YE AS MUCH AS ME MY *DUKEDOM.*

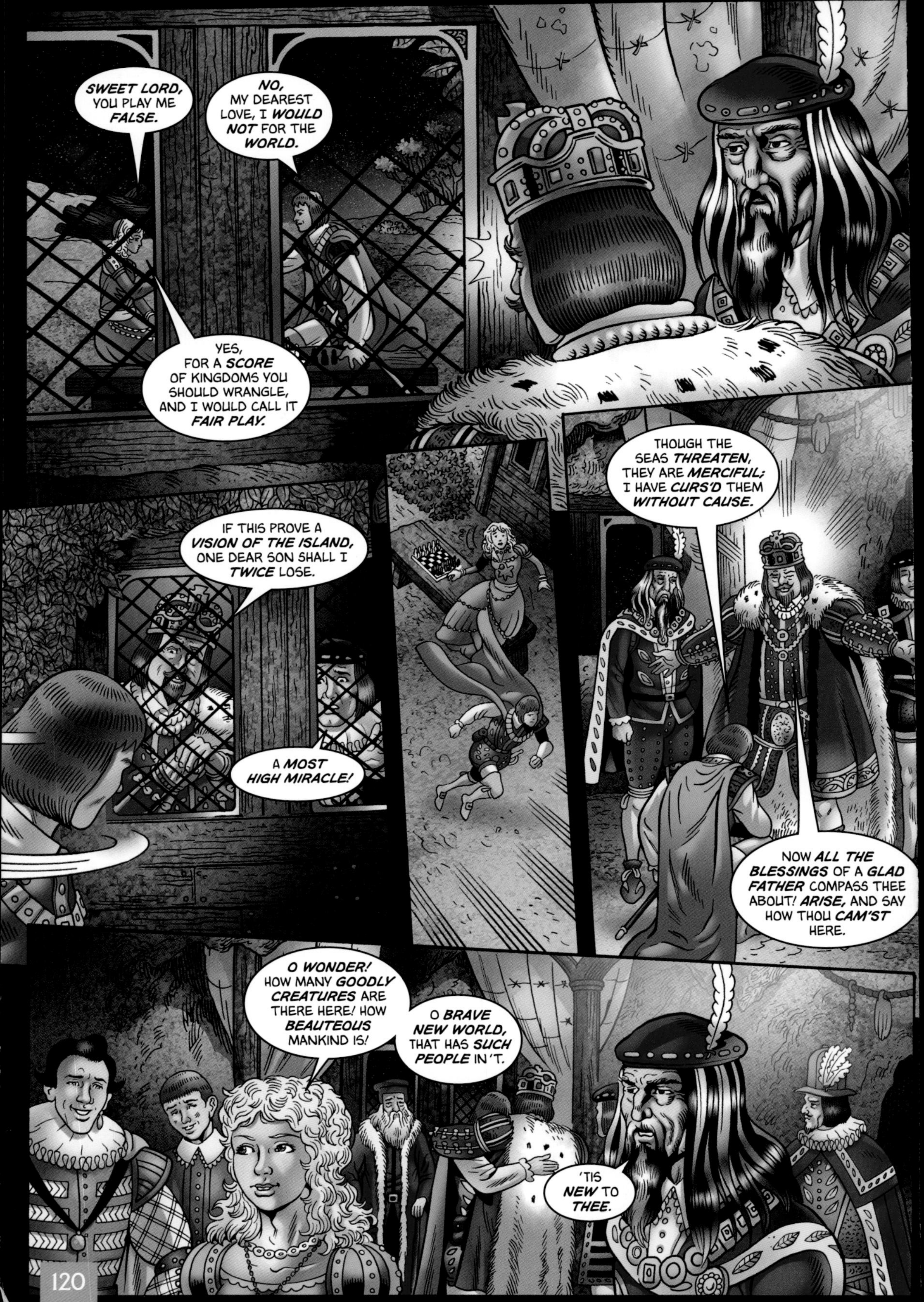

SWEET LORD, YOU PLAY ME FALSE.
NO, MY DEAREST LOVE, I WOULD NOT FOR THE WORLD.
YES, FOR A SCORE OF KINGDOMS YOU SHOULD WRANGLE, AND I WOULD CALL IT FAIR PLAY.
IF THIS PROVE A VISION OF THE ISLAND, ONE DEAR SON SHALL I TWICE LOSE.
A MOST HIGH MIRACLE!
THOUGH THE SEAS THREATEN, THEY ARE MERCIFUL; I HAVE CURS'D THEM WITHOUT CAUSE.
NOW ALL THE BLESSINGS OF A GLAD FATHER COMPASS THEE ABOUT! ARISE, AND SAY HOW THOU CAM'ST HERE.
O WONDER! HOW MANY GOODLY CREATURES ARE THERE HERE! HOW BEAUTEOUS MANKIND IS!
O BRAVE NEW WORLD, THAT HAS SUCH PEOPLE IN'T.
'TIS NEW TO THEE.

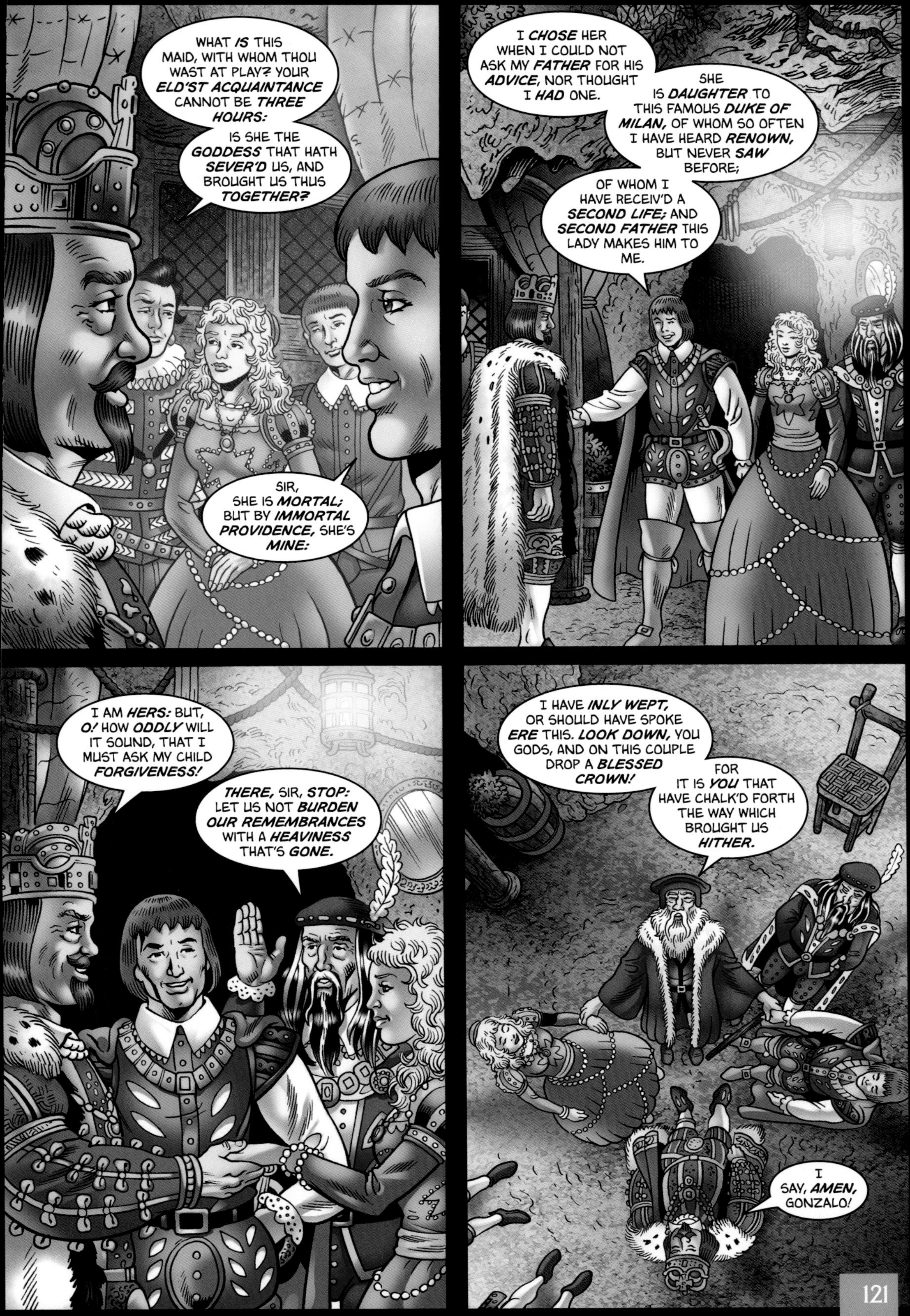
WHAT *IS* THIS MAID, WITH WHOM THOU WAST AT PLAY? YOUR ***ELD'ST ACQUAINTANCE*** CANNOT BE ***THREE HOURS:***
IS SHE THE ***GODDESS*** THAT HATH ***SEVER'D*** US, AND BROUGHT US THUS ***TOGETHER?***
SIR, SHE IS ***MORTAL;*** BUT BY ***IMMORTAL PROVIDENCE,*** SHE'S ***MINE:***
I ***CHOSE*** HER WHEN I COULD NOT ASK MY ***FATHER*** FOR HIS ***ADVICE,*** NOR THOUGHT I ***HAD*** ONE.
SHE IS ***DAUGHTER*** TO THIS FAMOUS ***DUKE OF MILAN,*** OF WHOM SO OFTEN I HAVE HEARD ***RENOWN,*** BUT NEVER ***SAW*** BEFORE;
OF WHOM I HAVE RECEIV'D A ***SECOND LIFE;*** AND ***SECOND FATHER*** THIS LADY MAKES HIM TO ME.
I AM ***HERS:*** BUT, ***O!*** HOW ***ODDLY*** WILL IT SOUND, THAT I MUST ASK MY CHILD ***FORGIVENESS!***
THERE, SIR, ***STOP:*** LET US NOT ***BURDEN OUR REMEMBRANCES*** WITH A ***HEAVINESS*** THAT'S ***GONE.***
I HAVE ***INLY WEPT,*** OR SHOULD HAVE SPOKE ***ERE*** THIS. ***LOOK DOWN,*** YOU GODS, AND ON THIS COUPLE DROP A ***BLESSED CROWN!***
FOR IT IS ***YOU*** THAT HAVE CHALK'D FORTH THE WAY WHICH BROUGHT US ***HITHER.***
I SAY, ***AMEN,*** GONZALO!

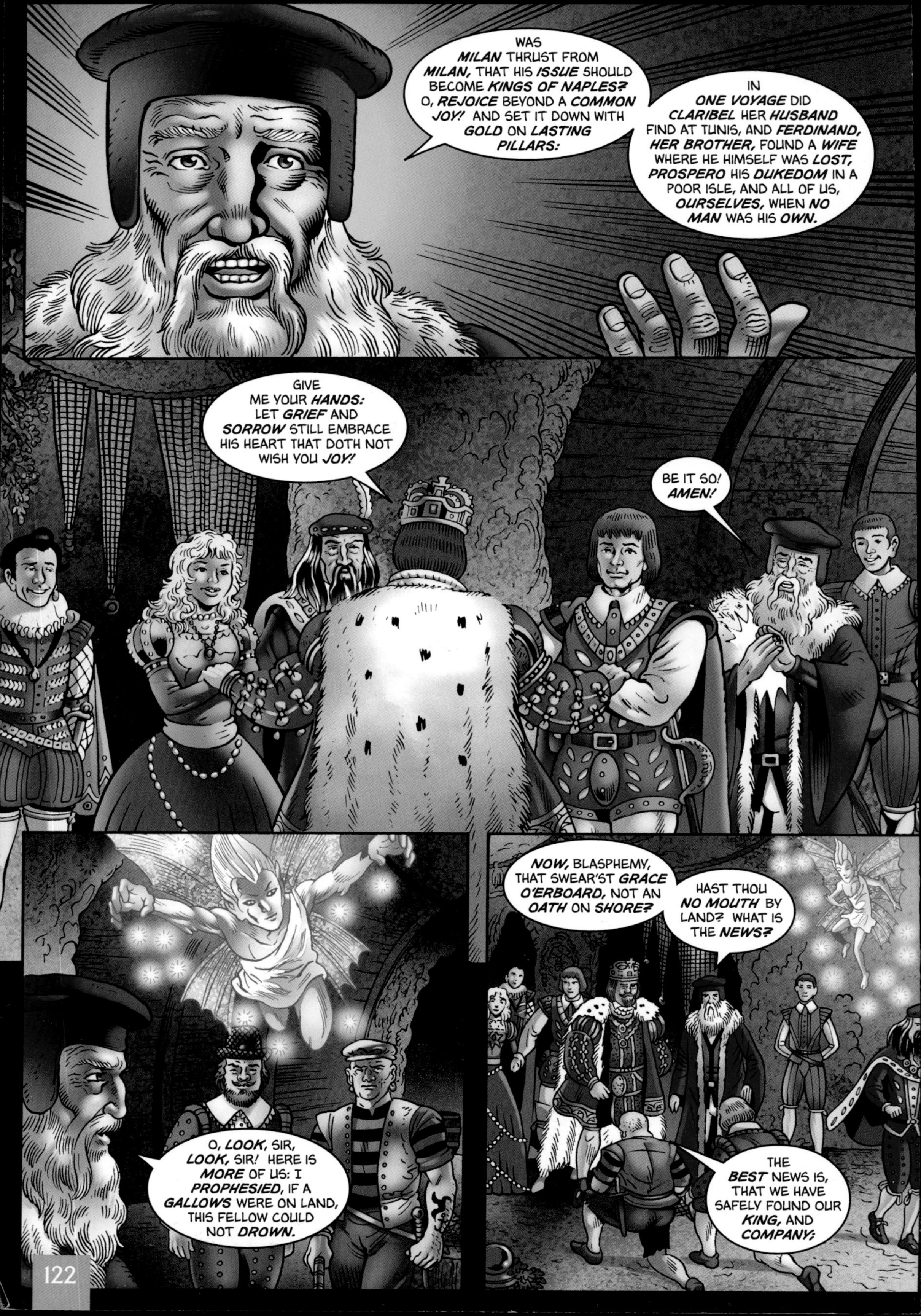
WAS MILAN THRUST FROM MILAN, THAT HIS ISSUE SHOULD BECOME KINGS OF NAPLES? O, REJOICE BEYOND A COMMON JOY! AND SET IT DOWN WITH GOLD ON LASTING PILLARS:
IN ONE VOYAGE DID CLARIBEL HER HUSBAND FIND AT TUNIS, AND FERDINAND, HER BROTHER, FOUND A WIFE WHERE HE HIMSELF WAS LOST, PROSPERO HIS DUKEDOM IN A POOR ISLE, AND ALL OF US, OURSELVES, WHEN NO MAN WAS HIS OWN.
GIVE ME YOUR HANDS: LET GRIEF AND SORROW STILL EMBRACE HIS HEART THAT DOTH NOT WISH YOU JOY!
BE IT SO! AMEN!
O, LOOK, SIR, LOOK, SIR! HERE IS MORE OF US: I PROPHESIED, IF A GALLOWS WERE ON LAND, THIS FELLOW COULD NOT DROWN.
NOW, BLASPHEMY, THAT SWEAR'ST GRACE O'ERBOARD, NOT AN OATH ON SHORE?
HAST THOU NO MOUTH BY LAND? WHAT IS THE NEWS?
THE BEST NEWS IS, THAT WE HAVE SAFELY FOUND OUR KING, AND COMPANY;

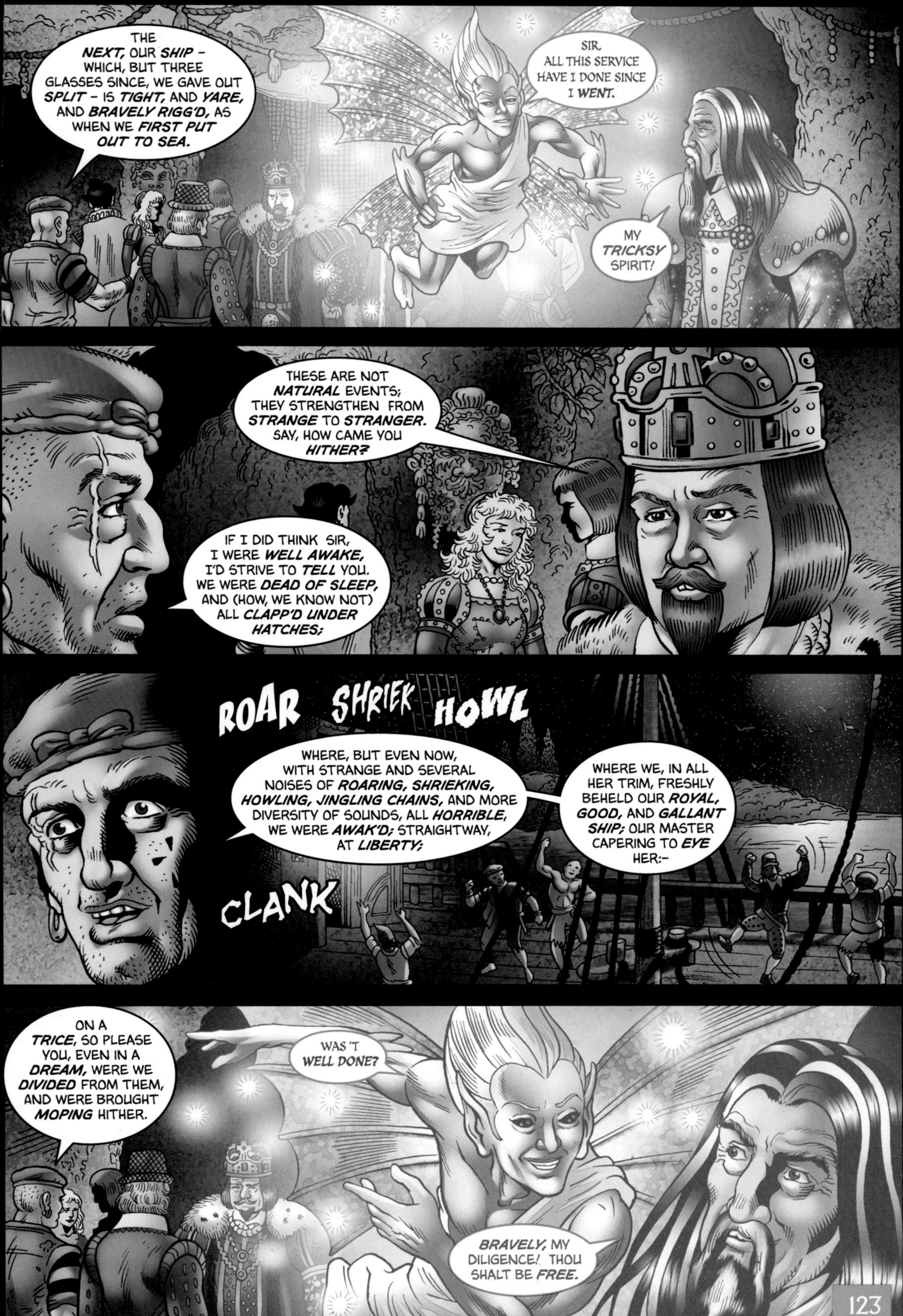
THE NEXT, OUR SHIP – WHICH, BUT THREE GLASSES SINCE, WE GAVE OUT SPLIT – IS TIGHT, AND YARE, AND BRAVELY RIGG'D, AS WHEN WE FIRST PUT OUT TO SEA.
SIR, ALL THIS SERVICE HAVE I DONE SINCE I WENT.
MY TRICKSY SPIRIT!
THESE ARE NOT NATURAL EVENTS; THEY STRENGTHEN FROM STRANGE TO STRANGER. SAY, HOW CAME YOU HITHER?
IF I DID THINK SIR, I WERE WELL AWAKE, I'D STRIVE TO TELL YOU. WE WERE DEAD OF SLEEP, AND (HOW, WE KNOW NOT) ALL CLAPP'D UNDER HATCHES;
ROAR
SHRIEK
HOWL
WHERE, BUT EVEN NOW, WITH STRANGE AND SEVERAL NOISES OF ROARING, SHRIEKING, HOWLING, JINGLING CHAINS, AND MORE DIVERSITY OF SOUNDS, ALL HORRIBLE, WE WERE AWAK'D; STRAIGHTWAY, AT LIBERTY;
WHERE WE, IN ALL HER TRIM, FRESHLY BEHELD OUR ROYAL, GOOD, AND GALLANT SHIP; OUR MASTER CAPERING TO EYE HER:-
CLANK
ON A TRICE, SO PLEASE YOU, EVEN IN A DREAM, WERE WE DIVIDED FROM THEM, AND WERE BROUGHT MOPING HITHER.
WAS 'T WELL DONE?
BRAVELY, MY DILIGENCE! THOU SHALT BE FREE.

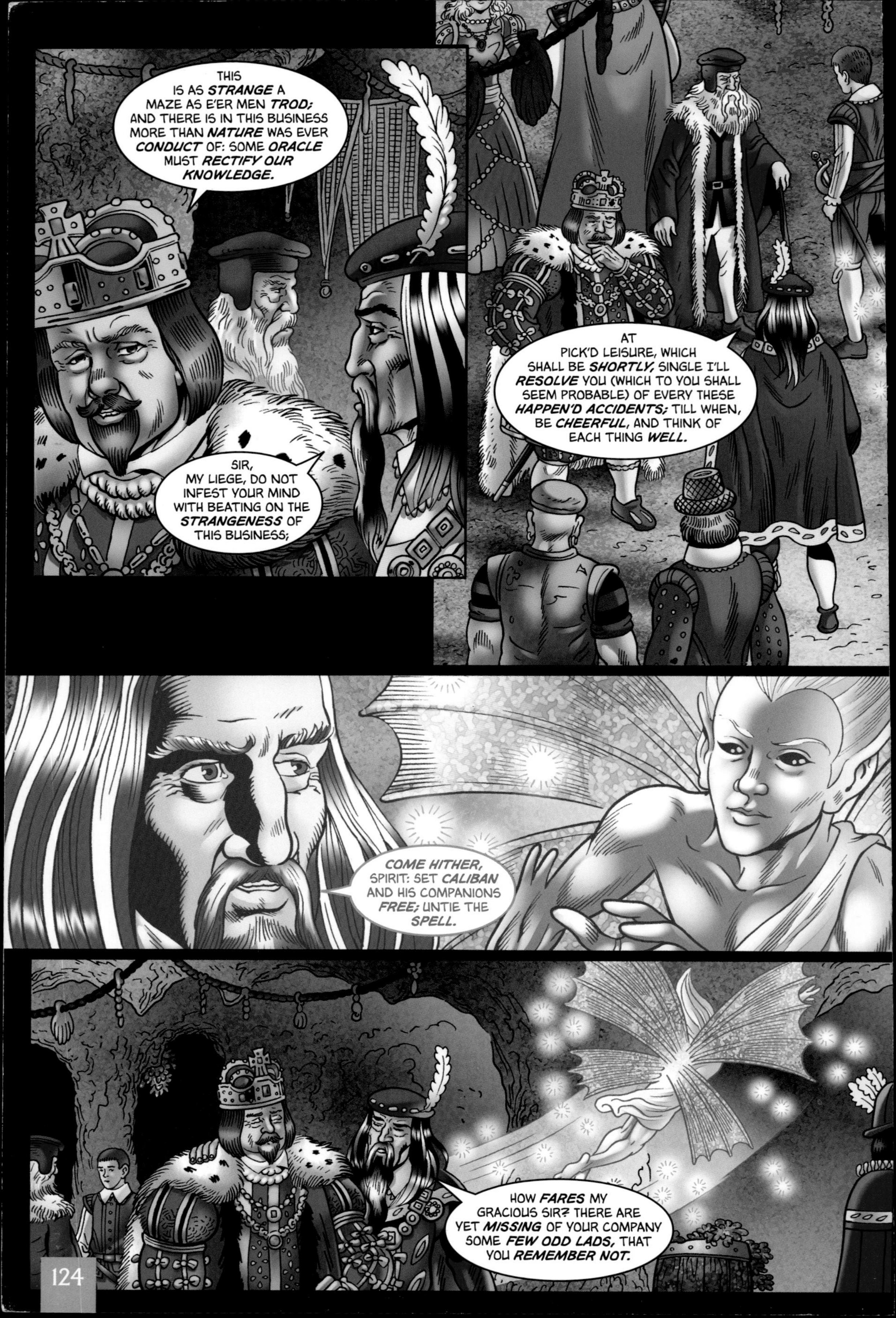
THIS IS AS STRANGE A MAZE AS E'ER MEN TROD; AND THERE IS IN THIS BUSINESS MORE THAN NATURE WAS EVER CONDUCT OF: SOME ORACLE MUST RECTIFY OUR KNOWLEDGE.
SIR, MY LIEGE, DO NOT INFEST YOUR MIND WITH BEATING ON THE STRANGENESS OF THIS BUSINESS;
AT PICK'D LEISURE, WHICH SHALL BE SHORTLY, SINGLE I'LL RESOLVE YOU (WHICH TO YOU SHALL SEEM PROBABLE) OF EVERY THESE HAPPEN'D ACCIDENTS; TILL WHEN, BE CHEERFUL, AND THINK OF EACH THING WELL.
COME HITHER, SPIRIT: SET CALIBAN AND HIS COMPANIONS FREE; UNTIE THE SPELL.
HOW FARES MY GRACIOUS SIR? THERE ARE YET MISSING OF YOUR COMPANY SOME FEW ODD LADS, THAT YOU REMEMBER NOT.

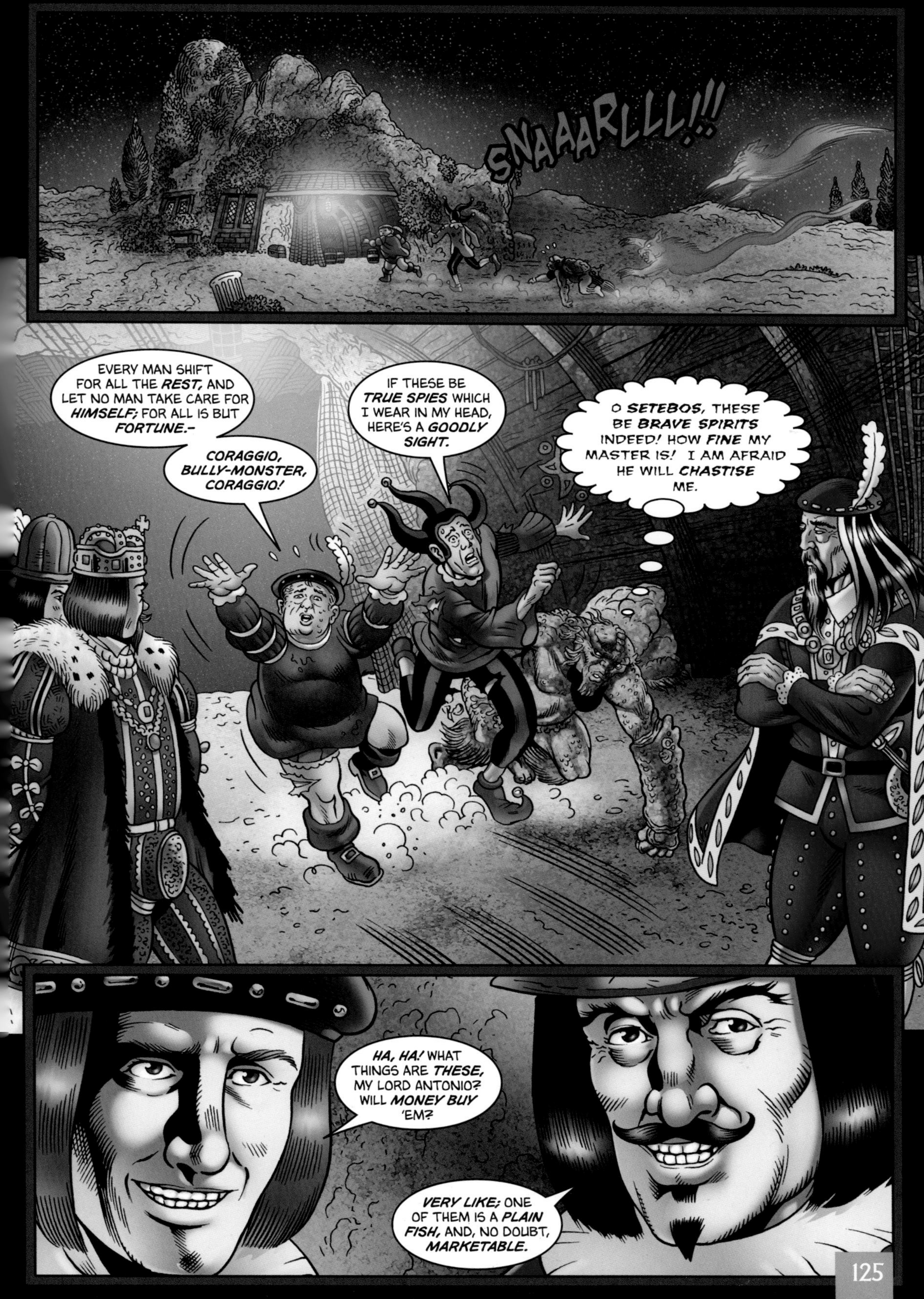
SNAAARLLL!!!
EVERY MAN SHIFT FOR ALL THE REST, AND LET NO MAN TAKE CARE FOR HIMSELF; FOR ALL IS BUT FORTUNE.-
CORAGGIO, BULLY-MONSTER, CORAGGIO!
IF THESE BE TRUE SPIES WHICH I WEAR IN MY HEAD, HERE'S A GOODLY SIGHT.
O SETEBOS, THESE BE BRAVE SPIRITS INDEED! HOW FINE MY MASTER IS! I AM AFRAID HE WILL CHASTISE ME.
HA, HA! WHAT THINGS ARE THESE, MY LORD ANTONIO? WILL MONEY BUY 'EM?
VERY LIKE; ONE OF THEM IS A PLAIN FISH, AND, NO DOUBT, MARKETABLE.

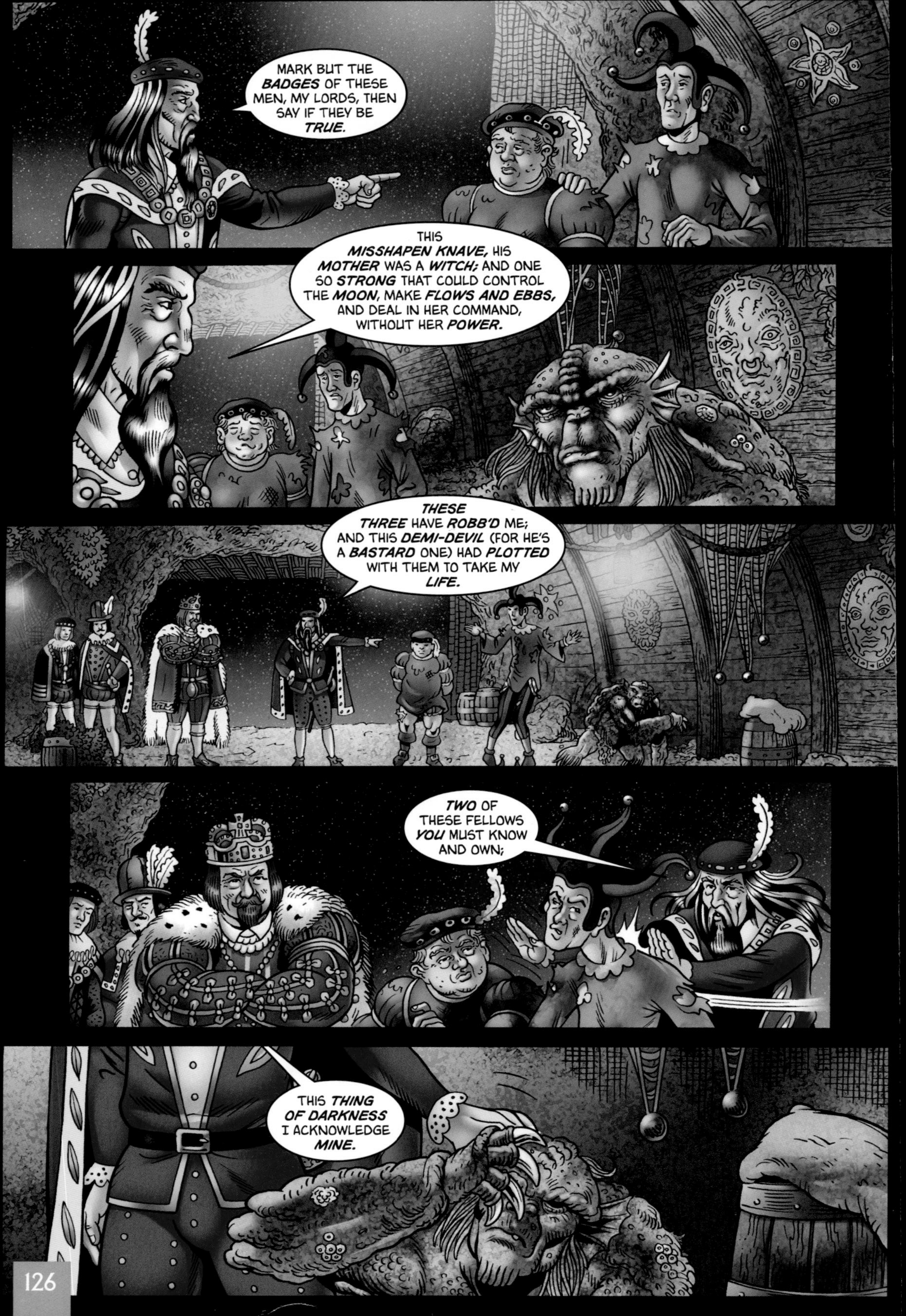
MARK BUT THE BADGES OF THESE MEN, MY LORDS, THEN SAY IF THEY BE TRUE.
THIS MISSHAPEN KNAVE, HIS MOTHER WAS A WITCH; AND ONE SO STRONG THAT COULD CONTROL THE MOON, MAKE FLOWS AND EBBS, AND DEAL IN HER COMMAND, WITHOUT HER POWER.
THESE THREE HAVE ROBB'D ME; AND THIS DEMI-DEVIL (FOR HE'S A BASTARD ONE) HAD PLOTTED WITH THEM TO TAKE MY LIFE.
TWO OF THESE FELLOWS YOU MUST KNOW AND OWN;
THIS THING OF DARKNESS I ACKNOWLEDGE MINE.

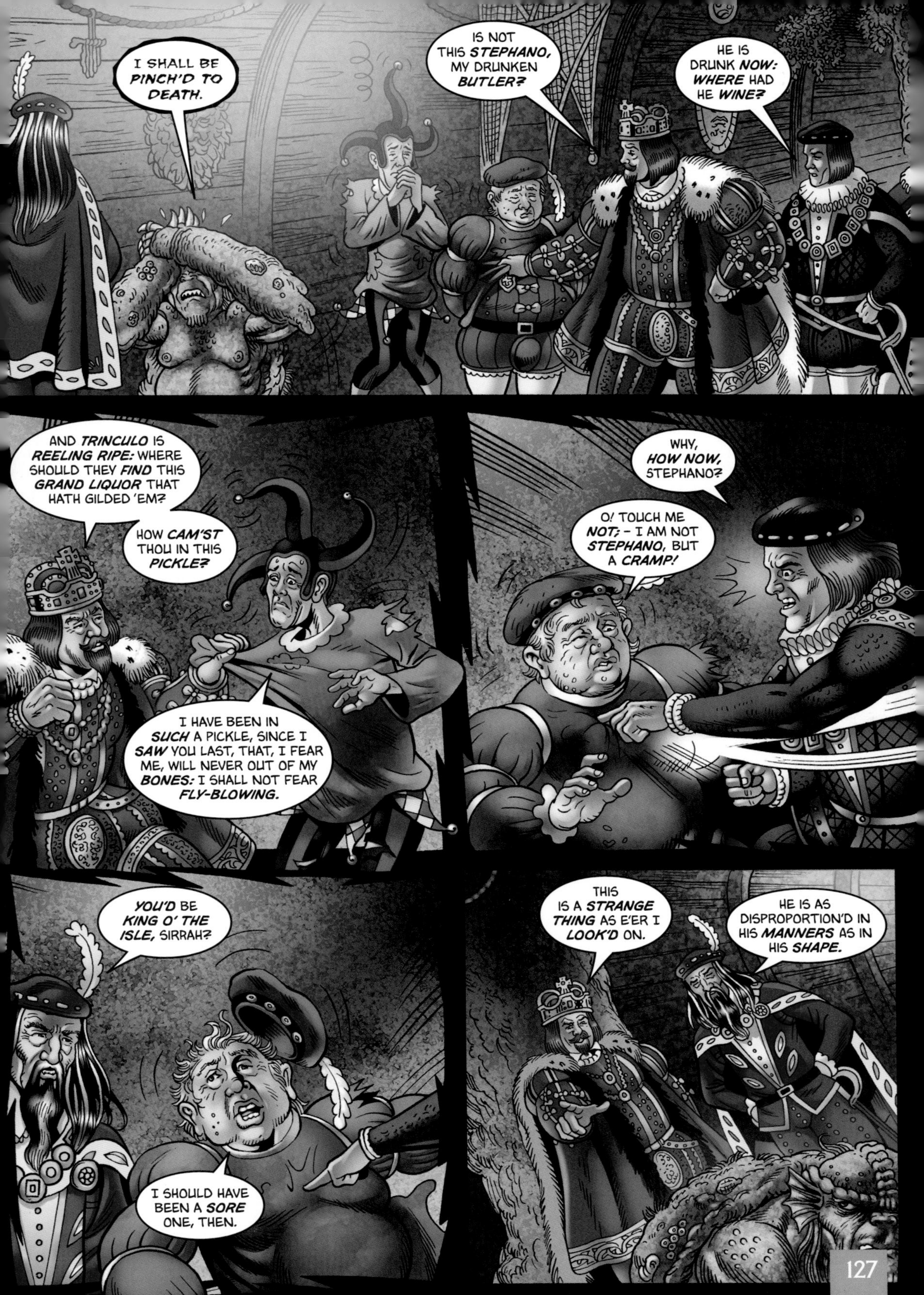
I SHALL BE PINCH'D TO DEATH.
IS NOT THIS STEPHANO, MY DRUNKEN BUTLER?
HE IS DRUNK NOW: WHERE HAD HE WINE?
AND TRINCULO IS REELING RIPE: WHERE SHOULD THEY FIND THIS GRAND LIQUOR THAT HATH GILDED 'EM?
HOW CAM'ST THOU IN THIS PICKLE?
I HAVE BEEN IN SUCH A PICKLE, SINCE I SAW YOU LAST, THAT, I FEAR ME, WILL NEVER OUT OF MY BONES: I SHALL NOT FEAR FLY-BLOWING.
WHY, HOW NOW, STEPHANO?
O! TOUCH ME NOT; - I AM NOT STEPHANO, BUT A CRAMP!
YOU'D BE KING O' THE ISLE, SIRRAH?
I SHOULD HAVE BEEN A SORE ONE, THEN.
THIS IS A STRANGE THING AS E'ER I LOOK'D ON.
HE IS AS DISPROPORTION'D IN HIS MANNERS AS IN HIS SHAPE.

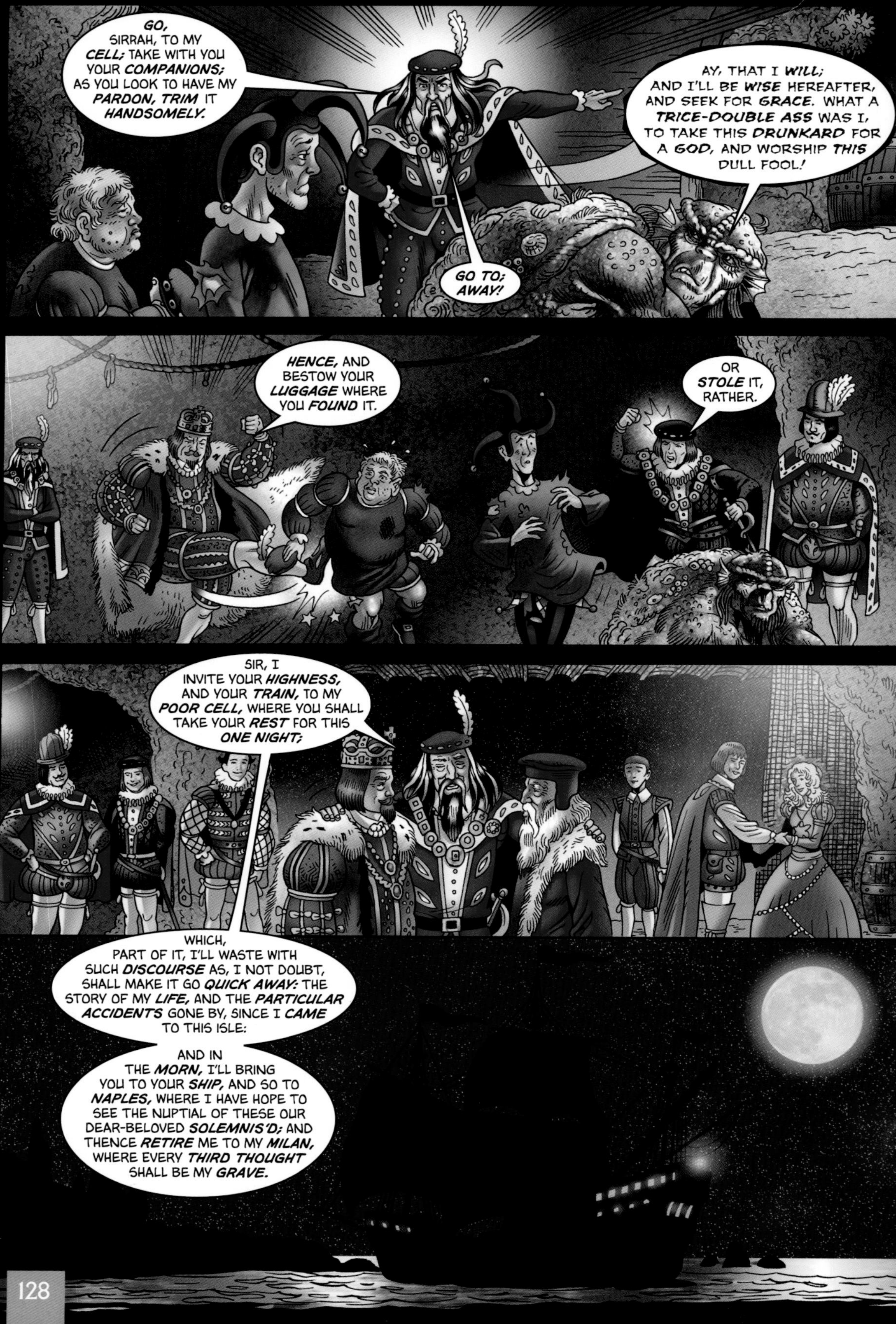
GO, SIRRAH, TO MY CELL; TAKE WITH YOU YOUR COMPANIONS; AS YOU LOOK TO HAVE MY PARDON, TRIM IT HANDSOMELY.
AY, THAT I WILL; AND I'LL BE WISE HEREAFTER, AND SEEK FOR GRACE. WHAT A TRICE-DOUBLE ASS WAS I, TO TAKE THIS DRUNKARD FOR A GOD, AND WORSHIP THIS DULL FOOL!
GO TO; AWAY!
HENCE, AND BESTOW YOUR LUGGAGE WHERE YOU FOUND IT.
OR STOLE IT, RATHER.
SIR, I INVITE YOUR HIGHNESS, AND YOUR TRAIN, TO MY POOR CELL, WHERE YOU SHALL TAKE YOUR REST FOR THIS ONE NIGHT;
WHICH, PART OF IT, I'LL WASTE WITH SUCH DISCOURSE AS, I NOT DOUBT, SHALL MAKE IT GO QUICK AWAY: THE STORY OF MY LIFE, AND THE PARTICULAR ACCIDENTS GONE BY, SINCE I CAME TO THIS ISLE:
AND IN THE MORN, I'LL BRING YOU TO YOUR SHIP, AND SO TO NAPLES, WHERE I HAVE HOPE TO SEE THE NUPTIAL OF THESE OUR DEAR-BELOVED SOLEMNIS'D; AND THENCE RETIRE ME TO MY MILAN, WHERE EVERY THIRD THOUGHT SHALL BE MY GRAVE.

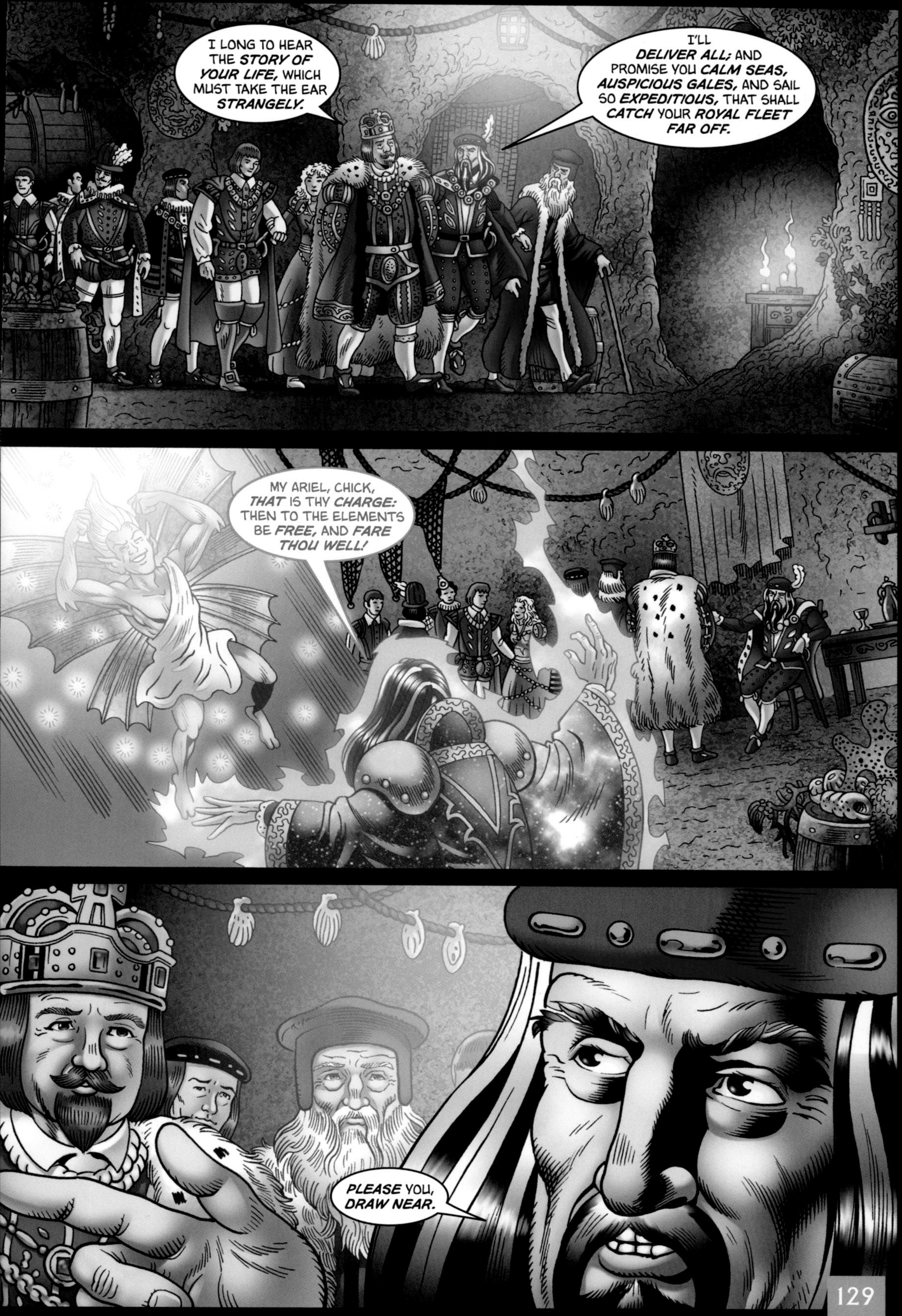
I LONG TO HEAR THE STORY OF YOUR LIFE, WHICH MUST TAKE THE EAR STRANGELY.
I'LL DELIVER ALL; AND PROMISE YOU CALM SEAS, AUSPICIOUS GALES, AND SAIL SO EXPEDITIOUS, THAT SHALL CATCH YOUR ROYAL FLEET FAR OFF.
MY ARIEL, CHICK, THAT IS THY CHARGE: THEN TO THE ELEMENTS BE FREE, AND FARE THOU WELL!
PLEASE YOU, DRAW NEAR.

Epilogue

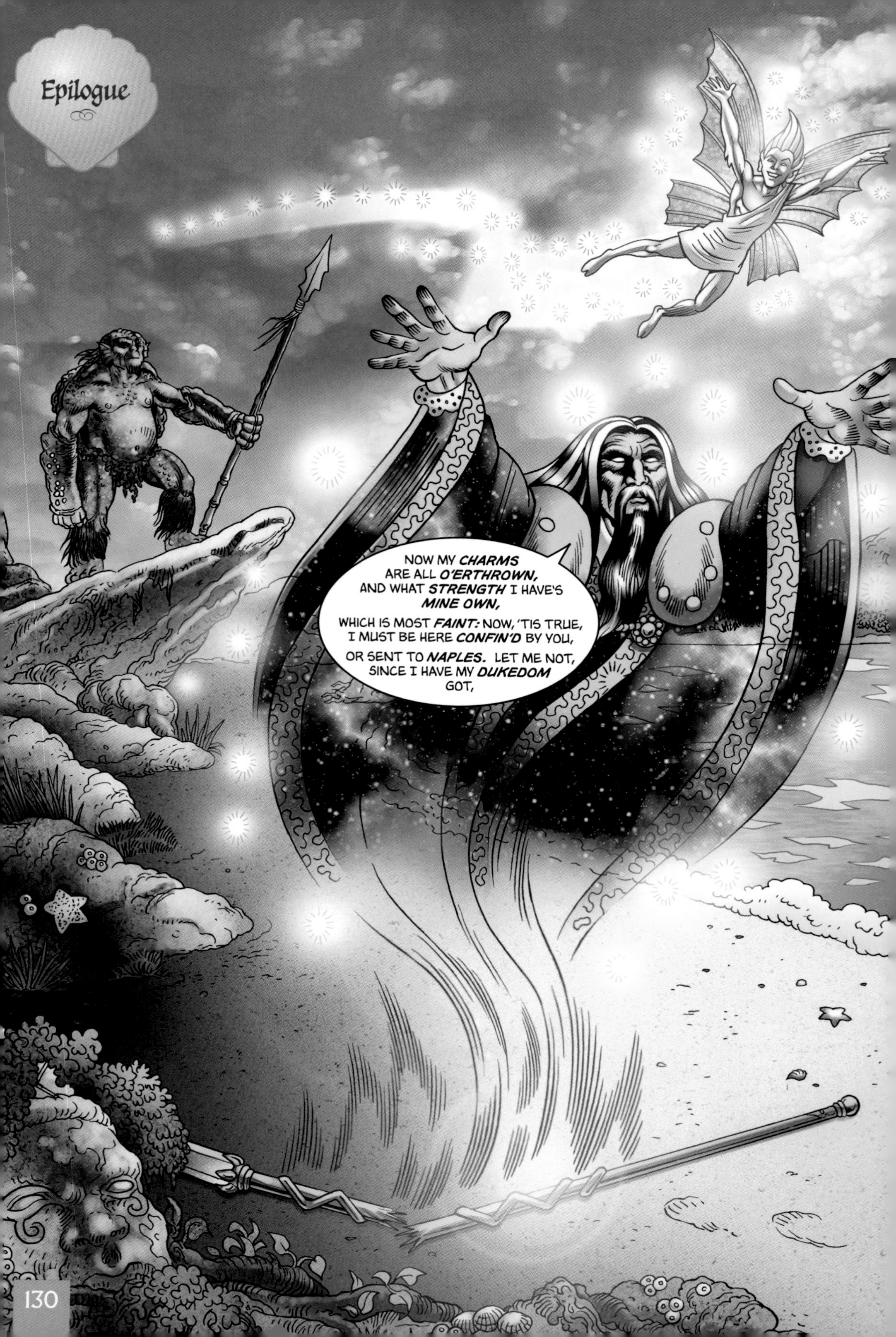
NOW MY CHARMS ARE ALL O'ERTHROWN, AND WHAT STRENGTH I HAVE'S MINE OWN,
WHICH IS MOST FAINT: NOW, 'TIS TRUE, I MUST BE HERE CONFIN'D BY YOU,
OR SENT TO NAPLES. LET ME NOT, SINCE I HAVE MY DUKEDOM GOT,

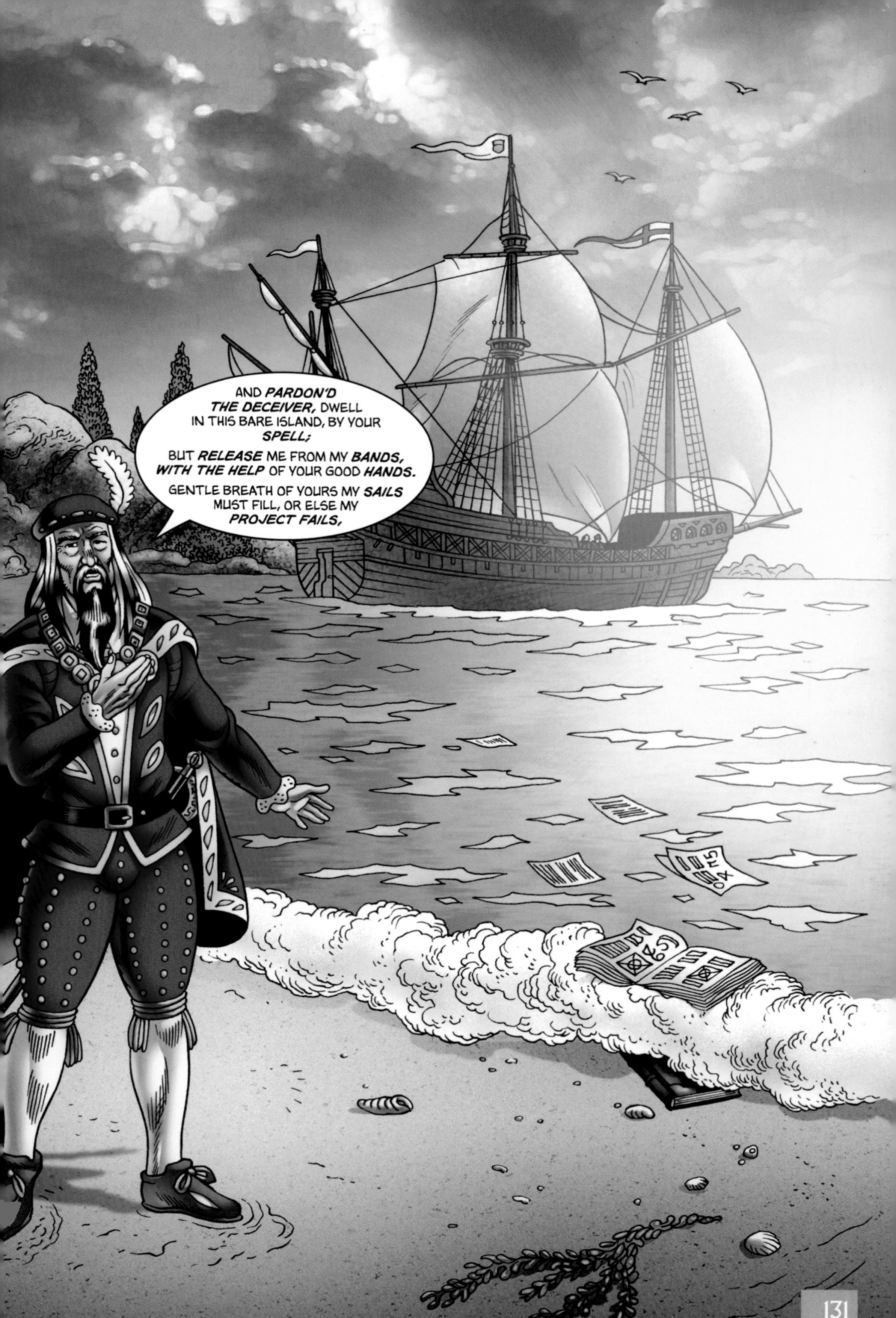
AND *PARDON'D THE DECEIVER,* DWELL IN THIS BARE ISLAND, BY YOUR *SPELL;*
BUT *RELEASE* ME FROM MY *BANDS, WITH THE HELP* OF YOUR GOOD *HANDS.*
GENTLE BREATH OF YOURS MY *SAILS* MUST FILL, OR ELSE MY *PROJECT FAILS,*

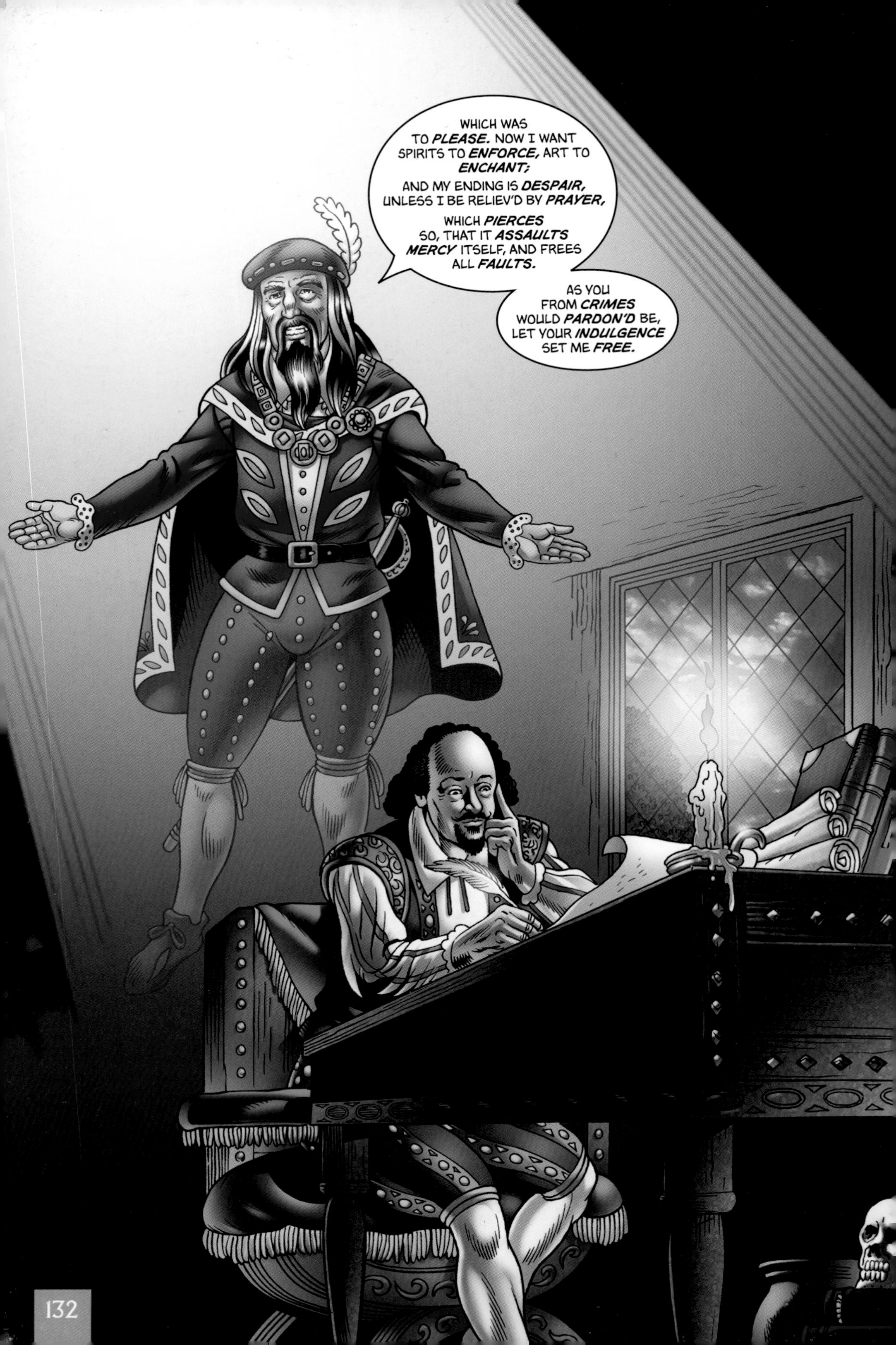
WHICH WAS TO PLEASE. NOW I WANT SPIRITS TO ENFORCE, ART TO ENCHANT;
AND MY ENDING IS DESPAIR, UNLESS I BE RELIEV'D BY PRAYER,
WHICH PIERCES SO, THAT IT ASSAULTS MERCY ITSELF, AND FREES ALL FAULTS.
AS YOU FROM CRIMES WOULD PARDON'D BE, LET YOUR INDULGENCE SET ME FREE.

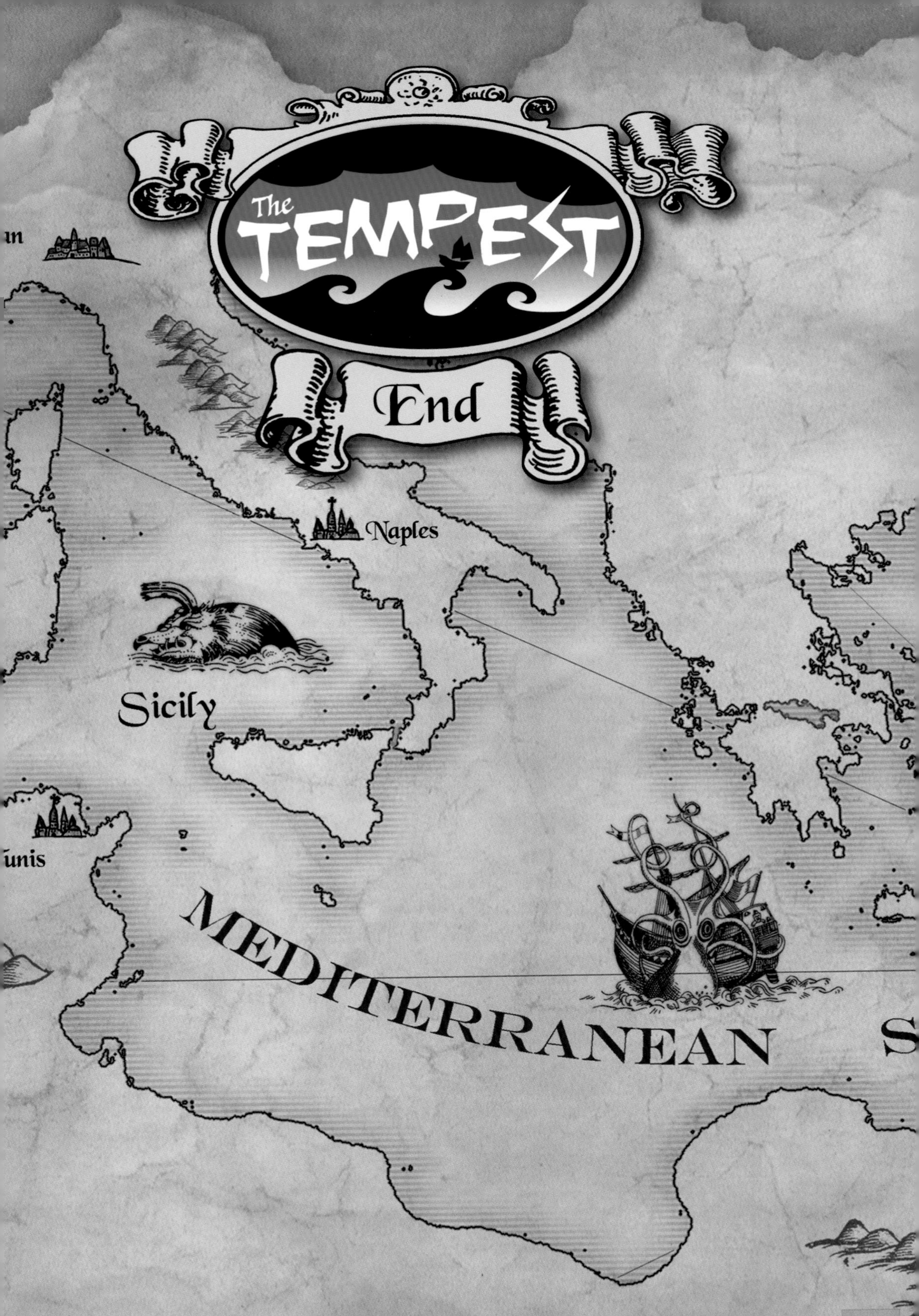

The TEMPEST
End
Naples
Sicily
MEDITERRANEAN

William Shakespeare

(c.1564 - 1616 AD)

Shakespeare is, without question, the world's most famous playwright. Yet, despite his fame, very few records and artifacts exist for him – we don't even know the exact date of his birth! April 23, 1564 (St George's Day) is taken to be his birthday, as this was three days before his baptism (for which we do have a record). Records also tell us that he died on the same date in 1616, aged fifty-two.

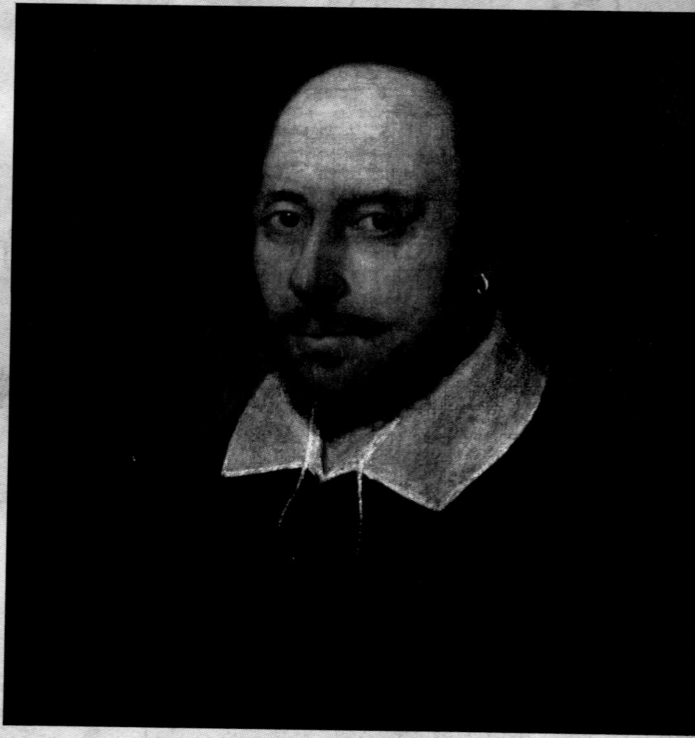

National Portrait Gallery, London

The life of William Shakespeare can be divided into three acts.

Act One – Stratford-upon-Avon
William was the eldest son of tradesman John Shakespeare and Mary Arden, and the third of eight children (he had two older sisters). The Shakespeares were a respectable family. The year after William was born, John (who made gloves and traded leather) became an alderman of Stratford-upon-Avon, and four years later he became High Bailiff (or mayor) of the town.

Little is known of William's childhood. He learned to read and write at the local primary school, and later is believed to have attended the local grammar school, where he studied Latin and English Literature. In 1582, aged eighteen, William married a local farmer's daughter, Anne Hathaway. Anne was eight years his senior and three months pregnant. During their marriage they had three children: Susanna, born on May 26, 1583, and twins, Hamnet and Judith, born on February 2, 1585. Hamnet (William's only son) died in 1596, aged eleven, from Bubonic Plague.

Act Two – London
Five years into his marriage, in 1587, William's wife and children stayed in Stratford, while he moved to London. He appeared as an actor at *The Theatre* (England's first permanent theater) and gave public recitals of his own poems; but it was his playwriting that created the most interest. His fame soon spread far and wide. When Queen Elizabeth I died in 1603, the new King James I (who was already King James VI of Scotland) gave royal consent for Shakespeare's acting company, *The Lord Chamberlain's Men* to be called *The King's Men* in return for entertaining the court. This association was to shape a number of plays, such as *Macbeth,* which was written to please the Scottish King.

William Shakespeare is attributed with writing and collaborating on 38 plays, 154 sonnets and 5 poems, in just twenty-three years between 1590 and 1613. No original manuscript exists for any of his plays, making it hard to accurately date any of them. Printing was still in its infancy, and plays tended to change as they were performed. Shakespeare would write manuscript for the actors and continue to refine them over a number of performances. The plays we know today have survived from written copies taken at various stages of each play and usually written by the actors from memory. This has given rise to variations in texts of what is now known as "quarto" versions of the plays, until we reach the first official printing of each play in the 1623 "folio" *Mr William Shakespeare's Comedies, Histories, & Tragedies*. His last solo-authored work was *The Tempest* in 1611, which was only followed by collaborative work on two plays (*Henry VIII* and *Two Noble Kinsmen*) with John Fletcher. Shakespeare is strongly associated with the famous *Globe Theatre*. Built by his troupe in 1599, it became his "spiritual home", with thousands of people crammed into the small space for each performance. There were 3,000 people in the building in 1613 when a cannon-shot during a performance of *Henry VIII* set fire to the thatched roof and the entire theater was burned to the ground. Although it was rebuilt a year later, it marked an end to Shakespeare's writing and to his time in London.

Act Three - Retirement

Shortly after the 1613 accident at *The Globe*, Shakespeare left the capital and returned to live once more with his family in Stratford-upon-Avon. He died on April 23, 1616 and was buried two days later at the Church of the Holy Trinity (the same church where he had been baptized fifty-two years earlier). The cause of his death remains unknown.

Epilogue

At the time of his death, Shakespeare had substantial properties, which he bestowed on his family and associates from the theater. He had no son to inherit his wealth, and he left the majority of his possessions to his eldest daughter Susanna. Curiously, the only thing that he left to his wife Anne was his second-best bed! (although she continued to live in the family home after his death). William Shakespeare's last direct descendant died in 1670. She was his granddaughter, Elizabeth.

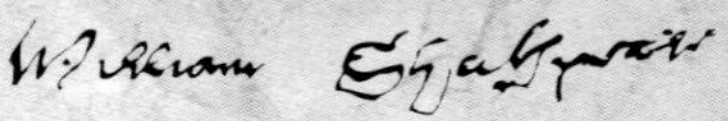

Shakespeare Birthplace Trust

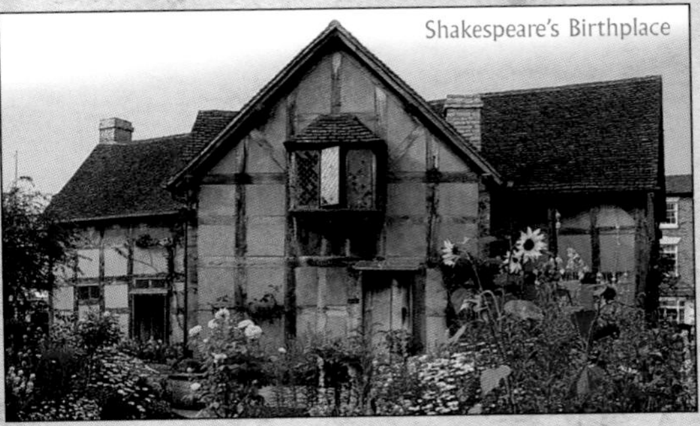
Shakespeare's Birthplace

As so few relics survive from Shakespeare's life, it is amazing that the house where he was born and raised remains intact. It is owned and cared for by the Shakespeare Birthplace Trust, which looks after a number of houses in the area:

- Shakespeare's Birthplace.
- Mary Arden's Farm: The childhood home of Shakespeare's mother.
- Anne Hathaway's Cottage: The childhood home of Shakespeare's wife.
- Hall's Croft: The home of Shakespeare's eldest daughter, Susanna.
- New Place: Only the grounds exist of the house where Shakespeare died in 1616.
- Nash's House: The home of Shakespeare's granddaughter.

www.shakespeare.org.uk

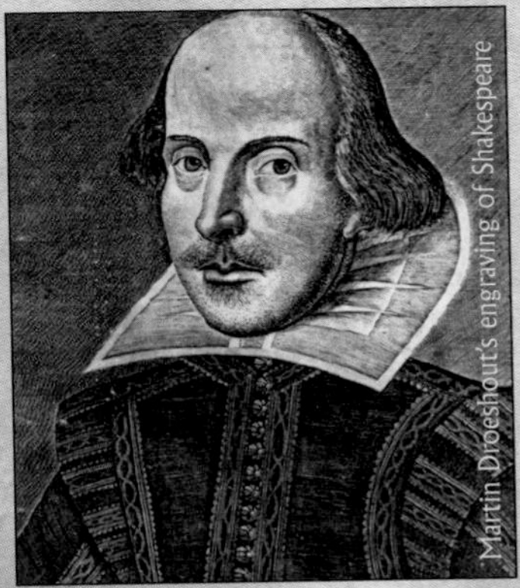
Martin Droeshout's engraving of Shakespeare

Formed in 1847, the Trust also works to promote Shakespeare around the world. In early 2009, it announced that it had found a new Shakespeare portrait, believed to have been painted within his lifetime, with a trail of provenance that links it to Shakespeare himself.

It is accepted that Martin Droeshout's engraving (left) that appears on the First Folio of 1623 is an authentic likeness of Shakespeare because the people involved in its publication would have personally known him. This new portrait (once owned by Henry Wriothesley, 3rd Earl of Southampton, one of Shakespeare's most loyal supporters) is so similar in all facial aspects that it is now suspected to have been the source that Droeshout used for his famous engraving.

www.shakespearefound.org.uk

History of The Tempest

The Tempest was almost certainly Shakespeare's last solo-authored work. Only *Henry VIII* and *Two Noble Kinsmen* were to follow, and they were both collaborations with John Fletcher. It is also the only Shakespeare play that features an original story — all of his other plays have very clear sources. Perhaps it is these two factors that prompt many to believe it to be his finest work — a view shared by the publishers of his first collected works (the "First Folio" of 1623), who gave pride of place to the play.

As with all of his plays, an accurate dating of *The Tempest* is near-impossible; however, we know that it was performed for King James I in November 1611, and this leads us to believe it was written earlier that same year (it was such a success that it was played again the following year to celebrate the betrothal of King James' daughter Elizabeth).

Shakespeare effectively retired after writing *The Tempest*, returning to Stratford-upon-Avon to live his final few years close to his family. Prospero's closing speech of the play appears to be a metaphor for Shakespeare "saying goodbye" to the profession and bowing out from the theater altogether. The fact that he was soon to write his will and tidy up his business affairs means that this is unlikely to have been a coincidence.

Although it was performed in court, it wasn't written for any particular royal performance; however, it was almost certainly written with the King and his daughter in mind. Not only does it feature magic and witchcraft to pander to the King's interests, but it portrays an all-seeing and all-knowing father who protects and looks after the interests of his own daughter. The play also features a "masque" (the dance performed by the goddesses Iris, Ceres and Juno on pages 98-103). Masques were extremely popular in the royal courts and here also served as an interlude or resting point in the progress of the story.

The opening storm of thunder, coupled with shouting and peril, was a wonderfully effective way to grab the attention of the audience. Shakespeare uses the device brilliantly, as the storm also cuts the characters off from one another and separates reality from fantasy — not only for the players, but also for the on-lookers, as the actors land on the mysterious, magical island.

Sources

Exploration and colonization of the "New World" were topical subjects in the early 1600s. Only 24 years before *The Tempest* was written, Sir Walter Raleigh had returned from his attempts to start colonies in North America. One such colony was established on Roanoke Island, off the coast of North Carolina, Virginia; but when supply ships revisited the colony four years later, all of the inhabitants had disappeared, and they became known as the "Lost Colony". Despite such stories, the expansion of British interests via colonization continued, building up a romantic notion of valiant expeditions and the "taming" of the savage inhabitants of far-off lands.

Travelers brought back many strange tales, and some were documented, giving Shakespeare the inspiration for his masterpiece. The reports talked of cannibals and primitive people who conducted bizarre rituals. They were only vaguely human — much like Shakespeare's portrayal of Caliban (it is thought that the name of Caliban purposefully sounds similar to the word "cannibal"). Caliban's primitiveness, forced into civilization by Prospero, reflects a positive view of colonization that would have found favor with King James, justifying the many expeditions that the King funded. Shakespeare also cleverly portrays Caliban's resentment of Prospero's intrusion

nd enforced civilization, which obbed Caliban of his ruling status on the island. This is quickly ismissed within the play. Not only oes Shakespeare reveal Caliban's oor character in the recounting of is attack on Miranda (pages 36-7), but he clearly shows how rospero was able to release the idden power of the island, making : a better place for his arrival.

he inspiration for the storm itself ame from a pamphlet printed in 610 called *A Discovery of the ermudas, other wise called the Ile of Divels.* It documented the story of ow a convoy of ships, traveling rom London to Virginia, ncountered a storm that separated he flagship from the rest. The lagship was blown towards ermuda and, although the ship was ost, no one drowned. The travelers ved on the island until they could uild boats and sail on to Virginia. he story captured the minds of he exploration-hungry citizens of ngland and gave Shakespeare a ramatic starting point for his play.

Prospero
rospero is shown to be a caring, brilliant and learned father with nagical powers (which would have ppealed to King James I). Like the King, his power is signified by his books, his staff and his robe. Books not only provided knowledge, but hey were seen as a source of mystical power; particularly by the argely illiterate public. The figure of rospero is thought to have been nspired by Queen Elizabeth's strologer, Dr John Dee (1527-1608). Dee had a reputation for performing acts of magic and was enowned for possessing a vast ibrary of books — at one time the

largest library in England. The mystical power that people believed he derived from his books was so feared that a group of people attacked his house and set fire to his library. King James I put an end to his financial support, and Dee was forced to sell his possessions. He died in poverty three years before *The Tempest* was written.

Theater Development
From 1608, Shakespeare's acting troupe started to perform his plays at *Blackfriars Theatre* on the north bank of the River Thames in London. His "spiritual home", *The Globe Theatre,* was an open-air performance space and subject to the effects of weather (the

"groundling" audience had no shelter from rain). *Blackfriars Theatre,* on the other hand, was a fully enclosed space that included lighting and a pipe organ. *The Tempest* was shaped by the availability of this facility. The play features the most music of any of his works, using the organ to full effect, as well as the backstage areas for sound effects and other "off-stage" music. Also, the "imaginary banquet" scene (pages 87-93) is stage-directed for the sudden appearance and disappearance of the table and the food. This was made possible by a trap door on the stage, with the area beneath open for the moving of props — something that *The Globe Theatre* didn't possess. This was theater at the forefront of technology in 1611. It was important for Shakespeare always to be coming up with new spectacles, and one can only imagine how ending his fulltime writing career "on a high" with *The Tempest* would have left him satisfied in his final few remaining years.

Page Creation

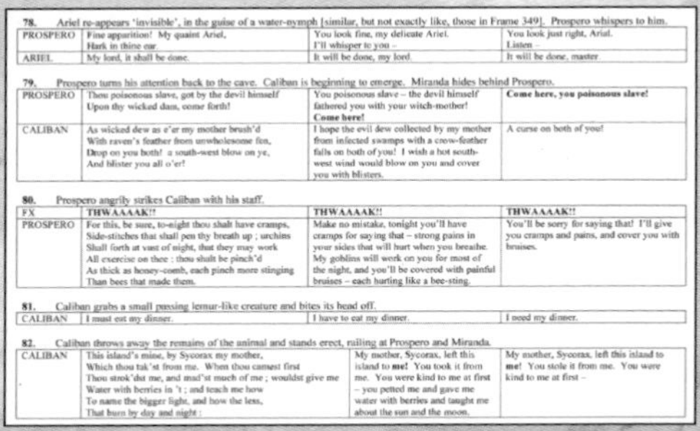

78. Ariel re-appears 'invisible', in the guise of a water-nymph [similar, but not exactly like, those in Frame 349]. Prospero whispers to him.

PROSPERO	Fine apparition! My quaint Ariel, Hark in thine ear.	You look fine, my delicate Ariel. I'll whisper to you –	You look just right, Arial. Listen –
ARIEL	My lord, it shall be done.	It will be done, my lord.	It will be done, master.

79. Prospero turns his attention back to the cave. Caliban is beginning to emerge. Miranda hides behind Prospero.

PROSPERO	Thou poisonous slave, got by the devil himself Upon thy wicked dam, come forth!	You poisonous slave – the devil himself fathered you with your witch-mother! **Come here!**	**Come here, you poisonous slave!**
CALIBAN	As wicked dew as e'er my mother brush'd With raven's feather from unwholesome fen, Drop on you both! a south-west blow on ye, And blister you all o'er!	I hope the evil dew collected by my mother from infected swamps with a crow-feather falls on both of you! I wish a hot south-west wind would blow on you and cover you with blisters.	A curse on both of you!

80. Prospero angrily strikes Caliban with his staff.

FX	**THWAAAAK!!**	**THWAAAAK!!**	**THWAAAAK!!**
PROSPERO	For this, be sure, to-night thou shalt have cramps, Side-stitches that shall pen thy breath up ; urchins Shall forth at vast of night, that they may work All exercise on thee : thou shalt be pinch'd As thick as honey-comb, each pinch more stinging Than bees that made them.	Make no mistake, tonight you'll have cramps for saying that – strong pains in your sides that will hurt when you breathe. My goblins will work on you for most of the night, and you'll be covered with painful bruises – each hurting like a bee-sting.	You'll be sorry for saying that! I'll give you cramps and pains, and cover you with bruises.

81. Caliban grabs a small passing lemur-like creature and bites its head off.

CALIBAN	I must eat my dinner.	I have to eat my dinner.	I need my dinner.

82. Caliban throws away the remains of the animal and stands erect, railing at Prospero and Miranda.

CALIBAN	This island's mine, by Sycorax my mother, Which thou tak'st from me. When thou camest first Thou strok'dst me, and mad'st much of me ; wouldst give me Water with berries in 't ; and teach me how To name the bigger light, and how the less, That burn by day and night :	My mother, Sycorax, left this island to **me!** You took it from me. You were kind to me at first – you petted me and gave me water with berries and taught me about the sun and the moon.	My mother, Sycorax, left this island to **me!** You stole it from me. You were kind to me at first –

Page 35 from the script of *The Tempest* showing the three text versions.

1. Script

The first stage in creating a graphic novel adaptation of a Shakespeare play is to split the original script into comic book panels, describing the images to be drawn as well as the dialogue, captions and sound effects. To do this, not only does the script writer need to know the play well, but he also needs to visualize each page in his head as he writes the art descriptions for each panel (there are over 460 panels in *The Tempest*).

Once this is created, the dialogue is adapted into Plain Text and Quick Text to create the three versions of the book, which all use the same artwork.

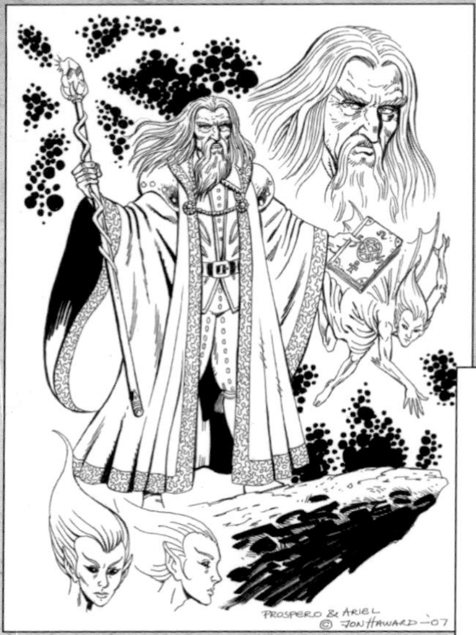
PROSPERO & ARIEL
© JON HAWARD -07

A character sheet of Prospero and Ariel.

2. Character Sheets

As well as creating the script, the scriptwriter (John McDonald) also supplies descriptions of each character. The artist (Jon Haward) couples these with his own ideas to create a number of character sheets. These sheets provide a point of reference when drawing the pages, but more importantly they allow the artist to familiarize himself with the characters – to the point where they almost take on a life of their own.

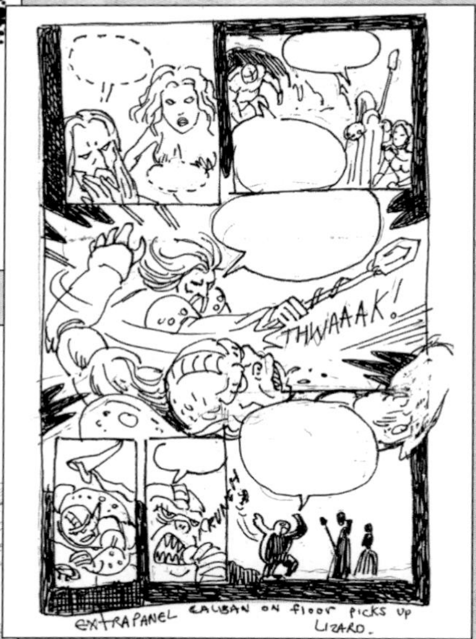
THWAAAK!
EXTRAPANEL CALIBAN ON floor PICKS UP LIZARD.

The rough sketch created from the script.

3. Rough Sketch

There is a wealth of detail in each panel of this book, and therefore it is important to solve any problems in the layouts through the use of rough sketches of each page. Here is Jon's sketch of page 35. Comparing it to the finished page, you can see how slight alterations were made during the artistic process.

Note how the characters were reversed in panel 2, to help with the lettering and also to have Prospero continuing in speaking from left to right, leading the reader on through the page.

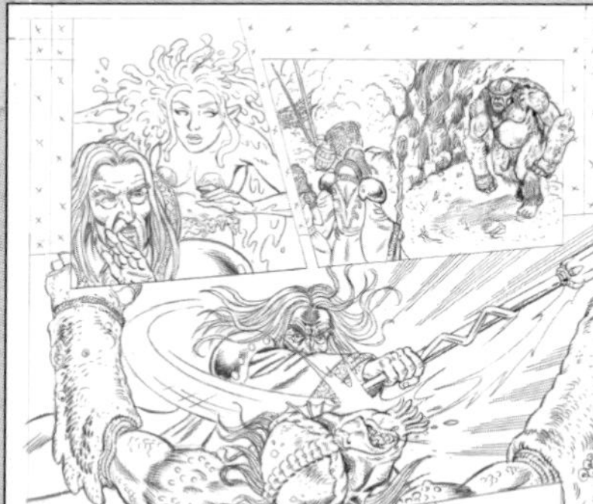

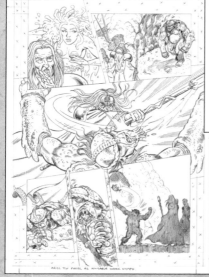

The pencil drawing of page 35.

4. Pencils

As soon as the rough sketch is approved by the editor, work starts on penciling the page. The artwork is drawn on A3 art board at approximately 150% of the finished printed size. Here you can clearly see the change to panel 2, and the amount of detail that goes in to each and every panel, even at this early stage.

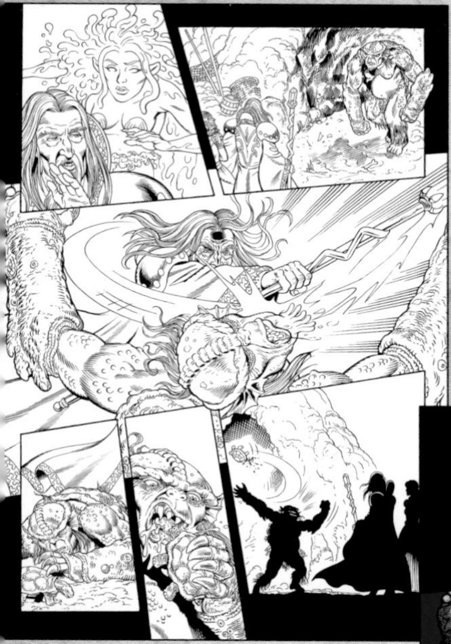

The inked image, ready to be colored.

5. Inks

The inking stage is important because it clarifies the pencil lines and finalizes the linework. There is far more to this than simply tracing over the pencil lines! The best way to view inking is as a pre-coloring stage, where deep blacks are created, and certain textures added. Different line weights are used to create a sense of depth in the image, and also to imply the types of edges being portrayed in the various materials.

6. Coloring

Adding color really brings the page and its characters to life. Coloring isn't merely a process of replacing the white areas with flat color. Some of the linework itself is shaded, while great emphasis is placed upon texture and light sources to get realistic shadows and highlights. Effects are also considered, such as the glow from Prospero's staff.. Finally, the whole page is color-balanced to the other pages of that scene, and to the overall book.

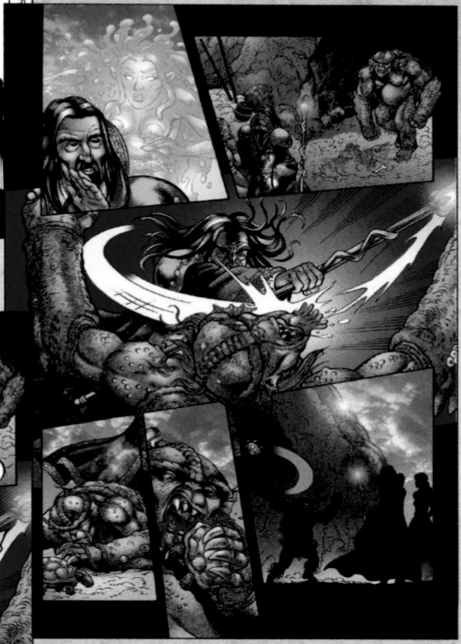

The final colored artwork.

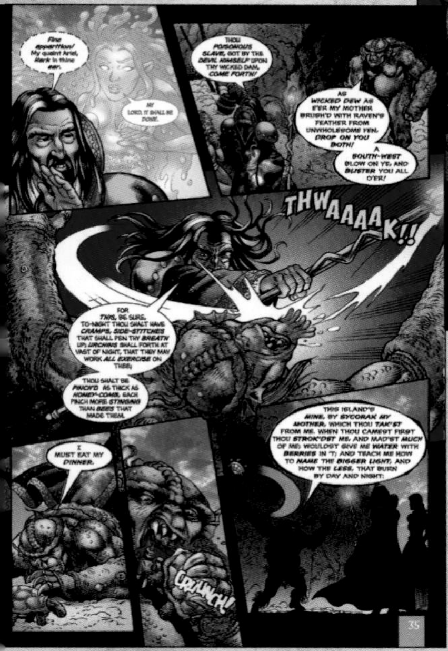

Fine apparition! My quaint Ariel, Hark in thine ear.
MY LORD, IT SHALL BE DONE.
THOU POISONOUS SLAVE, GOT BY THE DEVIL HIMSELF UPON THY WICKED DAM, COME FORTH!
AS WICKED DEW AS E'ER MY MOTHER BRUSH'D WITH RAVEN'S FEATHER FROM UNWHOLESOME FEN, DROP ON YOU BOTH!
A SOUTH-WEST BLOW ON YE, AND BLISTER YOU ALL O'ER!
THWAAAAK!!
FOR THIS, BE SURE, TO-NIGHT THOU SHALT HAVE CRAMPS, SIDE-STITCHES THAT SHALL PEN THY BREATH UP; URCHINS SHALL FORTH AT VAST OF NIGHT, THAT THEY MAY WORK ALL EXERCISE ON THEE;
THOU SHALT BE PINCH'D AS THICK AS HONEY-COMB, EACH PINCH MORE STINGING THAN BEES THAT MADE THEM.
THIS ISLAND'S MINE, BY SYCORAX MY MOTHER, WHICH THOU TAK'ST FROM ME. WHEN THOU CAMEST FIRST THOU STROK'DST ME, AND MAD'ST MUCH OF ME; WOULDST GIVE ME WATER WITH BERRIES IN 'T; AND TEACH ME HOW TO NAME THE BIGGER LIGHT, AND HOW THE LESS, THAT BURN BY DAY AND NIGHT:
I MUST EAT MY DINNER.
CRUUNCH!
35

The finished page 35 with Original Text lettering.

7. Lettering

The final stage is to add the captions, sound effects, and speech bubbles from the script. These are placed on top of the finished colored pages. Three versions of each page are lettered, one for each of the three versions of the book (Original Text, Plain Text and Quick Text).

Original Text

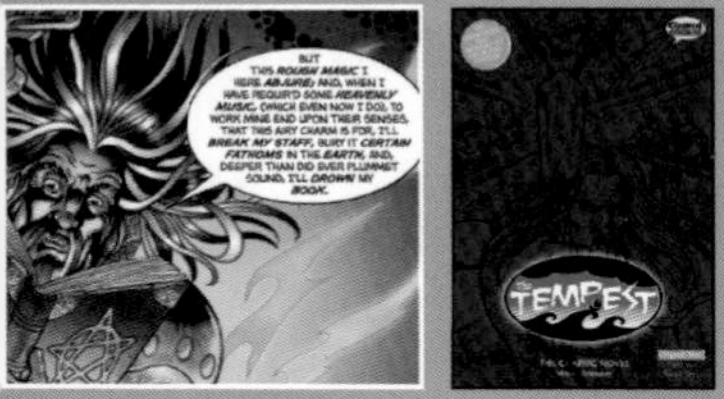

BUT THIS ROUGH MAGIC I HERE ABJURE; AND, WHEN I HAVE REQUIR'D SOME HEAVENLY MUSIC, (WHICH EVEN NOW I DO,) TO WORK MINE END UPON THEIR SENSES, THAT THIS AIRY CHARM IS FOR, I'LL BREAK MY STAFF, BURY IT CERTAIN FATHOMS IN THE EARTH, AND, DEEPER THAN DID EVER PLUMMET SOUND, I'LL DROWN MY BOOK.
TEMPEST

ISBN: 978-1-906332-69-3

Plain Text

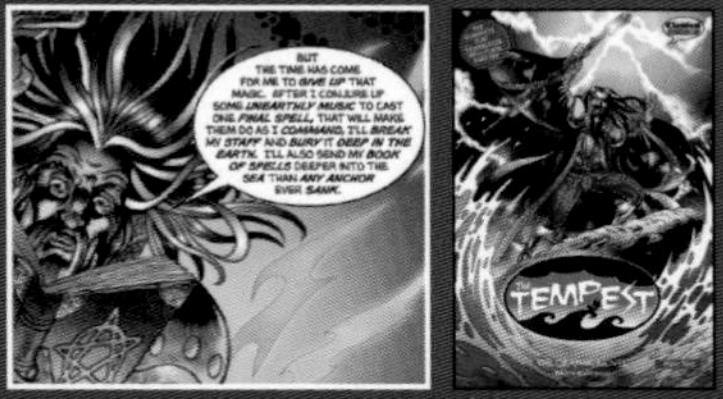

BUT THE TIME HAS COME FOR ME TO GIVE UP THAT MAGIC. AFTER I CONJURE UP SOME UNEARTHLY MUSIC TO CAST ONE FINAL SPELL, THAT WILL MAKE THEM DO AS I COMMAND, I'LL BREAK MY STAFF AND BURY IT DEEP IN THE EARTH. I'LL ALSO SEND MY BOOK OF SPELLS DEEPER INTO THE SEA THAN ANY ANCHOR EVER SANK.
TEMPEST

ISBN: 978-1-906332-70-9

Quick Text

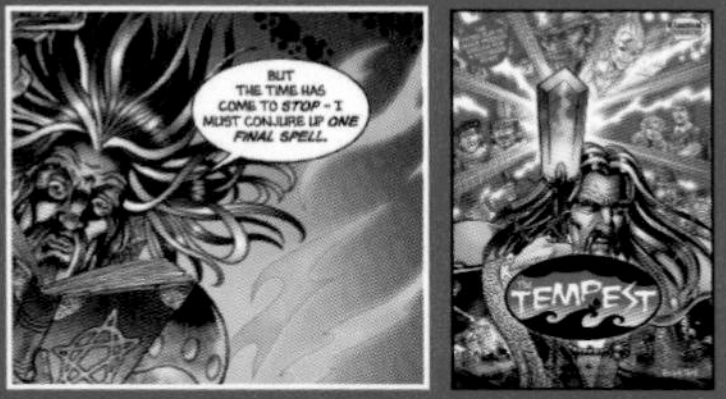

BUT THE TIME HAS COME TO STOP - I MUST CONJURE UP ONE FINAL SPELL.
TEMPEST

ISBN: 978-1-906332-71-6

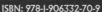

Shakespeare's Globe

The Globe Theatre and Shakespeare

It is hard to appreciate today how theaters were actually a new idea in William Shakespeare's time. The very first theater in Elizabethan London to only show plays, aptly called *The Theatre*, was introduced by an entrepreneur by the name of James Burbage. In fact, *The Globe Theatre*, possibly the most famous theater of that era, was built from the timbers of *The Theatre*. The landlord of *The Theatre* was Giles Allen, a Puritan who disapproved of theatrical entertainment. When he decided to enforce a huge rent increase in the winter of 1598, the theater members dismantled the building piece by piece and shipped it across the Thames to Southwark for reassembly. Allen was powerless to do anything, as the company owned the wood - although he spent three years in court trying to sue the perpetrators!

The report of the dismantling party (written by Schoenbaum)

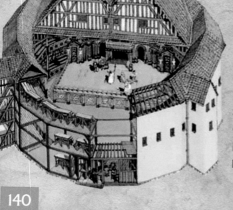

says: *"riotous... armed... with divers and manye unlawfull and offensive weapons... in verye ryotous outragious and forcyble manner and contrarye to the lawes of your highnes Realme... and there pulling breaking and throwing downe the sayd Theater in verye outragious violent and riotous sort to the great disturbance and terrefyeing not onlye of your subjectes... but of divers others of your majesties loving subjectes there neere inhabitinge."*

William Shakespeare became a part owner of this new *Globe Theatre* in 1599. It was one of four major theaters in the area, along with the *Swan*, the *Rose*, and the *Hope*. The exact physical structure of the *Globe* is unknown, although scholars are fairly sure of some details through drawings from the period. The theater itself was a closed structure with an open courtyard where the stage stood. Tiered galleries around the open area accommodated the wealthier patrons who could afford seats, and those of the lower classes - the "groundlings" - stood around the platform or "thrust" stage during the performance of a play. The space under and behind the stage was used for special effects, storage and costume changes. Surprisingly, although the entire structure was not very big by modern standards, it is known to have accommodated fairly large crowds - as many as 3,000 people - during a single performance.

The Globe II

In 1613, the original *Globe Theatre* burned to the ground when a cannon shot during a performance of *Henry VIII* set fire to the thatched roof of the gallery. Undeterred, the company completed a new *Globe* (this time with a tiled roof) on the foundations of its predecessor. Shakespeare didn't write any new plays for this theater, which opened in 1614. He retired to Stratford-Upon-Avon that year, and died two years later. Despite that, performances continued until 1642, when the Puritans closed down all theaters and places of entertainment. Two years later, the Puritans razed the building to the ground in order to build tenements upon the site. No more was to be seen of the *Globe* for 352 years.

Shakespeare's Globe

Led by the vision of the late Sam Wanamaker, work began on the construction of a new *Globe* in 1993, close to the site of the original theater. It was completed three years later, and Queen Elizabeth II officially opened the *New Globe Theatre* on June 12th, 1997 with a production of *Henry V*.

The *New Globe Theatre* is as faithful a reproduction as possible to the Elizabethan theater, given that the details of the original are only known from sketches of the time. The building can accommodate 1,500 people in all, across the galleries and the "groundlings".

www.shakespeares-globe.org

Teaching Resource Packs

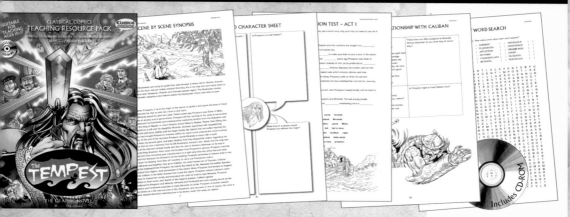

HELPING YOU PREPARE MOTIVATING AND STIMULATING LESSONS

CLASSICAL COMICS TEACHING RESOURCE PACK
The TEMPEST
THE GRAPHIC NOVEL
CENE BY SCENE SYNOPSIS
CHARACTER SHEET
ION TEST – ACT I
TIONSHIP WITH CALIBAN
WORD SEARCH
Includes CD-ROM

o accompany each title in our series of raphic novels and to help with their pplication in the classroom, we also publish eaching resource packs. These widely cclaimed 100+ page books are spiral-ound, making the pages easy to photocopy. hey also include a CD-ROM with the ages in PDF format, ideal for whole-class eaching on whiteboards, laptops, etc or for irect digital printing. These books are ritten by teachers, for teachers, helping tudents to engage in the play or novel. uitable for teaching ages 10-17, each book rovides exercises that cover structure, listening, understanding, motivation and character as well as key words, themes and literary techniques. Although the majority of the tasks focus on the use of language and comprehension, there are also many cross-curriculum topics, covering areas within history, IT, drama, reading, speaking, writing and art. An extensive Educational Links section provides further study opportunities. Devised to encompass a broad range of skill levels, they provide many opportunities for differentiated teaching and the tailoring of lessons to meet individual needs.

"Thank you! These will be fantastic for all our students. It is a brilliant resource and to have the lesson ideas too are great. Thanks again to all your team who have created these."
B.P. KS3

"As to the resource, I can't wait to start using it! Well done on a fantastic service."
Will

"...you've certainly got a corner of East Anglia convinced that this is a fantastic way to teach and progress English literature and language!"
Chris

OUR RANGE OF TEACHING RESOURCE PACKS AVAILABLE

he Tempest
78-1-906332-77-8

Romeo & Juliet
978-1-906332-74-7

Macbeth
978-1-906332-54-9

Henry V
978-1-906332-53-2

rankenstein
78-1-906332-56-3

Jane Eyre
978-1-906332-55-6

A Christmas Carol
978-1-906332-57-0

Great Expectations
978-1-906332-58-7

- Only $22.95 each
- 100+ spiral-bound, photocopiable pages.
- Electronic version included for whole-class teaching and digital printing.
- Cross-curricular topics and activities.
- Ideal for differentiated teaching.

AVAILABLE IN THREE TEXT VERSIONS

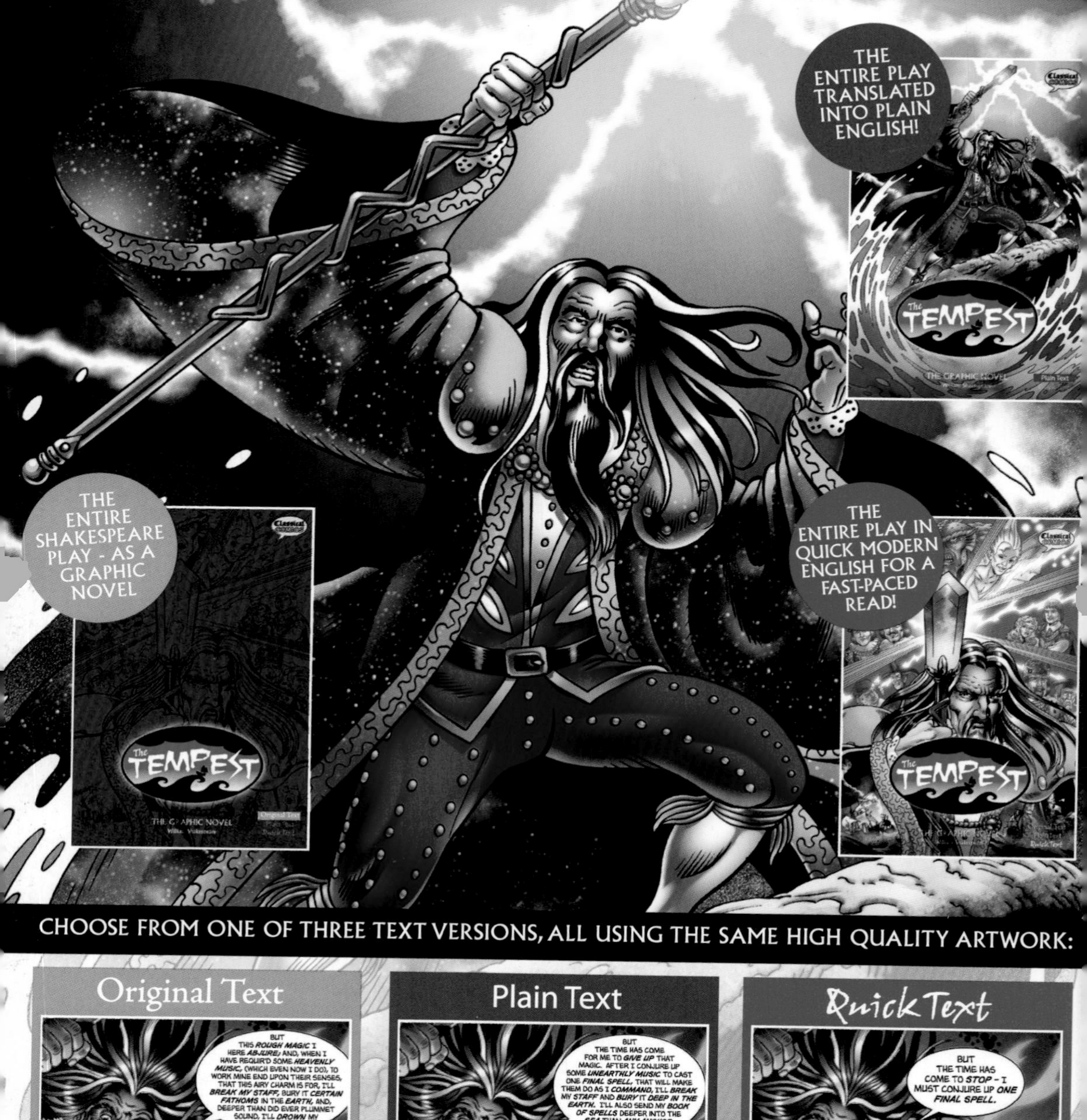
THE ENTIRE PLAY TRANSLATED INTO PLAIN ENGLISH!
The TEMPEST
THE GRAPHIC NOVEL
Plain Text
THE ENTIRE SHAKESPEARE PLAY - AS A GRAPHIC NOVEL
The TEMPEST
Original Text
THE ENTIRE PLAY IN QUICK MODERN ENGLISH FOR A FAST-PACED READ!
The TEMPEST
Quick Text

CHOOSE FROM ONE OF THREE TEXT VERSIONS, ALL USING THE SAME HIGH QUALITY ARTWORK:

Original Text

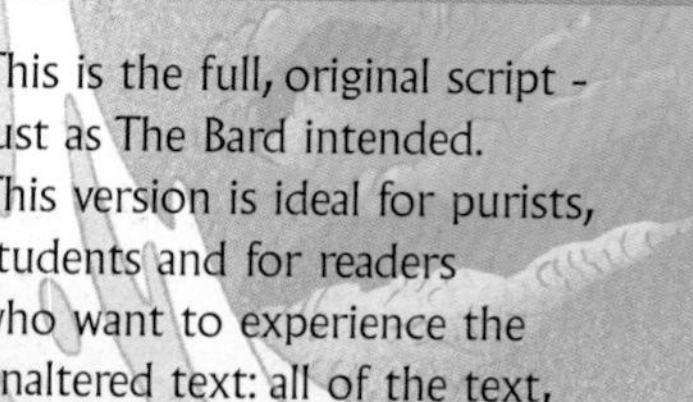
BUT THIS ROUGH MAGIC I HERE ABJURE; AND, WHEN I HAVE REQUIR'D SOME HEAVENLY MUSIC, (WHICH EVEN NOW I DO), TO WORK MINE END UPON THEIR SENSES, THAT THIS AIRY CHARM IS FOR, I'LL BREAK MY STAFF, BURY IT CERTAIN FATHOMS IN THE EARTH, AND, DEEPER THAN DID EVER PLUMMET SOUND, I'LL DROWN MY BOOK.

ISBN: 978-1-906332-69-3

This is the full, original script - just as The Bard intended. This version is ideal for purists, students and for readers who want to experience the unaltered text: all of the text, all of the excitement!

Plain Text

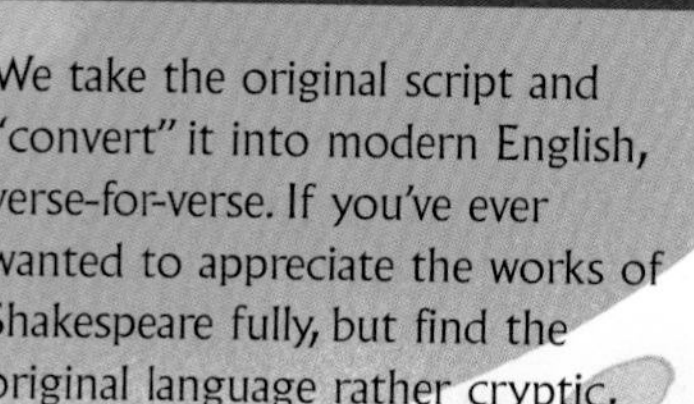
BUT THE TIME HAS COME FOR ME TO GIVE UP THAT MAGIC. AFTER I CONJURE UP SOME UNEARTHLY MUSIC TO CAST ONE FINAL SPELL, THAT WILL MAKE THEM DO AS I COMMAND, I'LL BREAK MY STAFF AND BURY IT DEEP IN THE EARTH. I'LL ALSO SEND MY BOOK OF SPELLS DEEPER INTO THE SEA THAN ANY ANCHOR EVER SANK.

ISBN: 978-1-906332-70-9

We take the original script and "convert" it into modern English, verse-for-verse. If you've ever wanted to appreciate the works of Shakespeare fully, but find the original language rather cryptic, then this is the version for you!

Quick Text

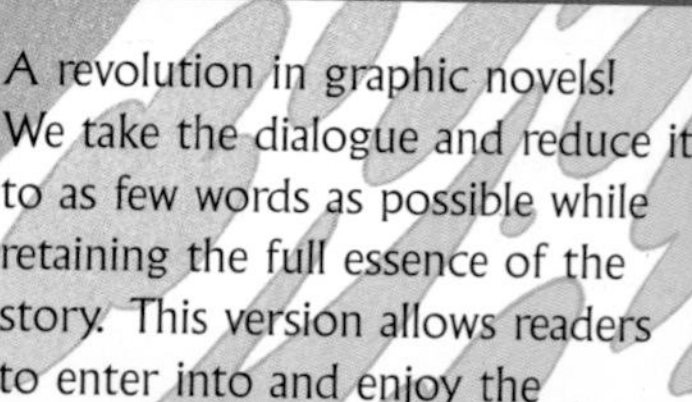
BUT THE TIME HAS COME TO STOP – I MUST CONJURE UP ONE FINAL SPELL.

ISBN: 978-1-906332-71-6

A revolution in graphic novels! We take the dialogue and reduce it to as few words as possible while retaining the full essence of the story. This version allows readers to enter into and enjoy the stories quickly.

CLASSIC TITLES IN THE SERIES

Out now and available in Original Text and Quick Text

Frankenstein: The Graphic Novel

• 144 Pages • $16.95

• Script Adaptation: Jason Cobley • Linework: Declan Shalvey • Letters: Terry Wiley
• Colors: Jason Cardy & Kat Nicholson • Art Direction: Jon Haward

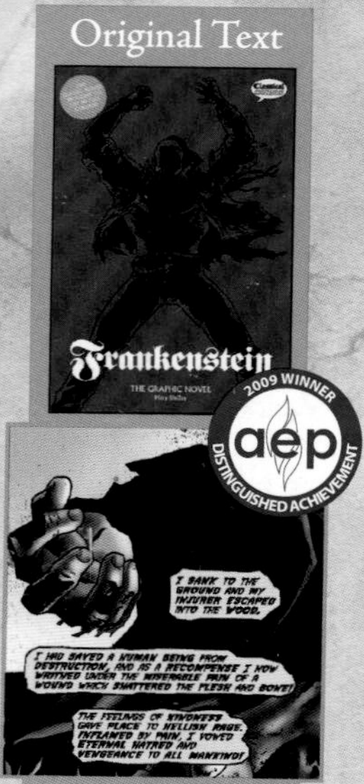

Original Text
Frankenstein
2009 WINNER
aep
DISTINGUISHED ACHIEVEMENT
I SANK TO THE GROUND AND MY INJURER ESCAPED INTO THE WOOD.
I HAD SAVED A HUMAN BEING FROM DESTRUCTION, AND AS A RECOMPENSE I NOW WRITHED UNDER THE MISERABLE PAIN OF A WOUND WHICH SHATTERED THE FLESH AND BONE!
THE FEELINGS OF KINDNESS GAVE PLACE TO HELLISH RAGE. INFLAMED BY PAIN, I VOWED ETERNAL HATRED AND VENGEANCE TO ALL MANKIND!

ISBN: 978-1-906332-49-5

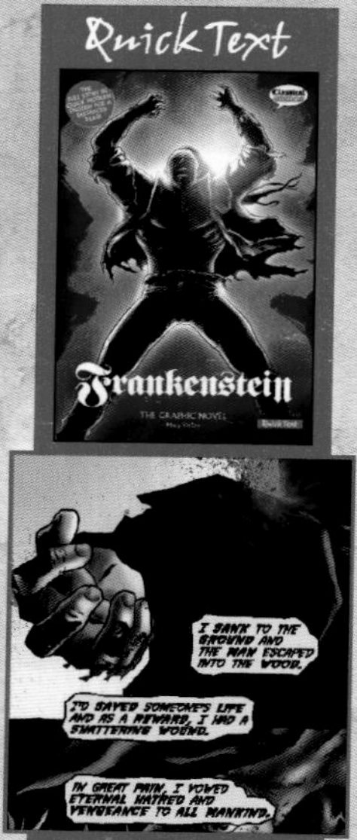

Quick Text
Frankenstein
I SANK TO THE GROUND AND THE MAN ESCAPED INTO THE WOOD.
I'D SAVED SOMEONE'S LIFE AND AS A REWARD, I HAD A SHATTERING WOUND.
IN GREAT PAIN, I VOWED ETERNAL HATRED AND VENGEANCE TO ALL MANKIND.

ISBN: 978-1-906332-50-1

Jane Eyre: The Graphic Novel

• 144 Pages • $16.95

• Script Adaptation: Amy Corzine • Artwork: John M. Burns
• Letters: Terry Wiley

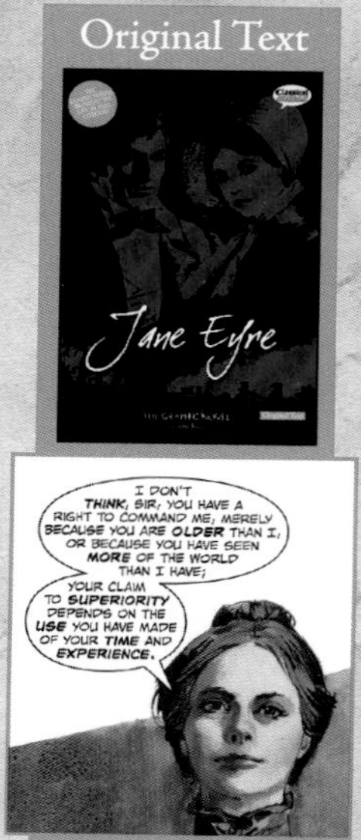

Original Text
Jane Eyre
I DON'T THINK, SIR, YOU HAVE A RIGHT TO COMMAND ME, MERELY BECAUSE YOU ARE OLDER THAN I, OR BECAUSE YOU HAVE SEEN MORE OF THE WORLD THAN I HAVE;
YOUR CLAIM TO SUPERIORITY DEPENDS ON THE USE YOU HAVE MADE OF YOUR TIME AND EXPERIENCE.

ISBN: 978-1-906332-47-1

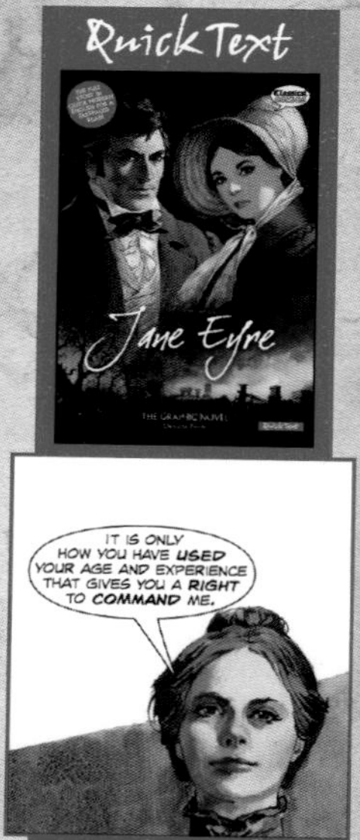

Quick Text
Jane Eyre
IT IS ONLY HOW YOU HAVE USED YOUR AGE AND EXPERIENCE THAT GIVES YOU A RIGHT TO COMMAND ME.

ISBN: 978-1-906332-48-8

A Christmas Carol: The Graphic Novel

• 160 Pages • $16.95

• Script Adaptation: Sean Michael Wilson • Pencils: Mike Collins
• Inks: David Roach • Colors: James Offredi • Letters: Terry Wiley

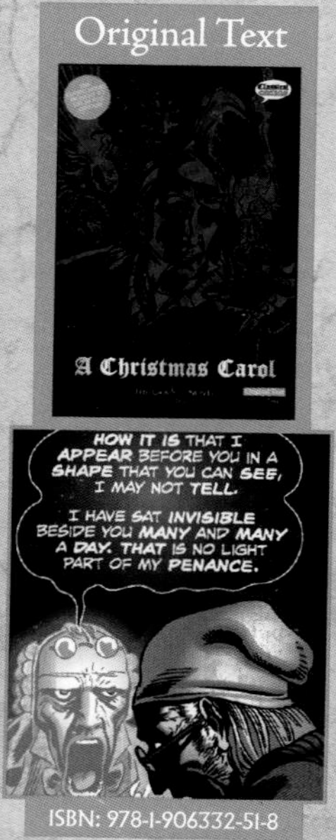

Original Text
A Christmas Carol
HOW IT IS THAT I APPEAR BEFORE YOU IN A SHAPE THAT YOU CAN SEE, I MAY NOT TELL.
I HAVE SAT INVISIBLE BESIDE YOU MANY AND MANY A DAY. THAT IS NO LIGHT PART OF MY PENANCE.

ISBN: 978-1-906332-51-8

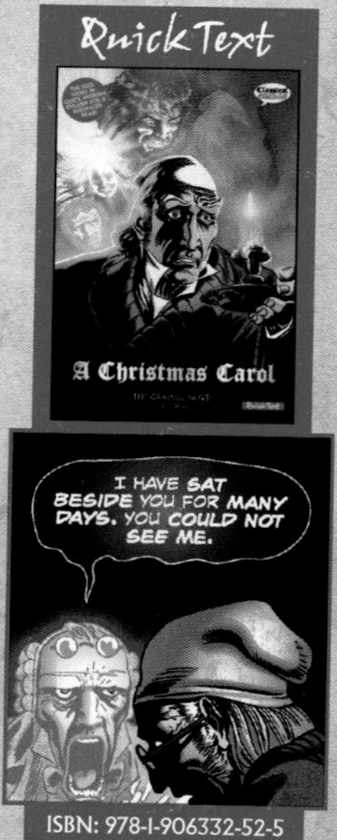

Quick Text
A Christmas Carol
I HAVE SAT BESIDE YOU FOR MANY DAYS. YOU COULD NOT SEE ME.

ISBN: 978-1-906332-52-5

Great Expectations: The Graphic Novel

• 160 Pages • $16.95

• Script Adaptation: Jen Green • Linework: John Stokes • Letters: Jim Campbell
• Coloring: Digikore Studios Ltd • Color Finishing: Jason Cardy

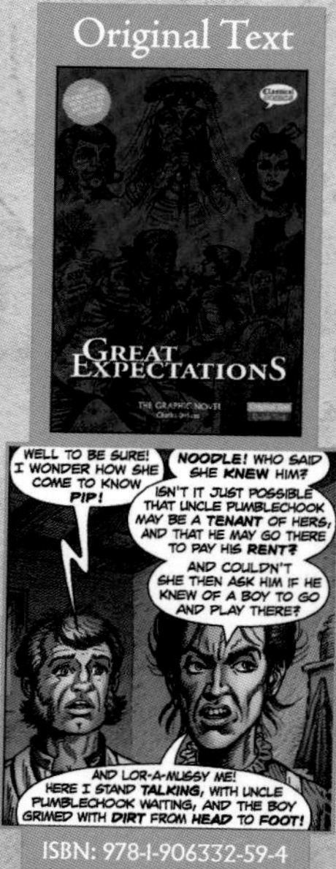

Original Text
GREAT EXPECTATIONS
WELL TO BE SURE! I WONDER HOW SHE COME TO KNOW PIP!
NOODLE! WHO SAID SHE KNEW HIM? ISN'T IT JUST POSSIBLE THAT UNCLE PUMBLECHOOK MAY BE A TENANT OF HERS, AND THAT HE MAY GO THERE TO PAY HIS RENT? AND COULDN'T SHE THEN ASK HIM IF HE KNEW OF A BOY TO GO AND PLAY THERE?
AND LOR-A-MUSSY ME! HERE I STAND TALKING, WITH UNCLE PUMBLECHOOK WAITING, AND THE BOY GRIMED WITH DIRT FROM HEAD TO FOOT!

ISBN: 978-1-906332-59-4

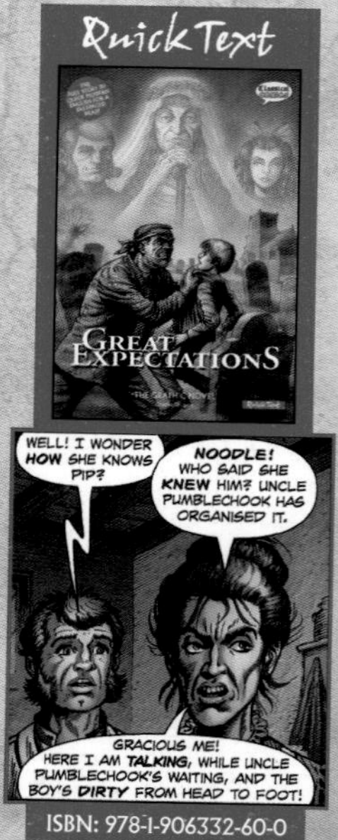

Quick Text
GREAT EXPECTATIONS
WELL! I WONDER HOW SHE KNOWS PIP?
NOODLE! WHO SAID SHE KNEW HIM? UNCLE PUMBLECHOOK HAS ORGANISED IT.
GRACIOUS ME! HERE I AM TALKING, WHILE UNCLE PUMBLECHOOK'S WAITING, AND THE BOY'S DIRTY FROM HEAD TO FOOT!

ISBN: 978-1-906332-60-0